Praise for
The Pea

"Beautifully constructed and highly emotional. Massey's knowledge of Japanese antiques and downtown D.C. enhances the story."
—*USA Today*

"A superb book, with wonderfully realized characters, a deftly woven plot, and a vulnerable, heroic, unforgettable sleuth."
—Diane Mott Davidson

"Massey's pungent take on mixed marriages and East-West culture clashes is first-rate."
—*Kirkus Reviews*

"Adept at crafting dead-on dialogue and juggling serious issues with humor, Massey has produced another triumph."
—*Publishers Weekly*

"Sujata Massey gracefully weaves Japanese art, history, and social mores into a series narrated by a Japanese-American antiques dealer."
—*New York Times Book Review*

"A riveting story."
—*Library Journal*

"The clever mix of the . . . restaurant opening with the serious investigation of a disappearance, perhaps a murder, makes this seventh novel of Ms. Massey's enthralling."
—*Dallas Morning News*

"A feast of delights, sure to make readers impatient for Rei Shimura's next adventure."
—*Sun* (Baltimore)

"Sujata Massey's mysteries are breezy and girly and . . . tartly funny."
—*Philadelphia Inquirer*

Also by Sujata Massey

The Samurai's Daughter
The Bride's Kimono
The Floating Girl
The Flower Master
Zen Attitude
The Salaryman's Wife

The Pearl Diver

Sujata Massey

An Imprint of HarperCollinsPublishers

A hardcover edition of this book was published in 2004 by HarperCollins Publishers.

First Dark Alley edition published 2005.

Dark Alley is a federally registered trademark of HarperCollins Publishers.

Designed by Nancy B. Field

The Library of Congress has cataloged the hardcover edition as follows:

Massey, Sujata.
    The Pearl Diver / Sujata Massey.—1st ed.
        p. cm.
    ISBN 0-06-621296-0 (acid-free paper)
    1. Shimura, Rei (Fictitious character)—Fiction. 2. Women detectives—Washington (D.C.)—Fiction. 3. Japanese Americans—Fiction. 4. Washington (D.C.)—Fiction. 5. Antique dealers—Fiction. I. Title.
    PS3563.A79965P43 2004
    813'.54—dc22   2003067614

ISBN 0-06-059790-9 (pbk.)

05 06 07 08 09 ❖/RRD 10 9 8 7 6 5 4 3 2 1

Acknowledgments

From the very beginning, when I was casting about for an idea for Rei's new adventure, my editor, Carolyn Marino, was inspirational. So, too, were longtime readers and e-mail friends, especially Reiko Okochi in Palos Verdes, Paul Sayles in San Francisco, and Ryohei Omori in Tokyo. I thank Gerard Busnuk for patiently answering my questions about American police procedure, and John Mann for his lessons on American warfare in Vietnam. I am indebted to the U.S. Marine Corps Historical Center, especially Frederick J. Graboske, head of the archives section, and Robert V. Aquilina, historian and assistant head of the reference section. Karen Oertel, a coowner of the Harris seafood business and Harrison's Restaurant in Grasonville, taught me all I know about Chesapeake Bay history and oysters. Julie Kehrli, chief of staff for the Honorable Senator Paul S. Sarbanes, D-Maryland, was kind enough to give me an office tour and teach me about the ins and outs of Senate life.

So many restaurants filled me with delicious food and ideas. I am especially grateful to the staff of the former Aquavit restaurant in Minneapolis, and in Washington, D.C., to restaurants including Burma, DC Coast, Poste, Zola, and Zaytinya. I also give special thanks to my husband, Tony, who manfully submitted to many restaurant dinners over the past year, and to Carina Casabón Inzunza, for giving our children dinner and a lot of fun during these times. I owe the writing of this book to Larry Horwitz and all staffers and friends, past and present, at the real Urban Grounds in Baltimore, as well as Mike Sproge and Glen Breining at its reincarnation The Evergreen. Without your encouragement, nickels for the meter, and single skim-milk lattes, this book would not have progressed past page one. Finally, to my children, Pia and Neel: You're the best—now eat your asparagus!

Sujata Massey
October 2003
Baltimore, Maryland

Cast of Characters

REI SHIMURA. A young antiques expert who is hoping to put an unsavory past in Tokyo behind her in exchange for a fabulous future in Washington, D.C.

HUGH GLENDINNING. Rei's live-in boyfriend who practices law and pillow-book maneuvers in the hope of getting Rei to the altar.

KENDALL HOWARD JOHNSON. Rei's Washington cousin, a former fund-raiser married to the preppy realtor Win Johnson and busy raising their twin toddlers, Jacquie and Win Junior.

HARP SNOWDEN. A California senator with a taste for Asian food and an eye on the White House. His press attaché, Martina, keeps him in line.

MARSHALL ZANGER. A restaurant entrepreneur in Washington who has deep pockets and deeper expectations of everyone.

JIRO TAKEDA. A former *Iron Chef* participant turned executive chef for Marshall's two restaurants, Mandala and Bento.

ANDREA NORTON. Bento's hostess, a Washington girl-about-town famous for her looks and attitude. Her mother's whereabouts are unknown, but her father, ROBERT NORTON, and his second wife, LORRAINE, and son, DAVON, live in rural central Virginia.

ALBERTO. A prep cook who keeps his eyes open and ears peeled.

PHONG. A bartender who makes wicked drinks.

JUSTIN. A waiter with ambitions.

LOUIS BURNS. A homicide detective on the Washington, D.C., police force.

NORIE SHIMURA. Rei's beloved aunt from Yokohama, who has a legendary *yosenabe* recipe and a yen for murder.

PLUS a motley crew of cooks, waiters, police, watermen, and war veterans.

Prologue

Their wedding was supposed to mark the beginning of spring, but it felt like winter. It was a small gathering, and everyone present looked cold—the men in their stiff uniforms and suits, and their women wearing spring dresses in candy colors.

Instead of a lacy, white American gown, the bride had chosen a wedding kimono. It was not a handed-down one, like so many people expected, but a brand-new one: red-and-orange silk brocade that shimmered with embroidered pairs of ducks, the sign of conjugal bliss. It had come from the Ginza, a district filled with enthralling boutiques that she could never have afforded until he'd come along—but shops where they weathered disapproving glares and hissed insults.

It didn't matter anymore. Here she was on the edge of the water, the water that stretched all the way from her country to his; the water that he'd flown over to discover her, and to love her. And in the new country she would be valued more than just for her toughness in cold water.

When it was time to put the rings on each other's fingers, she rushed so quickly that she accidentally dropped his. The guests laughed gently as he caught it, just before it hit the sand. She slid the ring on his finger, and he did the same for her. When they were done, he squeezed both her hands warmly. She paused, not sure if this was proper procedure, and he smiled a little, as if to let her know he'd gotten carried away.

I do, she said. In two tiny words, she promised to love and honor in sickness and in health. He promised to do the same for her. It all seemed so incredible: the chilly, wild shoreline; the man beside her; the fact that she was finally getting married.

He was kissing her now, as he'd done a thousand times before, but in front of all these people. For a moment she froze in fear, because at the start of the ceremony, when she'd scanned the crowd to see who had come, she'd noticed the two men she didn't like—the men who had suddenly appeared one evening a few months ago with a heavy black suitcase. Their voices had been harsh, and she'd quickly fled to the bedroom and shut the door, not wanting to know. She'd been so relieved when they'd gone a few hours later, but the feeling they'd left behind was bad. Why had they come to the wedding? She couldn't imagine that he would have invited them.

The world wasn't perfect, she thought as she closed her eyes and returned to the kiss. But now, she was no longer the girl-friend, on the outside. She was the wife. And if she used her new-found powers, she could find a way to make those men go away.

1

I'd scored a single line and a shadow.

Or were they double lines? I squinted at the plastic wand lying on the edge of the bathroom sink. One line meant negative, two positive. There was no definition for one line and the vague suggestion of a shadow.

"What's the verdict? I'm about to dash," Hugh called from the other side of the door.

"Inconclusive," I said, opening the door and holding out the EPT stick like an obscene hors d'oeuvre. "You do the math."

"One. That's easy."

"Don't you see that shadowy line next to it?"

"A line would be pink. That's just a wrinkle in the material." He was already pulling on his Burberry. It was early spring in Washington and had rained for almost a solid week.

"I wish there was an explanation for shadows—"

"Shadows that only you can see. Darling, if you're really anxious, you could call the consumer help line."

"If I do that, I'm sure they'll tell me to consult my doctor."

"Maybe this means you're a little bit pregnant." Hugh paused in putting on his coat and slipped his hand inside my flannel pajamas to stroke my bare stomach.

"A surprise pregnancy would be a delight, without even a wedding date on the horizon," I said, removing his hand. Hugh and I had been engaged for exactly three months. We had considered a quickie elopement, on the beach in Hawaii, but once our families had gotten wind of the idea, they'd guilt-tripped us out of it. Now we thought we should set the wedding in Washington. But progress was slow. I didn't know the area well and was totally stymied about locations and caterers. I had nothing to show for myself except the guy.

"My cousin was married with new baby in arms and it was the best wedding anyone had been to in years," Hugh said, spinning his rolled-up umbrella through the air before catching it neatly. He was such an optimist: about babies, about the outcome of the class-action suit he was trying to organize, about life in general. He didn't even mind the Washington rain, because it reminded him of Edinburgh. I preferred the hard, blinding rain that made a rock-and-roll sonata on the tile roofs in Japan in the fall, or the warm, humid rains that marked spring's rainy season. But I'd take the Washington rain, because it came with Hugh, and the promise of our future.

After we negotiated the night's dinner plan—risotto with browned onions and sea scallops if I could find them, and a simple green salad—Hugh left, and I made myself a quick *o-nigiri*. I'd kept last night's rice warm in the rice cooker, and I had a small piece of leftover salmon in the fridge. I tucked the salmon into the rice and folded the triangular wedge into a sheet of seaweed that I quickly roasted on the stove.

I ate the rice ball with my left hand and used my right to scroll through the *Daily Yomiuri* online. I'd been away from Japan about six months now, and I could feel the language beginning to slip. It was my duty as a *hafu*—a half-Japanese, half-American—to keep up. I bypassed woeful economic news and went straight to the language-teaching column aimed at foreigners. The word of the day was *zurekin*, which meant "off-peak commuting," an idea strongly encouraged by the government but not quite adopted by the working world. It was easier, calmer, better for people and the environment

At least, that's how it sounded on paper. My whole life had gone from frenetic to *zurekin*—and I wasn't sure I liked it. I'd spent my twenties working in Japan, where I'd lived simply and worked hard, and come to believe that everything Japanese was wonderful, even the crowded trains. The problem was, I couldn't live in Japan anymore. I'd been thrown out, for an indefinite length of time, by the government for a misdeed I'd committed in the name of something more important. Now, because of the black mark in my passport, I had to make the best of it in Washington, complaining like all the other Washingtonians about crowded Metro trains that I considered only half-full, and so on. The only thing I truly agreed with was that Washington real estate was as insanely priced as Tokyo's—though the spaces were bigger.

Hugh's apartment, for instance, a two-bedroom on the second floor of an old town house, had lots to admire—high ceilings, old parquet floors, a bay window in the living room. It was lovely, but so . . . foreign. The telephone rang, and even that sounded different. I picked it up.

"Hi, honey, what are you doing for lunch?" The throaty voice on the other end of the line belonged to my cousin Kendall Howard Johnson, who lived in Bethesda.

"Kendall?" It annoyed me when people didn't introduce themselves on the phone.

"Yes, Rei." She drew my name out in the exaggerated way she'd pronounced it since we were little. Raaay, it sounded like.

Kendall had grown up in Bethesda, so I'd run into her plenty of times on my childhood visits to my mother's home forty minutes to the north, in Baltimore. Grandmother always called Kendall and me the ladybug team because of Kendall's red and my black hair; a set of cousins the same age who seemed destined to go together, but didn't really. I'd never forget the humiliation of the summer when Kendall was fifteen and she'd taken me in the backyard bushes and produced a joint. I hadn't known how to strike a match, let alone inhale, and I was from the Bay Area, where everyone was supposed to know how to roll. But at the coed boarding school Kendall went to in Virginia, she'd already learned lots of things that I hadn't. Horseback riding, joint rolling, how to sneak backstage at concerts without being stopped. Kendall, who'd worked as a corporate fund-raiser for a few years after college graduation, was always more advanced than I, and she'd maintained her advantage. The trust fund our grandmother had set up was now open for her use. Kendall dipped into it for her wedding, her first house payment, and even political donations that she'd begun to make as she began her careful ascent in grown-up Washington. My mother hinted that if I spent more time with my grandmother, she'd feel more benevolent toward me, but the fact was, I didn't feel comfortable with Grand, as everyone called her, and the last thing I wanted to do was suck up to her for the money that all the Maryland cousins received, and that I, the lone Californian who hardly ever visited, didn't. Then again, my exclusion from the trust might have occurred because my mother had jumped into a marriage that had felt like a death blow to the Howards. If my father had been black, the marriage would have broken Maryland law at that time. An Asian husband wasn't quite as shocking as a black one, but my parents' wedding hadn't been a family affair.

Still, I couldn't resent Kendall for being one of the Howards, for as busy as my cousin was with the babies, running her household, and fund-raising for her favorite political hopefuls, she hadn't forgotten me. Kendall was the only relative who'd sought me out since I'd arrived in Washington a few months earlier, and I was grateful for that.

"How are the twins?" I avoided asking about her husband, Win, whom I couldn't stand. Win was a real estate agent and saw everyone as a potential target. The fact that Hugh and I hadn't been interested in buying a McMansion in the suburbs was still a point of contention.

"The babies are sick with strep. It's highly unusual in children under three, but my two have it, of course!"

"You must be tearing out your hair running from one to the other," I sympathized.

"At night, yes. By day our au pair is playing Nursie, thank goodness. I've escaped to the gym and had an hour to spin and then an hour for weights. I'm starved. Could you make a twelve-thirty lunch?"

"I don't know. The weather's kind of bad. I was thinking of doing some things around the apartment—"

"Rain's good for you, honey!" Kendall snorted. "And it's not just a gals' lunch at the coffee shop I'm talking about. It's at a good restaurant with Harp Snowden."

"You socialize with Harp Snowden?" I was amazed. Harp Snowden was a Democratic senator representing California, a liberal stalwart who voted against each and every war proposed. He was one of the few politicians who'd entered the new century unabashedly pro-environment, pro-immigrant, pro-peace. Kendall's meeting with him was interesting; she was a conservative Democrat, practically Republican.

"It's a new relationship. When he suggested lunch at Mandala— one of my favorite places—I knew he was on the make. I thought you might like to come along, too."

"What do you mean, he's on the make?" I asked. Kendall had been married for five years. I'd thought she was still crazy about Win.

"Not that way, silly. He wants me to raise money for him, you know, get involved with his campaign in this area, especially reaching into northern Virginia. It's kind of a challenge, not being a Republican there, although he does have the history of actually having fought in Vietnam and lost a foot, which earned him the Silver Star and a Purple Heart. He's kind of like John McCain meets Howard Dean meets the late Paul Wellstone."

Kendall was like that. She talked in shorthand, clichés, expressions that I was just beginning to learn everyone used, 24/7, in America. "But you're from Maryland," I said. "And if Senator Snowden and you are both Democrats, what are you doing talking about going after Republicans?"

"It's possible to get people to shift their vote, if the candidate is right," Kendall said. "Of course I'm a Marylander, but I went to boarding school and college in Virginia, which practically makes me a citizen. I know everyone, from the horsey set in Charlottesville to the techies in Reston. Harp desperately needs a friend like me."

Everyone meant people with money, I thought cynically. "So how much money do you have to give the senator to become his friend?"

"An individual can't give more than two grand because of all the soft-money reforms, but people like me can encourage our friends to give money. Lots of people, lots of money. You weren't here during the McCain campaign, but I threw a dinner for him that people are still talking about."

"McCain wasn't a Democrat," I pointed out. "What are you, a switch-hitter?"

"Usually I describe myself as a conservative Democrat with independent leanings," Kendall said. "Anyway, I promise you lunch won't be too political. I want you to relax. You can talk with him about Japan. He did some kind of Zen yoga thing there when he was in his twenties. Maybe you have some friends in common." She paused. "Oh, Rei. About your clothes?"

"Yes. What should I wear?" A private lunch with a senator was a first for me.

"Think Democrat, but dress Republican. Got it?"

I went through my closet furiously that morning, tossing clothes left and right as I searched for the outfit that Kendall had in mind. At one time, I had many conservative skirts and blazers from Talbots, but Hugh had encouraged me to toss them after I'd left my old life as a teacher. Now I wore sexier, casual things—leather jeans, blue jeans, T-shirts, miniskirts, boots. I also had a magnificent collection of cast-off clothing of my mother's that spanned the sixties to the nineties. The clothes were well made and beautiful, but none of them was Reagan Red or Bush Blue—after all, my mother was a lefty, too—but in the end, I settled on a cream Ultrasuede pantsuit worn with a black camisole. Looking at myself in the mirror after I'd belted its jacket, I appeared unhappily thick in the middle. Since returning to the States, I'd rekindled my love affair with bread and cheese. The scale said 121, which was horrific for someone who had hovered carelessly between 110 and 115 her entire life.

Still, the pants had an elastic waist, so I was able to wear them. I covered it all up with an aquamarine-colored raincoat that Kendall had made me buy a month earlier during a frenetic shopping expedition we'd made through White Flint Mall with her babies in tow. A raincoat was a necessity in Washington; it seemed as if it had rained all spring. Today was no exception. I hoisted my umbrella and left Hugh's Edwardian apartment building on Mintwood Place. The neighborhood we lived in, Adams-Morgan, was a real hike from the Metro; Hugh had chosen it when he was a bachelor, for the restaurants and bars. He hadn't thought twice about the twenty-minute walk to the Metro because he used a car to go to work downtown.

It was an odd habit, I thought, this insistence on driving a car in cities with public transportation.

Again, I was reminded of the city's deficiencies. When Hugh had courted me, taking me to jazz clubs in Georgetown and coffee shops in Dupont Circle, I'd been charmed; but now that I'd more or less explored every inch of the nation's capital, I felt otherwise. Sure, there were delightful late-nineteenth-century brick and stucco houses in Adams-Morgan, and you could dance at a real salsa bar, or get a reasonably priced Brazilian bikini wax from a real Brazilian, but that wasn't enough to make a world-class city experience. Outside Adams-Morgan, the situation was even bleaker. Downtown Washington was a bore, a far cry from my birthplace of San Francisco, and Tokyo, my adopted hometown since college. In Washington, there was nowhere to browse, no scene. Large office buildings were interspersed with ugly chain stores and just a smattering of turn-of-the-century buildings that had gone to pot—literally, from the looks of some of the people lounging outside them.

As I emerged from the Metro Center station and headed toward Ninth, where Mandala was located, I passed a woman sitting on the steps of an old row house, a child between her knees and a Styrofoam cup at her side. I didn't always give money to people who asked me for it, and the woman hadn't even looked at me, let alone spoken. Yet I was overcome with guilt for what I'd just been thinking about Washington. I dropped a dollar in the cup, but only the child looked at me. She had a typically round child's face, but eyes that looked much older. She seemed to see through me, back to the wild salmon I'd had for breakfast, and the expensive meal that lay ahead. A dollar wasn't much of a trade, but she nodded at me, and I nodded back.

I shivered, trying to put the moment behind me as I opened the heavy old temple door that led to Mandala. I hadn't been here before, but Hugh had, for some business lunches, and he'd told me it was fantastic. Judging from the atmosphere alone, it was my kind of place. Flickering electric candles in iron sconces illuminated a gorgeous mosaic tile floor with a floral mandala in its center. The dining tables were made from old Chinese altar tables or doors, I thought after a moment of study. Everything was rubbed to a soft reddish sheen, and the waitstaff wore dark-red shantung Mao jackets over black pants. It was quite a scene, about a million miles removed from the rainy, drab world outside its oversized brass doors.

The hostess, who had a long, blond pigtail and a hard-to-place European accent, told me that I'd have to wait for a table until my entire party was assembled. I glanced around the half-empty restaurant in irritation and spotted Kendall smack in the center of the room—as close to the mandala as she could get without being on top of it. Kendall, a leopard-patterned cell phone glued to her ear, looked perfect in a teal-blue knit suit and candy-red lipstick. She fluttered matching red-tipped fingers at me.

"I was just speaking with Harp. He said he's running a few minutes late," Kendall said after she clicked off. "Ooh, don't you look faboo. Did you get that at Neiman's?"

"I. Magnin," I said, which was where my mother had bought it about twenty-five years ago. The San Francisco department store didn't even exist anymore, but Kendall was an East Coast girl who wouldn't know that.

"Very cool. Hey, I was just about to order a martini—how do you like yours? Vodka, gin, dirty?"

"Not this early. I'll be happy with a glass of water," I said, studying the menu card in front of me with pleasure. I loved restaurants, especially ones that knew their way around a stick of lemongrass, as this one probably did.

"Don't tell me you're preggers already!" Kendall exclaimed.

"Of course I'm not." I flushed, feeling as if she'd been secretly watching the morning's activities.

"Oh, that's a drag. What kind of undies does Hugh wear?"

"What do you mean?" I put down my menu, not understanding Kendall's lightning change of topic. But the fact was, ever since Kendall had laid eyes on Hugh, she'd had a consuming interest in matters relating to him. Yes, the Scottish accent was sexy, as was his six-foot frame and his golden-retriever mop of hair. But he was mine.

"I mean, does he wear boxers or briefs?" Kendall looked at me expectantly.

"If Hugh wants to tell you about his underwear, I'll let him tell you directly."

"Now, honey, don't get *your* panties in a twist. It's just that if he's wearing tightey-whiteys, that could be overheating him and affecting his sperm count. Make sure he's wearing boxers, okay?"

"Kendall, why would I want to get pregnant before the wedding?" I was beginning to wish I hadn't come to lunch. If she kept up this kind of banter around the senator, I'd be mortified.

"To make sure it really happens! Come on, Rei, it's one of the oldest tricks in the book. And the best. I hear Grand did it to snare Granddad."

Silently, I vowed to myself to buy condoms on the way home.

"Believe me, it's better to get on these things right away. You don't want to have to go through IVF like I did."

"I hear that's pretty rough," I said in a low voice, because people at the next table were shooting us irritated looks. Probably the topic of sperm count wasn't what they wanted to digest along with tuna tartare.

"It is," Kendall said vehemently. "It hurts, it costs a fortune, and the end product is pretty damn unpredictable. The fertility specialist to whom I paid half a year's salary, thank you very much, had me impregnated with five fetuses at one point. I count my lucky stars that I wound up just with the twins."

"Oh, I'm sorry." I paused. "What happened? Did you lose the others?"

"In a manner of speaking." Kendall looked at me evenly, and suddenly I sensed that she was telling me she'd had an abortion. Or would it count as three? "Anyway, Rei, don't worry. I've seen the size of Hugh's hands and feet. From the looks of them, I'm sure he has no problem with anything down south."

She was so outrageous that there was nothing I could do but laugh, which was, I realized, what she'd wanted all along. The IVF conversation had probably taken a more depressing turn than she'd liked. So we laughed for a minute like a couple of high school girls. I broke off only when I noticed an elegant silver-haired man with a face I recognized from the newspaper. Harp Snowden was being helped off with his raincoat by one of the red-silk gang, at the same time that another male customer was trying to pat him on the back, and another was shaking his hand. Harp Snowden's briefcase slipped but was caught by someone. From the body language, it seemed as if the man who'd caught his briefcase was angling to accompany him to our table, but I saw Harp shake his head before raising his eyebrows at Kendall and shooting her a broad smile.

Kendall had risen to her feet, as had I. In Washington, it seemed that younger people always stood for older, more important people. He moved toward us with a very slight limp, and I recalled his missing foot. He walked without a cane, though, and from what I could make out from under the cuffs of his dark gray trousers, he was wearing two perfectly normal, polished wing tip shoes.

"Harp!" Kendall said, bringing her cheek to his mouth for a social kiss that he delivered smoothly upon his arrival. "I brought my cousin Rei Shimura to meet you."

"Senator Snowden, this is a real honor." I started to bow before remembering I wasn't in Japan. I came up and took the firm handshake he offered. "I'm a great admirer of your consistent stance on gun control. We heard about it all around the world, even when I was living in Japan—"

"Why thank you," he said, shrugging off the compliment with a warm laugh. "I hope you're from Virginia now."

"No, she lives in the District proper, where you'll have no trouble securing votes. My husband, Win, has been trying to find her and her fiancé something more family sized in the suburbs." Kendall looked at me indulgently. "Rei's used to historic San Francisco real estate. It's where she grew up."

"Oh, you're a past constituent!" Harp Snowden smiled at me. "No wonder you're familiar with my voting record."

I blushed with pleasure. I couldn't believe he was being so nice to me.

"Rei went on to Japan, but she's just moved back. I thought she could advise us on what to order."

"Actually, I've never been here," I said, feeling awkward about the position I'd been put in.

"Oh, everything on the menu's wonderful," Harp boomed as a handsome Asian man in his thirties with a short, gelled haircut and a spotless chef's jacket moved toward our table, a square black plate filled with hors d'oeuvres in his hand. "Jiro, my good friend. How are you?"

The chef was Japanese, I realized with a tinge of excitement as I heard his name. His English, as he started speaking, was soft but strong. "Very well, Senator. But what about you? How was your party last week? I called to check the next day, but you were away—"

"Back in L.A. The whole menu was terrific, and my wife wants the short-ribs recipe. I told her that it was probably classified."

Jiro's brow creased, and I sensed that despite his good English, he hadn't understood the metaphor. I said a quick couple of words in Japanese that explained what the senator had meant about the recipe being a valuable secret.

"Ah. You speak Japanese!" Jiro appeared to really notice me, for the first time.

"Yes, you certainly do, and it sounds fluent. What do you do with it?" Snowden asked.

I was beginning to replace the outsider image I'd had of Harp Snowden with that of a smooth-as-silk operator. "Well, I just moved here, like Kendall said, and I'm trying to sell Japanese antiques. It's a venture I started with a good friend who ships the furniture from Tokyo."

"Oh, so you were in Tokyo! Just like me." Jiro beamed at me and I felt warmly included. In Japan, so often I'd been reminded I was an outsider, but here in Washington, Jiro and I were both Japanese expats.

"Jiro was one of the iron chefs," Kendall said. "The cutest one they ever had. He was one for weeks and weeks."

"Until the day I made the terrible mistake of my lobster custard. I garnished with cilantro, and the sad fact was, one of the judges had an allergy."

"It's impossible to keep winning," I said. "Anyway, the show's finished now, so you have something else important to do."

"Yes, and the program brought me a wonderful job offer here in America. And now, before they become cold, I insist you try my *amuse-bouche*."

The little hors d'oeuvres he'd brought certainly were amusing: an assortment of sea scallops wrapped and grilled in lime leaves, cilantro risotto cakes topped with crisply fried seaweed, and miso-smothered rack of lamb ribs.

While I loved miso, I was trying not to eat meat, so I took a scallop first. I tasted the sea, the lime, and a slight hint of something else. "Hmm," I said. "Star anise?"

"Yes, yes! We roast and grind the spices here. It's not a Japanese ingredient, of course, but Chinese. This restaurant is what people call Pan-Asian. We mix European flavors with the Far East," Jiro explained.

"It's very delicious," I said. "I haven't had anything as tasty and sophisticated in a long time."

"Jiro's opening a new restaurant on H Street, near Fifth," Kendall said. "Win's selling the building next to it, so he's been watching the progress and says it's going to be great, like Mandala only more vintage-looking."

"Actually, it will be quite different from Mandala," Jiro said. "The new restaurant we are calling Bento, after the simple wooden box used to hold food. At lunch the service will be *bento* service, nice and quick, and for dinner, it will be *kaiseki ryoori*, when people have more leisure to eat slowly and appreciate."

"I ate *kaiseki* just once in Japan," Harp said. "They told me it was the highest form of Japanese cuisine. Each of the courses, as I recall, had something to do with the *yuzu* root. Why they chose *yuzu* is beyond me, though!"

"What do you think?" Jiro deferred to me, and I realized that he was being very Japanese—hesitant to tell the senator that *yuzu* was a revered food, and if he didn't appreciate it, it was probably because he was foreign.

"*Kaiseki* cooking is very intellectual," I said. "The goal is to send out a parade of exquisite small dishes that are linked, symbolically, and what they look like is sometimes more important than what they taste like. I've eaten *kaiseki* only a few times, but each time, the meal took up half a day—"

"Not here," Jiro said with a rueful smile. "We need to turn over tables faster than that. We are timing it for presentation over two hours."

"Well, I almost wish that was the timeline for lunch, not dinner," Kendall said with a laugh. "I like a nice long time to chat over lunch."

"You can always stay as long as you like, Kendall," Jiro said. "And actually, the problem is, we may not be able to do proper

Japanese lunchtime service. We were supposed to receive *bento* boxes last month, but the manufacturer is having trouble finishing our order. He says he does not have the resources to produce the amount we need in time."

"A Japanese manufacturer?" I asked.

Jiro wrinkled his nose slightly. "No. The boxes in Japan are made of pine or balsa and are too simple for what we are trying to accomplish. We found a woodworker in California with a supply of redwood. I wouldn't concern myself with these problems normally, but you see, the design of our food must coordinate with the kind of utensils we offer—"

"I could look into lacquered or stained wooden *bento* boxes for you," I said. "I know a good source for them in Kappabashi."

"Thank you, Miss, ah . . ." Jiro raised his eyebrows and I realized that I hadn't introduced myself to him. I told him my name quickly, and he smiled. Then, as if he'd sensed the needs of Kendall and the senator, he told us about the day's specials.

After listening to the recitation, Kendall went for salmon, the senator free-range beef, while I chose soft-shell crabs with a lemongrass-chili salsa and a salad of jicama and orange. I began a quick mental calculation of how much more I could afford to eat, since I had gone out with $40 in my backpack and had, in the course of ordering the two menu items, almost spent it all already.

Kendall and Senator Snowden had moved to second base, a general discussion of how the various Democratic candidates were doing. Kendall needled him a bit about whether he was going to jump into the race of Democratic hopefuls, and instead of answering her, he pumped her for information about the kind of fund-raising events that had worked best in northern, versus the rest of, Virginia. I became slightly bored by the talk about town-hall meetings and musical entertainment, but the food was wonderful, and I ate steadily.

Senator Snowden surprised me by turning the conversation to Japan. He'd been flown there for periodic spells of R and R during the Vietnam War, along with thousands of other men. "Two weeks' worth of Kirin and young women was supposed to put us in the mood to go back and reload our weapons," he said ruefully. "I made the fatal mistake of leaving the Yokosuka Honchō to visit a Buddhist temple. And once I sat down to meditate, I saw the truth. I couldn't go back to the old ways."

"Do you mean you went AWOL?" I asked.

"No. But I turned into the kind of man who was too frightened to pull the trigger anymore." He smiled, and I could imagine just how attractive—and un-wimpy—he must have been in his twenties. "Understandably, the Marines in my unit weren't too thrilled to work with me. Eventually, I lost my foot. I was sent to the hospital and then home."

"You received a Silver Star for heroism and a Purple Heart for being wounded in action, I believe." Kendall made her eyes look big and awed.

He shook his head. "I was awarded it, yes, but I never actually received it. I had left the military by the time they wanted to award it to me, but I decided I'd rather not take it. Wounded in action is nothing to be proud of, especially in my particular situation."

His particular situation—that sounded intriguing. I wondered whether Kendall, who had a "Support Our Troops" sticker on her Volvo bumper, would feel inclined to remove it if she participated in his campaign. But just as I was thinking about how she'd handle things, Jiro came back with another person, a tall, fortyish guy with dark curly hair just starting to turn gray. He was wearing a cashmere turtleneck under a suit that was either an Armani or an excellent runner-up.

"You know we love you, Senator, but you've got to keep your hands off my girl. I need her for more than the occasional fundraising dinner." He put his hands on Kendall's shoulders, and she giggled as if she didn't mind at all.

"Marshall, you know I've got to spread my energy around." Kendall winked at him, and went on in a cheerful voice, "Rei, this is Marshall Zanger, the owner of this restaurant. Don't believe a word he says about anything unless it's related to food. "

"I second that." Senator Snowden laughed heartily.

"I'm glad to meet you, Rei," Marshall said, taking my hand in his. It was cooler and somewhat damper than the senator's. "I heard from Jiro that you were interested in our next restaurant."

"Yes. It sounds very ambitious," I said.

"And what I like about your restaurant is the use of organic, local ingredients," Harp Snowden said. "The future of American farming is tied to the kitchens of places like Bento and Mandala. As long as there are people willing to seek out and encourage small farmers, they'll survive."

"So true, Senator. Because of people like you who can taste the difference, and chefs like Jiro Takeda, Bento will be the only place in Washington where a vegan can have a really upscale dinner," Marshall said. Then he glanced at the remnants on my plate. "What about you, Rei? Are you a vegetarian?"

"Semi." I smiled. "I used to be a vegan, but the truth is, I can't resist seafood. I eat anything that comes from the water except for sea urchin and raw oysters."

"Sea urchin I haven't tried yet, but I think oysters are delicious," Marshall said. "If I were a good Jewish boy, I wouldn't eat them, but I can't resist."

We all laughed, and then Jiro said, "I think this feeling about oysters is actually gender related. Male customers order them frequently, female customers hardly at all."

"Maybe it has to do with taste and texture," Kendall said, turning her lazy gaze on Harp, and suddenly I had an idea of what she was thinking. I blushed to realize that this might be a thinly veiled innuendo, but Harp was smiling right back at her.

"Interestingly enough, in Japan it's historically been women who dive for oysters. It's difficult work. The extra layer of fat is supposed to give women more endurance," I said, trying to bring the conversation back to more tasteful territory.

"And speaking of Japan," Marshall said, "it sounded, from what Jiro said, that you know how to make contact with some sources there."

"I'd be happy to ask around for you," I said.

"Super. But before you start calling, could I steal you away to my office to talk some more?"

"Sure. But we haven't finished eating." I was done, but the senator and Kendall were not. I couldn't just walk out on them, especially when the bill hadn't been paid.

"Go on, Rei! Harp and I need to get back to our powwow," Kendall said, drawing her pretty lips together. So her gentle inquisition of the candidate was going to continue.

"I want to cover my portion," I said.

"Absolutely not!" Harp said. "It's my office expenditure, if that makes you feel any better."

"But I want to! I really enjoyed myself!"

"Then just relax," the senator said. "I won't allow a good friend's guest to pay to eat lunch with me. When that kind of thing happens, ethics nightmares begin."

Kendall nodded at me and smiled. I was in, just like she was.

"Thank you," I said quickly, and left, hoping that my free lunch wouldn't wind up costing me more, later on, than I was ready to pay.

2

"We're very excited about Bento," Marshall Zanger said in his office after he'd nestled me in a turmeric-colored cotton love seat across from him. Compared to the austere elegance of the restaurant, this little room was a den of pandemonium—multiple telephones, cookbooks jammed next to telephone directories, file cabinets, a computer with a waterfall of paper on the desk around it. On the wall were framed photographs of Marshall or Jiro standing next to celebrities; in the short inspection I made, I saw the last two presidents, Martha Stewart, and a young white man with a shaved head who looked curiously familiar. Was it Moby?

"Jiro said the cuisine was going to be *kaiseki*. I'm trying to imagine how you'll do something as complicated as that for American diners," I said, dragging my gaze away from the wall of photographs.

"There's a small-plates trend in better restaurants," Marshall said. "In this neighborhood alone, Zaytinya and Jaleo have made their names because of tapas-style menus. *Kaiseki* is just a Japanese version."

"So, tell me, why do you need *bento* boxes—which enable you to serve several courses at once—if you want to do *kaiseki* service?" I was confused by the different visions of the restaurant that he and Jiro were presenting.

"Jiro's hot to do *kaiseki*, but the truth is, people have no time at lunch. They want to set their *tuchis* down and get a plate of food in five minutes, so *bento* boxes make sense. They allow for better turnover of the tables, too." Marshall studied me, as if all my questions had surprised him. "So tell me more about your source. Maybe I should speak with them directly, explain the rush."

I wanted to ask what a *tuchi* or *tuchis* was, but I was aware I'd been asking too many questions. "The sources I deal with don't speak English at all, so I would have to call for you. I usually deal with antiques, but because I cook, I know all the stores in Kappabashi, the kitchen district of Tokyo."

"Hold on, tell me more about the antiques."

"Well, I have a warehouse full of goods that I brought over from Japan—"

Marshall interrupted me. "I'd love to get some antiques in the restaurant."

My pulse quickened. Business was something that I badly needed. "I can take you to the warehouse. What are you looking for, exactly?"

Marshall drummed his fingers on his desk. "Accessories to decorate the place, art, the kind of thing that makes a restaurant more of a home. I don't want to be too Japanese-restauranty."

"You mean no blue cotton cushions, no pine, nothing too modern," I guessed aloud, and he nodded happily. "Maybe you should go historic. Late Meiji Period?"

Marshall laughed shortly. "When was that? Don't tell me five hundred years ago. That'll cost me more than I have."

I laughed, too. I was starting to like Marshall. "Don't worry. Meiji and later is what most dealers can afford. The end of Meiji coexisted with the British Victorian period. In Japan, just as in Europe and America, there was a fabulous amount of ornamentation and a design sense that combined East and West in an opulent, yet cozy, way."

"Hmm," Marshall said. "There's a great restaurant in San Francisco that's got the feeling I'm after. It has these fabulous oversize antique fans that flap back and forth on the ceiling—"

"Betelnut?" I hazarded.

"That's right. You do know the restaurant scene."

The truth was, Betelnut was a few blocks from my family home, which was why I'd eaten there plenty of times. I had a hometown girl's advantage, but there was no need to get into it. Instead, I said, "During the European colonial era, those fans were more in use in countries like Singapore or Malaysia. There might have been ceiling fans of that style in more tropical parts of Japan, like Okinawa, but in the old days, Okinawa wasn't even part of Japan. I'd have to research whether that style of fan was in use—"

"Oh, there's no need for that." Marshall sighed heavily. "It's too late to make major changes. I had such hopes for this place, what it could be, and now we're opening in thirty days without so much as tableware. Not to mention staff. I'm still trying to get line cooks. In fact, I have interviews scheduled there in about an hour. Hey, why don't you ride over there with me? While Jiro and I are interviewing staff, you could look around and get some ideas of what I need."

"All right," I said, pausing at the door. "Oh, I almost forgot to ask you something. It was a word I didn't understand when you were talking about the lunch service."

"Fire away."

"What's a *tuchis*?"

Marshall laughed for a full minute before saying, "*Tuchis* is Yiddish for 'ass.'"

Feeling like one, I got into his Mercedes.

Bento was housed in an old brick building on H Street, more on the edge of Chinatown although it was technically within the boundaries of Penn Quarter, the faded section of downtown that was coming back because of a number of hip new restaurants. I hadn't been in Washington's Chinatown since my college years, when I'd occasionally driven with a carful of other hungry Asian studies majors for dim sum. It seemed as if a lot of the Chinatown restaurants had evaporated since my day. There was no shortage of Starbucks cafes, though. Starbucks was strange. In Kendall's suburban neighborhood of Potomac, Starbucks was full of blond power moms like herself; but in my neighborhood, it was solely inhabited by Spanish-speaking men. I would have liked to scope out the situation in the Chinatown Starbucks, but Marshall seemed impatient.

"Chinatown doesn't seem very—Chinese—anymore," I said to Marshall. It seemed that all over H Street and Fifth, drugstores and Irish bars had replaced the small restaurants I remembered.

"The rents went up," Marshall said. "It's going upscale. If we could only drive out the gangs, it'd be perfect."

Now there was something I could comment on. "In San Francisco, there were some gang wars when I was really young. There was a shoot-out in a Chinese restaurant that decimated the restaurant business in Chinatown for a few years."

Marshall looked at me. "I'm not anticipating a shoot-out in Bento, but there's hostility from our neighbors. I don't know if having a real Japanese chef is the problem—because of the grudge the Chinese still bear against Japan since the war—or if it's just plain competition."

"What's happened so far?"

"Another restaurant owner tried to keep me from putting in a parking area out behind our kitchen. No matter that it freed up more space for street parking—he didn't want me having anything he didn't have."

I didn't comment on that, because it seemed pretty minor league to me, but concentrated on the building's facade. The restaurant site was typical of the early-twentieth-century Washington vernacular, a redbrick, four-story building. It was built on a corner, and it had especially charming moldings, Gothic peaks over the windows and doors. There was a boarded-up building of the same vintage next to it, made of the same brick but with a peeling white-paint overlay. A shingle flapping outside confirmed that Kendall's husband, Win, was indeed handling its real estate transaction. You could see through the windows in this building to the peeling wallpaper and scuffed wooden floors. Marshall and Jiro's building had its windows covered in brown paper, so nobody from the outside could peek in.

For good reason, I discovered when I went inside. The place was in an utter shambles: drop-cloth-covered furniture intermingling with ladders, huge boxes of electrical fixtures, and other things I couldn't identify. Half a dozen men were at work in the room, hammering and drilling.

"The walls will be sea grass on the top half, and plum below the chair rail," Marshall shouted over the din. "Would that work with Meiji?"

"Perfectly. What will the floor be?"

"Underneath the tarps, we have old Georgia pine. We're going to sand it and stain it the color of teak." He pulled back the plastic covering a rosewood chair, straight backed, with a cushion covered in a cinnabar-and-gold patterned fabric.

"That looks like an old obi," I said.

"Yeah, but it's synthetic. Totally stain resistant, which is what we need. Which reminds me of something else. Jiro's fixated on this idea of redwood, but I'm not sure wood is durable enough for restaurant service. What's your take?"

I liked Jiro and his dream of the lacquered redwood *bento* boxes, but I knew how much effort it took to preserve the glossy finish on my own real lacquered possessions. After being used for food, lacquered wood had to be gently washed and dried. Its finish showed smeary fingerprints, too.

"I think we could compromise and still have beauty and durability," I said. "*Bento* boxes exist that are made of such high-quality plastic that they look and feel just like lacquered wood. I'll order some samples from Japan so you can decide—"

"I've already decided. That's just what I want. But don't tell Jiro it's plastic, okay? It'll be just between us."

I was about to tell him that it would be impossible to fool a Japanese person about such a thing when a young woman with a tawny complexion and a mop of springy, blond curls interrupted us. "Marshall, one of the cooks is already here, the guy from Nora's—"

"Excellent." Marshall winked at me. "If I can steal this guy, I know I'll be in good hands."

"But I thought Jiro would cook the food here." I was confused.

"He will be executive chef. The interviews going on are for line chefs who'll work under him. And who knows, from the line a star may be born—the guy who'll lead my next restaurant. Andrea will show you the existing interior-design elements, the paint chips, that kind of thing—"

"What do you mean? I'm supposed to be checking in the cooks for interviews, and getting all those returns done on the light fixtures!" Andrea narrowed her almond-shaped eyes.

"First you'll show Rei around." Marshall's voice was firm. "She's going to be taking over the interior-design stuff, which will make your life easier."

"Oh?" Andrea looked at me doubtfully.

"I could come back another day if it's better." I was thinking to myself that a Japanese employee would never have spoken to a boss like that. Even Marshall seemed disturbed because his voice rose and he waved his hand to include the whole room of workers.

"Come on, we've got to move! Thirty-five days from now, our doors will open. Andrea, it'll take you five minutes to show Rei around. After that, you can go on with your regular schedule. Rei, I'll need the proposal from you by tomorrow morning—it doesn't have to be final, but tell me what you think I need to buy and approximately how much it'll cost."

And with that, he disappeared through the swinging doors to the kitchen, presumably to interview the cook from Nora's.

"It's a good thing he pays people as much as he does, because he'd be impossible otherwise," Andrea muttered.

"I'm sorry to be making more work for you," I said. It was in my interest to get along with her, but I doubted it could happen. She was one of the gorgeous but mean girls who seemed to work exclusively in places like restaurants, fashion houses, and television stations. Andrea had slanting, catlike eyes, high cheekbones, and lips so full they must have endured a few collagen injections. She was model-quality beautiful—even in a chic, shrunken hooded sweater and low-slung yoga pants that revealed a navel pierced with a shining black stone. I sucked in my own abdomen and examined her again. Something had to be wrong with her or I wouldn't sleep at night. Now I decided that her short, blond, kinky hair could not possibly be natural.

"It's okay," Andrea answered grumpily. "Actually, you'll be saving me work if I don't have to hunt for those *bento* boxes anymore."

"What is your official title within the restaurant?" I wondered if she was some kind of sous-chef—or merely the waitress from hell.

"I used to be a hostess at Mandala, and I'm going to do the same job here. I organize people, not chairs. Did he tell you that we had an interior designer who did a lot of buying and choosing at the start of the project? No? Well, that girl quit after she got in a fight with Marshall about her fees."

Andrea took me down a set of creaky, dusty stairs to the restaurant's basement, where more of the furniture lay waiting, mostly chairs and tables, all the same style as I'd seen before. There was also a folder with a blueprint of the dining room and the hallway leading to the rest rooms, and a furniture-placement diagram.

"I don't suppose you could show me any other accent pieces you have?"

"Well, we've got forks, knives, that kind of thing. There's the maître d's station table up there already, and the bar—did you see it?"

I hadn't noticed it, so I picked up the folder and went upstairs again to look. Two more potential chefs and a dishwasher had arrived, so while Andrea took them back to the kitchen for their interviews with Marshall and Jiro, I wandered the room by myself, trying to piece it together. The things they'd chosen were all quite beautiful—hand-painted silk Roman shades for the windows, the plum wall color, and the light greeny-yellow sea grass covering for the top half of the walls. These weren't typical colors of modern Japan, but they could fit in well with late-nineteenth- and early-twentieth-century design. The rest rooms were boring, I thought, after I walked into both men's and ladies'. In my mind I was already papering the walls with the legendary arts-and-crafts textile designer Candace Wheeler's carp-patterned wallpaper. As I did so, another idea followed: stalls made of reclaimed wood from old storehouse doors, several of which Mr. Ishida had sent to our downtown warehouse.

The toilets were roughed in, I could see, as were the plumbing lines for the sinks. The fixtures hadn't been installed yet, which made me think of some slightly flawed, but handsome, *tansu* chests that could be transformed into vanities. Blue-and-white porcelain Imari bowls dropped in their centers would serve as sinks. I also had several antique blue-and-white china urinals that could come into play as planters, or toiletry holders. The rest rooms could be amazing.

I emerged from the lavatories to consult with Andrea, who was grumbling into a cell phone to somebody.

"What now?" she asked after she'd finally hung up.

What a sourpuss, I thought to myself, and asked how much of the bathroom furnishings had been purchased.

"Just what you see. The interior designer didn't get around to sinks, and Marshall was supposed to order them but I'm sure he forgot."

Great, I thought to myself.

I spent three hours in Bento, wandering around and dreaming. The job wouldn't be insurmountable. Spending thirty-five days polishing up the restaurant was something I thought I could do. This would be a good way to get me out of the apartment and the sense that everything in my life was standing still.

At five, I peered into the kitchen, where Marshall was chatting, rapid-fire, in Spanish with one of the cooks, and told him I was leaving.

"I'll see you tomorrow, nineish," Marshall said.

"Uh, afternoon would be better. I'll probably have to work through the night—that being the Japanese day. And then I think I'll need a few hours of rest."

"Of course. Take your time getting it right. I'll see you late afternoon at Mandala."

When Hugh arrived home at seven, he found me at the computer with dozens of design and antiques magazines fanned around on the floor. I'd already found three good choices for *bento* boxes, and now had been drawing and cutting and gluing together pictures of what I would try to accomplish at Bento. I had the speakerphone on, and my mother's voice was booming into the room.

"One hundred dollars an hour, sweetie, is a junior decorator's rate right now in San Francisco. And there's just as much moolah in Washington as out here. Now, the next thing you must determine is what percentage to mark up the merchandise, although if you can sell him some of your own *tansu* chests, you'll profit very nicely."

"Thanks, Mom. Hugh's here, so I'd better go start dinner." I suddenly remembered the risotto I'd promised to make.

"Give Hugh my love and tell him to examine everything carefully! I'll send over what I've been using, but you probably need more protection."

My mother rang off and Hugh kissed the back of my neck.

"Exactly what is your mother sending? I thought we were trying to get pregnant."

"Only you are," I said. Now I recalled that I'd forgotten to buy condoms, along with scallops, at the supermarket. I pulled away from the kiss and told him about the new job designing the restaurant.

"Is there anything you'd like me to do?" he asked, taking in the flood of papers around me.

"Could you take care of dinner? And after that, maybe you could advise me on the contract. I'm still trying to decide what my services are worth."

"Loads." Hugh smiled. "Exactly what else are you putting on offer tonight?"

"Not what you seem to be thinking about." Who had time for sex when such a crisis was looming?

I managed to divert Hugh into stirring the risotto and listening to everything that had happened at Mandala and the soon-to-be Bento. He agreed with what I'd been thinking of: offering antiques from my warehouse wholesale, and passing on any discounts I received for items bought elsewhere. I would bill my services at $90 an hour, to make it really seem like a bargain.

"Ask if we'll be able to eat free at Mandala and Bento, once it opens. You'll be working so many hours you won't have much time to cook," Hugh said when we sat down to the risotto flavored only with onions and cheese. The rice was undeniably hard. I felt guilty that I hadn't taught him the proper stirring and stock-adding techniques.

"I'm not sure I would really be relaxed having dinner there," I said, moving on to the salad, which was perfect—though completely lacking in dressing. "They're a bit uptight. I adore their chef—this Japanese guy, Jiro—but I'm supposed to trick him into thinking I'm buying real lacquered wooden *bento* boxes when I'm actually buying plastic—"

"Do you really want to do the job?" Hugh studied my face. "It isn't worth it to work with bad people, no matter how much you might earn."

"They're not bad people," I said. "Jiro and I already get along well. Marshall is not the kind to give anyone much time, but that's to be expected, with the opening in a month. On the other hand, Andrea, the one who is going to be the restaurant hostess, is pretty cold. I wouldn't want to spend more than a minute with her, and I can't imagine how she's going to make diners feel welcome."

"That opinion doesn't surprise me." Hugh grinned. "You're not much for the girls."

"What do you mean?" I took a sip of zinfandel.

"You've never had a really close female friend. Ever since I've known you, it's just been blokes. I thought maybe it was hard for you to connect with women in Japan, given how nontraditional you are, but I see it here, too."

"Well, I don't much care for Kendall. I admit that."

"Even though your cousin did you a very good turn taking you to lunch at the restaurant." Hugh shook his head. "And she left a message on the phone about my getting to see some boxers. I didn't catch all the details, but I gather there must be a match. How keen are you on going?"

"Argh!" I sputtered wine in an arc that hit my plate.

"What's wrong, darling?" Hugh passed me his napkin.

"That call was about your underwear, specifically, whether you wear boxer shorts. Kendall's on a rampage. When she was a child, she wasn't half this bad. But she's grown into a nosy, raving maniac!"

Hugh laughed. "Maybe you should join that club Kendall mentioned to meet a few others who might be more your sort."

I choked hard on the wine going down my throat. Finally, I sputtered, "I am not going to join the Junior League of Washington. I'm already part of the Washington Japan Friendship Society."

"Those are all old people!"

"Yes, there are many retirees, but at that open house last month, we both met some young students."

"But you aren't a student anymore, Rei. You need girlfriends your age. They'll be a lifeline after the baby comes."

I set down my glass. "It sounds as if you're presupposing that if I have a baby, I'm going to stop working and stay at home all the time."

"You stay home all the time now," Hugh pointed out. "And I'm glad about this restaurant job for you if it'll get you out and about and meeting people. Male or female, I really don't care. Just that you have someone to be with. I've got a work trip coming up, and I'm nervous because you've not stayed alone in an American city. You've forgotten how dangerous they are. It's not like Tokyo, where you can traipse home after midnight without a worry—"

"Where are you going?" I asked, my heart sinking. We were supposed to meet with a very-hard-to-get wedding caterer in four weeks' time.

"Japan. I'm sorry, love. I wish I could pack you in my suitcase, but the suitcase-screening procedures have gotten so tight."

But I couldn't travel, even if I had a ticket. Suddenly, the wine in my mouth was too tart. I pushed the glass away.

As if he understood what I was thinking, Hugh said, "I'm sure that the ban will cease sometime. Paul McCartney was banned from Japan after that marijuana charge, but they rescinded it recently."

"Yes, but I'm not going to be knighted." I made a face at him. "Hey, sweetie, I'll forgive all those sexist comments if you help me figure out how to do a spreadsheet for my presentation."

He did, and as we worked together that night, finally shutting off the computer at four in the morning, I felt more exultant than exhausted. I had put together a strong proposal, and Marshall was desperate. The job at Bento would be mine.

3

I'd thought that the month until the opening of Bento would pass quickly, but it didn't feel that way at all. For me, it was all about waiting—for the *bento* boxes to be airmailed from Tokyo, the wallpaper to come UPS second-day ground from New York. A master carpenter in the Virginia tidewater area had all my old Japanese wooden doors, but he was taking forever to nail together the stalls—even though he'd been paid a rush fee.

Every day, I would show up at Bento, ready to seize newly arrived items. They came in sporadically, and I had to assuage Marshall, who was vastly impatient. The only solace was in the kitchen, where I would lean against the long, stainless-steel counter, watching Jiro work on dishes that he allowed me to taste.

Crab cakes mixed with dark soy sauce, chilies, cilantro, and spring onions were a hit—soba noodles in a sweet potato broth were not. I made friends with the fleet of line cooks who'd be working under him, mostly Latin Americans, with the occasional white boy who'd graduated from culinary school. Spanish conversations simmered around me like chili-saffron bouillabaisse in a giant stockpot, and I stretched back to my youth in California to understand what they were saying. They respected Jiro but feared Marshall. They thought Andrea needed to get laid.

They called me the bride, because they knew I was going to marry in a few months. I didn't tell them how silly I thought that was, because I was secretly relieved they were calling me something less crude than usual. Jiro had told me that not a single woman had applied to be a line cook, but he had hired Jessica Olson, who had been a pastry chef at Citronelle, to make his desserts. Jessica was about my age, but blond and very voluptuous; there was always such a commotion in the kitchen when she made her deliveries that I could understand why she preferred to work at home. Not that Jessica was cowed by the comments made around her; she delivered a steady stream of obscenities back in a broad Minnesota accent that made me have to hide my smile.

Opening night was just a week away when Hugh had to fly to Tokyo. He was continuing the lengthy process of crafting a lawsuit on behalf of Asian nationals abused by the Japanese during World War II. The work was important, so I wanted him to go— but still, I was disappointed. I'd wanted him to be at my side on opening night.

"Can't I pop in a day early, just to get a peek?" he said as he packed his suitcase.

"I wish you could," I said ruefully. "Marshall has made the whole place off-limits until the opening night party. There's brown paper over the windows, locked doors, everything."

"Sounds like a terrorist cell," Hugh said. "Well, I'll just have to see it when I get back. Are you taking anyone with you to the opening?"

"Kendall and Win."

"Oh! I'm glad you're at last reciprocating their hospitality."

I didn't explain that it wouldn't cost me much at all. Bento was having a soft opening, a run-through of sorts, where specially chosen guests were invited. People could order anything off the menu that they wanted, gratis; there would be charges for bottles of wine, but that was the only thing. The following day, Saturday, the restaurant would open to the public.

Hugh hugged me and said, "What shall I bring you from Japan?"

"You don't have to shop for me. Just do your work and get home."

"But I *like* shopping. Come on, what do you want, more Shu Uemura makeup or books from Yurindo or a proper fish steamer—"

"How about some old kimono? Go to the flea market on Sunday morning, and scoop up twenty or thirty kimono without holes. I could resell them to a museum gift shop. I'll need something to do, now that the restaurant is almost finished."

"No, I mean something for *you*."

"I can't think of anything I need." Just you, I thought to myself, but didn't say for fear of being maudlin.

On a sunny Friday afternoon, Bento finally opened. I watched Marshall and Jiro tear down the brown paper from the glass windows that fronted the street. Suddenly, the room that had been so closed and dark was open. Late-afternoon sunshine made the plum walls suddenly bloom with color. The restaurant was much brighter than Mandala, I realized. A lot of the warmth came from the wood: the honeyed tone of the wide pine plank flooring, the reddish brown of the cryptomeria-wood kitchen *tansu*, a fabulous late-Meiji-period storage cabinet so expensive that I'd despaired of ever selling it. The *tansu* was filled with cocktail glasses now and stood behind the vintage zinc-topped bar.

Everywhere you looked, Bento was a mishmash of Japan and America: the immaculate white tablecloths set with Imari chargers, a design element that gave the restaurant the drama it needed for evening. Other dishes would be served in faux lacquer *bento* boxes—boxes that Jiro had, within minutes, figured out were plastic, but grudgingly accepted.

I continued my survey of the room. Most of the art I'd chosen was hanging already. A tryptich woodblock print of courtesans dining was hung along the north wall, as was another print showing a Tokyo food market in midwinter. More art was en route from Mr. Ishida's shop in Tokyo; I hoped to have it installed within the first two weeks. For the lavatories, I'd found charming vintage posters from the 1920s that advertised soap and sweets, which I'd had framed and hung on the doors. My idea of installing blue-and-white basins inside small *tansu* chests had worked beautifully for the vanities. The carpenter was just finishing the stall door locks, brass hardware from Japan that was quickly faux-aged in a substance I was afraid to ask about but that did the job beautifully.

I'd get an early sense of whether the interior was a success at the opening-night party, when the friends of the restaurant would test it. And far more important than my interior would be the kitchen's ability to assemble its dishes, the waiters' speed and finesse, and even the sommelier's choices of wine pairings. Not to mention how the food tasted. That was the most important thing of all.

The restaurant didn't smell of food now, just of the heady incense that I recognized from Japanese temples. Andrea, dressed all in black, had lit a stick of incense at the hostess's podium. She stared out at the passage of traffic beyond the glass window, the people streaming home from the Mall in cars and on foot.

"How many are coming tonight?" I asked.

"About two hundred," she said. "You have two guests, right? I'm putting you all at a four-top over by the west wall."

I glanced where she had gestured with her long red fingernails. The table in question was not in a great location, but I was hardly one of the people they needed to impress. "I see it. What's the VIP situation?"

"What do you mean?"

"Are any celebrities coming?" If Moby and Hillary Clinton showed up, my night would be made.

She rolled her eyes. "In Washington, celebrity doesn't usually coincide with very important."

"Of course," I said, feeling my face burn a little. Washington was like Japan in that way. Senators, International Monetary Fund bigwigs, C-SPAN journalists—these were the people who counted, and I was woefully inept at recognizing them. When I'd been over at Mandala one day trying to cadge some candles for Bento, the new Speaker of the House had been there, and Marshall had been shocked that I hadn't recognized him. The problem, I explained in a half-joking manner, was that I only recognized beautiful things, whether it was an antique vase or a particularly lovely waiter. Fortunately, there were many of the latter hired for Bento, and I'd learned almost all their names. There was Phong, a good-looking Vietnamese-American guy who ran the bar, concocting such drinks as *shiso* mojitos and saketinis; Justin, the moonlighting undergraduate with the tousle of black curls; and David, a languid blond from Australia. Marshall had hired two female runners, Carla and Joan, who were also young and attractive, but their responsibilities were limited to carrying out the plates as they were finished, not taking the initial orders. They earned a portion of the tips, as did Andrea, but not the kind of money Justin, David, and their male cohorts did.

As the old rosewood Seiko grandfather clock in the restaurant's side hallway chimed seven, the first diners arrived and their comments on the interior felt like strokes along my back. The *tansu* holding barware—how beautiful! The old china on the walls, the artwork—fabulous! Awesome! Marshall had me on his arm, taking me around as if I was his partner, making me tell everyone about the Meiji Period and the heritage of the pieces I'd chosen.

In the midst of it all, Kendall made her entrance. She'd pinned up her fox-colored hair in a French twist and was wearing a sleek black suit that ended mid-thigh. She wore spiky Manolo Blahniks and some extra accessories that I hadn't expected: a twin at the end of each arm.

I wish she'd told me, I thought to myself. I'd had to clear my guests with Marshall, and I'd definitely not mentioned children. At the moment, Marshall was scrutinizing the two children as if they were a couple of homeless beggars who had wandered in.

"Hey, sweetie," Kendall said. "The restaurant is just gorge. Winnie, look at the pretty color on the walls. What color is that?"

"Boo," said Win Junior.

"No, it's purpur! Purpur!" shrieked Jacqueline, causing heads to turn.

"Let's get them comfortable right away," I said to Kendall, handing an unsmiling Andrea the twins' tiny dirt- and mucus-smeared down jackets.

"I'll need two high chairs right away, and the kiddie menus," Kendall said to Andrea.

"We don't have any," Andrea said coolly.

"Really? You opened a restaurant with no high chairs?" Kendall countered with her own glare.

"We aren't geared to babies," Andrea replied coldly. "However, we do have a booster seat. But just one. And as far as children's food, Chef can prepare smaller portions of regular adult meals, if you like."

"Okay. I'll stash Winnie in the booster and Rei and I will trade off holding Jacqueline. I understand this is the opening night and all, but you will probably need to improve your seating. Lesson learned!" Kendall said cheerfully.

Without answering, Andrea led us to the table. Kendall made a face at me, and I mouthed my apologies to her. I *was* sorry. The restaurant should have had high chairs and at least a few booster seats. But how could I locate baby furniture that looked as if it was a hundred years old and Asian?

The children played underneath the table, tugging at the white tablecloth so vigorously that I was on the verge of saying something. Finally, Carla the runner appeared with a plastic booster seat. Kendall strapped it around a chair and hoisted Win inside.

"I didn't mean to bring them," Kendall said. "The problem is that I'd forgotten I gave our au pair the night off to go to a dance at the Naval Academy. I didn't want to stand you up, and I have big news I wanted you to be the second to know about."

"Another baby?" I could ask happily, because a week earlier I'd gotten a tiny bit of proof that I wasn't going to have one myself.

Kendall looked as if I'd slapped her. "I guess you can tell that I missed last week's sessions with my trainer. When I stop lifting weights, my metabolism goes haywire." She sighed. "Actually, I've been so busy because I agreed to organize a fund-raising dinner for Harp Snowden. I'm considering this as a possible location."

"Wow! If you have the dinner here, Marshall and Jiro will be ecstatic!" And I would be, too, if pictures of my beautiful restaurant showed up on television and in news magazines all over the country.

"It's going to be fun, but a ton of work. We're meeting next week to start thinking about the logistics of it all. Food, music, the works!" Kendall snapped her fingers, and the twins started to giggle. "For music I'm thinking about trying to get Coldplay—they're interested in liberal politics, you know. And doesn't Hugh just love them?"

"We both do, but you know, Hugh isn't a citizen, he can't vote—"

"No biggie. He can still donate; there's no law against that yet." Kendall made a face. "I'm going to have a hell of a time convincing Win to write a check, though. He's gotten so cranky about money lately."

"Well, he was a Republican before he married you, right?"

"Still is." Kendall made a face. "Thank God I have Grand's trust to tap into for my own use. He'd never go for me spending his money on my candidates."

"Is Win joining us later?" I inquired.

Kendall shook her head. "He has a late appointment in northern Virginia. It drives me crazy, but that's what I deserve for marrying a real estate guy. Where's your own hubcap?"

"Japan." I would have elaborated, but Jacqueline was starting to try to wriggle off my lap. Kendall had said she'd hold her daughter after she finished reading the menu. That reminded me that the twins would need some dining suggestions.

"Jacqueline, do you like noodles?" I entreated. "There are some nice noodles on the menu in a yummy sweet sauce."

"Ooh, let me have the steak," Kendall said, studying the menu.

"After that weight gain, I'm back on Atkins. And for dessert, it's got to be fruit and whipped cream. Hmm, I don't see it listed on the menu, but Jessica Olson's doing the desserts, so I can ask her to put together something special for us. You should have it, too, Rei. No carbs in whipped cream!"

"But why?" I objected. "I've tasted Jessica's cakes and tarts before, and they're not to be missed."

"I took a cooking class from her at the Smithsonian once, before I'd started watching my weight. Let me tell you that she's a real bitch. She went ballistic when I suggested substituting Pepperidge Farm puff pastry for homemade in one of the recipes she was teaching us."

"Well, Jessica is a La Varenne–trained pastry chef—" I cut myself off, distracted because Jacqueline started to burble about wanting macaroni, and Win Junior started grabbing all the beautiful faux-ivory-handled tableware; Kendall's cell phone rang. She slipped it out of her Kate Spade diaper bag.

"Yes, Harp!" she said loudly, giving me a significant glance. "I'm sorry, but you'll have to speak up. The acoustics in here suck."

Justin appeared at our table with two complimentary saketinis. When he saw Kendall, he said to me, "Didn't you tell her about the cell phone policy?"

"No. What's the policy?"

"No cell phone usage in the dining room. They're supposed to go in the hall by the rest rooms if they want to talk."

"I can't interrupt her, Justin. She's talking to Senator Snowden. By the way, could you bring some juice for the kids? Apple juice, say, in plastic glasses?"

Justin wrinkled his beautiful nose. "We have neither apple nor plastic. The best I can do is Perrier with a twist of lime—"

"Do you two like fizzy water?" I asked Win and Jacqueline.

They shrieked with excitement, and I placed the order. But Justin wasn't done. Sternly, he addressed Kendall. "Miss, you'll have to take your call in another place."

"Just a minute, please, Senator." Kendall paused and stared at the waiter. "What kind of restaurant is this that you're so rude to the patrons?"

"House rules. Out in the hall," Justin said firmly.

So Kendall swept out carrying her saketini and the telephone, leaving me with her little twosome.

Since I had no adult to chat with, I indulged in a little people-watching. While there were some people dressed elegantly, there were a surprising number of casual dressers. At least a dozen young men were wearing regular dress shirts, untucked, over shorts or trousers, and I spotted a woman walk by who'd tied an Hermès scarf around her torso to serve as a blouse. People had said Washington was not a fashion city—I was beginning to see that Kendall was an exception, and not a rule. I hadn't expected people wearing scarf tops and shorts to be sitting at my elaborately decorated tables, but they, in turn, probably hadn't been expecting to see kids.

Justin came to take the rest of our order, and I gave it: a carrot-ginger salad, noodles with *ponzu* dipping sauce, and a sweet bean–chocolate pâté for the kids' *bento* meals. Instead of the lengthy *kaiseki* menu, for myself I went for the convenience of a quick *bento* containing a *daikon* salad, *soba* noodles, and red snapper, and for Kendall asparagus with *wakame* seaweed and soy-glazed filet mignon, because of what she'd said about the Atkins diet. What kind of a country was it, I thought, where a diet book could hold sway over so many people's dining habits? Jiro had talked seriously with Marshall about it beforehand. There were at least three dishes on the menu that met Atkins requirements. I couldn't remember if soy was on or off the diet. I became nervous thinking about it, so I asked Justin to find Kendall and ask.

"What do you think I am, suicidal?" he snapped. "Rei, I've got lots of tables to serve—oh, damn, look what that little boy of yours did to the flowers."

Hers, not mine, I could have said, but didn't. Win Junior had rearranged the camellias that a Georgetown florist had so carefully arranged in a low bowl earlier that afternoon. One camellia was in his hair, and the other on his sister's plate. She was picking up her blossom to eat it.

"Not for supper! Supper's coming soon," I said, taking the camellia from her lips and tucking it back into the dish. "Please check for me, Justin. I beg you. I'm not a child care expert—you need to get her back or who knows what will happen."

Justin came back with the news that Kendall wasn't in the hall, and that Marshall wanted me to stop by table 5, because the patrons had a question about the origins of the *tansu* behind the bar. I glanced across the room and saw Marshall sitting with them. Great. I had to do it, but I couldn't abandon Win and Jacqueline, leaving them alone at the table.

I hung on to Jacqueline's sticky little fingers with one hand while I unbelted Winnie from his booster seat with the other. We proceeded slowly to table 5, hampered by Winnie's attempts to grab things off the tables we passed.

When we reached the table, I did my best to talk intelligently about the *tansu* with a pleasant older gentleman who'd spent some time in Japan. But Jacqueline kept up a patter about where her mommy was, and Win grabbed a menu out of the hands of the man's female dining companion. I decided to make a quick exit. Glancing across the room, I saw that Kendall still hadn't returned.

"Let's visit the lavatory," I said in my most cheerful voice.

"No potty!" Jacqueline cried.

"You don't have to go potty there, don't worry. I want to show you some—fish! Fish on the walls. Don't you like fish?" I led the two of them into the ladies' rest room. Win decided he wanted to try to potty, and I undid his pants and struggled to undo his diaper. I spent too long figuring it out, because Win wound up exploding on the Italian-tile floor.

I pulled up his diaper in horror and scrubbed quickly at the floor with paper towels as a couple of women walked in and gasped at the sight before them. I concentrated on cleaning up, and after I'd washed and dried everyone's hands and was leading them out, I caught sight of Andrea.

"May I make a quick phone call from the maître d's stand?" I grabbed her sleeve, because she seemed as if she was trying to ignore me.

"Those are for incoming calls only." She pulled away her arm and examined it, as if I might have torn the lace on her long-sleeved blouse.

"This is an emergency." I planned to call Kendall's cell number, which I knew better than her household one, since she was always out.

"What kind of emergency?" Andrea prodded.

I was losing my patience. "A child care one. These kids are going to be in the restaurant all night if we don't get their mother to come back from wherever she's hiding."

Andrea grudgingly let me use the telephone, but my call just went into her voice mail. She had to still be chatting with Harp Snowden. But where *was* she? Kendall couldn't have gone far, because I could see, through the restaurant's front door, her Volvo parked on the street.

Maybe she'd stepped out back. Trundling the children along with me, I moved through the masses and then the swinging doors that led into the kitchen. I was blindsided by a tray carried by one of the runners. The tray teetered and broth leaped from a bowl and onto me.

"Wrong door!" the girl carrying the tray practically spat at me. Right door in, left door out. I repeated it to myself as I led the children into the kitchen.

It was pandemonium. The children gazed in awe at the white-coated cooks moving fast at their stations, sautéing and stirring and flipping. There was a boom box playing salsa that was over-powered by the sound of hissing meat on the grill, the clattering of iron pans.

"Has anyone seen a woman come through here?" I called out.

"I'm the only one around, unless you count him." Jessica, the pastry chef, shot a naughty glance at Justin, who was pinning up a dinner order on the line.

"Yeah, girlfriend, but at least I'm not built like a Midwestern milk truck," Justin shot back.

"I'm looking for my cousin, has anyone seen her?" I pleaded. Then I remembered that half the kitchen staff didn't speak English. "*Dónde a chica—*" I flubbed, then pointed at the children with me. "*Madre.*"

"You have children, Rei? I didn't know." Jiro, who was showing one of the line cooks how to roll and then cut a *shiso* leaf, looked up with a beatific smile. He seemed to take a Zen approach to the chaos of opening night.

"Not mine, my cousin's. I'm looking for her—she's an attractive redhead in a black suit. I think she went into some part of the building or just outside it to make a cell phone call."

"Ah. Let me ask." Jiro fired off something in Spanish. I couldn't hear it clearly because I was in the midst of retrieving Win from tumbling into a gigantic standing mixer.

A small, dark-haired man answered Jiro in Spanish and pointed to the door over which hung a spanking-new exit sign.

Jiro wrinkled his face in a way that I figured meant thank you. Then he translated for me. "She was outside. When Alberto removed some boxes about ten minutes ago, he saw her talking on the phone in the parking area."

That was all I needed to know. I grabbed both children and went out the back to the trash area. It was dark out now, but I could make out a Dumpster piled high with garbage bags.

"Watch out, kids, there are steps here. We're not going to tumble down them, are we?" I held tight to each child's hand as we stood on the top of a short flight of steps. Maybe this was where Kendall had been standing; I couldn't imagine her going down to lean against the Dumpster in her beautiful suit. I glanced down the steps and saw broken glass and was about to caution the children about it when something occurred to me.

The glass came from a broken martini glass like the one

Kendall had walked off carrying, when she was talking on the phone.

So Kendall had been out here, talking and sipping. Something must have happened that had caused her to break the glass.

She could have tripped, I told myself. Her heels were high.

But why hadn't she come back?

4

Justin brought me a second cocktail, but I didn't touch it. I kept returning to the facts: Kendall's car was still parked outside the restaurant, but she had vanished.

Win had fallen asleep in his booster seat, as impossible as the ergonomics seemed. He drooped sideways, his mouth half-open, snoring contentedly. It was eight-thirty.

Jacqueline squirmed in my lap and said, "I want Mommy."

Our dinners had come and gone. The red snapper I'd ordered had been tasty, but I'd barely had a nibble because I'd been busy cutting up the children's noodles and feeding them by hand. I thought back on the pregnancy-test wand that had turned out to be negative, after all, and again felt relief. I wasn't ready to give up the right to eat my own meals. Kendall's steak had remained lonely and uneaten. My cousin had left her Kate Spade diaper bag underneath her chair. I picked it up and rummaged through it until I found her Palm Pilot.

In it, I found three numbers for Harp Snowden: office, home, and cell. I jotted them down on a business card and took that, and the twins, to the restaurant foyer.

Andrea looked askance when I told her I needed the phone. "I guess you don't care if Marshall gets mad at you, but he's going to fire my ass if I let you tie up the line. Phones are never for restaurant staff to use—"

"A woman is missing, okay? I just want to try to connect with the person she was talking to when she disappeared. It would let me know if she's safe or—"

"What's going on?" Marshall demanded. He'd come up behind us, and was scowling. "Rei, you're done with your table, right? I'd like the busboys to set it up for the next group coming in."

"Yes, but their mother has *vanished*. I need to use a telephone to make some calls to figure out where."

"You're talking about Kendall? I heard there was a problem about a high chair, but nothing more serious than that."

"Yes, it's Kendall. I want to call the person she last spoke to—Senator Snowden—to find out if she said anything about where she was going."

"Did you try to call her on your cell?"

"Um, I don't have a cell phone." I'd received one as a gift when I'd left Japan, but I'd thrown it away when I'd found its technology was incompatible in the U.S.

"Use this." Marshall reached into his chocolate-colored flannel trousers and pulled out his own cell phone. "Just be sure to remove all the children and whatnot from the table, because we need to use it in case Hillary and her friends show up. Go into Jiro's and my office to do it so nobody else hears this nonsense. And don't forget to give me back the phone."

Marshall and Jiro's office in Bento was even more chaotic than the one I'd visited in Mandala. The children built towers out of the piles of cookbooks while I tried Senator Snowden's various numbers. His office was closed. That left home and cell; I tried home first, and reached a woman who sounded like she might be his wife. I introduced myself and attempted, as quickly as possible, to tell her that I was trying to track down a fund-raiser to whom the senator had just been talking.

"Why don't you call his chief of staff?" She sounded irritated.

"Mrs. Snowden—you are Mrs. Snowden?"

"Yes, I am," she answered testily.

"My cousin and the senator were just talking on the phone, but she's nowhere to be found. I think he might have a clue as to what happened."

"My husband's left the office, but he isn't home yet. I really have no idea."

"Does he carry his cell phone?"

"Yes, he does, but I'm not going to give you the number. You should call the office, just like everyone else." Mrs. Snowden hung up on me.

Thanks a lot, lady, but I'll trump you. I turned back to the final number on the Palm Pilot: cell. Please answer, I prayed as the phone rang.

"Marshall?" The male voice on the other end sounded surprised, but not upset.

Harp Snowden must have had a caller-identification feature on his cell phone to have guessed that Marshall Zanger was calling. "Senator Snowden, it's not Marshall. It's Rei Shimura, using his phone. I don't know if you remember me."

"Harp, please." His voice was jovial. "You're Kendall's cousin. I was just talking with her, actually, but we got cut off."

So they weren't together. "Did she tell you where she was going?"

"No. We were talking about the upcoming party and then she made a sound—something like a gasp or a cough—and the line went dead. Why are you calling? Is she okay?"

"I'm not sure. Can you remember what time the call ended?"

"Twenty minutes ago, I think. Actually, I'm going to have to get off the line, I'm in heavy traffic and I've got to get over a lane—"

He hung up before I could say good-bye. Using Marshall's cell phone, I dialed Kendall's cell number again.

Beep. Beep. Beep.

"Hootis," a male voice answered.

"Ah, I'm calling for—"

It sounded like the phone receiver fell hard, against something, and then I heard nothing.

I kept the phone to my ear, and one hand on Jacqueline. No more conversation, even though I said "hello" a few more times. From the digital display on the telephone's face, I knew I'd gotten the right number for Kendall. But someone else had answered. "Hootis." It had sounded like a strange name at first. But as I thought about it more, I realized what it meant.

Who dis?

Who is this?

My empty stomach was turning nauseous, and my forehead was warm. My cousin was not alone. Maybe I was being melodramatic, assuming too much. But Kendall had been gone half an hour, and someone else had her phone.

Andrea popped her head in. "What's going on?"

I laid the cell phone aside without disconnecting it. Then I took her a few steps away and told her, in a low voice, what was going on.

"That doesn't sound good." All the hauteur had dropped from her, for once.

"I'm going to call 911. There's another phone in here, somewhere, isn't there?" I scanned the overloaded desk.

Andrea slid open a drawer, and voilà, there was a cordless phone and receiver. "They won't believe you."

"What?" I asked, my fingers punching in 911 on the new phone.

"I'm telling you, they won't care. This is D.C. Somebody missing for twenty minutes isn't exactly viewed as urgent."

As the operator patched me through to the police, I thought quickly about how to get the best result. Andrea was right that Kendall's absence wasn't long enough for her to qualify as a missing person. So when the police dispatcher came on the line, I told him about the cut-off phone call, the smashed glass, and the strange male voice on the other end of the cell phone.

The dispatcher switched me to a cool voice that said, "Homicide. Detective Burns."

Homicide. I couldn't fathom Kendall having reached that point already. I told my story again, layering the fact that a U.S. senator with whom she'd been speaking was concerned for her safety. This was D.C., as Andrea had said, and every connection counted.

"Do you still have the connection open to the cell phone?" he asked.

"I'm not sure," I said. "I didn't hang up, but I heard a noise on the other end. It might be on or off."

"Give me the number for your cousin and we'll test it from here," he said. "And whatever you do, make sure nobody disconnects the phone you were using. We have a mobile phone-trace unit we can bring in to hook up to that cell phone if it comes to that. Hang on for me. I'll be right back." The detective came back on the line after about two minutes. "We can't get through. We'll bring the mobile phone-tracer—probably be there in ten minutes or less."

I took the time to drag Marshall to privacy and tell him that I had to temporarily hand over his precious phone to the police.

"You couldn't have picked a better night for this," Marshall said as he watched me coax the drooping twins to the restaurant foyer, where I planned to wait for the police.

"I'm sorry for the inconvenience," I answered coldly. "However, it shouldn't impact things too much. They're really mostly interested in talking to the cook who saw Kendall go outside."

"Great. The police go into my kitchen, everyone's going to think it's getting raided by the INS."

"Don't be such a fatalist," I said.

"Me, a fatalist? How about you? I don't think it's an abduction when a guest leaves the table to make a phone call in privacy."

"Look, I'm sorry about this. Maybe you can make an announcement about what's going on so the diners don't think it's an INS raid."

"Thank you, I will. I'll let everyone know that our restaurant is so fabulous that the district's finest criminals have discovered it already."

There was no point in talking with Marshall. He was angry, and if I hadn't been so worried about my cousin, I would have felt sympathy for him. But Kendall was in danger. Detective Burns's response made this clear.

Jacqueline had started to cry because Win was hitting her. Resolutely, I plopped myself on a bench in the foyer with one child on each knee. Andrea, from her position at the podium, watched, a distasteful expression on her face.

"It's okay, sweetie," I murmured, smoothing Jacqueline's hair back into its bow. "Everything's going to be okay. Win, do you like policemen? You're going to meet one soon!"

He didn't answer me, so I looked at him and saw that he had taken Marshall's cell phone from its perch on a shelf and was punching in numbers.

"No!" I blurted out, pulling it away from him. Now he was crying as hard as Jacqueline. I held the phone aloft, as high as I could.

Justin popped his head around the corner. "I hear that red-headed witch flew off on her broomstick."

"How can you say that!" I didn't bother to hide my anger. "She had to go outside to finish her phone call and she vanished. It's your fault this happened!"

"I didn't tell her she had to go outside," Justin said. "Just away from the dining area."

"If you had just let her finish—" I stopped talking, because I was on the verge of crying, and people were streaming in. A black man in a preppy-looking tan suit walked in with another man in uniform. I stood up to address them, but before I could do that, Andrea had swung into operation. "Sir, under what name is your party's reservation?"

"I'm not here for dinner. I'm Louis Burns, a homicide detective with the District police."

I jumped up from the bench where I'd been sitting. "I'm Rei Shimura, the one who called. I have the phone right here."

"Is there a quieter place within this restaurant where we can link our computer to your phone?" Burns said. Now I noticed that the uniformed officer with him was carrying something that looked like a laptop computer.

"There's an office shared by the chef and the restaurant owner. And about the cell phone, it belongs to the restaurant owner, Marshall Zanger, who needs it back as soon as possible."

"That might be a while. And the children don't need to come with us," Burns said as I gathered them up.

"They're Kendall's children. There's nobody else to watch them, just me." I was starting to feel defensive of Jacqueline and Win. Didn't anyone in Washington tolerate children?

"If you take them home, I can work faster and give you updates by phone on what's happening," Burns said.

I looked at the wilting, whining twosome and saw the sense of his suggestion. And the family Volvo, with its two child-safety seats, was parked just outside. I could ferry Win and Jacqueline back to Potomac, tuck them into their cribs, and wait for word from Kendall.

I fished around in the diaper bag, pulling out a makeup case, diapers and wipes and plastic cups, before latching onto a Gucci key ring. I opened the car easily, but found that snapping children into their car seats took some time to figure out, given that I had even less experience with child travel than child pottying. After that, I had to figure out how to get to Potomac without using the beltway, as I usually did; in the end I remembered that Massachusetts Avenue would lead me there, so I took it.

Traffic, at this hour of the evening, was light. As the car sped smoothly to the suburbs, I thought about how far Kendall might have gone already with the strange man who had answered her telephone. Far in terms of distance, far in terms of violation . . .

I fought back a lump in my throat and drove into Treetops, the development of hulking homes where my cousin lived. Its builders had made an effort to maintain a fringe of tall old trees between the houses and the road. Once inside Treetops, though, the houses were so large that there were only a few yards between them, barely enough to grow anything. I drove slowly, hoping I wouldn't pass the turn. It was hard to remember Kendall's street because, to me, they all looked the same. Harmony Way—yes, that was it. I recognized her home when I saw on the front door a eucalyptus wreath tied with a pink-and-green ribbon, and Win Junior's red Little Tikes car tipped over the front path.

I jabbed the doorbell hard, just in case Kendall's husband was home from his meeting, but nobody answered. Please let the alarm be off, I prayed to myself as I tried different keys in the lock. The door swung open with a soft chiming sound, not the siren I'd feared. Excellent, I thought, hurrying back to the car to bring in the children. With one tucked under each of my arms, it was a heavy load, but I couldn't risk leaving one child in the car unsupervised for even a minute. Despite the rough handling, Jacqueline kept snoring, but Win Junior woke up and wanted to play in his car.

"It's too late. Too dark," I said. Once we got inside, I unloaded Win on the Persian rug in the cavernous entry hall while I carried Jacquie upstairs to her crib. Then I hurried back downstairs to make milk for Win, who'd begun to whine for it. He showed me where the sippy cups were, and pointed out the soymilk in the fridge. As a cup of milk revolved in the microwave, I surveyed Kendall and Win's kitchen. It was state-of-the-art, in Kendall's words, with acres of black granite countertop, and faux-faded cream cabinetry. Near the Sub-zero fridge, a faux-antique framed chalkboard had neatly chalked-in names and phone numbers. Kendall's work and cell, as well as Win's. I'd call him after I got the children settled. As I was on my way to them, the telephone rang. Louis Burns told me that he'd determined Kendall's cell phone was moving at a pace that seemed to indicate it was in a car.

"Do you know for certain that it's a car?"

"Oh, no. It could be anything—a car or truck or van or even bus. There's really no way to tell, at this point. I'm sending someone over to get a picture of your cousin. Can you get one ready for us?"

Casting a last look at Win Junior, who was lying on his back sucking down the cup of warm milk, I took the cordless phone with me into the living room. I couldn't see any photo albums, but on the mantel I noticed a silver-framed wedding photograph of Kendall in a white gown leaning back against Win, before his hairline had begun to recede. I'd missed their wedding because I'd been in Japan. I picked it up and asked, "Would a framed photo work?"

"Sure. We'll take it out of the frame and put it back in when it's all over."

All over. That could be good, or bad. "The fact that you want the photo, does it mean you're seriously looking for her?"

"Yes," he said shortly.

"So you're tracking the telephone. What if the phone battery goes dead?" I asked.

"Sometimes we've still been able to locate the vehicle. But we can't pinpoint it exactly. We can track it to a quarter-mile area. If we know what the car looks like, it's usually pretty easy to find."

But nobody had seen the car. That was unspoken.

We made arrangements for an officer to come to the house to take the photograph from me. He also wanted to talk to Kendall's husband. I gave him the phone number that I'd seen on the chalkboard.

"How are the kids?" Burns asked gruffly.

"Okay. I'm about to put them to bed."

"Good idea. Is there anyone else who could help you? A grandmother, maybe?"

"Kendall's parents are on St. Barth's right now. Kendall and Win have a live-in baby-sitter. She's got to make it home sometime."

"If, for any reason, nobody can relieve you, there's always emergency help from social services."

I looked at Win, half asleep on the rug, and felt so much fear that I was on the verge of tears. I couldn't talk to Burns anymore. I whispered, "Why don't I let you go, so you can get back to tracking down my cousin."

I changed Win's diaper and put him in pajamas and laid him

down in his own blue-and-yellow bedroom. I turned off the light but left the door open a crack after he whimpered that the room was too dark. He still hadn't asked for his mother. I wouldn't have known what to say if he had.

I checked back in on Jacquie to adjust her covers, and when I heard the sound of deep, even breathing from both babies' rooms, I went downstairs.

Social services. Why had Louis Burns brought that up? Children went into social services only if there wasn't another parent or family member to care for them. Did the detective think there was a reason Win wouldn't be able to care for the children? When a woman went missing, was her husband automatically a suspect?

It was eleven o'clock now. I leafed through the family address book, looking for contact information for Kendall's parents on St. Barth's. Nothing. I put in a call to my mother, in San Francisco, who was packing for a long-anticipated holiday with my father, and some close friends, in Fiji. But when she heard what had happened, she started talking about canceling the eighteen-day trip.

"Rei, that's—oh, my Lord, so terrible! What kind of neighborhood were you in? Are you and the children safe right this minute?"

"It was a fine restaurant, and to answer your second question, I'm at Kendall's house with the children. I'd hoped you'd know where Aunt Deborah and Uncle Bill are staying."

"It's the Breakers—no, that's where they go in Florida. St. Barth's, let me think. I think it's a bed and breakfast they use. They sent a lovely postcard last year, which I'm sure I tossed in the spring cleaning—"

"I guess I'll have to wait for Win to get home, then," I said.

"Don't count on him to know anything." My mother's opinion of Win was about the same as mine. "Ask Dougie."

She was talking about Kendall's brother. "I don't know where he lives. Do you?"

"He lives in Howard County somewhere—Millersville, that's it. Haven't you seen him?"

"No. Since I've been here, Kendall's been the only one of the

Howards who has been interested in doing things."

"It takes two to tango. Have you gone to visit Grandmother yet?"

"Not exactly," I said. My grandmother and I had unfinished business that I meant to keep that way. "Mom, I'd better get off the line. I heard someone at the door. Maybe it's the cop."

"What?"

"'Bye, Mom." I clicked off quickly, because I didn't need any more flack from my mother about not seeing my relatives. And it was true that there was the sound of something happening outside the door. I walked toward the foyer, Kendall's wedding picture in hand. I'd been expecting a police officer, but from what I could see through the leaded glass pane next to the front door, this probably wasn't one. The shape of a tall man was clear through the pane, leaning against it as if he thought he could push it in. Adrenaline surged as I thought about the possibilities: a random break-in. Or maybe, the man who'd taken Kendall had brought her home.

5

I was glancing back at the kitchen, trying to decide whether to run back to the phone, when I heard metal sliding into metal. The chime went off as the door flew open and Kendall's husband, Win, staggered through. His hair was slick with the night's rain and his skin had a greenish cast.

"Hey, Rye. Whassup?" He blinked at the sight of me.

"Rei," I said, correcting his pronunciation. "Actually, I have bad news."

"The restaurant's going to tank?" He laughed shortly. "Don't let a slow first night scare you. And I'm sorry I couldn't make it, I had something else to do—"

"It's not a problem with the restaurant." I could hardly get out the next two words. "Kendall disappeared."

"You mean, she didn't show up?" He snorted. "She called me earlier today, bitching about child care problems. That's probably why she didn't come."

"She *did* meet me for dinner there, with the kids. But she stepped out to make a phone call and never came back."

"What the hell—did you call the police?" Was his expression

tightening out of concern for his wife, I wondered, or something else?

"Yes," I said. "They have been trying to reach you on your cell phone."

"I had it turned off. God, what happened to Kendall?"

"I don't know. Nobody does. But her cell phone is in motion. It's going across the city."

"I don't get it. What's this about the phone?" Win rubbed his temples, as if he had a headache. His pupils were huge, two shiny blue-black discs.

"She might have been abducted." I couldn't say *killed*.

"Oh, my God." He leaned against the wall, looking sick. My gaze moved from his face to the rest of him, thinking it odd that he had no briefcase, and that when his coat gapped open it revealed a rumpled business shirt peeking through his trousers. He looked as if he'd been rolling around with someone in a car—either that, or he'd forgotten to pull himself together after using the bathroom.

"Did Lisa put the kids down?" he asked abruptly.

"No, she's at a dance. Remember, there were child care problems? I brought the twins home and put them to bed." I still felt a flush of pride at the fact that I'd done it. "I can leave now, or I can stay a while longer."

"I can take it from here. What do I owe you?"

"Owe me?" I was confused.

"For watching the kids."

"I'm Kendall's cousin, remember? If you do anything for me at all, just phone the detective who's involved, because he's been on my back about where you are. He'll be sending over another cop to pick up this photograph." I put the framed wedding photograph in his hand.

"I can't believe it. If only I'd gone with her tonight," Win muttered, looking at the picture. "God, she's beautiful. She still looks the same, you know—"

"Where were you tonight?" I interrupted him angrily.

"At a meeting." He said it without expression.

"Where?"

"Ah, downtown."

"Kendall thought you were in northern Virginia."

"I guess you are like her, after all." There was an edge to Win's voice.

I made my voice softer. "I apologize if I seem harsh with you at this time of trouble. It's just that I'm very concerned about Kendall, and the children. If you don't feel, ah, well enough to take care of them right now, I'd be willing to stay until your au pair gets home—"

"Just leave, all right." For a minute, Win had pulled himself together into the kind of *über*man that I remembered from his university lacrosse days.

"Good night, then. I hope you don't mind if I take Kendall's car? I drove it over because of the kids."

He didn't respond, so I let myself out.

As I drove home, Friday night turned to Saturday morning. There weren't that many cars around; those I saw appeared to be driven by people in their late teens and early twenties, partiers, the kind I worried might have smoked or drunk something.

Win had been so strange. It was as if he'd been high on something. I knew all the signs of someone who'd drunk too much—having done that myself, every now and then—but I knew nothing about illegal mood enhancers. Drugs hadn't been at all big in Japan. Maybe if I stayed in Washington long enough, I'd be able to distinguish a crack high from a heroin buzz, or whatever it was called. I didn't want to know.

As I drove slowly down Columbia Road, toward Adams-Morgan, the road got busier, with street people steering drivers into parking spaces, dancers spilling out of nightclubs, drinkers leaning on the edges of doorways. A few weeks ago, I'd considered this one of my favorite parts of the city. But now I saw shadows everywhere, and in them, I imagined lurking men. Hugh's words about being careful in Washington came back to me.

There was no legal parking spot left on the block in front of our town house, so I parked illegally, in the no-parking zone at its end. I didn't care if I got a parking ticket tonight—at least I'd get into the apartment safely.

I was turning the key in the lock of the apartment when I heard the telephone within start ringing. I rushed in, grabbed the receiver, and discovered Hugh on the other end. He wanted to hear how the restaurant launch had gone.

I laughed shakily before telling him the whole story, including the disturbing part about Win's demeanor.

"Did he have a smell about him?" Hugh wanted to know.

"I didn't get close enough to tell. I don't think so—"

"It probably isn't pot or alcohol, then. Maybe it's heroin. I hear there's a big boom in the suburbs."

"Why would a preppy real estate agent do things like that? The father of twins?"

"You said he was unzipped when he came home," Hugh said. "If he's shagging someone while he's high, it probably isn't heroin. That would incapacitate him—"

"You, the expert on sexual function," I snorted. "Whatever he's under the influence of, I hope it's worn off. Because if the police encounter what I did, they might want to take him in."

"D'you reckon they'll be suspicious of him in Kendall's disappearance?" Hugh asked.

"I don't want to jump to any conclusions," I said. "He's a jerk, but I'm sure he loves Kendall. The way he looked at her photograph . . ."

"In any case, he's not like your Japanese relations at all," Hugh said. "I visited your aunt Norie for supper last night. She cooked that delicious tabletop stew, but with beef because you weren't there. I think it's called *nabe*?"

"I'm sorry, Hugh. I just can't concentrate on menus at this time." I wanted to keep the line clear for the police, for Kendall, for whoever might need to reach me.

"She misses you. She told me that you didn't say a proper good-bye in Japan."

"I know. I had to leave so fast—"

"What do you think about her coming to us for a visit? She could help us get sorted for the wedding—"

I cut him off. "Sure. Whatever. Tell her anytime. But, sweetie, I'm so tired. I don't think I can talk anymore."

I promised Hugh that I would take the Glendinning cure for severe anxiety—hot milk sipped in a hotter bath—and go to bed. The ritual unwound me enough to get between the sheets, but I found that I couldn't sleep. I lay there, listening to the silence, which gradually turned to radiators clanging, which meant that it was morning. Six o'clock. I decided to get up and attempt to jog off my nervous energy. As I was pulling on my shorts, the phone rang.

Burns was on the other end. He said words that I never expected to hear. My cousin was alive.

Euphoria washed over me. "Thank God. Where is she?"

"In an ambulance on her way to D.C. General. You were right in guessing that she'd been taken somewhere against her will."

"Was she hurt?" My feeling of joy turned back to anxiety.

"We don't know all that happened. She didn't have any obvious broken bones or injuries, but she's going to the ER just to make sure she's okay."

"How did you find her?"

"Well, unfortunately, our phone trace never panned out, but we located her through LoJack. Are you familiar with that technology?"

Hugh had it installed in his car. "Isn't it a chip, planted in a car, that can be used to trace it if the owners report it stolen?"

"That's right. A 1998 Mercedes was reported stolen by a Kalorama resident a few hours ago. Someone in the department was tracing it by using the LoJack feature. The car was found abandoned in southeast Washington. Mrs. Johnson was found in the trunk."

"Did she tell you what the kidnappers wanted?"

"She was able to give us the gist of what happened, but I need to talk to her some more. You can visit her in a few hours."

"Why did they take her?"

"We don't know that yet. All I can tell you is that she's alive and well and her husband is en route to the hospital to meet her."

"Who's watching the twins, then?"

"Apparently the au pair had arrived back at the house. Mr. Johnson said that the kids are still sleeping."

"Yes, it was a late night for them," I said, thinking about what a night they'd had: A night they'd never understand had almost changed their lives.

6

It was too early to call San Francisco to give my mother the good news, and Hugh, I knew, was at a business dinner in Tokyo. I felt at loose ends, so I decided to take the run that I'd planned. Usually I ran without thinking of much other than avoiding obstructions and beating red lights. The best thing was to leave Adams-Morgan and run through the wooded trails of Rock Creek Park, something I did only during peak running hours, because Hugh had cautioned me about a young woman intern whose body had been found near a jogging trail a few years before.

This morning was like all the others. Sun filtered through the tall, leafy trees, and the damp leaves and earth were gentle underfoot. I started to jog, but didn't have the power, or the desire, to push myself. So I walked quickly, glancing without really meaning to at every male who moved past. Nobody stared at strangers in Washington, just as nobody did in Japan. I dropped my gaze to the daffodils along the path. It was crazy to look at people like that. Anyone meaning harm would be lurking in the trees, not striding along a path full of morning exercisers.

I'd hardly sweated during the walk, but out of habit, I showered. As water drummed against my tight shoulders, I finally relaxed.

Afterward, even though it was slightly earlier than Detective Burns had suggested, I called the hospital. The emergency room receptionist told me that Kendall had already been released.

I decided to hold off visiting Potomac for a few hours to give her time for a reunion with the children. In the meantime, I could swing by the restaurant to share the good news and hear about how Jiro thought the restaurant opening had gone. It would be a relief to throw myself into some cheerful, trivial conversation—especially if I could forage for some good leftovers from the kitchen. My cousin was safe, and I had an appetite again. I was ready to live.

I drove Kendall's car to H Street, where because of the early hour, I landed a spot close to Bento. Through its spotless windows I caught the languid movements of a bus boy setting out silver, Marshall gesticulating over a table as he talked to Andrea. This was still family time; Bento would open to the public at six tonight. In the next week, it was supposed to start its regular schedule, open from eleven to eleven daily.

"Hello, everyone!" I made my greeting as I stepped into the dining room.

"You're cheerful today," Marshall said in a voice considerably less so.

"The police found my cousin," I announced. "She had been abducted, just like I thought. But she's alive and well and I'm going to see her after this—I'm just so relieved!"

"That's so great!" Phong punched his fist in the air.

"Yes, I heard already. They brought back my cell phone early this morning," Marshall said.

Andrea gave me a long look, shook her head, and went off into the kitchen.

"Has something come up?" I asked. I couldn't help but be shocked by Marshall and Andrea's lack of happiness at Kendall's rescue.

"Just a little bit of stress. Par for the course," Marshall said. "Actually, I've got to dash over to Mandala to get some coconuts. Alberto!" he bellowed.

Alberto, the prep cook who had noticed where Kendall had gone the night before, emerged from the kitchen wearing a white chef's coat and black-checked pants.

"I need you to come with me to Mandala. We'll be bringing over some produce that we need for tonight," Marshall said.

"Okay. I'll find my coat—" Alberto said in halting English before Marshall cut him off.

"No time for that. My car's parked right out front." And with that, Marshall swept Alberto out the door.

I wandered into the kitchen, where I found Jiro sitting on a stool at the stainless-steel prep counter. He had a half glass of an amber liquid in one hand and a newspaper folded neatly before him. I watched him read an article through, then start reading it again.

"Hi," I said. "What's doing?"

"Join me for a drink." He raised an eyebrow toward a bottle that I recognized as whisky. Whisky! I'd never seen Jiro touch alcohol before.

"It's a little early for me," I demurred. "But I could go for some leftover veggies from last night, if there's anything to spare—"

"Ha, you may as well have a fresh fish. I expect few people will come tonight."

"Why on earth?" I stared at him, finally noticing how upset he looked.

"Haven't you read the *Post*?"

I shook my head, recalling the rolled-up newspaper I'd tossed in my foyer before I'd gone out to exercise. I hadn't had time to read the paper while I was still in happy shock over the finding of Kendall.

I read the article over his shoulder:

Potomac Woman Abducted from New City Restaurant

Early yesterday evening, Kendall Howard Johnson, one of the District's youngest and most prominent political fund-raisers, vanished from the opening of Bento, a new Japanese restaurant just opened by restaurateur Marshall Zanger. District police were following several leads in an attempt to find Johnson, who, sources said, had left her table to make a telephone call to Senator Harp Snowden while a restaurant employee baby-sat her two-year-old twins. Bento, which is extravagantly decorated and priced to match, is located several blocks from Mandala, Zanger's popular restaurant in Penn Quarter.

Bento is directed by the former television chef, Jiro Takeda, who also collaborated with Zanger on Mandala. Bento features inventively named entrées and a mix of reproduction and antique Japanese furniture, including a grand nineteenth-century Sendai *tansu* that dominates the bar. As is almost requisite for ambitious restaurants in Washington these days, the restaurant has a staff of affected international waiters and a hostess with a manner as cold as the sake martinis served to all on opening night.

Despite its glamorous trappings, Bento is located on a stretch of H Street with a motley mix of establishments, including Chinese restaurants, an adult video shop, and subsidized housing. H Street has been the site of a variety of petty assaults in recent years; this abduction is the most serious crime in recent memory, according to Detective Louis Burns of the homicide division.

As I finished, I realized I knew who the reporter was. She must have been the quiet woman sitting with the man who called me over to ask about the age of the *tansu* chest. To Marshall, I said, "I can't believe she intended to write about us all along. That's not supposed to be done on a soft opening, is it? And what a shame the information wasn't reported that Kendall was found! But I know how these things work, they probably had to go to print before the police located her."

"Marshall called the editor to complain." Jiro paused to take another swig of whisky. "He said the reporter usually writes for the home and garden section, and she received an invitation from us to the opening. They'll run a follow-up piece that will include the information that your cousin was found safe."

"That should make things a little better," I said. "Don't you think?"

"The damage has occurred," Jiro said. "All morning the press have been crawling around, trying to photograph the restaurant. They even tried for me, but I said no. I refuse to become the laughing talk of the nation—"

"Laughingstock," I corrected gently. "And you aren't! You're a genius. It's too bad they didn't mention how good the food was."

"No, the newspaper observes very strict rules about that. The critic visits several times to have a good idea about the truth in cooking."

I sighed. "Well, the press isn't here because the story about the restaurant is over. Kendall's safe at home and being interviewed by every TV station I can think of in Washington. With this kind of happy ending, I'm sure the restaurant can go on."

"I think the kidnapping was—how do you say?—rigged."

"You mean someone set it up? Why?"

"We have several competitors in Penn Quarter. One of them might want to encourage the idea that our restaurant is in an area that is too risky. You know we have a difficult parking situation, and the valet service we hired was unusually slow last night. That could also have been part of the plot."

"I'm sure the police will look into that, if you mention it," I said diplomatically. I thought Jiro's ideas were crazy.

"My guess is that your cousin will not be able to identify the men who took her—and they wouldn't be the business owners, but criminals hired to do the job. I've seen it in Japan with *chinpira*, the boys who work for *yakuza*, and also with gangsters in Brazil. You know, in Brazil I had a bodyguard to protect me, and a car with bulletproof glass!"

"I will find out all that I can from my cousin. I'm actually headed that way, but I was going to give her a little time to spend alone with her children."

"You needed to eat. I'll cook for you." Jiro tipped his half-full glass of liquor into the sink. "I have a refrigerator packed with fresh seafood that will go bad if nobody comes tonight. What is your fancy?"

The jumbo Louisiana shrimp looked good to me, so Jiro taught me how to make Yin-Yang Shrimp, a dish in which the shrimp is fried with a black sesame seed coating on one side and white sesame seed on the other. The lesson seemed to cheer him up a little, and we were chatting about the health benefits of sesame seeds when Andrea came in. She wasn't dressed in one of her typically elegant outfits today, but, rather, in jeans that hung below her navel and a faded Montgomery College T-shirt. I saw a silver ring gleaming in her navel, which was quickly covered when she put a clean white apron over her attire.

She opened the fruit and vegetable refrigerator and turned to Jiro. "How many carrots?"

"Six pounds' worth, matchstick julienne. May I show you?" Jiro picked up a knife from his special cooking area.

"What's happening?" I was startled to see Andrea attempt to peel vegetables.

"Marshall called me this morning to say I couldn't be hostess anymore because of what the reporter said about my demeanor. This is my job now," Andrea muttered. "Kitchen gofer."

"'I'm sorry," I said. "So what's—who's the hostess now?"

"Marshall is training that asshole Justin to do it."

"But Justin was the one who caused the problem in the first place by not letting her talk on her cell at the table," I said.

"Yeah, well, I hope the loss in tips he'll suffer will feel like a punishment to him." Andrea put a hand on my shoulder. "Hey, I'm really glad the cops found your cousin."

"Thank you." I was surprised, by both the touch and the sentiment. Andrea was the only person who'd reacted with concern to Kendall's kidnapping.

I moved in next to Andrea to watch Jiro demonstrate his julienne technique. The carrots jumped in the air as his flat-bottomed cleaver came down fast. He wasn't turning them into matchsticks, he was turning them into shreds as fine as human hair. I cooked all the time, and I couldn't cut anything that small. How would Andrea cope?

"I'm working now, but I'd like to—talk to you about something. Can you meet me tomorrow? There's a coffee shop I like called Urban Grounds, in Adams-Morgan," Andrea said as Jiro moved off to let her work on the technique by herself.

"I know it. It's close to where I live." I looked at Andrea, surprised again by her attention. "Can you meet me in the morning? I have to go to the airport in the afternoon."

We agreed to meet at ten the next day. I left Andrea, slowly scraping carrots, to get into Kendall's car and drive it over to Treetops. This time, nobody could possibly miss her house. Harmony Way was filled by two police cruisers and three television station vans. When I rang the doorbell, a blond woman about my age peered out at me from behind long, overly layered bangs.

"Ms. Johnson is booked for interviews for the next two hours. You have to call first to schedule," she said.

"I'm her cousin, Rei Shimura. I came to return her car, and to see her if she's feeling up to it. Who are you?" I was horrified that my cousin, just hours after her trauma, was being bossed into an interview schedule by this woman.

"You're Kendall's cousin?" An unbelieving, arched eyebrow. Obviously, my Asian coloring didn't bear an obvious link to Kendall's. But then, Jacquie trailed across the foyer, a blanket in one hand, and saw me.

"Aunt Way! Aunt Way!" She toddled toward me eagerly, almost slipping on the polished wooden floor.

"You'd better come on in," the woman said, opening the door wider. "I have to be careful because we don't want to overexpose Kendall. I'm Martina Shattuck. I'm Harp Snowden's press attaché, but I'm helping Kendall out today. She called me from the hospital to meet her here an hour and a half ago. It's been crazy."

Shattuck. Like Howard, it was another good old name—this time from northern California. Maybe Martina Shattuck was one of Kendall's gal pals, but it seemed unbelievable that Harp Snowden would allow his attaché to be Kendall's personal assistant. Then again, Kendall and Harp seemed to have become very close.

"Kendall's in her study with the police right now. If you like, you can join the media in the sun room, where we've set up coffee and bagels for them while they wait."

"I'd rather hang out with this crew," I said, picking up Jacquie and inhaling the scent of her hair.

"Yeah, well, don't feel obligated. The au pair's here for that." She smiled brightly. "Hey, if you're able to help at all, it would be super if you could take over handling the press stuff for me at four? I need to get back to the office to follow up on some things for the senator."

"I have no press experience." Except running away from Japanese reporters, I thought bleakly.

"Oh, it's just manning the phones and booking interviews. If they press you for something immediate, there's a prepared statement."

"Whose statement?"

"Kendall dictated it over a hospital phone to me."

I sat down on the living room couch with Jacquie on my lap, and Win Junior playing ball on the carpet with Lisa, a slender, doe-eyed South African girl who seemed barely out of her teens. As she called to them in her soft, British-edged accent, they giggled and squirmed. Lisa seemed totally focused on them, and energetic, too—more energetic than I'd be after a late night out. It must have been her youth, and also the relief that Kendall was safe.

Martina brought me a cup of coffee and a sheet of paper with her name and work number on the top-right-hand side. It started off with a flattering description of Kendall as a chair of Harp Snowden's fund-raising efforts in Maryland, Washington, D.C., and Virginia. A graduate of the University of Virginia, a Junior League of Washington sustainer, and the Treetop community-garden club president, Kendall was a well-known member of her community, as well as the wife of one of the area's most successful real estate listing agents, Win Johnson, and the mother of fraternal twins.

I rushed ahead, because what I wanted to know about was the description of the attackers. As Jiro had suggested, there wasn't much there. The men had worn ski masks, so she could not see their faces. They'd put a pillowcase over her head before packing her into the empty trunk of a car. They took her cell phone so she couldn't call the police for help. Several hours of driving passed, which were marked by three stops. The sound of new voices made Kendall believe that perhaps other people were entering the car. At most, she heard four voices. Their speaking style led her to believe that they were African-American men under thirty from the Washington, D.C., area. At the third and final stop, there was only silence until the police opened the trunk.

The press release finished with a quote from Kendall expressing gratitude for the excellent detective work of the District police department. She mentioned that she had no known enemies and was confident that no political rivals of the senator would have been involved in such a despicable undertaking.

I sighed when I finished reading the statement. Jiro thought restaurateurs might have masterminded the abduction, and Kendall was raising the question of political rivals to Senator Snowden. Even though the statement was framed in negative language, it seemed as if it was meant to plant a question in the readers'—in this case, the news media's—collective mind.

I knew what I thought. It seemed most probable that the men had planned to rape Kendall. After all, the vehicle had stopped to pick up more men. Kendall had been lucky beyond belief to have been rescued untouched.

"What amazing bravery she had," Martina said when I put down the paper.

"Was it your idea to put in the business in the end mentioning political rivalry?" I asked.

Martina shrugged. "I told her she should address the issue straight on. She agreed. And I think there is a valid chance this might be a case of a rival campaign being afraid of Harp pulling ahead. We better expose it so it doesn't happen again."

"Where does he stand against the other potential presidential candidates in the party?"

"Well, he's fourth in terms of war chest, but he's first in terms of name recognition. He'll catch up with the money soon, I'm sure."

Especially since Kendall was now safe and sound and able to get on the phone and invite people to parties. I was anxious to see Kendall and Detective Burns myself. If it could be proved that Kendall was targeted because of her work, that might resolve any doubts about the safety of Bento's location. But this seemed unlikely, and a small thing to be happy about, when the men who'd kidnapped Kendall were still on the loose.

7

I had just finished talking to Martina about the press release when Detective Burns walked into the living room.

"I need to see the so-called press release," he said to Martina.

"Sure." She gave him a falsely bright smile and handed him a copy.

After scanning it, he tore it in two. "Get rid of these."

"We have a right to free speech—" Martina began.

"Ms. Howard now understands that she's jeopardizing the investigation with the description she gave of the assailants, and what was said about a possible involvement by political rivals to the senator is bound to be twisted and cause her, and us, no end of trouble."

Martina opened her mouth as if she were going to protest again, so I interrupted with some classic Japanese distraction. "Detective Burns, I can't thank you enough for saving my cousin's life."

He turned, as if seeing me for the first time. "Miss Shimura. Didn't I tell you that I wanted you to wait to see your cousin until after I'd talked to her?"

"Of course, but I thought you'd be through by now."

He rolled his eyes. "Well, I'm not. I'm only getting started. And she'd be better off with some quiet time rather than holding court for those media vultures. People in shock say things they later regret."

"How could someone in shock dictate a press release?" Martina countered.

"She's overdoing it. A common reaction after trauma."

Martina gave him a withering look and sailed off to the press-filled sunroom.

"I'll try to talk Kendall into taking it easy," I said to the detective when Martina had gone.

"You do that. And by the way, you made a phenomenal observation last night when you called us with the suspicion about the abduction. Most people would have waited until the next day, or at the very least, several hours." He looked at me again. "Any other reasons you thought your cousin might be at risk?"

"Well, I couldn't believe she'd leave someone as inexperienced as I am with her children," I said, although the truth was, Jacquie hadn't moved from my lap since I'd arrived, and Win Junior had been running back and forth with toys he wanted to show me.

"What I mean is, was there anything or anyone in your cousin's life who seemed disturbing? To put her at risk?"

"Nothing comes to mind at the moment." Except for the fact that her husband had told two different stories about where he'd been last night.

"At the hospital, the admitting doctor noticed a few old bruises. They've been photographed for the record."

Old bruises. I didn't like the sound of that. "Did you interview Win last night?"

"Yes, and I hope to speak to him again. After hearing Mrs. Johnson's story first."

Martina came back with a platter containing the remnants of the bagel brunch. "Rei, she wants to see you next. She's so happy you're here."

"I need to talk to Mrs. Johnson again," Burns said.

Martina looked at him coldly. "She said she wanted Rei, specifically."

"I'll be quick," I said apologetically. I didn't want to slow down the investigation, but I thought the longer Martina and Burns argued, the worse the situation would get.

I headed downstairs to the carpeted "lower level," as basements were called in modern houses like Kendall's. What Burns had said about the bruises shocked me. I would never have thought Win would hurt her. Last night, despite being stoned, he'd seemed shocked and upset about Kendall's disappearance. Perhaps in a more sober and calculating moment, Win could have ordered a hit on his wife, but I couldn't see the point. Kendall's family—her father's, and my mother's people—were descended from an English lord who'd once owned a large chunk of Maryland. Win name-dropped about the Howards shamelessly, so much so my own mother had sniped that it was a wonder Win hadn't changed his own last name after the wedding. On the other hand, the Howards in our branch didn't have land or money anymore. Kendall's father had a few great antiques, just like my mother did, but there was nothing more to be gained by the death of Kendall. If she died, the trust that my grandmother had given her would pass to the twins, not him—though he would probably be the executor of the will and the trustee of the trust itself—

I felt suddenly queasy, but my rapid and unsettling calculations were swept away by Kendall herself.

"Sweetie!" She peeked her head through her half-open study door, then rushed to me. I was gathered up in a blur of auburn hair and black cashmere. Everything felt the same, except for the fact that her wrists were thickly bandaged.

After we'd embraced, she drew back and said, "I am so damn grateful to you."

"Your wrists. What happened?"

"Those bastards bound them with duct tape. I tried to get loose by rubbing up against something sharp in the trunk, but all I did was cut myself."

"I'm so sorry," I said. "If only the waiter hadn't made you leave the table."

"He'll be sorry," Kendall said. "Or rather, Marshall Zanger will be, too, once he realizes I'm suing his company for reckless endangerment."

"What on earth—"

"A restaurant employee forced me to leave the table. That directly contributed to what happened. I'd like to give Hugh first crack at representing me."

The horror of the situation was growing exponentially. Not only would I have the whole restaurant staff furious with me, I'd have Hugh going bonkers as well. "Ah, you know, Kendall, I don't think Hugh's got the necessary American credentials to do that kind of work. And think carefully about whether you need to get a lawyer at all. Aren't you just relieved to be alive?"

"You don't think that I should sue? Win does. He thinks we have a very strong case."

"I think what we need to do is find and punish the guys who took you." I paused. "I read your statement, but there are still a lot of questions that I have. I know that they just drove up and grabbed you. Did they talk to you, you know, say what they wanted you to do?"

"They asked me to give them my purse. I said that I didn't have it. I was so scared, I dropped my glass. Then they"—Kendall paused, and her face scrunched, as if she was trying to hold back tears—"asked me my name. I didn't think of lying; maybe I should have. Now they can figure out where I live, especially since the news reports keep calling me a Potomac woman."

"What else did they say?"

"They told me not to scream or do anything stupid, just to get in the trunk, which was insanely difficult in my shoes—it broke the heel off one of my Manolos. The police gave it back to me, but the shoe will never be the same."

But Kendall would be the same. Her reactions were proof. I said, "Oh, my."

"When the lid came down, it was completely black in there. I didn't know which would be worse, to be killed in the woods or wherever they wanted to take me, or to die in the trunk, without air."

I put my arms around Kendall and hugged her. "I know how you feel."

"You can't possibly." Kendall stiffened.

I didn't argue with my cousin, but I did know. I'd been tied up in a dark cave once, a spooky, isolated spot that I knew no rescuer would ever find. Another time, I'd been locked in a pitch-black storehouse. It was scary in dark places where someone had left you to die. The saving grace was that I'd had resolution—the people in Japan who had tried to kill me had been caught, while Kendall's were still on the street.

"What physical details did you notice about them?"

"It was all so quick. They looked like—oh, the kind of guys you would see on the street anywhere. Baggy pants, down or leather jackets. They all wore knit caps, and the one who talked to me was wearing a balaclava. I was scared out of my mind. I kept hoping one of the cooks would bring out trash or something and see what was going on, but it all happened so fast."

"Any other details?"

"Well, not really about them. But in the car—the trunk—there was a box of, I think, take-out food, with a really strong smell."

"What kind of smell?" Jiro had said he suspected the kidnappers had been restaurant competitors.

"Chinese food. I saw the restaurant's logo on the bag around the container when I was being forced into the trunk. It came from Plum Ink."

Plum Ink was the Chinese restaurant whose owner had tried to fight Marshall on having a parking pad. Could he have masterminded an abduction from that parking pad to prove a point? Or was the food there for a more obvious reason? "Maybe the kidnappers stopped for dinner first. Whoever waited on them might be able to give a description."

"But the cops told me the car was stolen," Kendall answered. "Isn't it more likely that the owners of the car had gone to the restaurant and forgotten the food in their trunk?"

"It all depends on where the car was stolen. That will be easy enough to check out." I looked at my cousin, who suddenly seemed smaller than I'd thought. She was so thin, so breakable. "I don't like those men out there any more than you do. Until they're caught, no woman in the Washington area is safe."

Kendall sighed and said, "I don't think you have to worry about that. The guys were definitely focused on *me*. I had no money or ATM card. It wasn't a matter of wanting money."

"Do you think they were planning to rape you?"

Kendall pondered that for a minute. "I was scared, but I wasn't thinking about rape."

"So you don't think they wanted money or sex. What's left?" I asked dryly.

"It could be related to the campaign. I'm sure word spread over the last couple of days that I was going to work for Harp. I don't like to toot my own horn but"—she paused to drop her eyes modestly—"I'm pretty effective. If I and some other fund-raisers across the country can bundle enough of our friends' money together, he'll snag the Democratic convention. Everyone knows it. And this is a town where political rivals do commit crimes. Remember Watergate?"

"We were tiny babies then, Kendall. We can't remember Watergate. But if you really believe this theory, why did you write in your press release that you *didn't* believe your abduction was done for political reasons?"

"Subliminal persuasion," Kendall said. "I learned about it in a class on advertising rhetoric at UVA."

"That's what I was afraid of."

"It's a dog-eat-dog world in politics," Kendall said, looking at me. "Believe me, Rei, I know what some of these people are like."

"Win must be relieved that you're safe and sound," I said. "I'm sure he feels that's all that matters—"

"Yes, he's been very sweet. And, this morning before he went out, he told me that he was going to support Harp's campaign, since that was what I really wanted. He's a little tight on his own cash, so we're going to tap into Grand's trust to do it."

"Really," I said. Writing a check wasn't any proof to me that Win Johnson was a good husband. "I heard that the doctor saw old bruises on your body."

"What are you talking about?" Kendall sounded irritated.

"Bruises on your legs."

"Oh, that's probably from where Win kicked me."

"Kendall!" I sucked in my breath.

"Win Junior!" Kendall clarified. "Babies kick moms. Win hates having his diaper changed, so he kicks me when he gets the chance. Now, if you're so interested in what's going on with me, will you stay and help me troubleshoot the press?"

"Martina asked me already. I'm coming back at four."

"Great. And I have a favor to ask. How would you like to sleep over? Win's probably going to be out late again, and I'm just a little—nervous."

"Of course," I said. "You can count on me."

8

A night with Kendall and the kids. I had no idea what to expect. What I got was a TV marathon. As the children threw toys around the family room, Kendall ran around the house, double-checking that all the news shows were being recorded. She was working four different TV sets located in the master bedroom, the family room, the au pair's bedroom, and her own study. Hugh liked electronics, but nothing as extreme as this, I thought as I went upstairs to the au pair's bedroom, where I was supposed to record any mention of Kendall on the NBC affiliate. Saturday was usually a slow news day in Washington, and the airwaves had been full of Kendall during the supper news hour. Now it was eleven, and I was practically falling asleep, given my insomnia the night before, but I was duty bound to catch everything that Kendall said. She had been cleverly circumspect, volunteering none of the suspicions about the possible involvement of political rivals. Of course, because some of the press had read the release before Burns seized it, they asked her about political rivals of Harp Snowden, which was what she'd intended all along.

"I don't know, honestly," Kendall said for the cameras. "I don't know who took me, or the motive. The men never sought money from me and they did not harm me physically, except for my being tied." Here, the cameras flashed on her bandaged wrists, and the reporters usually went on to comment about the crime rate in Washington, and perhaps to flash the exterior of Bento. Marshall had refused to allow cameras inside the restaurant.

I was sitting on the floor, my back against the bed, watching the news. Sports footage was playing, so I ran my gaze around the au pair's room. Lisa had seemed to react normally when I'd seen her that morning. She'd been horrified about what had almost happened to Kendall, and full of hugs for the kids. I'd thought we should ask Lisa's permission to enter her room to tape the program, but Kendall said that if it had been okay at noon, it would be okay now.

It was such a teen girl's room, I thought; there was a poster of Britney Spears on the wall, a pink-and-purple Indian-print bedspread on the old spool bed, a bed that looked as if it had come out of my grandmother's house. Kendall had been given some nice furniture. There was a marble-topped Victorian vanity crowded with toiletries—moisturizer and lip gloss and perfumes and K-Y jelly—

K-Y jelly? I looked at it again. I shouldn't snoop, I told myself. The girl was nineteen, which was above the legal age of consent. She had to have a local boyfriend, that was it. I took another survey of her room. There, on the bedside table, was a cluster of family photos. Lisa smiling and holding flowers, standing in her high school graduation robe, flanked by her parents and siblings. Another one, Lisa with her friends in a rural area that, from the landscape, I guessed was South Africa. And finally, a solo shot of a serious-looking young man wearing a tuxedo, and herself in a long dress with a corsage on her wrist. The South African equivalent of a prom, I guessed. But if her boyfriend was in South Africa, why did she have K-Y jelly on her dresser?

Suddenly, the word "Bento" blared into my consciousness, and I rushed to hit the red button on the VCR. Kendall's kidnapping story was on. When the newscast finished, I rewound the tape and took it to Kendall, who was washing out the wineglass I'd barely used during dinner.

"Did I make it on NBC?" Kendall asked. "I was on our ABC affiliate but not WETA."

"Yes, you made it. I have the tape here."

Kendall smiled. "You probably think I'm a goof, getting so excited about being on television. But it's kind of exciting! I'm so used to putting the spotlight on other people, not having it on myself."

She was still in shock, I thought to myself. When she came out of it, she would drop the brittle facade and cry. To change the topic, I asked where Win was. I hadn't seen him at all during the day, and I half-wondered if he was staying away from me because of the awkwardness the night before.

"He got up around three and then had to go out to show some houses. Now he has another meeting. Let's hope it turns into a deal."

"Wow, he really works late."

"Twenty-four seven." Kendall smiled wanly. "I'm so glad you could be in the house tonight."

"Surely he'll be back by midnight," I said, glancing at the clock.

"Oh, he might be later. He says that the only way he can get things done is by working in the office when nobody's there."

"I see. And Lisa's out tonight with her boyfriend, then?"

"Oh, God, does she have a boyfriend? Did she tell you something like that?" Kendall groaned.

"No. I said very little to Lisa this morning, but I just thought she was probably seeing someone, given her age."

"One of the things I thought was great about her was that she had a fiancé back in Johannesburg. I thought that would mean less dating, you know, more availability for baby-sitting in the evenings. But it hasn't really worked out that way. She's got tons of girlfriends and they go out almost every night to Georgetown or anywhere they hear has boys. But who can blame her? Remember us at that age?"

I remembered Kendall: always so pretty, popular, and daring. "How do you get along with Lisa?"

"She's very sweet. I know the kids love her, and God knows, she has been a lifesaver during the times they had strep throat and colds and whatnot."

"But how do you and she get along personally?" I persisted.

Kendall hesitated for a second. "I guess okay. Sometimes I think she's judging me, you know, for spending so much time out of the house, and then needing a hand when I get home, but honestly, with Win being busy, I do need help."

I thought carefully about how to phrase my next question. "Are there ever times when you're out doing your charities, or whatever, that Win is home caring for the children?"

"If he's home, he wants Lisa to help with them. It's too much for him otherwise. Let me warn you: It's like that with all guys. Hugh may look perfect now, but . . . he's not a diaper changer. I can tell from his hands." Kendall poured the remaining few inches of wine from the bottle into her own glass.

"What can you tell about Hugh's hands?"

"They're too big. He'll be all thumbs." Kendall sipped, then smiled.

"Not long ago, you said his hands were a sign of fertility. Now it's parental incompetence."

Kendall giggled. "I guess it all depends on which expert I'm quoting. Fundraisers like to do that, you know."

I'd worried so much about Kendall, built up in my mind what a tragedy it would be to lose her. There were plenty of reasons to feel sorry for her, but her attitude was driving me crazy. Still, I'd try one more appeal. "Kendall, do you remember when we were little . . . the Barbies?"

"Barbies? You mean, like, drugs? I don't do anything like that anymore."

"When we were four, you taught me how to play with Barbie dolls. And then, at summer's end, you let me choose my favorites and take them back to California. You were so generous."

"No problem, Rei. I don't need them back. Jacquie's already starting to get them at birthday parties, can you believe, and she's not yet three."

"That's not what I'm talking about," I said. "I mean, when we were really young, things seemed so . . . easy between us. Last night, when you were gone, I just—I just knew something was wrong. It was like that communication was open again."

"Are you talking about woo-woo?" Kendall said. "Because actually, I was thinking about you. I hoped you'd notice that I'd been gone for a while, though of course, there was no chance of you finding me, once I went in that car."

"I was anxious right away. I still am. The thing is, Kendall, the police need to find out who took you—"

"Of course they do. But they'll never get to the truth. It's too political."

"Yes, the people who took you might have been connected with presidential politicking . . . or it might be someone else. Someone who chose you randomly"—here, I was referring to Jiro's thoughts about restaurant sabotage—"or someone who knows you personally. There might be something you haven't even thought about, like the odd person out in a"—how could I say this politely?—"a love triangle."

"You think I'm running around on Win?" Kendall's eyes glittered with strong emotion. "With whom? Let me guess, you think Harp Snowden."

"I really wasn't thinking like that." I'd been thinking of Win and Lisa.

"Well, let me tell you one thing, Rei. I hold the reins in the relationship, because I bring in money. No political hopeful would be stupid enough to try to seduce or sexually harass a woman fundraiser. Word would get around town so fast he'd be dead."

"Really." I was struck by her vehemence.

"That's right. To Harp, I'm the Virgin Mary. He can genuflect at my feet, but it stops there. I once thought you were smart, Rei, but it seems as if you're awfully naive not to know this—"

"I'm sorry, Kendall. I never thought about it that way." I had never seen her so enraged. Now I was afraid to bring up Win's stoned appearance. She'd have an excuse for that, I bet, and more harsh words for me. "Anyhow, I better go up to bed now. Tomorrow I have a ton of things to do."

"Like what?" Kendall seemed slightly mollified by my apology.

"Well, I've got to straighten up the apartment, since I've hardly been there long enough to put anything away. Then I'm meeting a friend at a cafe, and I have to hit the farmers' market, and finally, I'm picking up Hugh at the airport."

"The carefree, child-free life." Kendall winked at me. "Soon those cafe days will be over."

Maybe so, I thought after I said good night, went to the guest room, and settled in between the pretty, but scratchy, poly and cotton sheets. My cafe days might come to an end, but I wouldn't seek to replace them with what she had.

Around six-thirty the next morning, I went home. It was a complicated procedure, because I had to call a cab to take me to the Metro station; it wasn't worth it to wake Kendall, I thought. I was home an hour later, and used the next hour to clean the apartment. Then I jogged over to the farmers' market in Dupont Circle. The market was packed, as usual, with the assortment of foodies fighting over astronomically priced produce. I had wanted to get some morel mushrooms to sauté with garlic, but the last box was snatched up as I waited in line. Well, asparagus was in season. I was pondering which bunch to grab when I heard a familiar Japanese voice in my ear.

"Oh, hello!" I turned and saw that Jiro was wearing jeans and had a canvas shopping bag slung over his shoulder. He would have looked like a civilian, except for the fact that his shirt was a hip-length white cotton *kurta* that reminded me of what he wore in the kitchen.

"Take the thick one. Better texture," he said, eyeing the slim spears of asparagus I'd just touched.

"I always thought small ones had better flavor." With a feeling of skepticism, I took the stout bunch he handed me.

"I promise you, this is better for both taste and texture. Blanch it for just under a minute, then slice on the diagonal and toss with *mirin* and sesame oil. You can add some toasted sesame seed as garnish." He put the thicker bundle in my hand.

"Thanks for the recipe. Are you shopping here for business or pleasure?" I asked.

"Just the restaurant," he said with a light laugh. "I don't have the time to cook at home."

"Isn't it cheaper and easier to get the produce from a supplier?" I wondered aloud.

"Of course, but there are some really special things here. There is a farmer who grows *shiso* leaves, which you cannot get anywhere else. And sometimes, I can get quail eggs, which I need for the garnish on several dishes. What else have you bought?" He eyed my shoulder bag.

"Nothing," I said. "I got here so late. I wanted to make a nice meal to welcome Hugh home tonight. I missed out on our favorite mushroom for risotto."

"*Ah so desu ka*," Jiro said. "Why don't you cook a fish?"

"I thought it was a bad idea to buy fish on Sundays," I said.

"Try those fellows at the end. They caught the trout directly in a mountain spring in West Virginia. Now, I prefer the whole fish salt grilled. Do you know how?"

"Sure. It's a French technique—"

"And also Japanese. Watch out, I will have you cooking in the kitchen soon. *Sayonara*." He smiled and left.

As I was paying for the asparagus, a slim young man behind me asked, "Is that the Japanese guy who was on *Iron Chef*?"

I nodded.

"Cool," he said. "May I touch your asparagus?"

"How about trying his cooking at the new restaurant called Bento?" I said over my shoulder as I shot off for the fish vendor. I would try the trout, after all.

• • •

Half an hour later, I'd finished shopping at the farmers' market and bought an extra container of coarse sea salt at a bodega in my neighborhood. I parked the fish and vegetables in the fridge and jogged again to Urban Grounds, the cafe where Andrea wanted to meet. I'd been there before. It was just around the corner from Eighteenth Street's hodgepodge of Asian and African restaurants, incense and home-design shops. Urban Grounds was nursery-school cheerful, its pink and orange walls decorated with whimsical oversized sculpted coffee cups. A glass case held croissants, scones, and sticky buns in the morning, and lavish pastries and cakes in the afternoon. I eyed the chocolate hazelnut croissant but remembered how, just a month ago, Kendall had asked me if I was pregnant. I passed on the chocolate and ordered a toad in the hole: an omega-3 egg that was cooked in a hole cut in the middle of a slice of whole-wheat toast. Protein was what I needed.

Andrea was already there when I entered, sitting at a table in the back. I waved to her, and indicated that I was going to order my breakfast. As I did so, I thought it seemed strange that Andrea hadn't taken a better table, up front. There had been a few free when I'd walked in, but now they were filled with Adams-Morgan weekend regulars.

"Thanks for coming," Andrea said when I finally sat down. She was dressed in low-slung jeans and layered orange and pink camisoles that ended just above her navel. Today, her navel was studded with a purple crystal. How slim and sexy her midriff looked, I thought, reflexively touching my own softness under the spandex running tights I was wearing. Andrea sipped a cup of black coffee and looked incredulously at my latte, into which I was stirring three sugars. At least it was raw sugar.

"How are things going in the kitchen?" I asked as an opener.

"I'm surviving," she said. "I'm just keeping my fingers crossed that Justin will screw up so much that Marshall will give me my job back."

"It was bad luck," I sympathized. "That reporter was trying to do too many things, report on crime and decor and service. Overload, I guess."

"A good hostess is supposed to have attitude. I am who I am. It worked well at Mandala. If you only knew the kind of tips I used to get from the lobbyists . . ." Her voice drifted off sadly.

"Toad in the whole-wheat hole!" came a cry from the front counter. I excused myself to retrieve my breakfast dish. When I got back to the table, Andrea motioned for me to start.

"But your food isn't ready yet," I said.

"I'm not eating today." Andrea cleared her throat. "Actually, there's something I want to ask you."

"Do you want me to put in a word with Marshall?" I was instantly uneasy. The truth was, I did think Andrea was cold in her dealings with people.

"No, no, it's nothing to do with the restaurant. It's about you and me."

I paused, feeling relief. "I know we got off to a rough start. But I'm willing to try again, if you are."

"Never mind that. What I'm trying to say is that I don't tell many people this, but we—you and I—have something in common. My mother was from Japan."

9

"No way!" I said, and looked at Andrea, really looked at her, past the beauty that had made me so apprehensive when I'd first met her. "Of course. I should have noticed you have classic Asian eyelids. I guess I was a little distracted by your hair color."

"My hair is natural, but the color isn't." Andrea ran her fingers through her wheat-colored curls. "Anyway, nobody would call me an Asian-American like you. My father is black, which is a whole 'nother thing."

"To you, maybe, but there are plenty of people our age who are part Japanese, part American. There was even a documentary made about black Japanese kids ten years ago. It was great!"

"Really?" Andrea tilted her head, as if she was examining me more closely. "I haven't met anyone else like me. Here in America, any drop of black blood defines you. I never bothered telling Jiro I was half-Japanese because I knew it wouldn't count the way it counts for you."

"I have a Japanese name. That's the first tip-off for people from Japan." I changed the subject. "So how does your mother like it here?"

"I don't know. That's why I need a little help from you."

"You mean, to speak in Japanese?" I was confused.

"No. I want you to find her." Andrea leaned forward, as if she'd sensed my immediate desire to flee. "She's been gone since I was two years old. I don't even know if she's dead or alive."

"Andrea, I'm so sorry, but I—I don't know how I could help."

"You knew something bad was happening to your cousin," Andrea said, keeping her tough, sad gaze on me. "Any normal person would have thought she'd just gone out for a phone call, and maybe then ran off to do something. They'd wait around or blow the whole thing off and go home. But you knew, and then you made the cops listen to you. Maybe we could start with that guy, that Detective Burns, who found your cousin."

"Actually, another cop was tracking down a stolen Mercedes, and that's why Kendall was found. It was a matter of luck, I'm afraid." It still gave me the chills, in fact. Kendall wouldn't be around if it hadn't been for a car-theft tracking device.

"Did they catch the guys yet?"

"No, they didn't. This isn't Japan."

"What do you mean?" Andrea raised her eyebrows.

"In Japan, there are far fewer criminals. It's easier to stop people and hold them for questioning, too."

"I understand the Japanese police kicked you out of the country." I sputtered latte. "How did you hear that?"

"Well, I was a little curious about you when you started the decoration project. I wanted to see if you were really this high-powered decorator or not, so I did an Internet search. I came up with lots of links, most of which were in Japanese, so I couldn't read them. But from what I'd gotten in the English-language papers they print out there, I learned plenty."

"You told Marshall, I bet."

Andrea shook her head. "No. Growing up in the homes I did, I learned early on not to rat on anyone. But knowledge is power, you know? And what I read about you online, and then what I saw last night, made me think you could be a professional investigator."

I wondered what she meant about the homes she'd lived in, but I didn't have the time to ask about it. "I appreciate the compliment, but I really can't help you. You should contact the police or a PI."

"I already did that. Ten years ago, when I started making money, the first thing I paid for was a PI. He got a copy of the old police report, my father's statement, that kind of thing. Nothing of substance."

Her father's statement. I reflected on how odd it sounded, for a daughter to be cataloging a father's statement rather than talking to him. "What's the basic story of what happened?"

"Remember how I told you my father met my mother in Japan? Well, he was in the military. He was still in the Marines—he'd enlisted for a four-year term—when I was born in Virginia. He was based at the Pentagon at that point, but he was away on temporary additional duty when my mother vanished. The record states that she had left me with a next-door neighbor one morning and said she was going to a doctor's appointment and would be back by lunchtime. Well, she didn't come back that day or the next. The neighbor called the Pentagon and they sent word for my father to return. A day later a couple of tourists found her clothes and shoes at the edge of the Potomac River."

"A suicide?"

"Nobody ever found a body. And what kind of woman would actually take off her clothes if she was intending to commit suicide? I mean, if you knew your body was going to be discovered eventually, wouldn't you rather be clothed?"

"I guess I would." Especially now, when I was starting to hate the way my body looked.

"Furthermore, I found out from the report that while she lived in Japan, she'd been a professional pearl diver. Women like her worked underwater, without oxygen tanks. Someone who was that skilled underwater couldn't drown unless she was weighted down with something, and she had supposedly taken off all her clothes."

"As far as I know, pearl divers only work on the Shima peninsula. Is that where your father met your mother?"

Andrea shook her head. "I never heard of Ise anything. My dad was working at a base called Sasebo, and he said they met nearby."

"Really," I said, thinking that I didn't buy the pearl-diving story at all. In the nineteenth century, Japanese marine biologists had learned to culture pearls that were perfectly round and beautiful, far superior to the irregular natural pearls that women had dived for in centuries past. Given the time frame, Andrea's mother couldn't have been a pearl diver unless she was a tourism worker, and she was in the wrong geographic area to do that. Sasebo was on the Japanese island of Kyūshū. The pearl divers I'd heard about, the ones who put on a show for tourists, worked in Mie Prefecture, on the Shima peninsula, as I'd brought up already.

Andrea continued, "The Arlington, Virginia, police kept the case open for a few years but ultimately closed it. My mother's missing, presumed dead. That's not enough information for me."

"Those must have been tough years for you and your dad to wait through," I said.

"We weren't together." Andrea looked down. "He put me in foster care within a month of her disappearance. He couldn't take care of me because the military required him to travel, he said."

I was stunned by the mention of foster care. It reminded me of what Burns had said about social services for Kendall's children. "Why didn't you live with your American relatives?"

"He said he didn't think I'd be treated well there, because they didn't like my mom." Andrea sighed. "So I went into care, and like I said, the police kept looking for a few years. Then she was declared dead and my dad almost immediately remarried."

"Well, why didn't you join him then?" I asked.

"You keep putting it as if I was the one who could make the decisions." Andrea's tone was angry. "The fact was, he didn't want me. He hasn't been outwardly nasty, but his wife, Lorraine, has been, ever since the beginning. She still tries to keep him from seeing me. Believe me, I don't want to be close to him. All I want is to know what happened to my mother."

"I'm so sorry, Andrea." I didn't know what else I could say.

"There was something you said at the restaurant last night. What kind of mother would leave her babies?"

"'What kind of mother would leave her babies,'" I repeated. Last night, I'd said it out of desperation, the only thing I could think of to make people start to think it mattered that Kendall was missing.

"I think she was killed," Andrea said. "She wouldn't have run away without me. Even if she was so unhappy with Dad, she would not have left me there."

"She didn't take you in the water with her," I said gently. "Some mothers in difficult situations have done that. Yours cared enough to keep you safe."

"You know, I look at her face and try to tell. But I just can't." From her bag, Andrea withdrew a manila envelope. She pulled out old, faded color photographs, the type of photos that fill the 1970s section of my parents' photo albums. But Andrea's little three-by-three snaps weren't in any kind of album; each was placed in an archival acid-free paper envelope. How precious they were; I could tell by the way she handed the first one to me. It was a wedding photograph, a smiling woman in a red bridal kimono, hair blowing across her face, standing next to a black man with a similarly pleased expression. He wore a green military uniform and had his hands at his sides, the "at-ease" military position. The woman had her hands clasped in front of her, and I noted that they looked big. She, too, was large, not heavy, but closer in height to the man than I expected, and with a broadness to her shoulders that reminded me of Kendall's since she had taken up strength training. The sea lay behind them.

"Too bad the wind's got the hair going across her face. I really can't see it," I said.

"Look at this one, then." Andrea handed me a picture of her mother holding a baby. Andrea, at about two, looked a lot like she did now. She was a thin baby, unsmiling. Her hair had been tugged up into two pigtails and she wore a frilly pink-and-white dress with coordinating ankle socks and white lace-up shoes. Her mother, on the other hand, was quite natural. Her straight black hair hung to her shoulders without the benefit of any special styling, and it didn't look like she wore any makeup except for a faint gloss on her lips.

"What was your mother's name?" I asked.

"Sadako." Andrea pronounced it carefully. "My father called her Sadie. He thought her other name was too—"

"Difficult?" I had a grudge against people who invented new names for foreigners to help them integrate.

"No, he told me he thought her name was too sad. Her last name, I'm afraid I don't really know how to pronounce it. I think Dad was saying it wrong." Andrea handed me a copy of a marriage license that had been filed in San Diego in 1972. Here, her mother's name was listed as Sadako Tsuchiya.

"Tsoo-chee-yah," I pronounced for Andrea. "I've heard that name before. Where does her family live?"

"I don't know," Andrea said. "All I know is that way back when, the police did try to contact her family, but they didn't respond."

"Well, that's—ridiculous," I said. "They could have asked a Japanese police officer to call on the household."

"Dad said that she was written out of the register, whatever that means."

"There's a register kept in every town in Japan, with all the names of the families living there," I said. "When a woman marries, her name is crossed off and is entered in her husband's family register. What town did she live in?"

"Sasebo is all that I know," Andrea said. "Tell me more about family registers. Did they take her name off because she wasn't going to marry a Japanese guy?"

Andrea was coming uncomfortably close to a truth that I didn't like to think about. "Perhaps. If children make their parents upset, the parents might remove them from the register."

Andrea kept her eyes on me. "Because she married someone black?"

"Just marrying an *American* is a massive crime of dishonor, in many eyes. My grandparents wrote out my father because he married an American woman. Eventually, they changed their minds, and reinstated him." It was because I'd been born, everyone said. Babies made hard hearts soften.

Andrea pressed her lips together. "I doubt that would happen for me."

"I don't know." I decided to change the subject. "Tell me more about your mother's friends in the U.S., what they thought about her disappearance."

"The neighbor she left me with—Joanne Bridges—was supposed to be her best American friend. And she really didn't know anything at all about her. I talked to her in person once. She was nice, but not really helpful."

"Does your father still live close to D.C.?"

Andrea shook her head. "He left the Pentagon at the end of his enlistment, when I was four. He moved back to Orange, where he and Lorraine both came from. They were high school sweethearts. His thing with my mom was, as Lorraine puts it, the overseas fling."

I heard the pain in Andrea's voice, but I didn't want to get distracted from the facts I was trying to establish. "Orange County, near Los Angeles?"

"No, it's in Virginia. Charlottesville is the biggest town near it."

"Great wineries nearby," I said, then chided myself for my insensitivity.

"Restaurants, too," Andrea said. "If I was closer to my father, I might have looked for work around there."

"You say the relationship is bad. You could try to change it by going to see him," I suggested.

"It's not going to change. There's no point."

"You must press your father on some things." I picked up the detective's report. "I notice that the birth year for your mother on the detective's report is different from the one on the marriage license. Someone didn't do a very thorough job."

"You saw it. I knew you were the right one to help!" Andrea sounded happier than I'd ever imagined she could be.

"I think you should go back to your father. Ten years have passed since your last meeting, you said. Maybe he's mellowed. At the very least, he probably has a few more pictures or papers relating to your mother, which he could give to you."

"Every time I've called, there's some excuse for why they can't see me. It's not like a normal family. And besides, I don't have a car, and the train doesn't go out to those rural byways."

I felt terrible for Andrea: the loss of her mother, the betrayal of her father, the loneliness of her adult life. No wonder she spoke to everyone as if she had a chip on her shoulder. The chip was a mountain the size of Fuji. "Andrea, I can't help you with much. But I can give you a ride down there."

"You would? I didn't know you had a car."

"It's my boyfriend's car. I'm sure he'd think it was a good reason for a trip to Virginia. Especially if I swing by a vineyard to pick up wine on the way back." I gave her a serious look, the one I used to use on my students in Japan when I knew they were going to skip doing their homework. "I want this trip to be fruitful. I suggest you call your father to make sure he's there."

"If I call, Lorraine will answer the phone. And if say I'm coming, she'll tell me that they're going out of town. That's what happened the last couple of times I tried."

"Then don't give him a warning," I said. "And can you be more specific about the last contact you had? Surely it wasn't just that meeting ten years ago. Any phone calls, birthday cards in the meantime?"

"Zip," Andrea said. "I'd think he was dead if I didn't keep checking the Internet. I also put in a request to Veteran's Affairs for his military-service record. That was three months ago. I'm still waiting."

"Call the VA again to remind them. And what did you dig up on your father on the Internet?" I was still flustered that she'd found out so much about me.

"There was an updated alumni directory for his high school, a mention of his restaurant in a community newspaper—that kind of thing."

"A restaurant!" I wondered, instantly, if this was why she'd become a hostess.

"Well, it's actually a diner. You know, pancakes and burgers and all that. He owns the place, but he cooks."

"Can you look up the address for his diner?" I asked. "We might need to go there, instead of the house, if he's working."

"It's on Route 47, just outside Orange," Andrea said. "I know how to get there."

Since Bento was closed on Mondays, that was our obvious choice of a travel date. I agreed to pick her up at seven the next morning. I also made Andrea promise to photocopy all the photographs and reports so that nothing precious would be lost.

As I parted from Andrea, I thought about how strangely things were turning out. Hugh had said I had no women friends; now I was helping two women about my age with serious problems. Both of them were "pieces of work," to borrow one of Grand's favorite expressions.

The image came to me then, of Win and Jacquie playing desolately on the Persian carpet in the large playroom where the TV blared footage of Kendall. I had only to close my eyes to imagine Andrea, a small girl of the same age, sitting by herself in front of another bright television screen, in a house that was not her own.

I couldn't remake the lives of my nephew and niece, who were considered privileged, anyway. Andrea, on the other hand, had been alone as a child and still had nobody to call her own. And she was reaching out. I couldn't turn away from her now.

10

Hugh was coming out of customs, the zone in Dulles airport that was always the most jammed and chaotic. He often took a taxi home, even though it was about forty minutes from where we lived; but there had been a garbled message from the night before, of which I'd caught only the tail end, a warning to make sure the Lexus's trunk—"boot" in Hugh's Britspeak—was completely empty.

He must have gone on a shopping binge, I thought as I parked in the open lot across from the curved glass-and-steel terminal that looked like a cross between a space colony and a mid-twentieth-century high school. Hugh was the only man I knew who truly enjoyed shopping. What had he brought me? I began to fantasize pleasantly about objects that came in large boxes. I hoped he hadn't gone for something electronic; usually the newest and neatest things for sale in Akihabara weren't adaptable for U.S. electric voltage. Hugh had brought home from his last trip a Toto electric toilet seat with a built-in bidet. Unfortunately, it was sized incorrectly for our vintage toilet bowl.

Hugh's flight from Tokyo had landed ten minutes earlier, the arrivals board said by the time I'd walked in. Normally, he was off the plane pretty fast, thanks to business-class privilege, but luggage collection would take time. I pulled from my bag the mail I hadn't had time to read, given the last few days' excitement. The Washington-Japan Friendship League had sent me a quarterly newsletter. There'd be a potluck dinner on Children's Day in a few months, and volunteers were needed to help with decoration. I had some carp kites that I could lend them; it would mean a long Metro ride, but it would be worth going in early, especially if I could ask them about Andrea's mother. The WJFL's stated mission was to help Japanese immigrants, and it had been around forever. Maybe they would remember a Sadako Tsuchiya Norton . . .

"Darling!"

Hugh's shout broke through my meditation. I searched the crowd and spotted his red-blond head bobbing in a sea of dark ones. I'd missed him. I couldn't wait for the skin-to-skin reunion, but experience had taught me that it would probably come the next night, when he wasn't so tired. In any case, we'd have a wonderful dinner. The trout was clean and resting on ice in the fridge, the asparagus was done to Jiro's specifications, and a crisp baguette and a bottle of pinot noir were waiting on the counter. For dessert I would cut up strawberries and serve them with clotted cream.

I couldn't wait to hug Hugh, but there was a woman just in front of him, hampering his progress: a small, Japanese-looking woman with the perfect unlined face of Asian middle age, a face that looked almost like my aunt Norie's. I looked again. It *was* Norie.

I gasped aloud as Norie caught sight of me, too, and charged forward, rolling her suitcase over another traveler's feet.

"Obasan," I said, falling into the Japanese honorific for aunts, the term I always used to address her. While locked in an embrace with my aunt, I gazed over her shiny black hair at Hugh, trying to communicate my shock. "This is a wonderful surprise!"

"You heard my message about it, didn't you?" Hugh asked as he came up. "I asked you to leave plenty of room in the boot for her luggage because she's packed enough to stay for a year."

"Oh, my goodness," I said.

"I hope you have room for me in your apartment," Norie said, sounding shy. "I didn't ask you myself, but Hugh-san said you had agreed that it was a fine idea."

I smiled, searching my memory for what I might have said to Hugh. I'd been so distracted when we'd spoken. Well, it didn't matter now. I had a more pressing problem. My aunt didn't know that Hugh and I were living together, and I couldn't imagine that she'd feel comfortable staying with us sharing a bedroom in an unmarried state. It wasn't proper by Japanese standards; even my father, who'd been in the U.S. for over thirty years, wouldn't tolerate Hugh in my room until after we'd become engaged.

I took the handle of Norie's huge Samsonite suitcase and began pulling it quickly through the crowd. I had to get ahead of her, to get space to talk with Hugh.

"Rei, what are you doing?" Hugh caught up with me, just as I'd hoped. "Norie's a good ten meters behind you. It's not polite to go faster than she can—"

"Did you tell Norie we are living together?" I held my breath, waiting for the answer.

"Not exactly," Hugh said. "I thought that was better coming from you."

"She must not know that we live together. She'll lose face if she is forced to be a party to it. She'll insist on moving out, and our whole relationship will be ruined!"

"But we lived together in Japan." Hugh's tone was bewildered.

"That was just for a few months, before I got my own place. And she didn't like you very much at the time, do you remember? She thought you were taking advantage of me."

Hugh whistled softly. "What are we going to do? It's obviously my flat, full of my gear. Not to mention, I need somewhere to sleep. Especially after this last flight, when I normally would have drifted off but she kept me up the whole time, practicing English conversation—"

"You could go to Win and Kendall," I suggested desperately.

"No! It would be an imposition on them, not to mention that I want to be in my own bed at night, with you." He looked at me significantly.

"Then you'll have to go along with the plan that I suggest," I said.

"Which is?" Hugh sounded wary.

"To start, you can drop me off with all the luggage at the building, but don't you dare let her out of the car. You can drive her around to see the sights on the Mall. I'll need about an hour to de-masculinize the place. You'll join us for dinner, and then you'll go out again. I'll call your cell after she goes to sleep. Then you can sneak back in—oh, Obasan, I wish I had cleaned up the apartment for you!" I changed my tone as Norie caught up. "Anyway, Hugh is going to take you on a short drive while I organize a few things."

"But I'm a little tired," Norie started to protest.

"Don't you know that when you arrive in a different time zone it's important to spend time in the bright sunlight? That will help reset your body clock," I advised. "Our car's just across the way. Let me take another of your bags, Obasan."

"I brought my own sheets," Norie said. "Please don't worry about a bed. I am used to sleeping on the floor."

"There's a fold-out futon in my study," I said. It had been my bed once, in Japan.

"A study! My goodness, it sounds bigger than your last place, Rei-chan. You must be doing very well economically to have such an apartment. Of course, I will also have to see your parents' lovely home in San Francisco. Your parents invited me to stay there for as long as I like. But I'm here to work, to help you with the wedding preparations."

"Actually, I haven't been thinking about the wedding much. I've been so caught up in the opening of this new restaurant, you see."

"Yes, yes, Hugh said so. How is it?"

"Well, the food's wonderful," I said. "But there was a problem opening night that they are still trying to live down."

"'Live down'? What does that mean?" Norie asked.

I'd been speaking to her in English for Hugh's benefit. I tried again. "The restaurant, it suffered an embarrassment on the first night, which they hope will be forgotten."

"What kind of embarrassment? Some problem with the food?"

"Actually, my cousin Kendall was kidnapped from the place." Seeing Norie's shocked expression, I quickly added, "She was safely returned to her family the next morning. Unfortunately, the kidnapping was mentioned in the newspapers, which made the restaurant appear unsafe."

"Newspapers can be terrible for the image. We know that from our experience, don't we, Rei?" Norie nodded sagely. "I am not afraid to visit this restaurant. Shall we go there tomorrow?"

"Actually, tomorrow I'm driving to central Virginia. But on Tuesday we can go to Bento, if you like."

"Sightsee in Virginia? You are making such nice plans for me from the very start!"

"Actually, don't you want to rest tomorrow?" I asked.

"Oh, no. I am eager to, how do you say, adjust to American life. I will see the sunlight today, reset my body clock, and spend a full day of travel with you."

I took a few deep breaths and reminded myself that I should be happy. Norie had been my surrogate mother all those years I'd spent in my early twenties in Japan. She wouldn't stay with us forever; it was worth it to keep her approval during the time she was with me.

Hugh dropped me off with the bags, and I lugged them upstairs, then set about in a whirlwind of de-guying the apartment. Although I'd moved in plenty of antique Japanese furniture and placed a few woodblock prints on the walls, the apartment in general did not look like mine, chiefly because it had been painted and decorated by Hugh in the primary colors of blue and ochre. There was a leather sofa in the living room, which also had an elaborate stereo and high-tech-looking CD towers that housed every compact disc Hugh had collected from his college days on.

No point in doing anything about the CDs, I thought; Norie wouldn't know the difference between Grace Jones (mine) and Norah Jones (his). But I would sweep all the law journals off the coffee table and under his side of the sleigh bed. Hugh's mahogany sleigh bed in itself could be a problem, because Norie might remember that I only owned a futon. Well, I'd just have to tell her that I bought it, and the handsome Biedermeier armoire as well. Once the living room was done, I went to the bathroom and swept all of Hugh's shaving paraphernalia into a basket that I added to the underbelly of the bed. Then, Hugh's coats and shoes had to move from the hall closet to our narrow bedroom closet, which was already stuffed to the rafters. His rowing machine I couldn't hide—Norie would just have to believe that I'd taken up that form of exercise.

I was just changing the sticker on the buzzer downstairs from Glendinning to Shimura when Norie and Hugh came back.

"All set?" Hugh looked anxious as I crumpled up in my fist the old sticker bearing his name.

"Of course." I smiled encouragingly at him. "Welcome home, Aunt Norie! And, Hugh, now that you're back, won't you come up and have a cup of tea?"

When Norie entered, she exclaimed happily over the size of the place, and didn't seem fazed by anything, though she wondered aloud why Hugh had taken his own suitcase and carry-on upstairs.

"You can't leave anything in parked cars around here, Obasan, there's so much crime," I said smoothly. I showed her into the study, where she'd be sleeping, and offered her the chance to have a hot bath before dinner. The fish was delicious—I'd only bought two, so I cut them up beforehand; that way it didn't look as if someone had been counted out. I felt terrible for Hugh, who gobbled his portion promptly and then practically nodded with exhaustion over his plate.

"You'd better go home to your own place, but I'm worried about you driving. Where is it?" Norie asked kindly.

"Closer than you'd expect," Hugh said, then swept out with a long look, but no kiss, for me.

I chatted with Norie until she made her departure to the futon in the study. Twenty minutes later, I called Hugh on his cell phone. He was at the Irish pub near Union Station with his rugby friends, who were making bets on how long the single-girl apartment ruse would work. I reminded him to tell his friends to call him only at work or on his cell phone, and he groaned.

"Frankly, if living together unmarried is such a sin, we should marry posthaste," Hugh said. "Tomorrow I'll apply for a license. The hell with fancy weddings."

"But that would disappoint our parents," I said. "Darling, just come home. She's asleep now. We can talk about it."

But Hugh returned too exhausted to talk. He washed up quietly in the bathroom, put on the pajamas I'd laid out for him, and was snoring within a minute of hitting the pillow. I tossed and turned for a while, thinking about how hard the situation was going to be, but eventually fell asleep. I was still tired when Hugh kissed me awake the next morning. So he wasn't angry with me. I was relieved.

"Here. Your present," Hugh said. He was still damp from his shower, and was wrapped up in a terry-cloth robe.

Sleepily, I tugged the box open and saw what he'd given me: an impossibly tiny pink-and-black cell phone.

"It looks like a sex toy," I said.

"It could be." He grinned at me. "But really, it's high time you got one of these things. If Kendall didn't have one with her that night, where would she be?"

"Thank you. Do you know if it will work in the U.S.?"

"Yes, it's an export model. The thing I like about it is that you can use it all over the world to make and receive calls, so I can get in touch with you wherever you are."

Of course, he was the traveler, not I—though I still cherished my little dream of returning to Japan. I put the phone on the bedside table and slunk back down under the duvet.

Hugh shed his robe and crawled in after me. From the feel of him, he wasn't after a catnap.

"We'd better not. My aunt might overhear—"

He cut me off with a long kiss, then said, "I left the shower running in the bathroom. She won't hear a thing over that. And by the way, I'm armed!" He held a brand-new, microscopically thin Japanese condom for me to inspect.

"That's awfully wasteful," I sighed, as he disappeared under the covers again.

"The condom? Not really. I think we can afford them more readily than a baby, at the moment—"

"No, the water." I could hear it pattering against the tile, just as my body was starting to tighten in anticipation.

"There's no drought. Not in Washington, not down here either," Hugh said suggestively.

He was right. He was too good. All the things any normal woman would have thought of during first-thing-in-the-morning sex—lack of tooth-brushing and showering—flew out of my head. Hugh didn't care, obviously. His mouth was all over me in all the ways I loved, and he'd picked up an amazing new trick with his hands.

Sex with Hugh was perfect because it kept changing, growing, just as the feelings in myself, as I headed toward thirty, became more powerful. I was more responsive now, more daring. The days that Hugh had been gone had been full of work, but almost every night, once I'd gotten in bed, my mind had turned to what I was missing. I didn't change his pillowcase until just before he came home because I wanted to inhale his scent.

I found myself daydreaming, after we were through, about what sex would feel like postmarriage. Would it become boring? Would there ever be a time when Hugh, like Win, came home unzipped because there was something more exciting out there?

"What is it, darling?" Hugh stroked my hair, as if he'd sensed my worry.

I didn't want to seem too neurotic. "That new, ah, little finger trick of yours."

"Did you like it?" Hugh practically crowed.

"Tremendously. Where did you learn it?" I said.

Hugh laughed softly. "I saw it in a pillow book I bought at Kinokuniya. They sold it to me in a plain brown wrapper! I can show you now, if you like."

"I would love to see it."

Hugh hopped into his underwear and started digging in his suitcase, giving a running commentary on the reaction of the young female salesclerk when he'd asked for the title. He brought the book over to me, and we were giggling over it when suddenly, the pattering of water in the bathroom ceased. There followed a light knock on the door separating the bathroom from our bedroom.

"The water is very cold. I turned it off!" Norie's voice called out. "How can I turn on your water heater?"

Hugh's eyes were laughing at me, silently, as he started buttoning up his Thomas Pink shirt. I had no time for fashion choices; I bundled myself into his bathrobe and went to the door, through which I loudly explained that there was no water heater in the bathroom itself, but if she waited ten minutes or so, there would be enough hot water running through the system again for her own shower.

"If she went into the bathroom while the water was running, how many more boundaries is she going to cross?" I whispered to Hugh as we finished dressing inside the bedroom.

"We might have to run away," Hugh whispered back.

"I hear you," I said. "But where?"

11

While driving through the Virginia countryside a few hours later, I started a few fantasies about that escape. The rolling green hills dotted by grazing sheep and decrepit old barns were almost obscenely picturesque. Not that there would be many opportunities for practicing international law or decorating houses—Hugh and I would have to shear sheep or make artisanal cheese.

Andrea was sitting silently in the backseat; I'd introduced Norie to her, after picking her up, and she'd accepted the situation without much protest—or friendliness, either. By now I knew that Andrea's prickliness was probably a sign of how worried she was about the upcoming events. She was dressed in a manner that, for her, seemed semicasual: a long-sleeved voile blouse patterned with orchids, and fluid cream silk pants. She was wearing impossibly high heels, which she kicked off in the car.

After taking off her shoes, Andrea withdrew a package of Virginia Slims from her Coach bag. I told her to put them back.

"Shoot," she said, "I didn't know you were one of the anti-smoking Nazis."

"It's Hugh's car," I said. "He'd never lend it to me again if I brought it back smoky. And frankly, I can't imagine why anyone in the food business would smoke. Doesn't it ruin your ability to appreciate food?"

"More than half the kitchen smokes," Andrea said. "It's normal for restaurant people to smoke. Our palates are fine; in fact, a cigarette at the end of a meal is perfect."

"Andrea, if Bento were a smoking restaurant, you'd hate it," I said. "Just think of what working for six hours in a three-thousand-square-foot ashtray would do to your clothes every night."

"And your skin would be hurt," Aunt Norie chimed in. "Your beautiful golden skin would look old too young. As well as your eyes. Rei-chan, don't you think your friend's eyes look almost Japanese?"

I glanced back at Andrea through the rearview mirror. "May I tell her about you?"

"Go ahead. I can't get any more stressed out than I already am."

I wound up explaining Andrea's story in Japanese, just to make certain Norie understood how important the trip was. By the end of it, Norie looked as if she could use one of Andrea's cigarettes.

"There must be a way that I can help. I can find your Japanese relatives when I return home," Norie said in English. I'd noticed that on foreign ground, it was much stronger than it had ever been in Japan.

"Let's think about today, Obasan. Actually, I'm worried that your presence might bring back memories for Andrea's father," I replied in English, so Andrea would understand.

"Mrs. Shimura, how old are you?" Andrea asked, surprising me with her intrusiveness. But without seeming embarrassed, Norie answered that she'd been born in 1951.

"Really! I would have guessed you were younger," Andrea said. "What I'm thinking is, you could pass for my mother's sister, because she had a younger sister born in 1954."

"What's the point of passing for someone she isn't?" My hackles rose.

"I can use your aunt," Andrea said. "I can use you both. If you let my father believe that you are family of my mother's, come all the way to find out the truth, he'll have to talk to us."

I braked suddenly, causing the car behind me to honk. I pulled myself together and drove on. When I had calmed down, I said, "Andrea, I won't lie. And I won't let my aunt do it either. I've gotten in trouble for little lies. It's why I was kicked out of Japan."

"You won't have to say a word," Andrea drawled. "I'll do all the talking."

An hour later, we were at the JL Cafe. Andrea opened a glass door plastered with signs telling us to support state troopers, American freedom, and Jesus Christ, and we all filed in. Inside there was no hostess stand, rather a cheery, hand-lettered sign that said "Seat Yourself!" with a smiley face.

It was a picture-perfect diner, just like the ones from my childhood, when we drove into the farm belt for pick-your-own fruit or to go shopping for antiques. The only difference in this diner was that everyone inside it was black. I immediately felt that every eye was on my aunt and me, and wondered if this was what it felt like for black customers at Bento—there were some, but a minority compared to whites.

More than a few people glanced at us as we took the booth that Andrea selected instead of more public spots along the long, Formica-topped counter. Behind the counter was a vast griddle, where a tall, slightly hunched man of sixty was flipping pancakes. He glanced at us, nodded, and called out, "Marie!"

Marie, a slim woman in her forties with a sprinkling of freckles across her caramel-colored skin, came to our table with a pot of coffee in hand. We all nodded that we wanted coffee even though it was already eleven in the morning, and the thought of more caffeine made me anxious for the rest room.

After Marie had left, Andrea said very quietly, "That's my dad behind the counter."

Norie looked blank, and I guessed she hadn't understood what Andrea had said. I translated, and my aunt shot the cook a disapproving look. "He hasn't greeted us. In any restaurant in Japan, we would have been greeted!"

"No more English, okay?" Andrea said in a low voice. Marie was heading back to take the breakfast order. When she arrived, Andrea asked if they had any specials. I noticed Andrea's voice was changing its timbre, becoming more Southern. I could understand the phenomenon. The Japanese I'd spoken with the people at the friendship group and even with Jiro at the restaurant had been formal. With Norie, my Japanese was faster and more casual.

"Yep," Marie said. "Y'all just having breakfast or are you gonna order something from the lunch menu?"

Norie looked totally uncomprehending, and I realized how difficult this Southern dialect must sound to my aunt, who could barely understand Hugh's Scottish accent after two years. I spoke under my breath to her in Japanese, and together we consulted the menu. Norie ordered fried rockfish, which didn't surprise me since Japanese usually ate fish at every meal. Just that morning—after Hugh had slipped out unnoticed, of course—Norie had presented a dried bonito fish from her luggage and insisted on grating it to make soup for our breakfast. For some reason, the soup hadn't sat well with me that morning, so I was now in the mood for starchy comfort, a grilled-cheese sandwich. Andrea ordered a BLT. Afterward, she added, "By the way, you could tell Robert Norton he's got family here from out of town."

Marie's eyes passed rather incredulously over the three of us. "You sure about that?"

"Very," Andrea said. "I'm his daughter. I grew up in D.C."

"Oh, for heaven's sake!" Marie looked at Andrea again. "You got his height and his nose, that's for sure. What's your name, honey?"

"Andrea. Andrea Norton." My friend seemed to grow as she spoke her name.

Marie's eyes widened and, tucking her order form in her apron pocket, she went off without another word.

"Do you think people around here ever heard about you?" I asked Andrea when we were alone again.

"It doesn't seem like it. Ssh, I think it's him coming out from behind the counter."

I was sitting next to Andrea, so I shared her view of her father. He wore a white apron over a short-sleeved checked shirt. The apron was spotless, I noticed, and he had a kind of net over his close-cropped, graying Afro. When he saw our table, he did a double-take, then fixed his gaze on Andrea.

"Why did I do this?" she muttered.

"Don't lose your nerve," I whispered. "See, he's coming over. Norie and I will visit the rest room. That'll give you the first few minutes alone."

When we came back out, I looked over at the booth where we'd been sitting and saw that lunch had been served. The time elapsed since the order had been given was five minutes. Just good service—or were we wanted out?

Robert Norton was sitting across from Andrea. I could see her face, but not his. Once I would have thought it a haughty expression, but now I knew it meant that she was scared to death.

"She wants us to come. She motioned her hand to me," Norie said.

We walked back together, side by side. Norie bowed first, and I followed.

To my surprise, Andrea spoke up quickly. "Aunt Norie, may I introduce my father, Robert? And this is her daughter, who is my cousin, Rei. Rei studied English in school, but Aunt Norie doesn't speak much."

"Do you still live in Japan?" Robert Norton said. He didn't stretch out a hand to greet us, but that made sense. Japanese were bowers, not shakers. He'd remember that from his time in Sasebo.

"Until recently, I lived in Toe-kyoe." I drew out my vowels, trying to pronounce the city name the way Japanese did.

"Oh. Well, this is a surprise."

"Oh, rearry?" I changed my *l*s to *r*s, and Aunt Norie nodded and smiled. I was speaking English the right way at last, the way she and her friends did.

"Yes. When, ah, I married Andrea's mother, your family wasn't too happy."

"There is a Japanese saying, water washes everything away," I said slowly, continuing to exaggerate my accent. "That means time makes forgiveness."

"What Rei's trying to say is that the family wants to understand what happened to Mom. Especially Aunt Norie here." Andrea nodded at my aunt. "They need the rest of the things that were in the storage box, so they can bury them."

"Bury them?" Robert asked.

"In the cemetery. If Mom's really dead, she should have a marker somewhere. Her Japanese family wants to do it."

"This is the first I heard of it." Robert sounded uneasy.

Andrea was making mistakes. The Japanese wouldn't bury mementos, they'd make a family altar around them. Would Robert know that?

"We have family altar, so pictures and personal items would be welcome," I said slowly. "We seek the true story of what happened. You can say in English. I will translate for my aunt."

"Not here," Robert said tightly.

"We'll wait for you to get through," Andrea said.

Robert stared at Andrea, and it seemed to me a mix of emotions was running through him. He looked angry, sad, and, finally, very tired. "All right. I'll have to call in Davon. When he gets here, you-all can follow me to the house. I still have a couple of boxes of odds and ends relating to your mother. I'll give it to you."

"Thanks. I'll bring it back," Andrea said.

"Keep it! Please."

"Can you also tell us what you know about what happened?" Andrea asked.

"I told you ten years ago—"

"They haven't heard it," Andrea said. "And I'm sure they'll have questions of their own."

Robert Norton didn't look happy at that. He got up, he said, to go back to the kitchen to call in Davon. When he was gone,

Andrea told us this was her half brother, Robert's child by Lorraine. I attempted to eat my grilled cheese, but it had long grown cold, and I got a faint feeling of nausea from its taste. I guess I'd gotten too used to really good restaurant food. Aunt Norie, I feared, wouldn't like the cornmeal-dipped fried fish in front of her; but after the first bite, she closed her eyes in rapture.

"*Oishi!*"

"Delicious," I translated for Andrea. Then, I got down to business. "I don't know how you want me to play this."

"You're doing fine. You, too, Norie-san."

"You must try the fish!" Norie started cutting off a piece for me with the fork I wasn't using. "It is so good. Do you think, when we visit your house, your father can teach me how to cook this?"

I toyed with the sandwich, and Andrea, too, didn't seem hungry. After about fifteen minutes, a tall, slim black man who looked barely twenty walked in the diner. He wore a baseball cap backward and overalls over a muscle T. He had a warm, open expression: A baby face, I thought to myself.

"Davon," Andrea said under her breath. Her eyes widened as she looked at him; he glanced at her without recognition and went behind the counter and into the kitchen.

"I guess your father didn't tell him why he was coming in," I said.

"I'm sure the staff will let him know." Andrea sighed. "I never met him before. Lorraine kept him away."

"You should let him know who you are. He'd probably like to have a half sister."

"I'm sure he's heard no end of crap about me," Andrea muttered.

"There's always a chance to change that image—"

"Here's my father. Come on, we better catch up with him just in case he plans to bolt." Andrea laid a twenty on the table.

"We haven't gotten the check yet," I worried.

"This'll cover it, easy. And it'll make Marie happy."

"Thank you for the lunch," Norie said, rising to her feet and bowing. "But really, I am older than you two, so I should be pay—"

"Ssh. Not so much English, okay?" Andrea said as we moved toward the exit. Outside, Robert Norton was getting into the pickup truck I'd noticed earlier.

"Do you remember where the house is?" he said out the open window.

Andrea shook her head. "Not really. I'll follow you."

12

"Of course I remember where the house is," Andrea said between gritted teeth once she was in the Lexus beside me and Norie had taken the back. I had to slam the car into gear, because after pulling out, Robert Norton picked up speed so quickly he raised a small cloud of dirt behind him. I was edging toward fifty miles an hour to keep him in sight, and the speed limit was thirty. Was this his game, getting me to speed past a cop who would of course give me a ticket, since I was from out of state?

A few turns, and again, these nightmare speeds past fields of fledgling corn shoots and soybeans, fields that should have been enjoyed at a leisurely pace.

"He's talking on a cell phone!" I could make this judgment based on the way his head was cocked to one side.

"He's probably calling Lorraine," Andrea said. "Don't miss this left coming up. He's not using his turn signal. I guess he wants us to miss it."

"He doesn't have a hand free to hit the lever," I said, making the hairpin turn right behind Robert Norton. We were on a gravel road now, and going so fast that a piece of gravel struck the windshield, chipping it. I hoped Hugh wouldn't notice.

The farm was five minutes farther down the road. As Andrea had said, it was a brick ranch house that I guessed had been built in the sixties. A huge satellite dish was the only ornament in the front, but fields stretched on either side of it; the corn that Andrea had mentioned, and something else, low and creeping and green. As soon as we parked, Norie was out of the car, photographing the fields.

"What's this all about?" Robert Norton, standing outside his pickup truck, gestured toward Norie.

"Of course she's going to take pictures," Andrea said smoothly. "My aunt came all the way from Japan."

I wandered off in Norie's direction, planning to warn her to rein in her photographic impulses. I could still hear the conversation behind me.

"So they convinced you to bring them down. How did they locate you?" Robert Norton asked Andrea.

"Oh, you can find anyone on the Internet these days."

"So what you been doing with yourself?"

"I'm the hostess of a restaurant in D.C.," Andrea said. "You may have heard of it. It's called Bento."

"A restaurant?" He sounded incredulous. "I thought you'd do something more than that, with your schooling—"

"Yeah, the D.C. schools are really wonderful," Andrea said, sarcasm heavy in her voice. "And that community college you sent me to afterward! Wow, that really opened my future!"

He sighed. "You look like an uptown girl. Sound like one, too. Seems like you're doing all right."

I gently coaxed Norie out of the field and back to the two of them. As we reached them, Andrea said to us, "My dad's going down to the basement to bring up the box with my mother's things. He said we can wait on the patio or in the house."

"It's such good weather today," I said. The last thing I wanted to do was get holed up in some *Silence of the Lambs* basement.

"Do you ladies, ah, want something to drink?" Robert Norton offered.

I translated for Norie and she shook her head.

"I could use something," Andrea said. "You have any Cokes in the fridge?"

"Pepsi," he said.

"Whatever. I'll get it while you're downstairs," Andrea said.

"Lorraine'll be stopping by on her lunch hour," he said. "That's any minute."

"Looking forward to it," Andrea said.

Norie and I settled on plastic lawn chairs set on a newly built cedar deck and looked at the view. I could just make out the soft line of the Blue Ridge Mountains in the distance, so I pointed it out to Norie.

"I don't think he is an easy person," Norie said to me in Japanese.

"Really? I'm not sure he's all bad," I said. There had been something, in his conversation with Andrea, that made me understand that he'd struggled with guilt over the years. And the presence of guilt meant the presence of feeling, I thought. It was a good omen.

"He seems dishonest," Norie said.

"Why do you say that?"

"Let's see how he answers our questions," Norie said.

I put a hand on her wrist. "Obasan, please remember, you're not supposed to speak English."

"I will ask questions in Japanese, just as I have been doing. You shall translate for me," Norie said primly.

There was the sound of a door opening behind us, and I turned, expecting to see Andrea. Instead, I saw a very tall, light-skinned black woman of about sixty. Her hair was elegantly upswept, and she wore a black-and-red knit dress with a matching jacket. She had gold bangles on her wrist and a plastic ID card hanging from a chain around her neck.

"Well, this is a surprise. I'm Mrs. Norton."

Lorraine Norton's voice was so authoritative my first thought was that she was a school principal, but after I took a quick glance at her huge ID tag, it became clear that she worked at the local Social Security office.

"Herro, Mrs. Norton. How do you do? My name is Rei Shimura, and this is my aunt Norie Shimura. We are visiting from Japan."

Norie popped to her feet, bowed, and murmured the proper Japanese words of greeting someone for the first time. Lorraine Norton arched a pencil-thin eyebrow at her and said, "I thought you were mother and daughter, not aunt and niece."

Oops. "I—we are aunt and niece. It is sometimes difficult to translate to foreigners, we make mistakes," I said.

"Uh-huh." She sounded unconvinced. "I heard you-all came to collect the remaining possessions. A call ahead of time would have been nice. I don't know if Robert will be able to find anything down there on such short notice."

The door opened again. This time, Andrea came out with a can of Pepsi in her hand.

"We've been here twenty years," Lorraine said, then her head whipped around. "Andrea, hello. I see you've helped yourself to the refrigerator. Please close that door behind you. I don't want bugs getting inside."

"Dad said it was okay to get a drink." Andrea slid the door closed.

Norie said to me in Japanese, "Ask the new Mrs. Norton about Sadako's things. Why did they save them when they moved from the old house to here?"

I translated, "My aunt is very grateful that you have saved her sister's valuable things all these years. I know it must have been a burden to carry, can you please tell us why you saved them?"

"We don't really have much left. Robert gave her clothes to charity. It wasn't worth much, except for the kimono. We donated that to a church auction."

"Do you remember what the kimono looked like?" Andrea asked.

"Red. Real stiff and shiny. Or was it orange?" Lorraine asked herself.

"If it's red, it was the wedding kimono," Andrea said. "I saw it in the wedding picture Dad gave me. I'm sure her family would have liked to have it."

"Well, I hate to say it, but where were y'all thirty years ago when this was an issue?" Lorraine retorted. "We had no idea you-all would be interested. Since the time of the wedding, your family had apparently cut her off. Pretty cold, I thought."

"Do you think so?" Andrea said, giving Lorraine the evil eye.

The moment of tension was broken by the sound of the sliding door. Robert poked his head out. "I found it, but because of my back, I can't carry it up. I'm sorry."

"I'll help," Andrea said quickly.

"No, Andrea, you'd better keep me company. We have a lot to talk about," Lorraine said.

I expected Robert to protest, but he didn't. So I stood up and headed through the door and into the house before anyone could object. Just a half hour ago, I'd felt hesitant to come to this house. But in the time that had passed, I'd lost my fear of Robert Norton and become aware of two things: one, that Lorraine was going to do everything possible to keep Andrea and her father from spending any time together, and two, that I wasn't afraid of Robert Norton. I felt sorry for him, almost.

Robert was now leading the way through a tidy living room filled with 1980s-style bleached wood furniture, all upholstered in pastel florals and covered carefully with clear plastic slipcovers. Matching end tables were decorated with vases of silk flowers and little glass animals. My mother would have winced at the horror of it, but I tried to refrain from passing judgment—except for the thought that the room had been designed by Lorraine. There was nothing on the beige walls except pictures: Lorraine and Robert on their wedding day, Lorraine with her sorority sisters. I read along the names underneath to identify her: Lorraine Neblett, third from the left. I hadn't needed to; she looked exactly the same, with a handsome, high forehead and commanding eyes. She wasn't a girl I'd want to have as a roommate, I thought to myself, and moved on to the large, framed family portrait of her with Robert standing behind her and Davon at her side, age about ten.

"Your room is wide," I said, again translating Japanese to English the way so many of my former students had. "May I see?"

"Ah, okay." Robert seemed uncomfortable as I made a slow sweep through the living room, looking at everything. "Are you sure you can handle this box?" he asked.

"I'm quite strong," I said. We were passing through a small kitchen, avocado appliances and a coordinating vinyl-tile floor. The color scheme was so out, it was actually in again.

"A little thing like you." He shook his head. "Well, I know Japanese women can be small, but strong. Sadie told me there was a saying, something about small peppers—"

"'The Japanese peppers may be small, but they are hot.'" I said it first in Japanese, then in English.

"I think that was it. And Andrea, well, she's a tall one, but she fits that bill, too. Takes right after your aunt."

"*Heh?*" I was confused. Aunt Norie was so small, smaller than me, even.

"She's like her mother was. Always asking questions, and then getting upset about the answers." As he spoke, he was opening a door papered with notices about recycling and their church choir. Then he snapped on a light, illuminating a steep staircase covered in golden-brown plaid. Robert held tightly to the rail going down; I could see that he had some stiffness to his gait. Nothing was going to happen with a man whose knees hurt, I thought to myself.

Once downstairs, I discovered that the basement was brightly lit and tidy, with a pool table covered in smooth green felt and a case behind it containing some basketball and track trophies won by Davon. On the wall here, there was a line of plaques recognizing Robert for his military service. It seemed to me that the basement was the men's domain, while upstairs was Lorraine's.

There was a pile of boxes in a corner. A medium-sized one was on its side, papers spilling out of the top.

"It was up high, and I knocked it over coming down," Robert said. "Lorraine says I should use a stepladder for things like that, but I was in too much of a hurry to get one."

I squatted to pick it up. Forty pounds, maybe; it wasn't bad at all.

"Don't hurt yourself," he said.

"It's not so heavy." I moved toward the stairway, with him behind me.

"My back's not good because of all the standing in the diner," Robert said. "And my knees are bad from the war."

"Oh, what happened?"

"I received some friendly fire to one of my knees. It was shattered."

"War is a very bad thing," I said.

"Yes," he said shortly and started up the stairs.

In the kitchen, I paused. "Please, where shall I put this?"

"Right in your car would be fine," he answered, heading toward the front of the house.

I put the box down on a counter instead. "Norton-san, my aunt and Andrea-san may still have question."

"I'm sorry, but I can't talk about these things now. My wife, Lorraine—"

I was beginning to lose patience with this man who'd fought in a war and been shot, and who was afraid of his wife. "We have made trouble for you. I am so sorry. Maybe we should not have made travel."

"No, I apologize. I still feel real bad about what happened back when—back when we married. I guess that's why I hung on to everything, hoping it would mean something to somebody later on."

"Can you tell me the reason for Sadako-san's death? I don't understand it completely," I said, making my face look puzzled, not suspicious. "They say she drowned in water."

Robert seemed to reflect for a moment, then spoke. "I always thought it would be hard for her to die that way. As your family knows, she was a very strong swimmer."

And, I thought to myself, she'd supposedly gone in nude. She wouldn't have been able to weight herself down with stones, like a depressed Virginia Woolf had, to help herself sink.

"Was she ever found?" I asked, expecting him to tell me what Andrea had.

But he surprised me. "There were some remains of a female body found in the river a couple of years later. They thought it might be her. I couldn't tell, but I guessed they were probably right. I said yes. The case was closed."

For him, maybe, but not for me. "What about teeth?"

"We had no dental records because Sadie refused to visit the dentist. It was all I could do to get her to go to the obstetrician."

"One other thing," I said. "You and Mrs. Norton married close to the time that Sadako-san was declared dead, didn't you?"

"Two weeks later," he said. "Lorraine said she'd waited long enough."

"But . . . that must have meant you and Lorraine were seeing each other for a while. During the time you had no idea what had happened to Sadako."

"I'd known Lorraine since high school. Then, she was working at the Pentagon while I was . . . she was a great support for me. I needed that. All along I thought that even if Sadie *hadn't* committed suicide, she wasn't coming back." I must have looked blank, because he added, "I thought she'd deserted me."

"*Honto*? Is that the truth? Japanese women are usually very devoted." I couldn't think of a single woman I'd met in Japan who had divorced.

"She found it hard to become American, make friends, fit in. It was real different in Virginia during the seventies. There was a Japanese-American group in Washington, but she never wanted to go, said it was too far. She didn't drive, and the Metro lines were just getting built. She felt trapped."

I perked up at the mention of the Japanese-American group— could it be my group, WJFS, that he meant?—but stored the thought away as he continued talking.

"A lot of marriages like ours were breaking up. After Sadie left, when I went through her things, I found that she'd taken her passport. It seemed clear that she wanted to go back."

"Did the police check to see whether she traveled back to Japan?"

"They checked with Japanese immigration, sure. There was no record."

"What time was this investigation?" I asked.

"Right away, in 1974. The investigation remained open—I mean, I kept hearing from the FBI—until '77, when the body washed up."

But if Sadako was still alive, she could have traveled later, and not been noticed. That was a happy thought except for the fact that it would mean she'd abandoned her daughter.

"I don't understand," I said carefully. "If what you say is true, that she didn't commit suicide but pretended, and then ran away, why didn't she take Andrea with her?"

"I don't know," he said. "It seemed like the baby was the only thing that made her happy."

13

We left half an hour later. I'd tried to linger, to give Andrea and her father a chance to talk, but Lorraine made it impossible. She cut Andrea off every time she tried to say something, kept looking at her watch and commenting on how she had to get back to work. I thought we might be able to outlast her, or sneak back to the restaurant so Andrea could talk to Robert, but he announced a sudden need to drive into Charlottesville for supplies.

"Y'all are welcome to the rest room before going back. It's a long trip," Lorraine said pointedly.

We all declined.

"Well, when's your flight back?" Lorraine persisted.

"Not for several months," I said, smiling widely. "Not until we learn all that can be learned about Sadako-san's death."

"Oh, really?" Lorraine's expression froze.

"Yes, maybe you come see us in Washington if you remember something. We can meet at Andrea's place," I said, because Hugh's apartment would not seem a likely living space for two ladies visiting from Japan.

"I don't know about that—" Andrea started to say, just as Lorraine began exclaiming about how the pollution had caused her such bad allergic reactions the last time she'd been in D.C. that she'd had to get a prescription.

So we left with the box of papers, but not much else. I backed out slowly from the driveway, Robert's truck on one side of me and a sparkling silver Honda Accord parked on the other side. The Honda had to be Lorraine's car. She'd parked it so close to the Lexus that I had to hold my breath when I got in the driver's-side door.

Only Aunt Norie was pleased with how things had gone— we'd secured the box of papers, after all. But I'd hoped for more. I couldn't imagine what Andrea was thinking.

As I drove north on the country roads at a safer speed than we'd traveled them before, Aunt Norie's head lolled against the window. The jet lag from her long trip had hit her at last.

"What happened in the kitchen? I thought I heard you talking," Andrea said.

"I asked your father more about what happened." I filled Andrea in on the body that had been found and identified as her mother's.

"It can't be her," Andrea said flatly. "I know it can't."

"Well, the problem is, your mother didn't have dental records to be used as a comparison. But it is possible, don't you think?"

"You want it to be her. You want to have a quick, easy answer like the rest of them." Andrea sounded bitter.

"Look, I was able to help you obtain the box of papers," I said. "Now you have them and you're welcome to go through them on your own. And now your father knows where you work. He might want to get in touch when he's not being scrutinized by that horrible second wife of his. Or Davon might want to, as well."

"It's a good idea," Aunt Norie said between yawns from the back seat. "A family should know all members. I am going to find your Japanese family for you, too, when I return."

"Say what?" Andrea erupted so loudly that I jumped and started to swerve off the road. "Listen, it's pretty clear that my friggin' relatives here don't want me, no way and no how. These are black people pushing me out. I can only imagine how it'll be with the Japanese."

"Obasan, maybe she has a point," I said. "I may have gone too far, and I'm sorry for that. But, Andrea, you have to admit that you asked us to bring you here. You didn't want to do it on your own."

"Yeah, but I didn't want you to try to remake my life. I'm totally humiliated."

"Let's forget about it, then." I needed to calm her down. "You've got that box of information. It's yours, not mine to look at. And I suppose you don't want to hear more of what your father said to me."

"Of course I do!" Andrea exploded. "I want to know everything."

"Well, your father said that she led a very closed life. She had trouble making friends. He said that she vanished with her passport, but there was never any indication she returned to Japan—although he admitted that the police hadn't followed up with the immigration authorities every year. My thought is that she might have stayed in the U.S. for a few years longer, perhaps working, and then, when she had enough money, she could have flown back."

"That I can find out," Norie said sleepily. "When I return, I can check."

There was silence all the way to 495, but as we surged into traffic—the afternoon rush hour, so slow moving that it put Aunt Norie to sleep—Andrea spoke again.

"I'm sorry I was so sharp. I thought maybe, because ten years had passed, it would be better, but it wasn't. It never is."

"I felt for you," I said simply. The fact was, her father had been disappointing and her stepmother dreadful, but Andrea herself had been combative. Nobody had won prizes in the family Olympics that day.

"It's okay now," Andrea said shortly. "I'm starting to chill, a bit. And now that my dad knows where I work, maybe he'll look me up sometime."

I nodded in agreement, although I didn't believe it for a minute.

• • •

The next morning, after Hugh had slipped out of the apartment just after dawn, I sleepily showered and went in the kitchen to set up a breakfast that I thought my aunt would enjoy: French toast with a homemade strawberry sauce, coffee, and freshly squeezed orange juice.

"You must be very clean." Norie greeted me in Japanese when she stepped into the kitchen while I was sautéing strawberries in butter.

"*Heh*?" I looked down, and caught sight of a strawberry stain on my sweater. What was she talking about?

"This morning, you took two showers. I overheard the shower at five and then six-thirty. What's wrong with you?"

I was speechless for a moment, then recovered. "I awoke early, showered, then went running. I had to shower afterward."

"*Ah so desu ka*," Norie said, nodding. "Yes, that is a good idea if you will be trying on clothing this morning."

"What do you mean, trying on clothing?" I asked, setting the French toast before her.

"We need to shop for your wedding dress. And in the evening, I was thinking about visiting your restaurant." Norie tasted the French toast with strawberries, chewed, then smiled. "Delicious."

"I could take you to Bento for lunch. I'd be happy to." I was trying to remember what Marshall had said about my bringing guests. I was fairly certain that I had a house tab of some sort. I'd need it, because I was momentarily low on cash.

"Wouldn't dinner be better? Then Hugh-san can join us."

"He's working late tonight. I'll cook for the two of us." In fact, Hugh had told me he was sick of the pub and had decided to eat and stay late at his office, where there was a couch.

"Don't feed a caught fish," Norie said in Japanese.

"What do you mean?"

"It's an old Japanese saying. Before a fish is caught, it is fed and kept alive and treated very nicely. But once it is caught—" Norie raised her eyebrows. "No more special treatment."

"Are you saying I should stay unmarried?" I was shocked.

"Of course not," said Norie. "Just don't cheat yourself of any pleasure while you still have a chance."

"You and I will go out to dinner tonight," I said with determination. "I'm sure that you'll enjoy meeting Jiro, our Japanese executive chef."

"Very good. Don't you think seven o'clock will be about right? Now, we need to decide where to go for your wedding dress."

Without much hope, I suggested we visit the close Maryland suburbs of Chevy Chase and Bethesda. Neiman Marcus, Saks-Jandel, and Saks Fifth Avenue would be considerably smaller than Japanese department stores, I warned her, but there were bridal boutiques in other suburbs that we could visit. But I wanted to start off in Chevy Chase so I could drop off my Japanese kites at the Washington-Japan Friendship Society. I also thought there was a slight chance WJFS might have, within its membership, someone who had known Sadako.

We traveled on the Metro against the morning rush hour, so we had seats, and Norie enjoyed the view of suburban northwest Washington and Maryland. It brought up her recollections of how undeveloped Yokohama had once been. I couldn't think of the D.C. suburbs as undeveloped, but I could understand what she saw, from her Japanese perspective: a sky that was not filled up by boxy apartment complexes, but small houses, fifty years old, surrounded by green lawns. Hugh and I hadn't come close to buying a home. I knew that a simple brick ranch house in one of these neighborhoods would go for more than a million. I mentioned the prices to Aunt Norie, but she nodded sagely.

"The houses are large, but they are too expensive, still. It's better to have an apartment in Japan. Fewer rooms are easier to clean, *neh*? I notice you have no time to clean the apartment here. If only it were smaller."

I ignored the comment about my halfhearted cleaning attempts. "I'm trying to get back to Japan, Obasan."

"How are you doing that?" she asked. We were both speaking in Japanese, which made me comfortable enough to relay the joke Hugh had made over a month ago.

"I've been advised that I need to accomplish something great that will be noticed by the Japanese government. Maybe I'll become a singing sensation, earn millions of dollars, and then get knighted."

"Very funny, Rei-chan, but ladies cannot be knighted. Actually, I've been thinking, *neh*, that if you can do something to aid the nation of Japan, you might be readmitted."

"'Aid the nation of Japan'?" I echoed her words. "If that means showing around a Japanese citizen and giving her a good understanding of the life and people here, I'd be happy to do it."

"And, you could find the killer of an innocent Japanese citizen, a woman forgotten long ago by society, but who deserves justice. If you can do that, the government will be grateful and surely relent."

"I don't know that she was killed, Obasan. There's no indication—"

Norie interrupted me. "What kind of Japanese woman disappears with her passport and then doesn't go home?"

"A passport's an important document to have, whether or not you plan to travel right away. Perhaps she wanted to start a new life in another part of the United States."

"I wondered about that, too, except for what new Mrs. Norton said."

"Oh?" I stopped looking out the window.

"While you were downstairs getting the papers with Mr. Norton, Andrea-chan was speaking with new Mrs. Norton. Andrea-chan said something about her mother perhaps being alive and somewhere else in America, but new Mrs. Norton said it was impossible. She works for a security administration, and she knows."

New Mrs. Norton. I wished Norie had used that phrase in conversation with Lorraine so I could have caught the second wife's reaction. "It's called the Social Security Administration. She was wearing an ID tag on a chain around her neck."

"New Mrs. Norton said to Andrea that if Sadako-san was alive and working anywhere, going to any hospital, or receiving any kind of benefit, her personal number would have been active.

Mrs. Norton has checked herself, the last time ten years ago, and there is no evidence. She says Sadako-san probably died in a tragic accident."

"I wouldn't believe everything Lorraine Norton says," I told my aunt. "She has a powerful reason not to want Sadako to surface. If Sadako is still alive, it means that Robert committed bigamy by marrying Lorraine." At least, I thought so. I would have to ask Hugh how the law would apply in that case.

14

In Bethesda, we bombed out at Claire Dratch's salon because we hadn't made an advance appointment. So we went on to Chevy Chase, where we visited shop after shop and I tried on the few dresses my aunt and I agreed on. I didn't like the way I looked in any of them. Maybe it was because I wasn't as rail thin as I'd been in Japan, or because I wasn't used to seeing myself dressed like a cupcake.

Fortunately, the salesclerks at the boutiques seemed very familiar with this phenomenon of brides who tried but were hesitant to buy—especially when they heard it was my first day of shopping. Norie, on the other hand, was disturbed that I couldn't commit.

"At least I haven't spent thousands of dollars on something I don't like," I said as we dodged traffic on Wisconsin Avenue to get to Saks.

"If money is an issue, you must let me help you," Norie said instantly. "You are saving me thousands in hotel bills. I should buy your dress."

It was a good deal, but I couldn't accept it—especially since I wasn't in the mood to like anything at Saks. I also had other things that I wanted to do, such as grab lunch and then drop the kites off at the WJFS office, which kept afternoon hours only.

"How about sushi for lunch?" I said brightly.

We went to Tako, a casual Japanese restaurant on Wisconsin Avenue, right around the corner from WJFS. Hugh had introduced me to the deliciously smoky grilled eel here when I'd first visited Washington. Grilled eel should go on Bento's menu, I decided as I looked around the packed restaurant. I wondered how Bento was doing, now that it had started serving lunch. I should have checked yesterday, I thought guiltily. I should have let Marshall know when the woodblock prints we'd chosen a month earlier would be back from the framer's and ready to hang. All in all, it was fortuitous that I was going to see him at the restaurant that night.

We each had miso soup to start. Norie pronounced it undrinkable, but it tasted yummy to me. My red snapper sushi was fresh and tender, but Norie was bent on comparing it to *tai*, a superlative, light-tasting fish that you couldn't get in Washington, let alone most parts of the world outside Japan.

"You liked an American fish yesterday," I reminded her.

"Yes, but it was cooked in the American fashion. That made it superb."

I scrutinized my aunt. "I think you observe a double standard. You think that Japanese food should only be cooked and eaten in Japan, and American food here?"

"Usually, that would be the case. However, I'm sure the restaurant you are helping is wonderful. It has a Japanese chef, *neh*?"

"Yes. An Iron Chef, actually. He's called Jiro Takeda."

"I haven't heard of him." Norie frowned.

"He's very good," I said. "I've learned a few recipes from him already. Andrea's working under him in the kitchen right now, learning all about food preparation."

"I thought that she was a restaurant hostess?"

"She ran into a little trouble the first night, so Marshall took her off that duty. I think she'll be restored to hostess later on."

"But kitchen work is very special. Maybe she'll learn so much that she can become a chef someday. Wouldn't that be incredible?" Norie clasped her hands together.

"Not exactly," I said. "There are women chefs here, as I'm sure there are in Japan."

"Very few," Norie said. "When I was a young lady, it was not considered a proper profession. Even today, I can't say I've ever seen a woman sushi chef. They say our hands are too warm! Ridiculous, *neh*?"

Would Norie have liked to cook as a professional? I didn't ask her, but as we left the restaurant and walked around the corner to the Washington-Japan Friendship Society, I thought about how good she would have been. Her *nabe* dishes—simmered, deep-tasting complex broths in which a variety of seafood, vegetables, or meat cooked—were like nobody else's. So many cold nights in Japan I'd gone to her house for dinner, and huddled with the others around the *kotatsu* table draped with a quilt to keep the warmth of the heater going below, to warm our legs. But the real warmth was Aunt Norie's *nabe* pot.

We were at the friendship society building now—or rather, the half of a 1930s single-story duplex that housed it. The other side of the building was a printing press, a little New Age venture that consisted of two long-haired, middle-aged white men infatuated enough with Japan to offer to help out with the printing of the forthcoming history. I explained this to Aunt Norie as one of the printers bowed solemnly to us through the window.

"I just have to drop off these kites for the festival," I said, holding up the shopping bag that I'd been lugging around all morning. "It will take only a few minutes."

The office was a small, cheerful room decorated with old Japan Tourist Organization posters advertising tourist destinations in Japan. There was a long table someone had probably gotten from a school, and it was covered with papers and envelopes.

Evidently, a mass mailing was in progress. A seventy-something Japanese-American man in a striped sweater sat at the table folding papers with precision, then sliding each one in an envelope. I didn't know him, so I just nodded and smiled and tried to catch the attention of Betty Nagano, one of my better friends in the group. Betty was somewhere in her seventies and very well preserved, with a face the shape of a full moon—a happy, smiling moon, like out of children's storybooks.

She was smiling at me now as she continued her conversation on the telephone. "Just get the cans of *inari-zushi-no-moto*, it comes in cute little cans with a picture of the stuffed tofu skins on the outside. And then, you'll need to make rice." Another pause. "Borrow or buy a rice cooker. They sell them at Asian stores as well."

Under my breath I said to Aunt Norie, "It sounds as if she's trying to teach someone to make *inarizushi* for the festival."

"*Inarizushi*? Who needs a recipe for that?" Norie sounded incredulous.

Betty had hung up the phone and was smiling at us. "Sorry, Rei. I was just speaking with one of our younger members. She's never actually made rice, only had it in restaurants. Isn't that a shame?"

I didn't know whether to feel flattered, or unnerved, that Betty didn't consider me one of the group's younger members. "Mrs. Nagano, I'd like you to meet my aunt Norie Shimura. She's visiting from Japan."

"Betty, please." Betty Nagano gave me a mock-scolding look, then bowed deeply and greeted Norie with the customary words in Japanese. Norie bowed even lower and uttered the matching pleasantries. Then the two ladies stood stiffly, smiling at each other. And the older man folding envelopes was looking with interest at Norie now.

"This is my husband, Yuji," Betty said. "You haven't met Rei before, have you, Yuji? And this is her aunt, Shimura Norie-san. "

From Yuji Nagano's grunt, I could tell he was really from Japan, unlike his wife, Betty, who spoke good, ladylike Hawaiian Japanese.

Now I remembered her telling me that Yuji had immigrated to Hawaii in the early 1940s with his rice farmer parents, but their dreams were put on hold when the whole family was sent to an internment camp after Japan's attack on Pearl Harbor. The Naganos lost their farm to unscrupulous people who'd promised to protect it for them during the war years, but at least Yuji had found the treasure of Betty—a close childhood friend from the camp whom he married in the 1950s.

I wished I could tell this all to my aunt, who was bowing to Mr. Nagano and asking him where he came from in Japan. Nagano, fittingly, the province that bore his name.

"I've brought you two carp kites," I said. "I thought it might be useful at the festival. They really do fly, so the children might enjoy them."

"Oh, how nice of you. May I see?" Betty said, and motioned for me to take the first kite out of the shopping bag in which I'd been carrying it. As I laid it out, Mr. Nagano gathered up his papers and envelopes carefully, giving me room to unfurl the faded red-and-orange fish.

"But this looks antique!" Betty exclaimed.

"Oh, no, it's just a bit old. Fifty years, I think. The other one's the same vintage, but blue and green. I wasn't sure which color you'd like better, or if you could use both."

"The kite was my brother's," Norie said. "I gave it to Rei years ago, when I was helping my parents organize. I couldn't imagine why she wanted it."

"It's so beautiful," Betty said, looking at the kite in awe. "But I'm worried that it might be damaged if the children get their hands on it. It's certainly not the kind of durable polyester kite we usually let them play with."

I paused and thought about what she was really saying. Maybe she didn't like the kite, thought it looked too drab compared with the brightly colored ones wrapped in plastic that I saw stashed in a corner of a room.

"If you'd rather we didn't use it, that's fine," I said.

"It looks old and a bit dirty," Norie said quickly. She was identifying with me and denigrating, in the true Japanese fashion, what we'd offered.

"No, no, I really like it," Betty insisted. "I just think we should put anything this special in a place of honor . . . maybe a display area where we'll be promoting our community history book. Yes, that might draw people over to it quite nicely."

"I saw your call for submissions. I don't think I've lived here long enough to be helpful in telling your history, but I could help in editing or something like that," I offered. I had done so little for the society that I was embarrassed.

"We don't have much yet," Betty said. "My husband's not much of a writer, but he has the best memory of anyone, so he's been talking at night and I've been trying to record it."

"Betty, was the society active during the 1970s?"

"Yes, indeed. It was formed in the late forties to help the war brides who'd started coming over."

"Are there records of members from the seventies?"

"Sure. It's all in that file cabinet in the corner." Betty paused. "If you don't mind my asking, why are you interested in this particular time period?"

I took a deep breath. "I'm curious about your membership rolls because I have a close girlfriend whose mother came here from Kyūshū during that time. The daughter and mother lost touch, and the daughter's hoping to find out what happened."

"Oh, really? What's the range of years that you want to see, and what is her mother's name?" Betty had already gone to the file cabinet, and had opened the middle drawer.

"1971 through 1974," I said. "The woman's name is Sadako Tsuchiya. Her married name was Norton."

"Oh! The girl from Kyūshū who was married to a black soldier?" Betty asked.

"Yes, actually." I was stunned by Betty's quick response.

"Your friend is her baby girl!" Betty's voice rose. "Oh, I always wondered what happened to her! The police came to us after

Sadako-san disappeared to ask if anyone had seen her. Unfortunately we hadn't. I always wondered how the husband and baby got along."

"After Sadako disappeared, her husband put Andrea—the baby you remember—in foster care. She's thirty now. We work together at Bento," I said.

"She's a very troubled girl," Norie said in Japanese. "She doesn't know if her mother is alive or dead. And she has no real family to care for her now."

"It was a tragic situation," Betty said, looking at a paper she'd pulled from a file. "We had a subcommittee of ladies who would visit all the war brides to make sure that they were all right. Sadako Norton was very resistant to help. I went a few times with them to see her—yes, here's my name in a progress report."

"What do you have there?" I moved close to Betty, to read over her shoulder.

"This is a progress report—we did them for all the people we visited, whether it was war brides or invalids. Most of them are pretty brief, but with Sadako, there was so much visiting and follow-up there's a fairly extensive record. You can look at this one, if you like."

I sat down at the table, across from Mr. Nagano, and examined the report written in ballpoint pen on a sheet of ruled paper so old that it had yellowed. It was a monthly report on the war brides visited, with a number of different women's names, addresses, and phone numbers. Three women—Betty, Joanie Iwata, and Fumiko Sugiyama—had sprung a surprise baby shower on Sadako by arriving at her apartment in Arlington three months after she'd given birth to a girl. The basket they'd brought contained baby clothes, books, bottles, and diapering essentials, all paid for from the gift fund at WJFS. They'd also brought along sweet-bean cakes that Betty had made, and brownies from Joanie.

How kind they were, I thought as I read on. Sadako's door had been chained, and she'd looked out nervously at the ladies, who'd spoken to her in Japanese, reminding her that they were her friends. At last, she'd unlatched the chain and let them inside. The apartment was sparely furnished but clean, and the baby named

Akiko slept quietly in a cradle.

"Akiko!" I exclaimed aloud. "Andrea doesn't know she was ever called that. I wonder if it's the same baby."

"Yes, of course. We knew her real name was Andrea, but we went along with Sadako to make her feel better. A lot of us have Japanese and English names. I'm not really Betty, you know, but I've gotten used to it. Yuji's just—Yuji. I can't imagine him any other way." Betty glanced fondly at her husband, whose ears pinkened.

"What else does it say?" Norie entreated, squeezing onto a chair next to me.

I continued my translation of the English-language document I was reading. "Sadako asked them to sit down in the living room, and she made tea to serve with the sweets. She thanked everyone for the gifts, and confessed that Akiko-chan had a difficult disposition. Her husband was disturbed by the baby's nighttime crying."

"I'll tell you why. She wanted to breast-feed, but her husband was against it," Betty said, shaking her head.

"Why on earth?" I asked, instinctively crossing my own arms over my chest. It felt slightly fuller. I guessed that was a by-product of my weight gain.

"At that time, there was still a debate about which was better, breast or bottle. To some, the breast was considered old-fashioned and backward," Betty said.

Mr. Nagano's chair made a loud scraping sound as he moved away from us. Clearly, we were embarrassing him.

"Would it be better if I just photocopied this and took it home to read?" I asked Betty quickly. I also wanted something to show Andrea.

"You know, the records really shouldn't leave the office—especially this business because it's such sad personal information." Betty sighed. "But, it's been interesting, living through this story again. This makes me think we should include some mention of the stresses war brides faced, not naming names, of course."

"What were the stresses?" I asked.

"The girls who came with their husbands to America lost that Japanese family support, so it was like landing on a new planet. Not only would the women be dealing with an alien world, but their husbands were seeing them in a new way. The girls who had been so alluring now couldn't navigate the supermarket or chitchat with the neighbors or drive a car or bake a casserole."

"Just a minute!" Norie interjected. "Japanese ladies can drive, and we shop in huge supermarkets, and some of us have ovens— I do, for instance—"

"Obasan, she's saying that thirty years ago it was different," I said.

"Yes, and I'm sorry, I didn't mean to offend anyone. It *was* different then. It was a hard, hard world for the women, and many times the husbands would be impatient or bored with them and file for divorce. Unfortunately, the war brides didn't know about their right to alimony. So they lost everything after the divorce except for their children. That's why we stepped in."

"Now I am hearing this, I am worried about Sadako even more," Norie said. "Will you read some more, Rei-chan?"

"All right," I said, still feeling a bit tentative. "The ladies' committee reported that someone in their group suggested that Sadako sleep with the baby in the baby's room, the way it's done in Japan."

"Very correct," Norie said. "I slept with my children until my daughter was six and my son eight. Males need more coddling, don't they?"

Yuji frowned, and I looked down quickly to continue reading. "Sadako said that they had only one bedroom and her husband preferred that the baby sleep apart from them so his sleep wasn't disturbed. So the baby stayed in the living room." I raised my eyes from the paper and added, "At least she had friends to whom she could vent these frustrations."

"Not as much as she needed," Betty said. "I remember, we tried so hard to get her to join our young mothers' group, but she said she couldn't. It was the time before the Metro connected everything, and, of course, she couldn't drive. And I seem to remember that she was nervous about the American buses. She thought she wouldn't get off at the right place and she'd be lost forever. Not that we could help her anymore. I recall that when we attempted to visit her two months after that welcome-baby call, her husband wouldn't let us in."

I shivered. "What did he say?"

"She was resting. It could have been true, or maybe not. But we never went out there again because he'd been so unpleasant and some of the ladies became nervous."

"And if she was afraid to get on buses, she would have been virtually trapped at home." I shook my head. "It's such a strange perspective for someone from Japan, where there's so much public transportation."

"She was from the sea, not the land. That was why she was afraid," Mr. Nagano spoke up, surprising me.

"What do you mean? I heard she was a pearl diver, but I didn't believe it," I said.

"Maybe she was an *ama-san*," Norie suggested.

"Yes, yes, that's what she did. She was an *ama-san*," Mr. Nagano said.

"What exactly is an *ama-san*?" I asked both of them.

"*Ama* means 'sea,'" Norie said. "So an *ama-san* is a woman sea diver—someone who dives for things like oysters and abalone. There are some still working in Ise and other areas."

"Andrea's mother was supposed to have come from Kyūshū." Now I felt sorry that I'd so quickly dismissed Andrea's belief that her mother had been a pearl diver. She had been a diver, all right, but probably for something like abalone.

"She was from a small place, she told us once," Mr. Nagano said. "Her town still has several hundred women divers. They can earn, in a single day, what a woman would have to work all month to earn as a shop clerk. The men might row the boats, but it is the women who do the underwater harvesting. They work with a female partner, from after the tide goes out in the morning to two in the afternoon. In the old days, they used to just work in summer, but now, with wetsuits, they can work year-round."

"It sounds as if you know about the town," I said. "Do you recall its name?"

"I'm sorry. And actually, it's hard for me to remember what it was that she told me and what I just remembered from growing up in Japan."

"I can understand that challenge." I was totally discombobulated sometimes, between my old life in Tokyo and my new life in Washington. "Anyway, it sounds like the life of an *ama-san* beats the daily grind of a salaryman slaving in an office, doesn't it?"

"Well, because the women are so valuable, they are only allowed to marry men who are born into sea-diving families as well. The men usually drive the boats. It's a matter of tradition," Mr. Nagano said.

"There are reasons for that tradition," Norie said. "Women simply find things more quickly than men. Underwater, while holding her breath, a diver must locate a mature abalone quickly, and then pry it off with a knife without killing any of the baby abalone growing nearby. That sensitivity is a woman's special touch."

Betty was nodding enthusiastically. "That makes perfect sense. And now I feel ashamed of myself for assuming that Sadako had been in the water trade."

"But she was in the water," I said, before realizing that the Japanese word Betty must have been thinking of was *mizu-shobai*, which meant prostitution and bars.

"Bars were where a lot of girls met their military husbands. We didn't ask them, and they didn't tell."

"So she was a woman who was used to hard, honest work, and earning her own money. This transition to America, where she became a wife under the thumb of a man who was the sole provider, must have been very difficult—" I broke off, realizing that it sounded as if I was describing my own life.

"I remember that she'd never gone to a dentist, and refused to go, even though she now had all those military benefits," Betty said. "Getting her to the doctor when she was pregnant was pretty hard. Someone either drove her or rode the bus with her, to make sure she really went."

"Walter Reed Army Hospital is where Andrea was born," I said. "And you know, on the day that Sadako disappeared, she was supposed to have had a doctor's appointment. I wonder if she'd gone back to Walter Reed to see a psychiatrist or psychologist. Her life with her husband sounded pretty depressing."

"I really wouldn't be sure about that," Betty said. "That visit we made was when the baby was only three months old. Andrea was already two when Sadako vanished, and two is a much easier age to cope with."

"It is?" I was doubtful, thinking back on my chaotic moments in the restaurant with Kendall's twins.

"Yes, Rei-chan! When you have a baby, you will see."

"That's right, you should be getting married soon." Betty turned a warm smile on me. "And how is your fiancé, Henry, or—"

"Hugh," I said. "He's doing well. He was sorry to have missed the last dinner, but he should be there for Children's Day."

"I am organizing the wedding," Norie said. "Without me, I fear it will never happen."

"Is that so? How lucky for Rei." Betty winked at me, as if she understood that this was a mixed blessing. "How many days will you be here, Shimura-san? I would like to visit with you again."

"How kind. I will have plenty of time, as I plan to stay through the wedding," Norie said.

I had to stop myself from gasping. Until the wedding? She'd be here for months. I'd never be able to keep up the ruse that Hugh's apartment was mine, and he lived somewhere else.

Betty was opening the file drawer again, and Yuji Nagano mumbled something that I couldn't quite make out.

"I'm sorry, could you repeat that again, sir?" I asked.

"I said that you should bring Sadako-san's daughter to meet us, at our home," Yuji Nagano said.

"I'll talk to her about it. Please be aware that she's a little—prickly. All those years in foster care, I guess, left a permanent mark." I began gathering up my bag to leave.

"We should have helped her," Yuji Nagano said. "We should have returned to make sure she was all right."

Betty cast her eyes downward for a moment, and I was silent as well, thinking. So many missed cues, so many mistakes. Andrea's life could have been quite different.

Yuji Nagano spoke again. "Bring Sadako's daughter to our house. We must see her to explain, to say that we are sorry."

15

Now I was happy that we were going to Bento for dinner. I had so much to tell Andrea. I thought I could slip into the kitchen to talk to her, at which time I could introduce Norie to Jiro Takeda.

Norie asked me for advice about what to wear, and I told her, with some regret, that Washingtonians wore practically anything out to dinner. My aunt chose a mulberry-colored silk suit and shiny black pumps. I wore a black sleeveless turtleneck that was tighter than I remembered, with a knee-length black-and-white zebra print-skirt. Once I'd zipped up the knee-high black suede boots I'd gotten from my mother, I thought I looked pretty good, but Norie shook her head and sighed.

"Now I understand your difficulties in finding a wedding dress that suits you. Ah, well, at least you are young and trendy."

The walk from the Chinatown Metro station to the restaurant took a while, because my aunt was enthralled with the old, gaudy Chinatown gate spanning H Street. After she'd photographed me standing under it, we finally arrived at the restaurant. It was six-thirty.

Justin, the waiter who'd taken over Andrea's hosting job, gave us a disapproving look. "I don't see a reservation under your name."

"I forgot to call, but can't you fit us in?" I could see that about half the tables were unoccupied. I'd gotten a call from Hugh about half an hour earlier, saying he'd made it to the restaurant and was waiting for us. I couldn't see him at any table, though.

"Is there a difficulty?" Norie asked in English.

"Not at all. Obasan, this is Justin, the waiter who is substituting at the host desk. Justin, this is my aunt Norie, who has traveled all the way from Japan and really would like something to eat. And I know that somewhere in this place the third member of our party is here. He might even have made a reservation under the name Glendinning."

"You're with the, ah, Scottish guy?" Justin's hauteur evaporated.

Norie smiled and said, "He is her fiancé."

"Well, luckily for you, he did book a table for three for seven-fifteen. He's in the bar with some movers and shakers. Hmm, he's really a doll. It's a pity to think of him all buttoned up in flannel pajamas."

"Pajama? What does he mean?" Norie asked in Japanese.

Justin was insulting the two of us for being square enough to be engaged, but the truth was, Hugh did own a few pairs of pajamas—regular cotton ones, but I'd been thinking about getting him some in warm German flannel for winter.

"He is talking about a new form of casual dress," I said as I began guiding my aunt through the restaurant, toward the bar. "You know how fashionable Hugh is. Well, men here are starting to wear the clothes of other cultures—*kurta* shirts come from India, you know, as do pajama pants—"

Hugh was dressed rather more conservatively in one of his favorite Hugo Boss business suits. I spotted him on the outer fringe of a group of men surrounding Senator Snowden. Phong, the bartender, moved quietly behind the bar, making sure everyone had a drink. And these were serious drinks—not cute saketinis or *mojitos,* but glasses of whisky, bourbon, and the like.

I caught Hugh's eye right away. He moved away from the circle of people who were listening raptly to the senator. The words "allocation" and "budget" floated out to me: the business of the nation, the things that made Washington what it was.

"Do you want to sample an oyster? They're delicious with this wasabi sauce." Hugh proffered a small plate to me.

"None for me, thanks." He knew perfectly well that I hated oysters, I thought with irritation.

"Norie-san, how about you? We can take the plate over to our table."

"Where do these oysters come from?" Norie inquired.

"These are called Kumamoto oysters," Phong interjected from his position behind the bar. "From the Pacific Northwest. They are among the plumpest and most delicious, supposedly."

"Kumamoto is in Japan, but these days, it's not a place where oysters are grown. Why not serve oysters from the Chesapeake Bay? I read about them in a Japanese food magazine," Norie said.

Phong was tongue-tied, so I told my aunt what I'd heard about oyster populations having shrunk to near extinction in the Chesapeake Bay after having suffered two major diseases.

"The watermen want to implant new, hardy Asian oyster populations in the bay, but the verdict's still out on whether that's safe," said a new voice, and I glanced away to realize that Senator Snowden had stopped talking about the federal budget and had joined our conversation. "The question is, is the risk of introducing an alien better than letting an ecosystem perish—especially since this so-called Asian oyster has been reproducing successfully in California and the Pacific Northwest for the last forty years. When does a foreign species become domestic? That's the question that nobody can answer, and one of the few areas in which I sound like a pro-business Republican."

"Senator Snowden, hello!" I said, completely flustered. "I didn't mean to distract you with our worries about the oysters—it sounded as if you were talking about the budget—"

"You weren't distracting me. And I'm delighted to have met your future husband. Before you arrived, we were talking for a bit."

I glanced at Hugh in surprise, and he smiled at me. "Kendall was here earlier on. She did the honors of an introduction. We were having a fascinating conversation, like you said, about the national budget, and how it differs from the way we fund things in the UK."

"Who is this lovely lady with you, your older sister?" Harp Snowden nodded toward Aunt Norie.

Norie beamed as if she hadn't understood he was handing her a standard line. Well, that was all right with me.

"I'd like to introduce my aunt Norie Shimura." As I pressed my aunt forward, I murmured in Japanese that this was a senator she was meeting, one of the best-known men in the country.

"The no-gun senator," she said, smiling at him. "You don't like guns, do you? We heard about you on the Japanese news!"

"The No-gun Shogun." Hugh repeated the line the Japanese media had used to describe him.

"It's almost mortifying that I'm such an oddity for my stance." Harp Snowden shook his head. "Are you from Japan, Mrs. Shimura?"

"Yes. I come from Yokohama, which is one-half hour south of Tokyo," Norie said.

"Oh, yes. The lovely city with the famous iris gardens, and a Chinatown full of delicious restaurants—"

"You know it!" Norie beamed.

"I was in Japan first in the seventies, and it is still one of my favorite countries to visit," Harp Snowden said. "I love all the traditions, how time seems to have stood still."

A babble of men's voices increased as if they wanted to move on to something really important. But Norie's voice rose as clear as a *shakuhachi* flute above them. "How nice!" she said. "You must visit again. The women drive, the stoves have ovens and so on."

"Excuse me?" The senator put down his glass and looked at her more closely.

"A mineral water, and a glass of the Horton viognier!" I blurted out, desperate to change the subject. But Phong ignored me, as if he'd become spellbound by the increasingly bizarre exchange between my aunt and the senator.

I turned back to the two conversationalists. "Actually, Senator, I've been wanting to apologize for bothering both you and your wife on the phone the other day. I was desperate to locate Kendall, as you know, and I saw your numbers in her little phone book and just dialed."

"Don't mention it." Harp Snowden's face flushed slightly, and I wondered what I'd said wrong; probably, that Kendall had his home numbers in her address book. "It all turned out for the best, didn't it? Like your fiancé said, Ms. Johnson was here a few minutes ago looking very much alive. We were even talking about using Bento as a location for my dinner."

"Kendall wanted me to tell you that she's sorry, but she had to run home," Hugh said. "And I made sure she got in her car safely; don't worry about that!"

"Was she here to see Marshall?" I was still puzzled by the situation, and the way Harp, who'd seemed so close to Kendall before, was now calling her by her married name.

"In a manner of speaking." Hugh turned the two of us slightly away, so our conversation wouldn't be audible to the others. "I offered to serve as a mediator when she unexpectedly dropped in at my office this afternoon."

"What do you mean, you offered to serve?" I felt my hackles rise.

"We came here about an hour ago, and we had a short but productive conversation with Marshall. He seemed a bit defensive, and, of course, your cousin wanted to vent about her treatment that night, but I like to think the crisis has been averted. She's not going to sue."

"But I thought you couldn't represent her!" I said. "You do contract law, class actions, that kind of thing."

"Mediation is a way of staying out of court, which is what I thought you wanted?" Hugh raised one eyebrow.

"It is, but . . . what's Kendall getting out of it? There must be some payoff from Marshall."

"He's offering her the food at cost for Senator Snowden's dinner."

Hugh turned from me to my aunt. "Norie-san, we'd better see about our table in the dining room."

"Please don't leave just yet, Mrs. Shimura," Senator Snowden said to her. "I'd like to offer you a sample of an hors d'oeuvre the chef brought to us, a combination of *yuzu* and sweet potato."

I couldn't help thinking, as I watched my aunt open her mouth and begin to chat knowledgeably about *yuzu*, that one of her favorite proverbs fit Harp Snowden perfectly: "It stinks, but it's *tai*."

Harp Snowden had acquired a patina of superficiality. Still, he was like *tai*—the best kind of fish, even beneath the oiliness that came from his time swimming among the sharks of Washington, D.C.

Hugh walked me with one hand on my back into the dining room. "Before your aunt joins us, I'd better mention that I won't be sleeping at the apartment tonight. Kendall offered me her guest room, and given the circumstances, I think it'll be easier."

I stopped walking. "Easier? What are you talking about, she lives in Potomac!"

"Darling, you've made it clear to me that it's critical your aunt not discover that we're living together," Hugh said, urging me toward the table where Justin was pointedly hovering with menu in hand. "So, to avoid the inevitable discovery, it's probably easiest if I just stay away. You suggested Kendall's place a while ago, anyway."

"I changed my mind," I said.

"Rei, she is still shell-shocked from the abduction. She doesn't feel safe at home because Win stays out quite late. She was vastly reassured once I agreed to stay. Her face lit up like Christmas!"

"I can imagine other body parts igniting, too," I said grimly.

"Darling, you're not jealous of your own flesh and blood, are you?"

"Not exactly," I said. I was more anxious about Hugh. He had strayed a couple of years ago, when we were separated by an ocean and countless misunderstandings. He was engaged to me now, but that didn't make him invincible against a woman with an absentee husband and who had already expressed far too much interest in his underwear.

"All right, darling. I'll see what I can do to suit both you and Kendall. But in the meantime, I'll head over there tonight. When you and Norie are having dessert, I'll duck out to the apartment to pack my kit. I'll swing back here with the car and take you both home, then continue on to Kendall's place."

"You don't need to do that. We can take the Metro home."

"Ah, but then you have to get out at Dupont Circle and make it the rest of the way. Two women walking that distance at night is a terrible idea."

"Oh, really? I've done it before. And like you say, there will be two of us. Look, Norie's coming over. Do me a favor and start talking about something else."

We all settled around the table, menus in hand. Hugh and I were quiet, but Norie had enough to say for both of us while she showed off the stored picture on her digital camera that someone had taken of her with the senator. Then Marshall came over. I had just begun to introduce him to Aunt Norie when he cut me off.

"There's trouble with the ladies' room. I wonder if you could go in there for me and check it out."

"Sure." I just hoped it wasn't a toilet problem. I jumped up, relieved to leave my aunt and Hugh.

"This day is shot to hell," Marshall said. "The bartender quit, two of my line cooks called in sick, and one of the two dishwashers is in jail. His sub is so incompetent I've had to put Princess Andrea at the sink, and you can imagine how she's enjoying that. Our monkfish delivery never came, and the five pounds of morel mushrooms meant for tonight's special arrived disintegrated. Not to mention, we think the *Post* critic is at table 10."

"Shouldn't he be in disguise?" I asked.

"Yes, of course, but Justin saw the caller ID when the reservation was made a few days ago."

"Wow," I said. Justin was better at his job than I'd expected. I longed to ask Marshall about the dishwasher who was in jail, but I could see he was more upset about the kitchen chaos.

"I think there are some women in there," Marshall said. "I'll wait outside while you go in."

"Is it the, ah, toilet or something? I have to warn you that I'm not a plumber."

"Andrea said it was a problem with the vanities, and those, I believe, are your province. I was going to put in normal sinks, but you wanted *tansu* chests," he added.

Marshall was being unfair, I thought as I slipped my *kuginuki*, a special Japanese tool I always carried, out of my bag. When I went into the bathroom, I saw the problem. Water had leaked from the cold handle on one vanity and colored its beautiful red-brown paulownia surface whitish, right at the back. I turned off the water and did some work with the tool, but it was really better for prying off nails than unscrewing a faucet. What was needed was a wrench, and a real plumber.

The leak was the main problem, but there were secondary problems, too. The tansu's surface sloped very slightly backward—the plumber had grumbled about it to me when he'd cut holes for the blue-and-white ceramic bowls to be dropped in. The wood also hadn't been waxed. Without a protective finish like wax, water would continue to damage the wood. I eyed the paper towels, which were too rough to use to dry the wood, and used a corner of my cotton skirt instead. I slipped the *kuginuki* back into my skirt pocket and went out to give Marshall the bad news.

"I think a plumber needs to look at the installation of the faucets, and then you need to have someone else come in to wax the *tansu*. Also, during the dinner and lunch hour, someone should come in occasionally to wipe up any water drops with a soft cloth."

Marshall stared at me for a moment, then made an exasperated sound. "What do you mean, someone needs to wax it? This isn't a beauty salon."

"Okay, I'll do it," I said. "I'll come tomorrow morning."

"With regard to your other suggestion, our cleaning people come in at ten-thirty in the morning. They don't hang around with soft cloths during the dinner hour touching up sinks, let alone keeping the johns in decent shape."

I met his outraged gaze. "Like I said, I'll wax the piece tomorrow. That may take care of the problem entirely. I'll wipe up the surface tonight, as long as I'm here."

When I returned to the table, Hugh was studying the menu, but Norie wasn't around.

"She ran off for the kitchen tour," Hugh said, answering my unspoken question.

"Tonight hardly seems the time for a tour. I heard that two of the cooks never came in and the dishwasher's in jail." I was determined not to discuss his sleeping plans any further. I'd act as if I just didn't care.

"Your friend Jiro said it was petty larceny," Hugh said. "The police caught him with a tank of lobsters that he was trying to sell on New York Avenue."

"Really! Maybe he's the reason the monkfish delivery Marshall mentioned didn't arrive. I'm surprised he didn't think of that."

"It seems like quite a small thing to be booked for, but I gather this bloke had a record. Meanwhile, the kitchen's in chaos. Your friend Andrea's washing dishes, apparently, and Jiro says she's too slow."

"Oh, no. I should go back and give her a hand—"

"Washing dishes? Don't let them take advantage of you. You haven't even been paid for your labor yet, have you?"

"Marshall needs to sort a few things out before he writes my check," I replied. "I'm sure he's good for it."

Hugh shook his head. "I don't like the sound of that, nor do I think it's appropriate that you clean the ladies' cloakroom. You're a freelance professional, not a doormat."

"When you work in a restaurant, it means you work as a team," I said, trying to calm him down. "Just like you and your friends with your rugby games. You cover for people when they need help."

Hugh snorted. "Well, we might as well order. So what do you recommend to start, the Sashimi Flower Garden or this carpaccio thing called Red Paper? This poetic name business is so . . . nineties."

I looked at him and felt my anger building. "I don't eat red meat, so I can't speak for the beef carpaccio. But if you'd like to tear apart some more flesh, this is surely the dish for you."

"Well, I'll try it. At least it doesn't have carbs." He patted his abdomen, which, to my eye, looked flatter than ever. Since coming back from Japan, he'd been spending extra time swimming and lifting weights at his gym. It was my doing, because he couldn't hang around his apartment relaxing anymore.

Even though Justin was supposed to be hosting, not waiting tables, he personally came to take our order. In his flirtiest manner, Justin addressed every word to Hugh, who just smiled back and asked his opinion of the carpaccio. Two beefcakes talking about more of the same. I'd had enough and decided to go locate my aunt. I left the table without a word, not that the two of them noticed.

16

Bento's kitchen felt like a greasy version of a steam room. The fans were going full blast, but they were no match for the stoves. Flames leaped under pans while freestanding stockpots simmered. Everyone, it seemed, was busy cooking. The Salvadoreans who usually peeled vegetables were cooking on the line. Next to Andrea, I noticed a new dishwasher, an olive-skinned man with a long, lank ponytail and an elaborate snake tattoo on his bicep. Still, he looked old and down on his luck, the opposite of most of the young, fit-looking staff.

Andrea was working at a second sink near him, wearing jeans and two strappy tanks that were covered up by a long apron. Her strong shoulders pulled together as she lifted a pan to rinse it. She had a tattoo on her shoulder, a small black butterfly that I hadn't noticed before. Tattoos and piercings, my father had said, were signs of body mutilation, evidence that a person wasn't comfortable in the skin in which they'd been born. I didn't know about that. The tattoo looked pretty on Andrea's muscular shoulder— but maybe, after fifty, it would look as tacky as the other dishwasher's multi-colored snake.

"Hi," I said. "Need any help?"

"Nah. They shifted Toro, the guy who torched the tuna, to dish-washing, so we're doing fine." Andrea angled her head to indi-cate her companion, who didn't look up, just kept washing pans with a dull expression. Now I noticed that he was wearing rubber gloves. Andrea wasn't, and her hands looked red. I asked, "Hey, shouldn't you wear rubber gloves?"

"Honey, the last thing on my mind is dishpan hands," Andrea said. "Guess what? I got my dad's service record in the mail today. What you said about calling the VA again worked."

"Anything interesting in it?"

"Well, it raised a few questions in my mind. My father's tour in Vietnam was supposed to be thirteen months, but he had a change to Japan after just eleven months. I knew he'd gone to Japan, but I didn't know he'd gone *early*. I wonder why."

"Vietnam was pretty difficult duty," I pointed out. "Maybe they let him transfer because of his knee injury." I wanted to hear what Andrea had to say, but I felt distracted by my desire to find my aunt. She was supposed to be in the kitchen, but I couldn't see her from where we were standing.

"He had the injury much earlier in the tour, and after being treated for it, he went back to fighting," Andrea pointed out. "I also don't understand why anyone would do my father any favors. He had some disciplinary actions against him when he got to the U.S., to the Pentagon. He wound up with a general discharge."

"Maybe he just wanted to get out of the military after he got here and your mother disappeared," I said. "Anyway, what about the box of papers we brought home from your dad's house? Anything interesting there?"

"I haven't gone through it that closely because I was so sur-prised by the stuff from the VA, which I could read. The box my father sent is full of papers written or typed in Japanese. About the only thing I can read are the addresses on some letters she sent over there that were returned unopened."

"Are these letters your mother wrote to her family in Japan?"

"I can't tell for sure because it's all in Japanese except for the very last part, Japan and the zip code. And, of course, the return address to Arlington."

"It doesn't matter that they're written in Japanese! My aunt and I can translate. Now we may have an address for your Japanese family. To think it was there in the box all those years!" I hugged Andrea, not caring about getting wet.

She patted my shoulder and released me in the manner of people who don't really like to be hugged. "I don't need to contact those relatives, but I do want to know what the letters say. I'm a little shy about having your aunt translate, though. What if she reads something that makes her think badly of us?"

"Whatever Sadako may have done, it is no reflection on you," I reassured her. "By the way, I was over at the Washington-Japan Friendship Society and met some people who knew your mother when she lived here. They're eager to talk to you. Did you know that she called you Akiko?"

"Akiko," Andrea said. "No. Yes. I'm not sure—"

"Maybe you have a buried memory." I was getting excited.

"We need sauté pans!" Carlos called out, interrupting us.

I realized now that we had talked for too long. The other kitchen workers were shooting us annoyed looks. I felt worried, all of a sudden, that we'd been talking about personal things in public. I said, "Andrea, I'm going to go back to the table. I think I saw our order go out, and I need to round up my aunt, too."

"I don't think she has time to eat," Andrea said.

"Of course she does! She came here to eat."

"Look at her, over there next to Carlos. She's cooking. She put on an apron when she heard we were short a few cooks tonight."

I stared at my aunt. When I'd entered the kitchen, I had walked straight past her, assuming from the back that she was a small Hispanic man. She wore her hair short, so the mistake could be made, and the heavy white apron she wore camouflaged her silk suit. The two other line cooks were working docilely next to her, leaning in to listen as she told them something.

"She's making some kind of stew she calls yosy-nobby," Andrea told me.

"*Yosenabe*," I said. "Jiro let her cook?"

"He didn't want to, but Marshall said why not. She had a great idea when we were talking about what to do to make up for the screwed-up specials. She's using our standard Asian-style bouill-abaisse and just adding fresh vegetables, red snapper, shrimp, and cellophane noodles. Two orders have gone out already, and the customers specifically told the waiters that it was the best thing at their table."

"But—how can she work?" I dropped my voice. "She's here on a tourist visa. She's totally illegal."

"She told Jiro she was volunteering," Andrea said with a smirk. "Why so shocked? You're no stranger to bending the law."

I tried to talk my aunt into handing the ladle over to one of the other cooks, but she was too busy. No, she couldn't take a break to eat. She had been sampling the *yosenabe* anyway, to make sure it was perfect. Normally, the dish was cooked right at the table; it was more complicated to do it ahead of time, in small quantities, undercooking the fish, then having it rushed to the table in oven-heated earthenware-lidded bowls.

"I will try one shrimp now, just a minute." Norie lifted a ladle, dipped it in, and tasted. "Yes, it's a bit underdone. By the time it reaches the table, it will be perfect." She called out to signal the runners, "Fire on twenty, I request, please!"

I grabbed the ladle away from her just as she was about to dip it back in the pot. "You can't eat from a ladle and put it back in! This is a professional restaurant!"

"Sorry," Norie said cheerfully. "Rei-chan, please go back to the dining room and relax with Hugh-san. Takeda-san said that I must work at the highest possible speed."

I looked around and finally spotted Jiro Takeda. He was chopping vegetables. The executive chef doing vegetable preparation? It seemed crazy, but now I realized that he had one of the vegetable prep guys—the one who'd helped with information when Kendall had vanished—working the line, and another one was gently arranging sashimi. I went over to visit Jiro and discovered that he was cutting carrots in the shape of flowers. Carrot and daikon and lotus root flowers were my aunt's signature embellishment for dishes simmered in the *nabe* pot.

"Not my style at all," he said, surveying the sliced vegetables when I came up. "But for a *nabe* dish, it is traditional."

"You shouldn't have to cut vegetables, should you?" I asked.

"We are badly understaffed tonight. And, unfortunately, this dish will not even be served correctly because we are not set up with tabletop burners. Bento is not that kind of restaurant."

"I know what you mean," I said, sensing how upset he must be to have his authority usurped by a visiting Japanese housewife. "How can I help? You should be doing more important work than these flowers."

Jiro stopped chopping and looked at me. "Have you ever cut vegetable flowers?"

"Many times." I looked at a bundle of uncut scallions resting near the chopping board. "I know the Japanese scallion-cutting style, on the diagonal—"

"Please, no." Jiro raised his eyes heavenward. "On this, at least, I will make a point of having scallion curls. Let me show you." Jiro picked up a green onion, slivering out a long section and at the same time turning it against his blade so that it curved like a miniature lily frond.

I could do it, but we both agreed I should do the hard, less perishable vegetables first. I worked until my stomach began to growl and I realized that I'd forgotten about Hugh, in the dining room. I put away my knife and went to the rest room to wipe up the water, as I'd promised Marshall I'd do.

In the dining room, the table where Hugh and I had been sitting had turned over to another couple. I went off to look for Justin to find out what had happened, and he reached into his pocket and pulled out a note written in Hugh's elegant loopy hand.

> *Enjoyed dinner thoroughly, but tell them not so much red chile in the carpaccio dipping sauce. I've paid for it and have gone home to drop off your uneaten food in the fridge and to sort out my kit. I'll be sleeping where I told you, so call if you need to talk. And remember, if you're running late, take a taxi instead of the Metro.*
>
> *Love to your aunt,*
>
> *H.*

Something caught in my throat. Love to my aunt, but not to me.

I went back to the kitchen, and worked like a dog until eleven-thirty. The last people were leaving. All had gone well—the *nabe* had been a success. I'd let Norie pour me a small bowl of it. It was fabulous—even better than what I'd eaten in her own home. Somehow, Jiro's luscious fish stock combined to perfection with the ginger, and the seafood within was buttery and crisp at the same time. A slight bite from the scallion and *shiso* leaf on top gave the dish a stunning complexity, as complex as a wine, I realized, though I didn't have a glass of Riesling to sip with it, as some of the kitchen crew were doing. All had gone well with the restaurant's standard dishes, too—the tuna and steak supplies had been depleted. It was impossible to tell how the food critic had liked his meal, but the waiters had made sure that all the food that went to his party was as perfect as they could make it. Every plate was cleaned, and the five guests had consumed three bottles of wine. Over the dinner period, 201 covers had been served if you counted my uneaten meal that Hugh had paid for. Marshall didn't say what the evening's proceeds were, but he was smiling when he came in to say good night to everyone in the kitchen.

"D'you want to go around the corner to Plum Ink for a glass of wine?" Andrea asked me. "I can tell you about the papers."

Plum Ink. I felt a frisson of something go down my spine. This was the restaurant that Kendall had mentioned. A take-out package from Plum Ink had been inside the trunk of the car in which she'd been kidnapped. "I'd really like to, but you know, my aunt is too tired. I should take her home."

"Please go and enjoy with your friend, Rei-chan," my aunt spoke up from her position next to Andrea, where she was drying dishes. "Takeda-san is taking me home by car. If you can write down the address and give me a key, I shall let myself in."

"Sure." I hesitated, thinking about how hard I'd been on Norie when I'd discovered her cooking. "Obasan, I think your dish was a great success. I'm really impressed that you had the energy to step in."

"It is no *problemo*." Norie said, showing she had picked up some kitchen Spanish.

"Yes, thank you very much." Jiro had come up, and he bowed stiffly to Norie. From his face, I couldn't tell what he was thinking. The dish had saved the kitchen, but it was a bit of an etiquette conundrum for a newcomer to accomplish so much.

Norie bowed back more deeply to him. "Thank you for letting me try. I know it wasn't much, but anything I can do to help, I will. I would like to come back whenever you have a problem. I will stay here for a long time, so I am quite available."

"*Ah so desu ka*," said Jiro. "But you are an esteemed lady. I insist that when you return to this place, you must be my guest. I humbly request the honor to cook your heart's desire for you."

I watched the smiling back-and-forth and tried to decode it. Jiro hadn't really wanted the help and he was actually rubbing in the fact that she was a woman, and a woman shouldn't have a leadership role in a kitchen. A girl like Andrea or myself was okay chopping vegetables, but no female should be the chief executor of a menu dish. Norie's face had tightened, and although she thanked him in her soft voice, she didn't look happy.

"Obasan, would you like to go with Andrea and me to the Chinese restaurant?" I asked again when Jiro was out of earshot.

"I cannot reject Takeda-san's hospitable offer. Besides, I think it will be interesting to spend more time with him. He's a strange Japanese."

"This is the only key I have with me right now," I said as I handed it over. "Can you leave it under the umbrella stand in the entryway?"

"Is that safe?" Norie worried.

"It always has been," I reassured her. "I don't think I'll be too long. Maybe an hour or two."

17

Plum Ink was upscale Chinese: glass-and-chrome tables, leather seating, and plum walls decorated with oversized calligraphy characters, a few of which I recognized. Water. Peace. Money. The important things.

I'd thought Bento had enjoyed a big night, but Plum Ink was even busier, with a young, night-owlish clientele. The prices were lower here, though, I thought, studying the details in the framed reviews from the *Washingtonian* and the *Washington Post* that hung on the wall of the bar. The restaurant looked glamorous, yet it was fairly priced. How could it lose?

The bar area was where Andrea, David, Justin, Phong, the sommelier named Kevin, and Carlos and Alberto had decided to park themselves. Everyone except for me lit up cigarettes. I realized that my colleagues were Plum Ink regulars, because there was a lot of friendly greeting back and forth between them and the bartender, a young Chinese-American with spiky black hair and one dangling earring shaped like a cross. I was introduced to Mark, and the jokes flew about how I was the mom of the bunch because I was practically married. I acknowledged it all with a strained smile because I didn't want to put off Mark. I'd already started thinking that I could ask him if he'd heard anything about the take-out food that had been in the trunk of the car in which Kendall had been kidnapped.

"We'll be able to talk after they all get their drinks and get really loud," Andrea murmured to me. "What do you want to have to drink? He makes good cosmos."

"How about a coffee?" I said. Midnight was late for me, but I had a lot to stay awake for.

"Irish coffee in a Chinese restaurant?" Andrea laughed.

I offered to get the drinks, to ensure that mine wasn't alcoholic, and also because I wanted to have a private conversation with Mark. After he'd taken the drinks orders, I reintroduced myself.

"Of course, Rei. You're the famous one who's going to be married. Let me look at your ring." He grabbed my left hand and started stroking it.

"Oh, that's not really why I'm known," I said, gritting my teeth as he kept hold of my hand. It wouldn't pay to appear uptight at the moment. "I'm more notorious because of my cousin in the news. Kendall Johnson."

"Sounds like a wine label. Is she from California, like you?"

So he'd caught everything Andrea had said about my background. "No, she's a D.C. girl. I'm surprised you haven't heard of her. She was the fund-raiser who was kidnapped last week during Bento's soft opening."

"Whoa, now I remember! The cops came by last Saturday because there was a bag from our place in the trunk of the car."

"So you know about it?"

"Yeah. We had to go through our list of receipts for that whole day."

"Did anything of significance turn up?"

"Don't know. The cops were hot to find out if anyone had come in to eat, or carried out, three particular dishes. The spicy spinach, the scallops with ginger, the chicken fried rice—" He cut himself off as a fiftyish Asian man with a round belly covered by a track-suit walked up to the bar and spoke to him rapidly in what I recognized as Mandarin.

Mark began bobbing his head and grunted back a few short syllables. The man looked at the group from Bento, made a slight face, and walked out.

"Was that the restaurant owner?" I guessed.

"Yeah. Mr. Chow. He was asking which restaurant you came from, because he hadn't seen you before."

"Was he upset that you were talking to me?"

"Naw. He just pointed out that the kitchen was closing soon, and if you wanted food, you should be advised to order now."

"Hmm," I said. Mr. Chow hadn't looked that happy to see the big group—maybe he thought we were keeping better customers out.

"Hey, are you hungry? It's true that you should order now."

I shook my head. "The others already gave an order to the waitress. I can't eat this late at night."

"But you like to do other things. Like talk." Mark tilted his head, and looked at me in the same appraising, flirtatious way he had earlier.

I smiled and asked if any dinner check for that night had included the spinach, scallops, and fried rice.

"There were three dinner groups who ordered the spinach and scallops as part of a larger meal, but only one table asked to take the leftovers home. And they didn't have fried rice."

"Who were they?"

"Well, I didn't personally serve them, but one of the waiters did, and he said they were crotchety old geezers, a man and a woman, who paid cash, so there was no record of their names. To me that sounds like the kind who might kidnap their next-door neighbor's newspaper, but not more than that."

I nodded. "Did the police blow the whole thing off?"

"They said they'd check into it, but they hardly looked excited."

"What about take-out orders?" I asked. "Are those orders written up just like regular dinner checks?"

"Hey, this isn't that kind of Chinese restaurant."

"Sorry. It looks like a great place. Thanks for the drinks."

"You starting a tab, or what?"

I glanced over at Andrea, who looked impatient. "I guess a tab."

At least that would prolong paying, and maybe Andrea would split the tab with me. And while all the waiters were crowing over the three-figure tips each had made that night, I had nothing to show for it. Andrea, working as dishwasher, probably had nothing, either.

"What were you talking about for so long?" Andrea demanded. "Was he trying to get under your zebra skirt, which actually is really cute?"

"Thanks, but no, nothing was going on. I think the way he talks to women is just normal behavior, isn't it? Restaurant behavior?"

Andrea smiled knowingly. "I know Mark from before, back when we both worked at Mandala. He's not bad in the sack. Actually, I'd recommend him—"

"Really?" Not that I was interested. After my encounters with Marshall and Hugh that evening, I was feeling pretty anti-man.

"Sure." Andrea shrugged. "I'm not in love with him or anything. I'm not into emotional attachments, you may have noticed."

"So Mark worked at Mandala. Why didn't he go over to work at Bento like you did?"

"Mark left Mandala before Marshall even thought of opening Bento. It was one of those typical restaurant-opportunity things— the guy who owns Plum Ink lured Mark away with a great starting wage."

"I've been wondering about something, Andrea." I paused, not wanting to be rude. "How are you making it, financially, now that you're washing dishes?"

"Not too well. I'm waiting for Justin to fall down and really humiliate himself. Then I'll get my spot back." Andrea looked at him coldly, then back at me. "Now, tell me more about what those people said. The ones who knew my Japanese name?"

There was so much, I hardly knew where to start. I told her about how Sadako had been afraid to leave home, even to take a bus ride to the doctor. I explained that she'd been cut off from any possible friends, and that she'd clung to Japanese ideas about baby care. When Andrea pressed me for more, I mentioned that Betty had said that Sadako had wanted to sleep close to her at night to breast-feed, but Robert had thought it better for her to sleep in another room.

"Your dad seemed as if he was having trouble coping. A lot of men do." I thought of Win and his distance from his children.

"Don't make excuses," Andrea said shortly. "Was there anything else that they said to you?"

"They were very sorry to learn that you wound up in foster care. They had no idea that had happened. In fact, they want to meet you to talk about that."

"I'll do that when I can," Andrea said briskly. "Right now, I'm pretty busy. I've located another report of my mother being seen getting on a bus out of town."

"From Arlington to Washington, you mean?"

"No. A different bus, from the Greyhound terminal, headed for Delaware. It doesn't make sense, especially since you said she was afraid to take buses," Andrea said. "Hey, are you ready for another coffee? I'm buying."

My cup had grown cold while we'd talked, but I shook my head. I didn't need anything more to set my head buzzing. The conversation of the other waiters and cooks became louder. The dishwasher in jail was roundly mocked for being stupid enough to get caught selling seafood on a major thoroughfare. Justin, who had a wicked ear for accents, did an imitation of Jiro having a meltdown. Then Phong did a pantomime of Andrea washing dishes, using his hands eloquently to show both her inexperience and her distaste for mess. Andrea laughed as hard as anybody.

Restaurant workers were wild, I decided as I sipped my coffee and watched them. The humor was sometimes mean, but they'd all worked so hard as a unit. Some of them, who'd started before lunch, had been working for twelve hours straight. I glanced at my watch and saw how late it was. The only problem was, I didn't want to go out by myself.

When Justin and David said they were leaving, I decided to tag along. We stepped out and almost tripped over a man slumped outside the restaurant door, head buried in his chest. Leaning against his legs was a paper cup with a few coins in it.

I hesitated, but realized I'd need all my change for the Metro or taxi or whatever form of transport I caught.

"Disgusting," Justin said. "Marshall doesn't let anyone beg outside the door. If you put your foot down, they stay away."

"I'm sure he's hungry," I said to Justin as we moved away.

"Yeah, right. If I gave him this"—Justin hoisted a plastic bag that I guessed was full of food from Plum Ink—"he'd throw it away."

"I could see if that's true," I said. "Give me the bag."

"Hey, it's my food! I'm gonna—" Justin's words were cut off as we were enveloped in a swarm of people. A concert had just ended; some seventies band, I guessed, looking at the ages of the patrons.

"You got anything on you?" David asked Justin after we'd made it out of the thicket.

Justin shook his head. "I'm in the mood to get wasted, though. Let's swing by P Street."

I guessed that they were talking about buying drugs. I decided at that moment I should probably do my own thing, travelwise. I'd go for Hugh's suggestion and take a taxi.

But after I parted from Justin and David, I realized I'd made my decision too late. The concertgoers had snapped up all the taxis. I stood no chance of getting one for myself.

I walked back to H, past Bento and the vacant neighboring building Win was trying to sell. I noticed that his name was no longer on the for-sale shingle, but there was another phone number and a name. Interesting. Was the building being offered for sale by the new owner? Maybe Kendall's kidnapping really had affected the real estate market.

I saw that Justin and David were slowly walking along just a block and a half ahead, and I quickly caught up with them as they entered the Chinatown Metro station. They were having a loud, animated conversation about marijuana varieties.

"I can't believe you still have the energy for that," I said, breaking my rule about staying out of things that weren't my business.

If only they weren't speaking so loudly. Once we'd boarded the Metro train, I'd noticed that the three of us were catching some cold stares from the older generation.

"Oh, don't be such a mother." Justin wrinkled his nose.

"You're not going to tell Marshall, are you?" David asked.

"No, I'm not going to tell. But honestly," I whispered, "you both have to go back to work tomorrow. It's not a day off. How are you going to feel in the morning?"

"Who cares? We don't work till the afternoon. The only possible issue is getting the munchies really bad, but Mark made sure we got all this yummy Chinese." Justin held up the plastic bag, which I noticed was leaking soy sauce out of a corner.

"You're friendly with Mark, which surprises me," I said. "I'd have thought there would be competition between the two restaurants."

"Oh, the restaurant world is very tight. Mark was at Mandala and now he's at Plum Ink. Maybe Justin will be there next week," David said.

"Yeah, I'm getting sick of this hosting thing," Justin said. "I expected extra tips, you know, for giving people good tables. There's not enough to make it worthwhile. I earned more as a waiter."

"Really. Maybe you and Andrea should bring it up with Marshall about wanting your old jobs back," I suggested.

"Oh, he never listens to anybody." But Justin's expression was pensive, as if I'd put an idea into his head that he hadn't considered before.

It was time for me to get out, at Dupont Circle, and I bid Justin and David good-bye. I exited by Q Street, where I thought I'd have a better chance at a cab than the busier circle itself. Besides, this was in the direction of Adams-Morgan, where I lived. It was after midnight, though, and the cabs were full of people leaving bars and restaurants. I was in the same predicament as when I'd been in Penn Quarter, where I'd watched so many cabs pass me by.

I checked my watch and debated whether to start walking. It was about a twenty-five-minute walk to the apartment. Connecticut Avenue going north had some quiet patches, but it was a good neighborhood. And Connecticut led to Columbia Road, where enough late-night restaurants and clubs were open that I'd feel safe.

I started my walk. I'd worn high-heeled boots because I'd wanted to look good walking into Bento, but now I was regretting them. The hardness of the concrete jarred my feet with every step. Running shoes would have been perfect, I thought morosely. I could have made the trip home in half the time, if I were running. But I hadn't had much energy for running lately. And running might cut five minutes off my trip, but not more.

As I passed Florida Avenue, the landscape turned to hotels. I thought back on how I'd once visited someone staying at the Sofitel, now a Radisson. The Hilton was still there, as was the Marriot. Hotels meant taxis, I thought eagerly. I hastened toward the Hilton, but an empty cab sped past me. Wait. Was there one with an unlit medallion just around the corner on T Street? I turned the corner.

As I turned into the darker street, I almost tripped. It took me a few seconds to regain my balance and turn to see what kind of car was roaring up the street, beside me. By the time I'd turned, the car had stopped with a squeal of tires, and a man had jumped out of it and was rushing toward me.

In the next instant, a hand was over my mouth, a hand that was half metal. An arm wrapped around my waist and I was being dragged to the car. I kicked the legs of whoever was holding me, and he swore before dumping me in the car's open trunk. Then the trunk lid slammed down. The engine roared again, and we were off.

18

When you pack a car trunk, there's never enough room, no matter
how many cubic feet the sales brochure insists are there. When
you're lying inside one, it's a similar phenomenon. I was not a
claustrophobic person—how could I be, and have lived successfully in Tokyo?—but in that car trunk, I was terrified. The dark-
ness was overwhelming, and the space was so small it felt like a
coffin. Late-model cars like Hugh's Lexus had a glow-in-the-dark
catch that you could pull to open a trunk if you were trapped
inside, but there was nothing like that in this car. All I could find
was a coil of rope.

Rope. What was its purpose? My panic mixed with overwhelming regret. I wouldn't be lying in the trunk of a car if I had-
n't been stupid enough to walk back to Adams-Morgan after midnight. And of course, I wouldn't have walked if I'd been more
patient about catching a cab. And finally, I wouldn't even have
been out on the street at this hour if I had taken the ride home
with Aunt Norie that Jiro had offered.

Kendall had been kidnapped and had lived, I reminded myself.
She'd vanished, and even though nobody had seen her get
snatched, she'd survived. And these might be the same people. I

didn't understand how they'd done it, though—if they'd shadowed me in their car from H Street, they couldn't have known where I'd go, once I'd entered the subway system. No, the situation had to be simpler. The men had spotted me somewhere along my Connecticut route, and grabbed me when I'd turned onto T. They'd targeted me for a reason that had nothing to do with Kendall Johnson or restaurants.

I felt myself over and touched a bulge in my skirt pocket. For a second I thought it was my new cell phone, but I remembered too soon that the gift meant to keep me safe was still in the apartment, where I'd left it to charge its battery. In my pocket was the Japanese tool I'd used to try to fix the vanity. It had a sharp end, but I couldn't realistically think that it could do much—except, maybe, poke out an eye if someone was right on top of me. But of course, there were two of them.

I was so lucky they hadn't taken the time to bind my hands. I undid my watch, which had a glow-in-the-dark face if you pressed the right button. Because I'd need both hands to use the *kuginuki* in the manner that I was planning, I balanced the watch sideways between my elbow and the hard surface of the car trunk. A tiny aqua circle of light cheered me. I could only illuminate the trunk in sections, but I no longer felt that I was in a coffin.

The car was going fast now. Very fast. The noise level rose to a roar, and I thought we were on a freeway. Bumpy. It had to be 295, the District's freeway, not 495, which was owned and maintained by the states of Virginia and Maryland. Of course, 295 did cross over into Virginia, eventually. Perhaps that was where I was going.

Nobody was going to look for me there. Nobody was going to look for me, period. I had to get myself out of the trunk. Even as I started working, I was filled with foreboding. I might undo the latch, but I couldn't jump out of a car going eighty miles an hour on a freeway.

I breathed. The space was so close around me.

I'm going to get out.

I broke up the words between each of my long breaths. *I . . . am . . . going . . . to . . . get . . . out.*

It was good that I was using the *kuginuki* while the car was going fast, because they couldn't hear the clicks and scraping noises I was making. No matter how many ways I moved the knife, the lock held fast. I didn't want to break the latch, just trip it so that it opened neatly. And then, when I got the trunk unlatched, I'd have to keep it held down tight, so they wouldn't know what I'd done. Finally, the jump. And afterward? I couldn't rule out the possibility that they'd come after me. But I would be harder to find in the dark. I could crawl somewhere and hide.

Between the exacting work, and the stress, I was soon wet with sweat. I dropped the *kuginuki*, and when I moved to retrieve it, the watch was jarred and its light went out. Now I realized that my feet had gone to sleep. This condition had crept up on me occasionally when I was sitting in a classic Japanese *seiza* position. I began to wiggle my toes, desperate to get the blood flow back. I'd need my feet to run.

Was it my imagination, or had the car slowed? I had no concept of time. Now I was beginning to lose my perception of speed. My fingers closed around the tool, its edge pricking my thumb as I picked it up. I got my watch back in position, turned on its light, and resumed my work on the latch.

The car was picking up speed again, but not as fast as it had been on the freeway. And I could hear sounds of other cars passing us. It might be a suburban road.

Finally, I felt it. The latch turned all the way. I'd opened it, I could tell, because I could lift the lid. I held it open just a sliver to see the dark sky outside, and to hear the rush of the car over the road. If I let go of the trunk lid, it would fly right open.

Keeping one hand on it, I began to ready myself, turning my body so that I was on my hands and knees. My feet weren't completely in working order yet, but I would move them.

How fast was the car going? Thirty, maybe forty miles per

hour? There were other cars around now. There might not be any, in a little while.

I thought about Kendall one last time. She'd been left alone in the car trunk, unharmed. But my situation was different. I couldn't trust them to leave me alone, and I couldn't trust anyone to rescue me. I put on my watch again and looked at the time. We'd been driving for almost an hour. We had to be at least fifty miles from Washington. Far was not good.

The car turned again, knocking me against the inside of the trunk. Another street. They were proceeding toward their destination. I took a deep breath and lifted the trunk a fraction. I'd thought we were on a smaller road, and I was right. It was a double-lane country road with farm fencing on either side. No streetlights, and no car lights behind me. Still, it would only get quieter. They were driving into the country, not the city.

I lifted the lid all the way and moved into a crouch. There was no more time to think. I launched myself out of the trunk.

I seemed so slow, compared to the car. I was free, for a few seconds, soaring through the air, tucking my head in position for an airborne forward roll. I'd flown off a bike once this way and survived.

I circled through the air too quickly and hit the ground on my left side, landing on the *kuginuki* that I'd returned to my pocket. Oh, God. It hurt so much. I wanted to stay there forever, but I couldn't. Either they'd come back for me, or someone would hit me. I was bleeding. I couldn't tell if I'd broken anything.

Already, in the back of my mind, the pain was squeezed out by a terrifying sound, that of squealing brakes. Whether the sound came from ahead of me or behind, I didn't know.

I heard a rumble of voices. The rhythm felt Southern, but the sound was still far enough away that I couldn't guess race or even gender.

I rolled over on my belly and began to crawl. Now the pain was radiating out from my belly, a strange cramping so intense I had to clench my teeth not to cry out.

A circle of light was crossing the road. *Don't see me*, I pleaded.

Let me disappear into the blackness of the earth. My turtleneck was black, and so was my hair. The zebra skirt had been torn all the way up to my waist. I curled into a ball, covering my legs as best I could.

The pain from my fall had intensified. Now I couldn't raise my arms or legs. I felt myself lifting out of my body, looking down. A small Japanese woman, left along the side of the road like a wounded animal. We were one and the same. Thirty years separated us, but time, as I'd learned tonight, meant nothing at all.

The light found me. I felt it hot on my head, and my back. I didn't bother to lift my head. I knew they'd gotten me. There was a hubbub of voices, now all men's. They were black and white and Southern and Northern. More than two men, worse than I'd thought.

For a split second, I came back down to earth, and I saw boots: not fashionable women's boots like mine, but the big, steel-toed ones, the kind that men wore to do construction work. The horror of the boots was the last thing I remembered before I felt hands turning my body, and I decided not to think anymore.

19

"She is waking."

I opened my eyes. I could see out of only one, and all I beheld was a fluorescent light that turned the white sheets covering me even brighter. The glare was overwhelming, so I closed myself against it, again.

The same woman's voice spoke again, in Japanese. "You're here with us. You're safe now, Rei-chan. You will be fine."

I opened my working eye again and deduced the blurry outline of a middle-aged Japanese woman. Was it Sadako? Even though the words were comforting, I knew the worst had happened. I was alive, but I was in whatever hell was reserved for Japanese women who ran astray in America.

"She doesn't recognize me, Hugh-san," the voice said.

Hugh? Now I was really confused. I forced my eye open again and saw him, out of focus.

I opened my mouth. How dry it was. "Where," I said, unable to finish the rest of my question.

"You're here with Norie and me in a hospital in Quantico, Virginia," Hugh said. "You were smashed up pretty badly. A group of Marines riding to their base found you lying on the road. They called for an ambulance, which brought you here."

Black boots. I'd thought that my time was up when I'd seen them, but they'd really been on the feet of the men who had saved me.

"I was taken," I said. "A car. Two men." I stopped. My tongue was working so slowly. Painkillers, I guessed.

"You can tell the police when you're ready," Hugh said, holding a glass of water for me. I sucked down the coldness greedily.

"What do they say happened?" I was starting to get my voice back.

"I haven't heard it from them, but the police told me they saw your body first, and then saw the car ahead. It took off when they stopped."

"They saved my life." Despite my grogginess, I felt a wave of relief wash over me. Marines. I immediately regretted the many times I had been antimilitary. If there wasn't a military, there wouldn't have been this group of sharp-eyed Marines who had decided to stop and help me.

"They did," Hugh said. Why was his voice so sober?

"Rei-chan, I should never have let you go home by yourself." I heard Aunt Norie's voice again. "I cared for you in Japan, but I did not care properly for you here. You will not forgive me, ever. I am not worthy of it."

I shook my head.

"Norie, could you do me a favor and find Rei's nurse, please? I want her to bring an extra pillow."

"Of course," my aunt answered. I heard the sound of a door closing.

"Rei, darling, I'm so very sorry. For all the reasons." Hugh put his face against mine. "If I hadn't gone out to stay in Potomac, you would have gotten home safely."

I shook my head. "It was meant to happen."

"What do you mean? That the bastards would have come after you another night, that they'd marked you as their target the way they had Kendall?"

"I don't know. It felt like fate." I couldn't explain the strange feeling I'd had while lying on the road, that Sadako's and my destinies had intertwined. I didn't believe in ghosts, but at that moment, I felt as if I'd seen her.

"I won't accept that it was meant to be. Never." Hugh's voice was hard. "Rei, I have to tell you something before your aunt returns. During your—abduction—a very sad thing happened."

"You mean, you and Kendall." I stopped, too depressed to spell it out.

"What about Kendall and me?" Hugh sounded puzzled.

"I thought . . . maybe . . . you . . . got together." Each word was so hard to utter.

"Your wonderful cousin," Hugh said dryly. "When I arrived at her place, she was having a teleconference with some Snowden campaigners, oblivious of me, not to mention the bairns, who were tearing the house apart. I helped the au pair put them to bed. Then Win returned, drunk as a skunk, and I had to put him to bed. I was frankly exhausted at the end of it all and tucked myself into the guest room without bothering to phone you good night. I'm sorry about that."

Hugh had sounded so normal and believable that I was filled with remorse. "I practically drove you into staying there. There's no need to apologize."

"The thing that happened." Hugh paused, as if he didn't want to go on. "It happened to you."

I thought about how I couldn't see. "Did I lose an eye?"

"No. Your right cornea was scratched in the fall, which is why it's got a temporary bandage on it. That'll heal. It's—oh, hell."

I lay still, waiting. How hurt was I? Was it paralysis? Would I never walk again?

"The baby's gone. You miscarried during the fall."

"Baby." I said. My one eye stared at him, shocked. "How could that be?"

"You were hemorrhaging during the transport to the hospital. That's when the tissue came out, the beginnings of our . . ." Hugh's voice trailed off.

"Oh, Hugh." So that had been the wracking pain as I lay on the road: the journey of a child, breaking apart and pouring out of my body.

"Did you know?" Hugh asked. "We haven't had any time alone together since I came back. I thought maybe you did suspect something, but didn't have a chance to tell me."

"I didn't know. If I had known I wouldn't have jumped—"

Hugh sighed heavily. "But if you hadn't jumped, you might not be alive today. And if that had happened, I don't know how I could have gone on."

"Who knows if they would even have done anything to me?" I was beginning to hyperventilate. "Kendall waited to be rescued. She did the sensible thing."

"You were brave to get out the way you did. It's just that—my heart is breaking," Hugh said. "I never thought I would feel this way. I didn't know about the baby, I didn't have any time to dream about it or get—attached—but I still feel so . . ."

"I was stupid not to know." I'd gained weight, I no longer had the energy to run well, and I had no taste for wine. Unconsciously, I'd been protecting the baby—protecting it until the moment came when I killed it.

"Usually there's a sign," Hugh said.

"I had a period about six weeks back." True, it had been light to the point of near invisibility, but I had just chalked that up to stress. There had been a lot. First, the preparation for the restaurant opening, then Kendall's kidnapping, and finally, my aunt's surprise visit. That raised a new question. "How much does Norie know?"

"Not everything," Hugh said. "She knows about the eye, and that you have multiple fractures of your fingers, and that you took a hard fall. But I didn't tell her about the baby, and I asked the doctors to keep it private. Actually, there are new hospital privacy laws that are extremely strict. Even though Norie is your aunt, the only way either of us could be at your bedside is through permission of your parents, who, as you already know, are in Fiji. I managed to reach them. They're in shock over the whole thing, but very glad that you're alive."

"How long do I have to stay in the hospital?" The longer I stayed in, I knew, the worse I'd feel about my life.

"They may let you out today. Then you're supposed to treat yourself gently for about a week. I'm taking leave from work and not letting you out of my sight until you're completely mended. I told Norie I was moving in to protect you both, and she didn't utter a word of protest."

I smiled. "So you don't have to live at the gym or the office anymore."

"No. And I'm really sorry—sorry that I was so hell-bent, last night, on getting to bed at a decent hour. If I hadn't gone to your cousin's, this never would have happened."

Hugh was interrupted by the sound of a door opening and my aunt Norie's voice. "Rei-chan, I have your pillow. And one of the soldiers is here to see you, if you feel well enough."

"Can you bear it?" Hugh asked in a low voice.

"Yes. I must thank him." I felt dazed again, like I was moving in and out of two worlds.

"The doctors said no more than two visitors at a time, so I'll leave."

Hugh departed, and I tried to focus with my one good eye on the tall man in camouflage standing in front of me, his hat in his hands.

"I'm Lance Corporal Henderson, ma'am. I was with the group who stopped. Just wanted to see that you were okay." From what I could see of him, he looked to be in his early twenties—a gangly blond with a faint haze of hair over his head. He was like a spring chick, all stretched out.

"I'm very grateful," I said. "Can you tell me how it happened?"

"Our driver had the brights on. At first we thought you were a dog—because you weren't that big, see—and my buddy, he really loves dogs, so he wanted to stop. There was an argument because it was already two in the morning, and we'd have to muster at sunrise. But then my buddy saw what looked like clothing, so we had to stop."

"Tell me about the car I fell from," I said.

"It was a sedan with its trunk open. The car was going backward, fast, heading in the direction of where you were lying. But when we stopped, the car changed direction and took off. I guess that was the car that dropped you, huh?"

"I dropped myself," I said. "I don't suppose you saw the license plate?"

"No, ma'am. I'm sorry. We didn't put two and two together, that you might have come from that car, until later, when we were giving the report to the police."

"I understand. I'm really grateful."

"Well, we're pretty disappointed we didn't get those guys who did it." The lance corporal bowed his head for a minute. "We could have taken them down, you know, if we'd seen them."

"You saved my life. I think that's enough for one night," I said.

"Thank you so much," Norie said. "I think she is becoming tired."

My aunt sat by my side after the Marine left. She didn't say anything, which was a relief.

As my aunt's hand slowly warmed my cold one, I thought about how every Japanese town seemed to have at least one temple with a special garden that held small statues of Jizo-sama, the Buddhist guardian of children who die too early. Women would buy a small stone statue, and then dress it in hand-sewn or knitted or crocheted jackets and hats. They laid before it offerings of fruit and flowers. The mothers visited their child-guardians as long as they needed to, sometimes until a second child was born, in other cases, for the rest of their lives.

But there were no gardens of stone babies in the United States. Even if there were such a place, I couldn't set foot in it. I had never known my child, never worried about it, never loved it. And now it was too late.

20

Three days after the ride back to Washington, I still hurt all over.

The ER attending had prescribed Percocet, which had upset my stomach so badly that I'd flushed all the pills down the toilet. My local doctor gave me a prescription for something that bothered my stomach even more. Fractured fingers I could live with, and my eye had healed enough for me to take off the patch, but my stomach ached for what it had lost.

My parents called me every day from Fiji, on a crackly connection that often cut out. They were the only ones I could bear to speak with. Hugh shadowed me from room to room, running loads of laundry, puttering, and going out to run the occasional errand. He also kept out people I couldn't bear to see. The press, for the first few days, were incessant. The Marines had been happy to speak and pose for pictures, but I'd refused to be interviewed and begged my police contact to keep my name private—which they couldn't legally do. At least it hadn't gotten out about the baby.

After three long days, the cameramen stopped hanging around. They went back to Kendall, who was willing to oblige with her comments on the situation. She'd called up right away to offer her sympathies—as far as she knew, all I'd suffered were the bruises and scars of a kidnapping. I decided to keep the story simple, like that, because I didn't want to become a family horror story. I could imagine the news of my lost pregnancy making the Howard family telephone rounds. "How California," Grand might say. And the rest would shake their heads, musing with each other about why I didn't know about birth control when, for God's sake, I was living with a man—and why a woman who was almost thirty didn't know it was unsafe to walk around the District of Columbia after midnight.

Kendall had offered to help me write a press release about the kidnapping, but I'd refused. Then she'd offered to take me out for a drink at Zola, but I'd declined. In the end, she promised she'd stop by one evening after work. I was anxious to have a face-to-face talk. I thought that, if we talked, I might remember more about the men who'd taken me. I wasn't sure if my memory was so vague because I'd lost consciousness after the jump, or because I just wasn't thinking hard enough.

Detective Burns had been frustrated with me, I knew. He'd come to visit the day of my return. I'd settled in for the morning on Hugh's long leather sofa with an old Japanese patchwork quilt wrapped around me when the downstairs buzzer rang. I spoke into the entry phone, and I recognized Louis Burns's voice.

When Norie opened the door, the detective nodded at her. Then he looked at me. "Miss Shimura. I'm very sorry about your loss."

"Thanks," I said quickly, hoping that would end it. He obviously knew that I'd miscarried.

"May I talk to you for a little while?" Burns's voice was gentle. "I've read the reports from Virginia, but since the crime originated in the city, and bears some similarity to what happened to your cousin, it's fallen in my bailiwick."

I nodded and looked at my aunt. In Japanese, I said, "Obasan, please could I ask you to make some of your cherry blossom tea for the detective?"

As she disappeared into the kitchen, Detective Burns looked after her. "Your mother?"

"No, she's my aunt, Norie Shimura, from Japan. My mother's American. She's in Fiji, so I'm really lucky to have my aunt here in her stead. But please don't say anything about the baby. She doesn't know."

"Don't worry, I'm not going to dwell on that sad issue. I'm here to ask you about the American side of your family. Is it your mother who has the link to Kendall Howard Johnson?"

"Yes. My mother is the sister of Kendall's father, Douglas Howard."

"And are there other cousins I could contact?"

"Just Kendall's brother, my cousin Dougie Junior. He lives in Millersville. I'm not close to him, so I don't know the phone number or address."

"Hmm. You say that you're not close. Was there some problem growing up?"

I flushed, feeling as if I was becoming a suspect for some reason. "No. It's just that we grew up on different sides of the country, and he—well, I get along with Kendall better." Although that wasn't saying much.

"So, any reason to think members of this family—the Howards—might be in trouble of some sort? The target of anyone?"

I shook my head. "The Howards are an old Maryland family, but our branch doesn't have any significant land holdings or money. I mean, Kendall and her brother both have trust funds, but we're just talking about a few hundred thousand dollars each—not millions."

"But you and Kendall both disappeared," Burns said. "And you're first cousins living in the D.C. area."

"Kendall said that the men who took her asked her name before they took her. In my case, I was just stupidly strolling toward Adams-Morgan after midnight, and I turned a dark corner, and they came after me. They didn't ask my name, just chucked me in the trunk."

"Do you think the men already knew who you were?"

"I thought about that, but it couldn't be," I said. "As you know, I started out on foot near Penn Quarter. Then I took the Metro from Chinatown to Dupont Circle. How could I be followed by guys in a car if I went underground for so long and later emerged at a point they couldn't guess?"

"You said there were two of them. One man could have tracked you underground, and used a cell phone to signal his partner after you and he reached street level."

"I didn't notice anyone." But the truth was, I'd been uneasy. Subconsciously, I'd felt something, but ignored it, because I was so eager to get home.

"Tell me about why you went to Plum Ink in the first place."

"I'd never gone there before," I said. "Some of the kitchen and waitstaff from Bento like to unwind there after the restaurant closes. I went because I wanted to talk to Andrea Norton—she's my friend who used to be the hostess. And then, once I got there, I decided to ask their bartender some questions that related to my cousin's kidnapping."

"Why did you want to do that?" He stopped taking notes and looked up at me.

"The take-out box in the back of the car Kendall was kidnapped in was from Plum Ink, remember?"

"Certainly. We've already investigated that angle."

"And come up with nothing?" I guessed aloud. "But you know, the thing about Plum Ink is, it's not just the people who *pay* for food who can carry it out."

"What do you mean?"

"Some of the restaurant friends I'd gone with—two of the waiters—were given a bag of Chinese food for free when they left. Based on that, I think that a kitchen worker might have just given someone the food that turned up in the trunk of the car. He wouldn't have told the restaurant owner about this, because it was a favor for friends, not paying customers."

"That's interesting." Burns stroked his chin, where I noticed that a slight goatee was growing. "But I'm more intrigued by the fact that your colleagues would patronize that particular restaurant. There's competition between Plum Ink and Bento."

"I thought the same thing and asked one of my waiter friends about it," I said. "He said that people in the restaurant world are very social. They like to go to other restaurants and bars to relax after they're done working."

"But there's bad blood between Marshall Zanger and Ken Chow, who owns Plum Ink."

I was glad that Burns seemed in the mood to gossip. I decided to volunteer more, to encourage him. "Mr. Chow didn't seem exactly warm when he saw all of us hanging out in his restaurant's bar."

"Ken Chow was the loudest of the local business owners who cried foul to the zoning board when Marshall Zanger was getting a permit to open Bento. Something about the property not being zoned for any back-of-the-building parking. Zanger got the permit to allow parking, and he called the city health department to report health code violations at Plum Ink." He cleared his throat. "Allergies, sorry. So, getting back to your visit to Plum Ink. You were talking about your friends getting a few free bags of food from the kitchen. If it was left over from someone else's plate, that's a health-code violation."

Aunt Norie came in the room with an Imari teapot and two small tea bowls on a lacquered tray. In English, she announced, "I have made tea from the fresh cherry blossom leaves. I hope you can drink it."

"It's actually rehydrated, packaged cherry blossom tea," I added, mindful of the detective's talk of health violations. If he thought Norie had brought in a live agricultural product from Japan, we might be in trouble.

"Whatever it is, it smells as beautiful as it looks," Detective Burns said, watching my aunt pour. "Have you been to see the Japanese cherry trees on the Mall yet? They're starting to blossom."

"No, I haven't seen them. I am too busy taking care of my niece," Norie said. "So you are the detective?"

"I apologize for not introducing myself earlier. I'm Louis Burns, with the District's investigative unit."

"*Ah so desu ka*," Norie said, sounding unimpressed. "I have some questions for you, if you don't mind."

"Please. I'll answer what I can."

"This car went to Virginia, *neh*?" Norie said. "Have you questioned Mr. and Mrs. Norton?"

"Who?" Burns gave me an irritated look, as if I should have said something earlier.

"The Nortons are the father and stepmother of my friend Andrea from the restaurant," I said. "I mentioned to the Virginia police that we'd all gone down to Orange County to see them last week."

"There's no mention of anyone called Norton in the report we got from Virginia. Why exactly are you concerned about them?"

I weighed things. Andrea had tried to get the police to reopen her mother's case, but she'd been turned down. If I said something now, maybe things would take a turn for the better. "It's a long story," I said. "I think Andrea should be here to tell it."

"I'll get Miss Norton's story later. Tell me what you know."

So I did. At the end of it, Burns said, "That is interesting." I was beginning to think that this phrase was Burns's own version of the Japanese use-anywhere phrase "*Ah so desu ka*." "Is that so?" was the meaning of the phrase, but it really was a catch-all conversation filler.

"I guess there are a few possibilities," I said, thinking over all that we'd talked about. "The first is that both Kendall and I were taken by the same or similar types of men, for no reason other than that we were women who were easy marks."

Burns nodded. "That's the most obvious idea."

"On the other hand, you've said things that present a new theory about a restaurant war. In that scenario, Ken Chow would have sent thugs to take Kendall from the parking lot, and ordered the same crew to sweep me up later."

"But what about the Nortons?" Norie interrupted. "Andrea-san believes her mother was murdered. If Mr. Norton did that, maybe he is trying to stop Rei-chan from finding the truth. Please, you must investigate that man and his wife."

"I'll research whether this Norton guy has any old criminal charges," Burns said. "I can also see if he's willing to have a conversation with me. But I can't descend on his home without a warrant. And to obtain a warrant we need some kind of evidence that gives reasonable suspicion he's connected to a current crime. It doesn't sound as if the visit, as you describe it, turned up that kind of evidence. You asked for some old papers, and he cooperated fully."

"I haven't had time to thoroughly read through those papers yet," I said. "There might be something there—"

"But those papers are old. What could have been written thirty years ago that could be linked to what happened to you a few nights ago? Now, Miss Shimura, I have a question for you."

Both Norie and I looked at him, but from the direction of his gaze, it seemed clear the question was for me.

"What do you want to know?"

"Why you jumped."

I was disoriented by the attention. "Because I thought that if I didn't, they would open the trunk, take me out and"— I looked at my aunt, and decided to mince my words—"perhaps hurt me."

"Your cousin was left unharmed in the trunk. You didn't think of that?"

"My niece is brave. Very athletic," Norie said. "That's why she tried."

"I could tell from the way the car was being driven that we'd left the city. And there was rope in the trunk, which made me nervous," I added.

"Rope? You didn't mention that to the Virginia police."

"Didn't I? The details come and go. I'm sorry." I had felt it in my hand. A synthetic rope, stronger than straw.

"Rope doesn't sound good. You were smart to make your getaway," he said.

"Maybe you should look in all the people's cars for rope," Norie said. "The Chinese restaurant owner and Mr. Norton."

"I need a warrant to do that kind of search. We have no evidence, at present, to obtain a warrant." Burns was beginning to sound like a broken record.

"But what can we do, then?" Norie asked. Now that she was out of Japan, she was becoming so assertive. Her traditional manners were falling away from her just like the cherry blossom was expanding in my teacup.

She was blooming under the most adverse of circumstances.

I wished I could do as well.

21

I'd been consuming regular amounts of Aleve and irregular amounts of food, and that had taken a toll. My stomach ached steadily—enough to keep me from wanting to put anything in it, which exacerbated the situation. Norie explained this to me in between offering bowls of her famous gruel, a classic Japanese cure for the ill. Interestingly enough, the sludgy substance was tolerable. Ten days after I'd come home, the waistbands of all my jeans had become loose, but my slight reshaping didn't feel like any kind of victory.

For days, Andrea had been telephoning. She'd wanted to come to the apartment and see me, and for a long time I hadn't wanted to see her. I didn't blame her for what had happened, but I was wary. I sensed there had to be a link between the trip I'd made to Virginia with her and the kidnapping that followed a few days later. The men who'd taken me were still out and about. I could only imagine them following her to Hugh's apartment, the one place I felt was my refuge.

So to assuage Andrea, who was beginning to sound hurt, I agreed to meet her. On the first day that Hugh returned to work, Norie and I set off for Urban Grounds.

We went on foot, because it was just a few blocks away. Norie kept hold of my arm. I doubted a five-foot-one woman could stop anyone who intended to kidnap again, and I couldn't believe anything like that could happen during the day, when so many people were on the street. The weather had turned at last; it wasn't rainy anymore, and the tulips were finally opening. I'd encouraged my aunt to bring her camera to shoot some street scenes, but she'd said that would distract her from taking care of me.

Andrea smiled widely when she saw the two of us walk in. She'd taken the same table, way in the back, where I'd met her before. I waved at her and headed to the counter to order coffee, but she called out, "I got it for you already. Skinny latte, extra sugar. And for your aunt, I've got a pot of green tea."

"How very considerate," Norie murmured as we made our way to the back.

"I'm so glad you made it." Andrea's voice was almost shy.

"Oh, it's good for me to get out. I was starting to grow roots into the couch," I joked.

"No, I mean I'm glad you made it. Survived. If you had disappeared, I would—it would have been—"A hint of tears glittered at the edges of her gracefully made-up eyes.

"It *didn't* happen." I knew, all of a sudden, what she was thinking. The loss of her mother was being replayed in her mind.

"That detective called me." Andrea wiped her eyes. "You know, the one who came to the restaurant. Louis Burns. He wanted to talk about all kinds of things, like why I went to Plum Ink, and who I know there. He said he might be able to dig up the old police records relating to my mother's disappearance, if I helped him."

"He should be looking into those things whether you help him or not," I said, feeling my exasperation rise. "It should be part of the investigation about what happened to Kendall and me."

"I guess he thinks of me as an informant." Andrea paused. "Not that I told him a thing. But I'm wondering why he took an interest in my mother's disappearance?"

Before I could answer, Norie answered. "I said to him, Andrea-san, that maybe those strange people in Orange County were the ones who took Rei."

"'Those strange people.' You mean my dad and Lorraine?" Andrea asked.

"Yes, exactly," Norie said.

"They'll freak if Burns goes down there!" Andrea set down her coffee cup with a bang.

"I don't think he will harass them," I soothed her. "He already told me there's not the evidence to get a search warrant. Besides, he is pretty gung ho on his own theories of who's behind the abductions."

"Hmm. I wonder if that's why he asked me if I'd ever seen Ken Chow snooping around Bento, which of course I hadn't, though he's sent over staff a few times to check out the menu and prices."

"The detective should look inside Bento for a clue," Norie opined. "A few nights ago, I mentioned that I found something strange about Takeda-san. I have not told you, because your heart is so heavy. I did not want to add more trouble."

"What do you mean, Jiro's strange? If you think he has an eye for guys, you're mistaken," Andrea said. "In fact, I could tell you stories—"

"I have the story for you, I think. Jiro Takeda is not Japanese."

"What?" Andrea and I exclaimed in unison.

"I know you say he is iron chef, and maybe he appeared on *terebi*, but he is not *Nihonjin*. He speaks Japanese, but there is an accent. And he cannot cut a beautiful vegetable flower!"

"Obasan, his personal taste is just not geared to vegetable flowers. And there are regional accents in Japan. Remember that accent Chika picked up when she was in Kyoto?" I was struggling not to laugh.

"Who is Chika?" Andrea looked in confusion from me to Norie.

"Norie's daughter—my cousin who lives in Japan. My aunt's theory can't be right. Jiro is as Japanese as—as Norie herself," I added, because I'd been about to say "you and I," which wasn't much, given that Andrea and I were both classified as *hafu*.

"There is nothing bad about being foreign," Norie said. "I have a friend who is Korean. Very nice lady, good at flower arrangement."

"Where do you think Jiro comes from?" Andrea's expression remained doubtful.

"That I cannot say. Mainland China, Taiwan, Korea, somewhere like that. There are very smart people in these countries. And most Asians can learn Japanese easily."

"So the root of all the terror is an Asian chef who is closeted about his national origin. Let's tell Louis Burns." I made my sarcasm obvious.

"It actually is a big deal," Andrea said slowly. "If you look around this area, most Japanese restaurants are run by Koreans or Vietnamese. Japan-born chefs are expensive because they're so rare. Jiro added prestige to Marshall's operation. If he's exposed as not really Japanese, it's a blow to Bento."

If Jiro was a fraud, maybe Ken Chow knew it. Maybe the Plum Ink owner was blackmailing Jiro, or something like that. Kendall's and my kidnappings could have been connected to that blackmail, or some kind of revenge. I could barely keep my theories straight because both Norie and Andrea had more to say.

"Takeda-san is not the only problem in the kitchen. Some of the other cooks do not cook like professionals. The whole kitchen is strange," Norie said.

"I agree," Andrea said. "What about that new cook on the line who came in last week to replace the guy who called in sick?"

"Toro-san?" Norie asked.

"Yes, he's the one. He supposedly had all this experience at Jaleo, but he doesn't cook like he has. He fries everything on high, like it's a hamburger. When Jiro saw what he did to a piece of tuna last week, I assumed he was going to fire the fool. But all Toro got was his nickname, and Jiro shifted him to washing dishes."

Toro was the name of a super-high-quality cut of tuna, so now I understood the nickname. I wondered how much of him my aunt had seen. "What do you think about Toro, Obasan?"

"I did not have time to watch him closely. I was busy cooking." Norie sounded very pious.

"Norie, that dish you created, the *yosenabe*? People are coming in and asking for it because it was mentioned in the paper.

Marshall asked Jiro to put it on the menu permanently and, of course, he doesn't know your recipe, so he's in a jam."

"When did the newspaper review come out?" I asked.

"Last Sunday. It was—mixed," Andrea said. "I can't believe you didn't see it."

I'd been lost in self-pity on Hugh's calfskin sofa. "I'll have to dig it out of the recycling."

"I'd like to taste Takeda-san's *yosenabe*." Norie's expression was almost mischievous. "Let's see if he can prepare a Japanese dish without a cookbook."

Andrea and I exchanged a quick glance. I didn't want a failure in the kitchen, and I was sure that she didn't, either.

"Why don't you go along with Andrea to oversee Jiro's cooking?" I suggested.

"But I cannot leave your side—"

"Rei, you come, then," Andrea said. "Marshall's been waiting for you to wax the ladies'-room *tansu*. And I made copies of those letters of my mom's for you, Norie. It's all in my locker there."

"Rei cannot use hands to do any work," Norie protested again.

"Really?" Andrea eyed the splints on my fingers.

The doctor had told me not to do anything to cause stress to the fingers, but I found myself wanting to go. "They're healing pretty well. I can do some things. If I'm in pain, I'll stop."

The truth was, doing something more strenuous than reading or drinking tea might lift me out of my emotional slump, though I doubted that it would lessen the sensation that someone was watching me, from behind every corner.

I was greeted warmly when I entered the kitchen about an hour before the lunch service started. A crowd of cooks and waiters surrounded me in a giant football huddle, one that smelled of sweat and garlic and ginger. But I didn't mind.

"You go, girlfriend," said Justin, surprising me with a kiss on the mouth. I'd thought he loathed girls, especially me.

Alberto, the line cook who'd helped me before, asked me what I wanted to eat.

"Nothing right now," I said. "I have to check in with Marshall and also see to the *tansu* in the ladies' room. And my aunt has a recipe to share with Jiro—"

"Marshall and Jiro are together in the office right now, confabbing about the review," Justin said.

"I can't believe I missed it."

"Well, you've had a lot on your mind, honey," said Justin.

"I hear there was mention of the *yosenabe*. I hope my poor cooking did not embarrass this restaurant," Norie said, playing her Japanese manners to the hilt.

"That was the good part," said Phong, who had just come in. "Come over to the bar, Mrs. Shimura. I have a copy of it there."

I was curious about the article, but I wanted my aunt to have a chance to see the good review of her dish first. So Norie went off to the bar with Phong, and I set to work in the ladies' room with my container of wax and a few soft cloths. I'd put gloves over my bandaged hands, and while I wasn't as flexible in my movements as before, I could manage.

After thirty minutes' work, the *tansu* was drenched in wax. I needed to wait a while before rubbing it off, and it was high time, I knew, that I talked to Marshall. I wove my way through the restaurant to Marshall's small office. Through the window set in the door, I could see that Marshall was at his desk, facing Jiro and talking. The office was soundproof, so I couldn't hear what was being said, but Marshall's expression was serious. I felt a flurry of anxiety that didn't stop when Marshall caught sight of me and beckoned me in.

"You poor girl," he said, getting up and taking a few strides through his clutter to embrace me.

Jiro had risen, but didn't make a move to touch me. "Are you well enough to be here, Rei-san? You must take care."

His manners were so Japanese; he couldn't be anything else.

"Some of my fingers had small fractures, but they're healing well enough for me to have waxed the ladies'-room vanity. Sorry you had to wait so long for me to do it. I don't think you'll have water-damage problems for a while." I smiled at both of them.

"Have the cops caught up with the guys who, ah, took you?" Marshall asked.

"No, they haven't had luck, but they assure me they're working on it." I watched my boss, trying to figure out his motives. "Anyway, I'm just glad to be alive and finally out and about. How has business been over the last week?"

"Not great." Marshall's voice was flat.

"It looked pretty busy out there," I said.

"Not busy enough. I'm sure last Sunday's review has something to do with it."

"Everyone keeps talking about the review, and I'm embarrassed to say that I missed it."

Marshall picked up a newspaper from the top of his desk. "Do you want to read it?"

"Yes. I can take it out of here, if you like. I didn't mean to interrupt your meeting," I said.

"Please sit down. Jiro and I will carry on," Marshall said.

"Yes, please take your rest. We are talking about tonight's special, *yosenabe*." Jiro sounded unhappy. It probably felt like a slap to him, having to add a dish to the permanent menu that wasn't in his personal repertoire.

I sat down on the yellow love seat and began reading. The critic pointed out the true meaning of *kaiseki ryoori*, the classical Japanese cuisine term that Jiro and Marshall used to inaccurately label Bento's cuisine. Then he went on to complain about the Kobe beef filet's toughness and the grit in the mussels, though he praised a few dishes, like the salt-grilled red snapper and the *yosenabe* stew that he'd found "heady with complex aromas." But the review was about far more than food.

Despite the prettiness of the antique furniture in the place, the restaurant doesn't have the glamour that Mandala does. In lieu of airy chic, this restaurant appears overly fussy and Edwardian. It's not uncomfortable, but it's not a powerhouse like Mandala or Ten Penh.

"Oh my God," I said. "They hate the interior because it's not modern. Marshall, I'm so—so sorry."

"I asked you to use antique furniture," Marshall said heavily. "The customers tell me they like our china and the *bento* boxes. I just don't get it."

But I'd moved on to the last few damning lines of the review.

Adding to the restaurant's challenges is location. Too southeastern to be part of the hip scene in Penn Quarter and too foreign to belong to Chinatown proper, the restaurant lies in a zone that is bereft of reliable parking-valet service. The recent abduction of a female customer points up the neighborhood's edgy status. The good cooking's there, but it'll take a mountain of good karma to make this restaurant work.

I refolded the paper and said, "I can see why you're upset about this. I am, too."

"We'll survive," Marshall said.

"You said business was slow. What are tonight's dinner reservations like?" I asked. In the back of my mind, I was thinking. I was going to have to drum up business, call everyone I knew to come eat. I'd get Hugh to drag over his colleagues, Kendall to coax in the politicos . . .

"We're half-full, and if we get some walk-ins, we'll do okay. But I doubt it. Everyone's afraid to come to H Street now."

It was on the tip of my tongue to protest that people shouldn't be such chickens, but I recalled what had happened. I hadn't even been near H Street, but in a supposedly much better area. No place was safe.

22

Norie was tired after our venture to Bento, which meant that she wanted to nap rather than start reading Andrea's mother's letters. I didn't push her, just took the letters into the room I shared with Hugh and began to puzzle through them myself. Some words I caught—more than I'd expected. My *kanji* studies on the Internet had paid off. Still, I couldn't possibly put pen to paper and start a translation.

While Norie was lying down, a phone call came from the Naganos. They were planning to fry tempura for dinner and wondered if Norie, Hugh, and I would like to join them. Tempura! It had been ages since I'd had the lightly batter-fried vegetables that were so delicious when homemade. I imagined myself biting into a tender slice of *kabocha* squash, or a sweet onion. I had wanted to stay home and read the letters, but this would be a nice thing to do first.

"How kind of you," I said happily. "Hugh's working too late to join us, but Norie and I are free. What can we bring?"

Betty Nagano demurred a million times, but by careful questioning, I deduced that she hadn't planned dessert. I volunteered to bring some green tea ice cream. I would stop by the Japanese store in Rockville to get it, before we went over. My aunt slept on, so I nudged her awake at five.

"How kind," she said when she learned of the invitation. "It is so generous of them, I must bring a gift."

I explained that Betty thought that green tea ice cream was fine, but Norie didn't think it was enough, so I had to agree to let her buy *manju*, sweet-bean-paste cakes, at the Japanese grocery in Rockville. We were stuck in traffic all the way from Rockville to Bethesda, and the ice cream was somewhat melted when we arrived, so I was very glad that we had the *manju* as well. Betty put the ice cream in the freezer, and Yuji was pouring everyone tall glasses of Kirin when a beeping noise started.

"Someone's cell phone?" I asked.

"We don't have one," Yuji said. "It's coming from your handbag."

I looked at my bag in shock, remembering at last the cell phone. Hugh had been adamant that I carry it everywhere, but I still wasn't used to it. By the time I dug the phone out, the call had been forwarded to voice mail, so I had to awkwardly click my way into the messages to find out who had called.

It was Andrea phoning from the restaurant to say that she'd just heard from a neighbor that her apartment had been broken into. She'd already called the police, but she needed someone to be around when they arrived. Could I be there?

"What is it, Rei-chan? Andrea-san does not sound happy," Norie said, standing behind me.

"I'm not sure I understand it all, but she needs help. I'll call her at the restaurant first." I was already dialing Bento.

"Good evening, this is Bento. How may I help you?" The accent was almost English, but clearly put on. I recognized Justin.

"Justin, it's Rei. May I speak with Andrea?"

"*Ach, nein.*" Justin had switched to a phony German accent. "It's verboten for staff to use this line—"

"I've seen a phone in the kitchen. Can't you put me through on that line? Justin, this is a real emergency."

"Oh, you mean Andrea's break-in? She's been moaning about

that ever since her neighbor called, but Marshall really can't let her go, as we're short-staffed again."

So Andrea really needed my help. But I didn't like the idea of going somewhere I didn't know, in twilight. "Where exactly does Andrea live?"

"Somewhere off Fourteenth Street, near Logan Circle. One of those blocks in transition," Justin added archly.

"Let me talk to Andrea," I insisted.

"Enter at your own risk," Justin said in his natural snippy tone as he put me on hold. After five long minutes, the phone finally rang through to the kitchen. Alberto picked up and handed me straight over to Andrea.

"Thanks for calling," she said in a low voice. "Lucy, my neighbor, called me just about an hour ago. I need someone to be there to talk to the police."

"Wouldn't Lucy be a better person to talk to the cops? I mean, she would have noticed more things, and she's on-site—"

"She's not there anymore. Lucy's not the kind who gets along with the police. After they left—and she didn't get a look at them because she was hiding in her own bathroom while it was happening—she split. That's another reason I need you there. Lucy said that my apartment door lock was ripped out. That means now anyone could go in and take stuff. I need you to take my mother's papers over to your place for safekeeping."

"But we already have the letters—"

"I know. I'm grateful for that. But the box has lots of pictures and files and records—all I have of her. Please, Rei."

"Andrea, I'd like to help you with the police, too. But I'm in Bethesda right now, actually about to have dinner with some people—"

"Never mind, then," Andrea said bleakly.

"Is there anyone else you could call?"

"It's the dinner hour. Everyone in the world I could ask is working, except you. Look, I understand. It was a crazy idea—"

But the papers meant so much. They were Andrea's only tie to the memory of her mother.

"I'll see if I can get someone to go with me," I said.

Before I'd finished what I wanted to say, Andrea had blurted out an address on P Street and hung up. Maybe she was under scrutiny in the kitchen, and had to end the call.

As I clicked my phone closed, I noticed that the Naganos and Norie were staring at me.

"It's Andrea," I said. "Someone broke into her apartment. The police are on their way, and she was hoping that I could go there to meet them. I don't mean to upset dinner like this—"

"But it's an emergency," Betty said. "Of course."

"I'm going to call Hugh, to see if he can leave his office and meet me. It's almost seven already—he shouldn't be working this late." As I spoke, I was dialing. The phone in his office rang into voice mail, so I left a message and tried his cell number. Again, nothing. He wasn't at the apartment either.

"I'll go with you," Norie said.

"I don't feel comfortable putting you at risk. Besides, this is a special dinner! Tempura can't wait," I reminded her. It would get soggy and awful.

"We shall all go," Yuji Nagano said firmly. "I will lead with Betty, and the two of you can follow."

"It's too much of an imposition—" Norie and I both cried this out in unison. Then we all laughed. We were being so Japanese.

In the end, we went in both cars, me following Yuji because it turned out that he had GPS in his Lexus sedan, and because I thought it mattered to him to lead. We drove in on Sixteenth Street, which was blissfully free of cars due to the hour. Yuji Nagano found a spot right in front of Andrea's apartment, but he motioned that I should take it. He turned around and parked a half block south, which made me nervous; I'd noticed a run-down building nearby that I suspected was a shooting gallery because of some hollow-looking people coming from it. Justin's words about the neighborhood being in transition didn't seem so snobbish anymore. I'd been rash to come here, especially with three older people.

I got out of the Lexus, stepping carefully around the car to help Norie out.

"What's that?" she asked. I followed her gaze to a syringe lying next to the curb.

"A syringe. Don't touch it," I added.

"Could a doctor's office be nearby?" Norie looked around with a frown.

"I don't think so, but Andrea's building is right there." I pointed to a narrow row house of about the same vintage as Hugh's place in Adams-Morgan. The building, like others on the street, had lots of charming architectural flourishes—a witch-hat roof, curly plaster moldings over the windows, and a bay window. But unlike most of the houses, which had small, fancy gardens filled with flowers and unusual shrubs, Andrea's building had peeling paint and a front yard full of weeds. The Naganos joined us, and we all moved forward to the building's vestibule. A panel of names and buzzers by the door informed me that Andrea's apartment was on the second floor. There was a door separating the buzzers from the staircase, but the lock was broken. Andrea's door, on the second floor, hung open as well.

I reminded everyone not to touch anything as we walked inside. I used Norie's clean handkerchief over my hand to flip on a light switch, to no avail. In the last bit of sunset coming through the windows, I could see that the place had been thoroughly tossed. Drawers hung open, furniture was overturned, and cushions were strewn everywhere.

The first thing I made sure of was that there was nobody still in the apartment. Walking through each room, I looked behind doors and under furniture. The Naganos and Norie clustered by the door. It was too dark for them; they were worried about bumping into things. I urged them to go back to Hugh's car to wait. They could signal to the police, I convinced them, and also keep an eye out for me, in case anyone suspicious headed toward the building. I gave them my cell phone number and showed them that I was keeping the phone in my hand, turned on and at the ready, for word from them.

As careful as I was trying to be, I still hadn't wanted them to hang at my side while I looked around. I felt terrible for Andrea, whose place had been ruined. It was obvious that she had really cared for it. Her windows were draped with tasteful sheers, the walls were hung with old, framed fashion photographs, and the few pieces of furniture were all special and vintage-looking, including a dramatic red velvet sofa with an art deco shape. She wouldn't want the Naganos to see the ruined, semi-shabby life of the daughter of a Japanese woman they'd once known.

I'd been so caught up in the atmosphere of Andrea's apartment that I didn't immediately look for the papers. But now I reminded myself that it was a priority. Andrea had told me that it was in her bedroom closet. I went back to the closet and opened the door. In it, I found dozens of skirts and dresses and blouses, neatly hung by color. And beneath it all was a jumble of high-heeled shoes, but nothing more.

23

I checked the other closet, just to make sure that I hadn't misunderstood. But there was no box there, either. So the reason for her burglary was clear.

I heard the sound of a car stopping and looked out the window. A police cruiser had pulled up, and the Naganos and Norie were standing next to it. Norie pointed to the building, and the police officer started toward it. He was a baby-faced blond, the kind of guy who looked young enough to be the perfect decoy for a liquor-buying sting. By the time he got to the top of the stairs, I'd come to the door to meet him. He squinted in the dark at me as I introduced myself as a friend of Andrea who, since Andrea herself was at work, was there to assist with the police report.

"I need to speak to the complainant," he said flatly. "When's she coming back?"

"Not until after midnight," I guessed. "But she told me she left the place at noon today, locked, and her neighbor heard somebody here around six o'clock tonight."

"And when did this neighbor call the police?"

"She didn't. She called Andrea instead, who called 911 directly."

"I see. Any reason that you're sitting in the dark?"

"None of the lights work."

"Probably had her power cut off for nonpayment," the cop said.

"I'm sure the power must be out for some other reason. Maybe the lights were cut by the guys who came in."

"Only in made-for-TV-movies." He snorted.

I ignored his cynicism. "I have a pretty good idea of what was taken, based on what my friend told me to look for. It's not an ordinary burglary, but one relating to information theft."

"Computer hard drive?"

"No, some personal papers," I said. "Andrea and I went on a trip together, you see, and we were given these papers by some people who, well, might have regretted giving them. My guess is that they came to grab them back."

"Papers, you say. Any idea of the estimated value?"

"There's no dollar amount on them. It's just that the papers are of great personal value."

"Have you looked at them?"

I shook my head.

"Well, then how do you know they're valuable?" The cop appeared pleased with his deductive skills.

"I don't know exactly. I just wish you'd forward this report on to Detective Louis Burns."

"He's not in this division," he said. "When your friend comes back, tell her to call and we'll come out and write the report. In the meantime, she should get someone out to change the locks. Bunch of freaks live around here. They'll be here in no time for that TV."

What Andrea would worry about, I thought, was not a TV, but her clothes. What I'd seen in the closets was definitely worth stealing. When the cop departed, I used my cell phone to call the restaurant again, asking for Andrea.

"She's gone," Alberto told me after I'd been patched back by an insolent Justin to the kitchen.

"What?"

"She was so upset, she was dropping things. Marshall gave her the rest of the night off. She left about twenty minutes ago. I think she went back to the apartment, you know, to pick up things. Hey, your boyfriend called here, too, which really made, you know, Marshall crazy. We gotta stay off the line if it's personal business."

"Just tell me how Andrea's getting home." The sun had set at seven-thirty, around the time we'd left Bethesda. By now it was solidly dark.

"By the Metro. She takes that all the time."

"Alberto, do you know if Andrea has a cell phone?"

"I think so," Alberto said. "Doesn't everyone?"

"Do you know the number?"

"No, I'm sorry. Marshall would have that on file in his office, but I don't wanna disturb him because of a phone call—like I said, it's not good to talk on the phone."

"Thanks anyway. I'm sure she'll be here soon." I hung up feeling uneasy. Andrea would almost certainly be coming from the Howard University Metro stop because that was technically the closest stop on the Green Line—but it was a dicey walk at night. In fact, it made my solo walk from Dupont Circle to Adams-Morgan look as safe as a stroll through a shopping mall.

I heard voices downstairs, and stepped out into the hall.

"Rei-chan?" my aunt called in Japanese. "What are you still doing upstairs? Come downstairs and we'll go back to your kind friends' home for dinner."

"Please, you go ahead," I urged. "I heard Andrea will be arriving shortly, and I want to help her move her clothes or any other valuables that are left."

"I don't want to leave you here."

"It's perfectly safe. And please, I don't want to put the Naganos through any more trouble. I'll be over there within an hour or two to take you home."

"You'll miss the tempura."

"It's okay. I'll walk you to the car." I went with the three of them, apologizing profusely for the inconvenience I'd caused. Nothing seemed to be going on at the shooting gallery, I noticed with a great deal of relief. But as their car sped away, I hurried back to the apartment, not wanting to take any more risks than were needed.

I made it up the stairs to the apartment, but just as I was about to step inside, I felt a presence.

By now, I'd learned to trust my instincts. Someone must have entered when I was outside. Now I was stuck, because the cell phone was halfway across the living room, over by the window where I'd used the last bit of light to look through my address book for the Bento phone number. All I could do was leave. I started to tiptoe back down the stairs.

"Who's there?" a cold male voice asked—a voice that I recognized in a flood of exasperation and relief.

"Hugh!" I said, hurrying back up the stairs and through the apartment door. He was all the way over by the living-room bay window. "You scared me to death."

"You're scared?" He grabbed me tightly by the arms. "You—idiot! How could you come out here by yourself at night?"

"I didn't come alone. I came with my aunt and the Naganos. Actually, I was just out sending them away, because the police had come and now I'm just waiting for Andrea—"

"When I finished swimming and checked my phone for messages, I couldn't believe what I heard you'd done," Hugh said. "I don't think I've ever been as angry in my life."

"That's got to be an exaggeration," I said. "As I just told you, I didn't come alone—"

"But you sent them away! What kind of reckoning went into that situation?"

"Settle down, Hugh. Everything's all right," I said tightly. I wished he'd never come.

"For you maybe, but not for me. Let's go!" He put his arm around me, and started down the stairs.

I balked. "Don't manhandle me."

Hugh let go. "I'm sorry. But don't you feel—urgent—in an environment like this?"

"The theft has already happened," I said. "Whoever came in took what remained of Andrea's mother's papers. Now I'm waiting to meet her, because she's going to be devastated."

"Meet her? How can you, in the dark? Rei, you've got to walk away from this girl and her problems. You've already lost our baby and I'm not going to stand by and lose you, too."

"You do blame me for the baby," I said, feeling an inward chill. "I knew you did."

"I—I don't blame you," Hugh said in an unconvincing tone of voice. "But if you love me, you'll listen for once. I want you to step back, to get out of this before something terrible happens again."

I thought back on the past three years, the ones I'd spent with Hugh and also without him. We had survived misunderstandings and arguments galore, but he had never ordered me to do something.

I said, "No. I won't stop helping her."

Hugh was silent for a minute. When he spoke, his tone was frigid. "If you'd rather put her ahead of me, that's your choice. But this is it for me. I will not marry someone bent on self-destruction."

"What are you saying?" I was horrified.

"I'm saying that I'm leaving! Give me the car keys, okay? I had to take a taxi over here and it wouldn't wait around."

"If this is the end, you'll want more than the keys." I yanked the engagement ring off my finger and shoved it toward him. Of course, being dark, he didn't see it and it bounced off him and onto the floor. I made a disgusted sound.

"What now?"

"I dropped the engagement ring. Don't worry, I'll find it. I can turn on the light on my watch." I did that, and moved the tiny circle of light across the floor, looking to no avail.

"You can't even give back a ring like a normal person would do." Hugh sounded bitter.

"Well, you always said that I was not like the others."

We were quiet then. There was nothing left to say.

24

Our strained silence was finally broken by the sound of footsteps on the stairs, footsteps that were lighter than a man's.

"Hello?" Andrea called out as she entered the apartment.

"It's me," I answered swiftly. "Hugh showed up, too, but he's not staying long. Andrea, I'm so sorry. Whoever broke in took the box."

"I was afraid of that," Andrea said. "So it's all gone? The pictures and the papers?"

"Not the letters," I reminded her. "You still have her words. I'm sorry I haven't chained my aunt down to do the translation yet, but I promise you I will later tonight."

"If you hadn't picked them up at the restaurant today, I don't know what would have happened," Andrea said. "Someone went through a few people's lockers there tonight. My wallet was taken. I had to borrow money from Alberto to take the Metro home."

"It sounds as if someone's quite interested in you," Hugh said.

I was thinking the same—and also, that when I'd talked to Alberto half an hour ago, he hadn't mentioned the locker theft at all. Was it because he didn't have time to talk, or was it because the thefts weren't something that he was upset about?

"I'm too shaken up to stay here tonight," Andrea said.

"I understand that. I think you should just take anything that's really important to you, and we'll find you somewhere to sleep." I stopped myself, realizing that I couldn't volunteer Hugh's apartment. Maybe she could go to the Naganos, but I'd have to check with them first.

"David from the restaurant already gave me his key. But he lives on Capitol Hill—"

"Splendid. We'll drive you." Hugh made a move toward the door.

"Actually, I was hoping to take most of my clothes with me."

"I'd be glad to carry them out," Hugh said, not sounding glad at all. "The problem is that I can't see a damn thing in here."

"I've got two flashlights in the kitchen. Just wait." Andrea moved off.

"Did the lights go out before today?" I called after her.

"Yep. The electric company turned them off last week. When I pay off the bill, I'll get them back, but it's been tight, now that my wages are lower."

Andrea came back holding two turned-on flashlights in her hands. I aimed the one she handed me at the floor so I could find Hugh's ring. Its emerald sparkled like green fire in the tiny spotlight. I picked it up and handed it back to Hugh, who stuffed it in the breast pocket of his suit, and then started hauling clothes.

By the time we were all in the car, it was clear to Andrea that there was serious tension between Hugh and me. She did most of the talking on the way to David's apartment on Capitol Hill. She told us that she'd spoken to her landlord about the broken locks, and he had said the locksmith would come the next day. But David didn't mind if she stayed awhile. He was worth a roll between the sheets, every now and then. I saw Hugh stiffen at this comment; he wasn't used to girls talking like that. But he didn't know the restaurant world. I made a big point of laughing uproariously at what Andrea had said. For a few minutes, it took my mind off the fear.

Andrea handled the key in David's front-door lock as if she'd used it before. Then we hustled the clothing into the first-floor apartment of a narrow row house. Andrea waved us away, telling us she could hang things up by herself.

Finally we were done and back in the car. Hugh made a move toward the driver's seat, but I stopped him.

"Why don't I drive, because I can drop you off at home before I go out to Bethesda to bring my aunt home?" I suggested.

He looked at me for a long moment. "I'm not going home."

"Why's that?" I asked.

"I've too much bloody work to do! I need to go back to finish some writing."

"But that's crazy! It's eight-thirty now."

"I've been away from the office for seven days, taking care of you. Now I realize there are other people who need tending."

I wasn't going to ask him how he planned to get home. Another taxi, probably. He could call one to pick him up from his ivory tower when he was good and ready.

I turned on the radio to cover up the silence as we headed back downtown to K Street. He got out of the car on K Street without saying good-bye, and I didn't wait to see if he got into the law firm's steel-and-glass tower. I flipped through the CDs in the changer to find the artist I really wanted to listen to: Rachael Yamagata. Just like the woman in her song, I was worn down like a road—an extremely bumpy and patched one. But the irony was that I was behind the wheel of my lover's car, and still had a place in his bed. This was going to be a complicated break.

Norie, as I'd expected, was distraught when I finally arrived in Bethesda. I picked at the plate of tempura they'd left in the oven for me as I described how Hugh and I had moved Andrea and her valuables to the home of a restaurant friend.

"Where does this friend live?" Yuji Nagano asked. I started to answer, but then stopped myself. Outside of Norie and me, and the Norton family in Virginia, the Naganos were the only ones who'd known about the existence of Sadako's letters. I'd thought they'd been trying to help me with their stories about her—but what if they hadn't? What if something had happened between the Naganos and Sadako that they needed to keep secret?

"He lives in the city," I said slowly. Sadako had been a sad, lonely, and beautiful young woman. It was Yuji Nagano who'd known she was a diver—she had told him things she hadn't told the women in the group. Could he have loved her? And could there have been complications, a threat to his own marriage?

"He? Akiko is staying with a man?" Yuji Nagano sounded worried.

"We also stay with a man: Rei-chan's fiancé, Hugh," Norie interjected. "It's best to have protection in a city like Washington. A woman should not stay alone."

I was amused by my aunt's quick display of old-fashioned logic to throw off Yuji Nagano, but she wasn't going to let me off easily. After we made it into Hugh's apartment and I started to make a pot of tea for the two of us, she pointed to my hand.

"Where is your engagement ring?"

"I returned it." I couldn't meet her gaze, because I felt tears starting at the edges of my eyes. As angry as I'd been, I would never have broken up with him. I wouldn't have given up, the way he had.

"What are you saying?" Norie's voice broke. "I'm here to help with your wedding!"

"We're not getting married after all. And let's talk about something else, please." I held up the packet of letters. "I tried to start this, but I'm hopeless at it. Do you have enough energy to help me with it tonight?"

"Rei-chan, I think it's more important that I help with your marriage!"

I shook my head. "Let's not think about it. Please. These letters are all Andrea has left."

Norie settled down on the couch with the letters. I brought over two cups of green tea and some *sembei* crackers and sat, with a pen and paper, cross-legged on a *zabuton* on the floor. I was all ready to transcribe.

Sadako's early letters were written to her sister long before the wedding. Robert Norton had been sent on temporary duty to a U.S. Marine base in California. The letters describing how Sadako flew by plane for the first time, and then moved into a small apartment off base, were filled with a mixture of sadness about the break from her family, but also wonder at what lay before her.

A letter from the plane said:

> *Robert tells me that it will not be too difficult to find a judge. Here, weddings can occur in many places. Churches and hotels, of course, but also office buildings, even outside in gardens. It is so dry here, though, that I do not think a garden would be a nice place. Robert asked me my dream, and I said it was to marry beside the sea. I explained to him that if we were beside the sea, I could think of you on the other side, with nothing between us but the water.*

The next letter talked about the wedding itself.

> *We had many guests, American and Japanese. Omura Reiko-san and Kiyoshi Junko-san, those friends from Tokyo I told you about, are now called Mrs. Jones and Mrs. Wilder. They wore their best kimono to the wedding. You would have liked Jones-san's kimono. It was a silk crepe patterned with lily flowers. Wilder-san's was a crepe with a design of orange and gold roses. As for mine, it was a deep-red-and-orange silk brocade with a pattern of ducks embroidered on it in gold thread. Unfortunately the weather was cold, and I fear the ladies were as chilled as I. Another surprise was to see some guests who were not invited, two men who served with Robert in Vietnam. At our wedding party, they talked to him for such a long time that when he returned to the festivities, he did not seem to be enjoying himself. I asked Robert if he had invited them, and he said he hadn't. Maybe it is an American custom, to visit weddings without an invitation. If so, it is a custom I do not care for. Despite the surprises, the wedding was joyful. After*

the ceremony we had a tall cake with many layers, all white, decorated with
sugar roses.

There was a letter about married life.

> *Dear Atsuko,*
>
> *I am trying hard to be the kind of wife Mother taught us to be, but it is a*
> *challenge. Robert is eager to eat handmade American food, but I have trou-*
> *ble making it correctly. They have a leafy green vegetable here similar to*
> *horenso that they simply call green. It is a green color, but a more bitter*
> *taste. Since Americans have a sweet tooth, I could not imagine that this*
> *could be considered delicious alone. To improve the taste I added sweet*
> *mirin syrup. Robert noticed right away and instructed me that the correct*
> *flavoring to add is a piece of pork, preferably from the pig's bottom. I was*
> *embarrassed because there were some people who had come to our house to*
> *eat, people from his hometown. There is a woman who I think would like to*
> *have him. She follows him with her eyes, and she talks loudly about their*
> *happy times in high school. She said very little to me except for hello and*
> *good-bye and how different the greens tasted.*
>
> *I am determined to cook correctly. Wilder-san says that I should buy*
> *this green already cooked in a can. I will do that next time. Sometimes I*
> *think Robert is so particular about cooking that he would like to cook him-*
> *self! I am not complaining, of course, but it certainly is a surprise.*

Norie read on in Japanese, the intentness of her voice showing to
me that she was as fascinated as I. Sadako's letters were haunting,
because even though they were written to her sister, it was clearly a
one-way conversation: a monologue, stories told to which there was
never a response. All the letters had been returned, unopened, to
America, yet Sadako had resolutely written on.

> *Dear Atsuko,*
>
> *You will be the first to know that I am going to have a baby. I can imag-*
> *ine how Mother and Father will feel about it, so please don't tell them.*
> *Robert and I are very pleased, though it will mean a lot of hard work. We*
> *have finally been offered a house on base, which is a good thing, because it*

will save us money. Unfortunately, I'm not as strong to pack and move things. I don't have a friend who can help me organize now that Wilder-san has been transferred to Kansas and Jones-san went back to Japan. You may recall me telling you that the marriage did not succeed with Mr. Jones. It was a big shame because she tried very hard to be a good wife. Robert says that he will ask some of his friends to help us move house. I hope they are friends who will speak politely. Some of the ones I've met say they can't remember my name, so they call me Mama-san and laugh. It's disrespect- ful, I told Robert. He told them to call me Sadie. I don't like that either. We agreed that if we have a boy, he will name the child, and if we have a girl, I will name her. I can promise you she will have a good Japanese name, and I will make sure people know how to say it.

After Norie read that particular letter, I tried to blink back the tears, but I couldn't.

"What is it, Rei-chan?"

"It's just—" I couldn't tell her that the mention of the baby's name made me think of my own lost, nameless child. "Will you read some more?"

There were letters about the pregnancy and about the decision in the end not to move on base. There were letters about the birth and the first few months, brief windows into the intimate world of a mother and baby.

Akiko sleeps well during the night, waking me only three or four times for milk. She falls back to sleep close to my heart. Her hair is becoming curly, like Robert's; I love to tangle my fingers in it. I think her nose is quite like yours, Atsuko, and her eyes, everyone says, resemble mine. She can hold my glance for a very long time now, and I think she is beginning to smile.

Sadako told her sister that while she always called Andrea by the name Akiko, Robert insisted that Andrea was the name on the birth certificate. Comments like these showed that the strains between husband and wife were growing. Sadako's letters began to shift from adoration of the baby to complaints about her own fatigue, and about Robert's increasing absence from the home. There was also a letter mentioning the return of the men who'd crashed their wedding party.

I have asked my husband their names, but he said I wouldn't be able to pronounce them. I think I could. My English is poor, but not so poor that I can't learn a name. There are two of them, one black and the other white. They came to my door one afternoon, just after Akiko had fallen asleep. They wanted to wait for my husband to come home from work. I told them they could not wait inside since the baby was napping in the living room.

They came in, though. They pushed right past me and sat down. They had come before; I had not told you much about it, but every time they've come, I've been frightened. There's something between them and Robert. He won't tell me what it is. Usually, they have ignored me, but that day, it was not the case.

One of them noticed me glance at our telephone and laughed in an unkind way. It was as if he was warning me not to call anyone. The other man went over to Akiko's crib and moved her blanket. I had been frozen in place, but that action made me move. I went to the crib and told them not to touch her, to get away. The man who had been standing over Akiko hit me so hard that I could not see anything for a minute. When I could move again, I grabbed up Akiko and ran into the bathroom and locked the door. It is a small lock on the door, and I am sure they could have broken it easily. They did not try that, but they did not leave. When Robert came home and asked where we were, they laughed. Robert convinced them to leave the apartment with him, to go to the bar on the corner. After they all had gone, I unlocked the door and came out.

They had gone through everything, Atsuko. Opened every chest and closet and moved things all around. I realized that they had come intending to do this to the apartment. It didn't matter if I was there or not. And surely, Robert had seen what they'd done, and they knew he, too, would be too frightened to report it.

From my window I can see water. Remember how we used to swim together? Diving deep, reaching in the secret places to find the oysters with treasure inside. I was not afraid of the water then. I would rather have played there than gone to school.

But this ocean, the Atlantic, frightens me. It tempts me, but I resist. Anyway, I know that you are not on the other side.

There was one more letter.

Dear Atsuko,

I hope that you are well. As you know, things are becoming more diffi-cult. I am looking for the answer to how I shall continue. It is clearly too dangerous here. I spoke to Robert about all of us leaving for some other place, but he said that would be against the law—he must stay and finish his duty. I told him then that he must report the men, but he said that it would be worse for all of us if he did that.

I have thought of simply traveling home to Japan, but I cannot obtain a passport for Akiko without my husband's signature. I know he won't let her go, no matter how tiring he finds having a child. I think, too, that since you have not written back to me, it would be best for me to stay away. You are on my side, I know, but it would ruin your prospects if your elder sister appeared again with a half-American baby and no husband. I don't know if three years is enough time for everyone to forget about me, but I hope that is the case.

Three years since the wedding. It seems like it happened last month. I think about it, that day so full of hope. But even then, there were signs. Before the ceremony, the judge said he wanted to meet with me alone. During my meet-ing he said to me that I could change my mind if I wanted to, that there might be a way for me to stay in America without having to marry. I realized then that he thought I was marrying Robert because I wanted America, not the man. I replied that I was fine, that I wanted to marry. I thought he looked very serious, maybe displeased with me. Afterward, Robert told me that until recently it was against the law for black and white people to marry. I'm not white, I said to Robert. In the eyes of the law, he said, you are not black, and that is all that counts. But it's not true, of course. I have lost my strength here. I still cannot speak English well. I still cannot drive. My world is this apart-ment. This child. And now, these men.

I asked Robert about the men, and at last he told me the truth about why they come. He cried afterward and said that he thought I would hate him. No, I told him, I could not hate you. You did what you were told to do. After our talk, he slept well—better than he'd slept since Akiko was born. But I could not sleep. Now that I know the situation, I finally understand that the danger will always be around us.

I would like to eat fugu, but I want to live. The next time I write to you, I hope that I will be able to say that I've made the right choice.

The last few lines disturbed me. Why was she thinking about eating blowfish, which had a toxin inside its pancreas so deadly that even a trace amount could kill? Was the danger she talked about so overwhelming she was considering suicide by eating blowfish?

"I don't understand why she was talking about *fugu* like that," I said. "I'm sure there was no blowfish available in American restaurants in the seventies. I can't think of a place where it's available now, even Bento. Jiro told me he doesn't have any supplier who can bring the restaurant really fresh blowfish, and he doesn't trust any of the cooks to prepare it safely."

"'I would like to eat *fugu*, but I want to live' is a proverb, actually," Norie began.

"I should have known." I looked at the proverb queen.

"Yes, Rei-chan. It is something people say when they have trouble making a decision. Is it worth it to eat blowfish, which is so delicious—or not to eat the fish and know that you have avoided risking death?"

"'Should I stay or should I go.'" Just like the words to the famous Clash song that Hugh loved. "Look at the postmark on the envelope."

Norie took it in her hands. "June tenth, 1976. Is that a significant date?"

"No, it's October sixth," I corrected her. Japanese and Americans wrote out dates differently. "She disappeared on October tenth," I said. "This might have been the last letter."

The last letter. And in my mind, it seemed clear that she felt under threat, and was searching about for an escape plan, but one that was supposed to include Andrea.

25

Even after Norie and I put the letters away and went to bed, I spent most of the night trying to think the way I imagined Sadako had, all those years ago, as she looked for a place to go. Would she have hidden out nearby? No, I decided. She wanted to put as much distance as possible between her and the men she feared. She couldn't return to Japan, as did other friends whose marriages had dissolved, because she had her daughter and no passport for her. Kansas, where one of her friends had gone, was a possibility. But if she couldn't return to Japan because she didn't want to abandon her daughter, why would she go to another place in America without her?

It seemed as if morning would never come, but eventually, I must have fallen asleep because I woke to find Hugh, lying like a fallen redwood, on the far side of the bed. He must have come in after three o'clock, when I'd finally turned in. Now everything that had happened came back: his ultimatum, and my refusal to submit. I cast one last look at him and got out of bed.

I would start looking for my own living space, maybe a place like Andrea had. I was no stranger to shabby neighborhoods. The difference was, in Japan you could find inexpensive neighborhoods that weren't full of drugs. If I stayed in any major American city, I'd have to coexist with drug users, find a way to live with them in peace. But I'd never be able to have my parents visit, let alone Aunt Norie.

I turned the shower on high, trying to pound away the revulsion I felt. Before I found a place, I needed money. I'd submitted my bills to Marshall, but had not gotten any payment yet. He'd said something about money becoming available after the restaurant had opened. I hadn't pressed him, but now I realized that I had to do that, just as Andrea would have to press Detective Burns about the theft of Sadako's papers.

I was anxious to talk to Andrea about what I'd learned from Sadako's letters. I had written down David's telephone number the night before, but nobody picked up when I dialed it. Maybe they'd gone out for breakfast, or she was over at her apartment, waiting for the police.

After breakfast, I worked on making a more clear-sounding English translation of the letters, searching for any meaning that I might have missed. The marriage was unhappy, but there was nothing spelled out about Robert Norton being a violent man. It sounded as if the men from his past were the suspicious ones. Maybe they were in a gang that Robert had tried to get out of, or they were blackmailing him. Sadako could have been killed as a warning to him not to get out of line again. If that was the case, he might not report it to the police, out of fear for himself and his baby.

I also wondered about the abrupt end to the letters. I had her sister's name and address. Maybe there were no more letters because she had returned, not because she'd died or moved.

I knew now that we had to find Atsuko, the sister she had written to thirty years earlier. The letters had all been returned from the address in a village called Okita. I wondered if it was on one of the small islands that surrounded Kyūshū. I couldn't find it on a map of the main island.

I was just starting a Google search for it when the telephone trilled. I jumped. I picked it up, hoping for Andrea, but heard Kendall's voice instead.

"I hear you're out and about again, honey. Good for you!"

"You must have heard that I was at the restaurant yesterday," I said.

"Actually, Win saw you walking on P Street with your arms full of clothes. Did you find a good dry cleaner in that area, someone I should know about?"

"Hardly. What was Win doing there?" If Win had been driving by when Hugh, Andrea, and I had been bent under the weight of her formidable wardrobe, why hadn't he pulled over to offer some help—or at least say hello?

"Oh, I'm sure he was checking out some real estate. That area is so up-and-coming it's unbelievable."

"I was helping my friend Andrea."

"Who?"

"She used to be the hostess at Bento, but right now she's working in the kitchen." I was surprised by my vagueness. I was becoming protective of Andrea.

"If she's the bitch who didn't want to give my kids high chairs, I think you've got lousy taste. What does Hugh think of your new friend?"

"It doesn't matter what he thinks."

"Oops. Sorry, honey. Do you have time to get together for lunch today?"

"Could we do it tomorrow? I have to stop in at the restaurant today—"

"If you have to be at the restaurant, why don't I meet you there? You've probably heard that Marshall and I have settled our differences and I'm on a mission to try out the whole menu before the Snowden dinner."

"Bento is a little bit rich for my taste right now," I said.

"Don't you have a discount on meals there?"

"Yes, but I haven't even been paid for my services yet, so I'm feeling rather poor," I said.

"Actually, I'm feeling broke, too. What should we do, get a hot dog from a cart? Remember how we always wanted to get them when we were kids, but Grand said no because it was low class to eat on the street? But the times we got them, when she didn't know, they were so good."

I smiled at the memory of those foot-long hot dogs eaten at Baltimore's Inner Harbor back in my preadolescent, prevegetarian days.

"What about a real Chinatown restaurant?" I suggested.

"All the oil and rice!" Kendall groaned.

"Let's go to a Burmese restaurant, then. You can have a green-tea-leaf salad." I'd been offended, and I wanted to get my way on at least one thing.

We agreed on Burma and made plans to meet at one.

After my conversation with Kendall, I went to Aunt Norie, in the kitchen. She had finished all the ironing and had now moved on to crocheting something tiny, out of blue yarn.

"What's that?"

"Oh, nothing." She folded it back into her sewing bag.

"It looks like a doll jacket," I said.

"It's sort of like that, yes," Norie said. "Now, if you have any holes in your socks, I can darn them for you—"

"Don't distract me. You're making doll clothes for a Jizo-sama, aren't you?" I stared at my aunt.

"It's a coat, actually," she said. "I'm going to make a little hat as well."

"You must have guessed because we're sharing a bedroom." After I'd come home from the hospital, I'd been too weary to resume the charade of sleeping apart from Hugh. Besides, we weren't having sex anymore—there was nothing going on to which an older relative might object.

"It's his apartment, isn't it? Why wouldn't you share?"

"I didn't want to make you uncomfortable—"

"I always suspected. But more important, I see that your belly aches. I can see by the way you touch it, the way you move. I am a Japanese, it is true. In our country, people don't live together before marriage, but still, many fall in love and conceive babies unexpectedly. At least we have a civilized way to mourn the babies we lose. Your child deserves that."

I bowed my head. "I feel so terrible about it."

"I understand. You will feel desolate for a long time. But when you see your Jizo-sama statue at peace in the temple near my house, you will begin to stop hurting."

She must have forgotten that I was banned from the country. I said, "I'll never see it."

"I'll send you a digital photograph. I'll be able to get the statue for you very soon since I hope to go home this week."

"Just to dress a statue?"

"Not just for that reason. I've been thinking about Sadako's letters, Rei-chan. We must speak to the sister, this Atsuko. You cannot do it because the government won't let you enter. Andrea cannot do it because she speaks no Japanese. As you know, my current plane ticket is open return. I'll fly back to Yokohama and pick up Hiroshi before going on to Kyūshū. I already called him last night. He's in agreement that he needs a spring holiday for a change."

"It's a great effort for you to undertake. It's really something the Japanese police should handle, don't you think?"

"They didn't succeed before, and they won't this time, either," Norie said briskly. "A woman-to-woman conversation is needed. Besides, Hiroshi and I have not been to Kyūshū. We shall visit the ceramics villages and bring home some lovely new *ikebana* containers for my hobby."

"I suppose that the sooner you go, the sooner you'll come back." A few weeks ago, I was frightened by the thought of putting Norie up for an endless amount of time. But now I had grown so used to her presence that I couldn't stand the thought of her going.

"I must remind you that I'm not coming back," Norie said gently. "I must return to my home life in Yokohama. I'll telephone you with my findings, when I get them."

"But—but aren't you worried about me?" The babyish words burst from my mouth.

Norie smiled. "If you truly want protection, you have a loving man who wishes to offer it. But you don't seem to want that, do you?"

"No." I wouldn't lead a curtailed life, not even for someone I loved. "Obasan, I have to go out for a few hours. I have a few errands to run, and then I promised I'd meet Kendall for lunch at a Burmese restaurant. Would you like to come along?"

But Norie didn't want to go. All she wanted to do was get on the computer to send an e-mail to her travel agent. I closed the door on her tapping away on my Japanese keyboard, feeling bereft already.

26

Traffic patterns had changed and had become downright terrible, I realized as I inched along Ninth Street. I'd had to go west to get the photocopying of the translations done, and then east to pick up the last framed pieces of art for the restaurant. I'd timed my trip carefully to avoid the morning rush hour, but I was still trapped in the midst of a huge wave of vehicles flowing down toward the mall. I doubted I'd ever be able to make the left turn I needed to get over to Bento. What was this madness? I scowled at a Mercedes, with a Pennsylvania license plate, that sailed through the yellow light, eliminating my only chance at making the turn.

As the cars lined up behind me honked in frustration, I remembered that the cherry trees were in full bloom. While I'd been lying in the apartment, curling into my own misery, the buds of the one hundred or so trees that were a long-ago imperial Japanese gift had been slowly unfurling, spreading their petals.

I'd been to the Mall many times, walking past its cherry trees when the branches were bare, or full of thick green leaves. I'd never seen them at full tilt. I looked at the clock on the dashboard and decided to stay with the straight-ahead wave of traffic to the Mall, make a left turn along with the rest of the cherry blossom–viewing travelers, and exit headed in the direction of Bento.

Once my mind was made up, it seemed that traffic moved faster, although the clock on the dashboard told me this was not the case. I felt my body start to relax as I passed into the realm of stately, neoclassical buildings and green lawns. When a station wagon slipped out of a parking place on my left, I parked.

I'd caught a glimpse of the trees—fluffy, lovely, and pink. Children were running underneath, letting the blossoms rain down on them. Behind them trailed parents, nannies, and grandparents, video cameras and juice cups in hand. Some of them smiled after their children, while others looked anxious. I thought about Sadako and wondered if she'd ever made it in to Washington to show her baby the cherry blossoms. No, I decided. She had been too nervous about the world to take her daughter out into it.

I walked along the border of trees, unable to choose the loveliest one. They were only in flower for a few weeks, after which time the petals collapsed and were eventually swept away.

What had happened to Sadako? Had she lost her life forever—or, like the Japanese cherry, had she found a way to renew herself? I looked up into the branches of the graceful but sturdy old trees, wondering about it. Only the siren of an ambulance brought me back to my morning in Washington. I decided to get on with it.

"Hello, stranger," Marshall said when I went into Bento.

"Hi, Marshall. I've got your woodblocks at last," I announced, though I didn't really need to, since I was balancing all of them in my arms as I waddled slowly into the dining room. My belly felt the familiar pulling, but I didn't stop until I'd laid the pictures against the wall.

"Let's see what you've got," Marshall said.

I unwrapped the Meiji-Period woodblock print of peasants readying themselves to go fishing in an ocean harbor. Now, as I gazed at it, I noticed that the people in the picture were diving for shellfish. A woman wearing a white cloth wrapped around her hips was poised to dive off the side of the boat. A bucket full of oysters rested in it.

"Hmm," Marshall said.

"It's an unknown artist, I told you before, but I thought the work was very unusual. I haven't seen this topic in a woodblock before."

"Let me see the other one."

I unwrapped the next print, which was of a man eating a bowl of soba noodles. I'd liked the way the noodles tumbled off the chopsticks, and the array of bowls and dishes in front of him. This was a slightly older picture, not in as good condition as the pearl-diving picture, but nevertheless a beautiful one.

"I don't remember that print," Marshall said.

"I guess you were overwhelmed," I said. "You chose these two pictures out of two dozen that I showed you a month ago."

"I don't think I need much more art in here," Marshall said. "Remember how the reviewer said it looked a bit cluttered?"

"I don't think 'cluttered' was the word. Pretty and Edwardian were the two words used." *Not a powerhouse* was another phrase used—a phrase that I'd prefer to forget.

There was a moment of silence. At last I said, "Shall I tell you where I think they should hang?"

Marshall shook his head. "I don't think they fit."

"What do you mean?"

"I'm rethinking the look around here."

"Well, the problem with framing is that they don't give you refunds. And I just wrote them a check for slightly over five hundred dollars."

"Can't you sell them through your business?"

I was so angry I could barely see straight. "Marshall, you said you wanted them. Then you gave me permission to get them suitably matted and framed. Do you see how the aubergine color of the mats perfectly picks up the color of the chairs?"

"Honey, it's my restaurant. I'm the one who ultimately decides what goes where."

Honey. I didn't mind being called that by Kendall. Sometimes, I even called Hugh that. It was a term for people you loved, in its best sense. Coming from Marshall, the condescension in the term was clear.

"All right, sweetie," I said back. "Whether or not you hang the pictures, they are yours to do with as you wish. Here's the receipt for the framing. I've also included a copy of the invoice I gave you four weeks ago."

"I have it already." Marshall eyed the envelope but didn't take it. "I told you I'd take care of it when the restaurant was making money."

"I've been working for you for over two months now. I would never have taken on this job if I'd known pay was contingent on the restaurant making it to a certain profit level. We have a legal contract that states what you will pay me." A legal contract that I'd have to fight for myself, because there was no way in hell I would ask Hugh to help bail me out.

"Yes, we have a contract, but it's my checkbook." Marshall patted the breast pocket of his elegant gray jacket. "I'll pay you when I'm ready to do it, and seeing you come in here shouting about your own special needs hardly makes me want to rush to do anything."

"You'd never refuse to pay your fishmonger!" I protested.

"If I did that, he'd send somebody to break my arm," Marshall said wryly.

"It's because I *won't* do it that you're taking advantage. Maybe that's why you chose me, a little-known freelancer, to work for you in the first place." I couldn't hide my fury any longer. Out of the corner of my eye, I saw Alberto, Toro, and several other kitchen guys standing in the doorway to the kitchen, viewing the spectacle. Suddenly I realized that I was finally having my own knock-down, drag-out restaurant fight—with the owner, no less.

"Listen, you know that I paid up front for umpteen things already. I wrote checks for a good twenty thousand dollars," Marshall said.

"Yes, you paid for things that were provided by outside companies. I need to be repaid for labor costs, and for some of the goods I supplied from my warehouse. The *tansu* vanities, the kitchen *tansu* behind the bar—"

"Oh, yes, the fabulous defective *tansu* vanity." Marshall rolled his eyes.

The *tansu* vanity hadn't worked out as well as I'd hoped, it was true. But anyone who bought antiques had to accept that old things wouldn't have silicone-shiny finishes. Still, Marshall had the right to use the furniture he wanted in the restaurant that he owned. In the end, I said, "If you want to return the vanity to me, that's fine, but the framer will not refund the cost of framing."

"If I have to buy a new vanity, I'm out even more money," Marshall said grumpily.

"True. I gave you discounts on everything. Remember? That was part of the generous deal I offered you. I didn't mark up things like some decorators would have."

My message must have gotten through, because Marshall paused a long moment, then spoke. "Okay, I'll write your check. It'll be ready tonight. But don't bother hanging the damn pictures."

The show was over. I gave Marshall a last look, then walked straight past him, toward the kitchen. The audience hanging in the doorway parted to let me through. After I was in, the door swung shut and the cacophony of voices resumed.

"You go, *chica*," said Alberto.

"Tell him the truth, sister! You take your money!" Julio grabbed me in a bear hug, and to my surprise and some discomfort, the other men latched on.

"Julio, where are the chopped *shiso* leaves? The miz is not complete without *shiso*!" Jiro's voice, calm but strong, cut through the din of congratulations. "The rest of you, back to your stations. This is not recess time."

"Yes, Chef," Julio said.

The huddle broke up. I thought to myself that Jiro was more of a partner to Marshall than a union member. He probably didn't approve of the scene I'd caused. I glanced at him, but he'd already turned away and was looking through one of the vast refrigerators for something.

"When will Andrea get here?" I asked.

"She should have arrived one-half hour ago," Jiro said. "Toro can't do it all himself. There are forty reservations already for lunchtime."

"I hope she's all right," I said. "Her apartment was broken into yesterday."

"I hear many excuses for coming late to work," Jiro said.

"But it's true. I was there last night. I know what was taken—"

"What?" he asked.

"Some papers," I said, not wanting to say too much in public.

"What kind of crazy would steal papers?" Julio spoke up. He kept his eyes on me even while chopping. He was too interested, and too good with a knife, I thought uneasily.

"Missing papers are not a valid reason to be late. I'm going to talk to Marshall about that and the continued lateness of many of you." Jiro surveyed his kitchen staff. "Please remember, this is a restaurant, not a primary school."

There was a marked quieting of the kitchen din. I looked at my watch. I had an hour until Kendall would arrive, and nothing to do in the meantime. I had the car. Maybe there was enough time to run over to Andrea's apartment to make sure she hadn't gotten in trouble there.

When I reached Andrea's building, I saw that a locksmith's van was parked in front. A long-haired man in a coverall was crouched by the front door, working. Behind him a white man in his fifties wearing a Baltimore Ravens T-shirt paced, talking on a cell phone. I glanced over at the shooting gallery; there was a woman sitting on the steps, scrawny, with her face older than her body. A tall, golden-skinned woman with a butterfly on her shoulder was talking to her.

I sat in the car, watching Andrea.

She finished her conversation with the junkie, then crossed back over to my side. She said something to the man in the T-shirt—her landlord, I bet—then started walking at a fast clip down the street. She was headed for the Metro stop near Howard University. I turned on the engine and drove after her.

I honked but she steadfastly looked ahead. Maybe she'd

learned that was the best way to handle herself in this neighborhood. Ultimately, I rolled down the window and called out her name.

She finally stopped and recognized me. "What are you doing here?"

"Well, you weren't at work. Jiro's on a rampage because you're late, and I thought I'd better make sure you were okay."

"I came back early this morning so I could get the report finished with the police. But nobody came until nine, and then my landlord wanted to talk to me." She rolled her eyes. "Can you believe he tried to get me to pay for the locksmith? I had to remind him that he's the one who owns the building."

"So what happened in the end?"

"He's paying, but he's pissed, and I'm sure he won't renew my lease." She sighed. "So, was your aunt able to translate the letters?"

"Yes. Your mother had an amazing story," I said. "I hardly know where to begin. It's all in the envelope back there."

Andrea twisted around to pick up the manila envelope I'd laid on the backseat. "Can you stop somewhere so I have a chance to read them? I don't want to take them to work after what happened in my locker."

"It's a good idea to be careful, and I'm willing to hang on to the papers if you don't want to take them into Bento, but I'm not going to stop anywhere. At this point you are over an hour late for work!"

"Yeah, yeah," she said. "I'm late, but what does it matter? I'm going to lose my job anyway."

"I don't know why you say that—"

"The restaurant's losing money to the tune of almost fifty grand a week, David told me last night. I'm sure they're going to start scaling back the kitchen help, and I want to get back to the front, you know, to hostess or wait tables again. I've already filled out an application for a new French restaurant in Georgetown."

"Has Marshall not paid you?"

"He's paid me, but like I said before, it doesn't stack up to what

I was earning, not by a long shot. I'm going to have to freelance if I ever want to get the electricity turned back on." Andrea was studying the translated letters as she spoke. I decided not to answer her so she could read as much as she could before we reached the restaurant.

"There's a lot there," Andrea said. "It sounds pretty scary. Those men who came to see them—what did they want? I wonder if they were blackmailing my father or something."

"So you read through to the last letter," I said. "I think there's something significant about those men, too."

"Well, the police are going down to Virginia to talk to my father. Burns came by this morning, too, to see me about it. I don't know whether to be relieved that they're finally doing something, or scared. My father's going to be really mad that I gave them his name."

"Lorraine will be mad," I said. "Your dad might actually be worried that you're in danger."

"What? If he cared about anything like that, he wouldn't have put me in foster care."

I saw a van pulling out from a spot near the Irish bar, so I pulled in close in order to take it. After I'd successfully parallel parked, I said, "You've never told me about those years, exactly whom you lived with and what it was like."

"I don't want to remember," Andrea said. She handed me the papers she'd just gone through. "You can keep them in your bag or something like it for now. But I'll want them back."

I zipped them into the handbag, committing myself to not letting them off my person as long as I had them. I said, "Actually, you don't seem like someone who grew up in a string of poor homes. I mean, the way you dress and speak. Your accent is, well, accentless."

"You mean, I don't sound like your average black girl?" Andrea snapped.

"No, I—I'm sorry, Andrea, I don't know how to put it."

"I grew up in a string of homes, like you say. They weren't all poor. I had black American foster parents and black Cuban ones and white people, too—the family I lived with the longest was white. An engineer in Silver Spring and his wife and their own four kids. I spent six years with them."

"Was there a possibility of adoption, somewhere along the way?" I asked.

"Nope. The white family was interested, but at the time, it was almost impossible for white parents to adopt black children. The black social workers had come out and declared that transracial adoption, especially for black kids, would cause irreparable damage. And who knows, maybe they were right. I mean, my parents' marriage didn't work out, and look at you and Hugh."

"You never met my parents. They're still so much in love." Suddenly, I longed for them. I tried to shake off my sadness. "Why don't you get back in contact with the family you mentioned?"

Andrea shrugged. "I was a bitch, that last year in high school. I didn't want rules, I didn't want to take the SATs, all that teenage rebellion shit."

"And if there's no longer a legal relationship, and so many years have passed, it must have been easy to lose touch," I said.

"It was. And my dad did wind up giving me the money for community college, and I worked in restaurants, so I had enough to share an apartment with some other people. I've been making it on my own since I was eighteen."

"But why did you give up the roommates to live alone?"

"I was doing really well, making almost thirty grand a year. And I don't have much need for people. I mean, not until recently." She looked at me sideways. "I've never had a friend who'd come looking for me when I didn't show up at work. It's kind of sweet."

"Yes," I said as I pulled up outside Bento and stopped the car so that Andrea could get out. "Now, I'll hang on to your letters within an inch of my life. And if you can make sure you don't lose your job, we'll be set."

27

From H Street, it was less than two minutes to Burma, and I got a metered spot on the street. Despite all that good luck, I was eight minutes late, and I jogged up the street when I saw Kendall waiting outside the restaurant's door. She was looking tense, and practically shouting into her cell phone. I had first thought she was leaving a message for me, but as I drew closer I gathered she was talking to Lisa, her au pair.

"No, I want you to give them Tylenol, not aspirin. Aspirin's not safe for children anymore. Right. One teaspoon per kid." She paused. "I'll get some on the way home. Okay. 'Bye."

"It sounds like the twins are sick?" I asked.

"Yes, as always. I'm beginning to think we live in one of those houses that makes people sick because there's mold growing in it or something."

I had heard that new houses were more likely to have problems like that. "Is anyone else in the household suffering?"

"Well, our au pair doesn't have much energy. Neither does Win. And I can't say I'm as chipper as I was before we moved in."

"Well, you do have the kids to run after," I said. "That can be pretty stressful."

"Yeah, living with the kids must seem like hell to you. I bet you're glad that's a problem you don't have." Kendall's voice was sharp.

I hadn't told Kendall about the miscarriage because I didn't trust her. Now I was glad I'd been so private. Keeping my anger in check, I said, "I think children are a gift. You're very lucky to have Win and Jacquie."

What was Kendall's agenda? I wondered as we entered the restaurant. She was in a terrible mood.

Besides us, there were only four other tables with diners. Burma was one of those places that food writers and true gourmets raved about, but its subdued decoration had kept it from attracting the glamour crowd. Those people went to places like Mandala and Zaytinya and Poste, with a few stragglers left over for Bento.

Kendall studied the menu. "Do they have a liquor license? I could use a glass of wine."

"I doubt it." My head started to hurt just at the idea of it.

Still, Kendall persisted in asking, and she was told they did, so she ordered a glass of house white to go with her meal. I took iced tea, the wine of the South. The caffeine went straight to my head, helping ease the cloudy, tired feeling that had hung on all morning.

Kendall told me she was counting on me, as usual, to put together our order. I selected the green-tea-leaf salad and another salad of papaya, cucumber, and tomato. I also ordered an appetizer of deep-fried calabash squash served with a tamarind dipping sauce. That would be enough for two women with too much on their minds.

The food came quickly. As I waited for the squash sticks to cool, I asked Kendall what was going on.

"Oh, everything's falling apart," Kendall said, taking a sip of wine.

"You mean, the campaign for Harp Snowden?" I hadn't read anything about him in the papers that week.

"The fund-raising's fine. I've already gotten ten friends to pledge the full legal amount to his campaign. Win has some associates who are willing to pledge, too, but the real estate business being the way it is, he's going to float them loans so they can make their contributions in time for the dinner. And if memory serves me, you haven't chipped in yet. You like Harp, don't you?"

"Kendall, I haven't been paid by Marshall yet for the work I've done. I'd love to contribute money, but at this point, I can't spare two hundred dollars, let alone two grand."

"What about Hugh?"

"He's not a U.S. citizen. Wouldn't it look bad for Harp to take money from a foreigner?"

"But Hugh's *British*. That's practically American," Kendall said. "I know there are a lot of rules about financial contributions, but there are ways to get around them if you truly believe in a cause."

"Hmm," I said, looking over my shoulder. The restaurant was not crowded, but this was Washington. I hoped nobody would repeat what Kendall had said.

"Anyway, the campaign isn't my problem. Home life is. Our au pair wants to bolt, and the agency's saying that they won't send us another girl because we made Lisa work too hard. It's like they expect us to hold to a forty-five-hour-a-week schedule for someone with only a high school diploma who's doing unskilled labor in the home—while I, of course, am at the beck and call of everybody twenty-four hours a day. I try to be at home when I say I'll be there, but I've been late a lot. It takes longer just to get from point A to point B in the springtime. I've been meaning to stop by to take your aunt shopping, or at least welcome her to the city, but between the jammed-up roads and my diminishing child care hours, I've been gridlocked." Kendall ended her monologue by flinging her head backward so her red locks spilled everywhere, like the girls in shampoo commercials.

"Cherry blossom traffic is bad, I agree. I was caught up in it myself today." I was surprised that all she wanted to talk about was herself. Still, household labor was a life-and-death issue for a working mother. "Could you get a second baby-sitter to serve as a backup for the au pair?"

"Do you know what baby-sitters in suburban Washington charge?"

"Six or seven dollars an hour?" I guessed.

"Try ten or twelve," Kendall said. "And frankly, I don't have that kind of spare change anymore."

I could commiserate with that. "It's weird living here, isn't it? It's expensive in a way that is different from Japan. I guess I was more careful there. If I ate at a restaurant, it was a small immigrant place like this one. By the way, I doubt that our lunch for two will cost more than twenty dollars, and just taste it! I think it gives Bento a run for its money."

"Not on decor, though. Plastic-topped tables aren't really my thing." Kendall sighed. "I just don't understand what's happening to us. I started doing some freelance consulting, so I'm making more deposits in the bank, but still . . . things are tight. I can't buy tickets to other people's fund-raisers and charity balls. People ask where I'm hiding myself, and I've been telling them Harp's keeping me busy, but that really isn't true."

"What about Win?" I asked.

"He's not going to the parties either. Anyway, he'd be too depressed to go. His work has slowed down."

"But real estate downtown is booming," I said. "Didn't he just sell the building next to Bento? I saw that his sign was gone, and the person who bought it is selling it again—"

Discomfort flashed across Kendall's face. "The sign changed because he lost the listing. Win doesn't like to talk about it, okay?"

"I won't bring it up with him. What about his other listings, the residential ones?"

"Well, he was supposed to be the exclusive listing agent for a new development near Potomac, but that fell through. Win likes that kind of work best, listing properties worth more than a million. The little stuff—two- or three-bedroom ranches in the middle of nowhere—is too much work for the return."

"So when's the last time Win bought or sold a property?" I inquired.

"He sold something between Christmas and New Year's. It was a great big stucco house in Chevy Chase, two million, five."

I didn't need to point out to Kendall that it was already April, but I did tell her that I thought she was overlooking a caregiver who would work for free.

Kendall rejected the idea out of hand. "Too demoralizing. Win needs time to pursue business possibilities. Yes, I'd love him to spend more time with the kids, but why push it when he's having a masculine-identity crisis?"

"Kendall, just listen to me for one minute. You may need to become your family's breadwinner for a little while. You must cut back on helping Harp Snowden and your other volunteer work so you can start earning money somewhere. Don't fall in the helpless trap. I speak from experience, okay?"

"What do you mean you speak from experience? Is Hugh having work troubles, too?" Kendall blinked, as if she was coming up from underwater.

"Actually, I don't know how his work's going." It struck me that I hadn't asked Hugh anything about the class-action suit he'd been working at so doggedly for many months—I'd been too caught up in my own drama. "It's only that our relationship is on the rocks. Now I understand what our mothers always said about living together before marriage being a losing proposition."

She gasped. "Oh, I'm sorry! Now I see that you're not wearing your engagement ring. Did you actually break up?"

"Hugh called off the engagement. We still live together, although I don't know how long that can last."

"At least your wedding plans weren't too far along," Kendall said. "You didn't lose any money on deposits or anything."

I nodded. I couldn't say any more. We hadn't lost money. We'd lost a child. There was no way to earn it back, just as there was no way to resuscitate the joy we'd once had together.

"You know, if he broke up with you, the ring is technically yours. That's what the etiquette books say. You could sell it, if you're really in dire straits."

I shuddered at her words. "I returned the ring to him. I would never sell off his family history."

"It's a shame. I know a cute jeweler in Georgetown who would love to get his hands on a gorgeous emerald in its original art deco setting. Come to think of it," Kendall said, with a mischievous wink, "he'd love to get his hands on you."

Kendall might have revived enough after our conversation to make her usual kind of jokes, but I wasn't feeling so chipper. What she'd said about Win losing the listing, and being unwilling to take on any but the poshest houses, didn't bode well for her future. Or Win Junior's future, or little Jacquie's.

As I walked back to my car, I passed the sign hanging on the building that Win had once represented. It bore the name of a person, not a real estate firm. I decided to call, just to hear the owner's version of what had happened.

"I'm confused about something. I wonder if you could help me," I told the owner, a Martin Schmidt, who sounded as if he was about a hundred years old and had been smoking for most of that century.

"Well, I'm no mind shrinker," Schmidt said grumpily. "You interested in the building or not? It's nine ninety-nine, firm."

Almost a million dollars. That sounded like the kind of money Win liked. "I'm more used to dealing with a real estate agent, actually. What happened with the guy listed on the old for-sale sign, Win Johnson?"

"The screwball," Schmidt said. "I kicked his ass out."

"Why?" I asked.

"He was a screwball," Schmidt repeated. "He priced the building too high for the market, he missed appointments he'd set up with potential clients. When I finally got an offer, he sat on the damn contract for a week before showing it to me. By the time I looked it over and made my counteroffer, it turned out that our buyers had gone and picked up a different property instead. But that wasn't the last straw—" Schmidt broke off in a major coughing fit.

"What was the last straw?" I asked dutifully.

"He smokes. I caught him doing it up on the third floor one day, when he thought nobody was around. He'd stretched out, made himself at home—"

"Do you mean he smokes cigarettes?" Why should that bother Schmidt, who sounded like he did the same?

"Not cigarettes." Schmidt sounded irritated. "I smoke a pack of Camels a day myself. It's crack he was smoking. Crack cocaine. He's a druggie, which, if you ask me, is why he can't do his goddamn job."

Win was an addict. Now everything made sense. The dilated pupils, the disorientation the night Kendall had been taken, and his presence on R Street, near the drug zone. Crack cocaine was probably the reason the Johnson financial accounts were being drained, and if he'd racked up debt, maybe that was the reason for his wife having been snatched. It had been a warning to pay up, or else.

The problem was, I didn't know how I could talk about it with Kendall. She was already deep in denial about who her husband was, but I had to conclude that she was right about one thing: Win was the wrong person to watch over the twins.

That afternoon at Hugh's apartment, my aunt was on a packing spree. Her travel agent had arranged a ticket for a flight that was set to leave Dulles the next day at noon. She would take a taxi if I couldn't drive her.

"Of course I can drive you," I said. "Hugh would insist that I take you."

"Oh, no, but he's going away for a few days," Norie said. "He's going to Boston. Maybe he'll take the car."

"That's too far. I'm sure he'll fly. When did he say he was leaving?" He hadn't said anything to me in the morning, he'd just left the apartment in silence. Come to think of it, he'd had a carry-on bag with him along with his briefcase.

"He left just an hour ago. He returned to the apartment to speak to me but went out again. He made his apologies." Norie looked at me sadly. "I don't like to leave you alone like this. I wish you were coming with me to Japan."

I brooded about my future, and before I knew it, my vintage Seiko clock had chimed six. I was of two minds about going to the restaurant now that I'd learned what kind of financial stresses it was suffering. It seemed greedy to again push for payment if the restaurant was going to fold. But I needed the money. If I didn't get it, I'd be on the street.

"Would you like to come to Bento with me for a farewell dinner?" I asked my aunt. Everyone there liked Norie. Maybe her presence would ensure a harmonious transition of the paycheck. Also, I had no idea what to give my aunt for dinner, and I didn't want her to have to cook for me on her last night in the U.S.

"Yes, but I must take you," Norie said. "I insist because I was not able to buy your wedding gown."

In the old days, I would have refused, but not this time, this night. "Thank you. I'll make sure Marshall gives us some sort of discount and doesn't put you to work in the kitchen again."

"That I would enjoy," Norie said. "I never solved the riddle of where that mysterious Jiro Takeda comes from. When you find out, be sure to tell me."

"There are so many worse things to worry about. Crime. Drugs. Broken homes."

"Yes, yes, of course," Norie said briskly. "But the truth about people is important. If we cannot trust the cleanliness of the hand that offers rice, how can we eat?"

28

For a restaurant that was supposed to be on its last legs, Bento didn't look bad. For one thing, Andrea was out front again, wearing high heels and a bias-cut black-and-white crepe dress. Her hair was swept up in a French twist and opals winked at her ears. But the bored languor she'd once displayed had been replaced by a smile—a bit tentative, but a smile. I watched her greet a couple who hadn't made a reservation and show them to a lovely table by the window. Then she came back to help us.

"Andrea-san, you are looking *steki*!" Norie's compliment on Andrea's revived appearance came out half-Japanese. Oddly enough, Andrea seemed to understand, because she smiled at my aunt and complimented her in turn on her beaded blue jacket.

"Did Marshall give you the job back?" I asked Andrea. Her clothing was an amazement after the grunge look she'd started off wearing in the morning.

"Uh-huh. That dishwasher they have now, Toro, is turning out to be enough, so Marshall moved me back. I had to return to David's to get dressed for tonight, and here I am!"

"What about Justin?"

"He figured out that he made more money waiting tables. I could have told him that before he started."

The unspoken question, of course, was why Andrea didn't want to wait tables, if it paid more. But Bento didn't employ women servers, except for the runners who brought things out from the kitchen. So Andrea wasn't likely to break any barriers that way. And if being a hostess was the gold crown for her, so be it.

There were a few booths along one wall, cushioned in aubergine velvet, totally prized seating that usually went to whoever was the coolest-looking, or most powerful, reservation of the night. Andrea cheerfully led the two of us over to one of the booths.

"Justin will be over in a moment. If he gives you any trouble, tell me and I'll make sure he gets what he deserves." Andrea winked and was gone.

"Unbelievable," I said in Japanese.

"Marshall-san is more kind than I had thought," Norie said. "He must be in a happy mood tonight. I think you will receive your money."

"I don't know about that." My stomach was already in knots at the prospect of having to ask him for my payment again.

"Don't worry. Now, what shall I have today? Tuna or crab? I shall miss such luxury when I have to cook again," Norie said.

"You'll have some good restaurant meals in Kyūshū," I said. "I hear the sashimi there is spectacular."

"Probably not as good as Okinawa," Norie said. "Anyway, the town we are going to, Okita, is not for the tourists, my travel agent said. There aren't any famous restaurants. But perhaps I will be treated to home cooking."

"You don't think Atsuko's family will offer you a meal, do you? That's so un-Japanese!" Aside from my relatives, I had hardly ever been invited to eat in anyone's home in Japan.

"We will see," Norie said. "I have a plan. I hope to have a moment tonight to tell Andrea-san about it."

"Maybe you should tell me first," I said. When Norie pressed her lips together without speaking, I added, "I thought you were going to just gather information on whether the letters continued to arrive in Japan. If it turns out they kept sending Sadako's letters back unopened, they're probably very uptight about even admitting she exists."

"So much time has passed," Norie said. "Perhaps they'll be grateful to hear what we've pieced together. That's the most important thing, isn't it?"

I knew what the answer about family acceptance would be: a resounding no. But my aunt was making the trip at her own expense because she'd gotten caught up in the sad story of Andrea's life. It was a great thing for her to do.

As we sat down to dinner, I surveyed the crowd. The restaurant was about two-thirds full, again with many underdressed people. I couldn't imagine dropping $150 on dinner while wearing a pair of khaki shorts and sandals, but apparently many Washingtonians could.

Like the diners, our entrées seemed slightly off-kilter. My tuna was cooked to a light gray color, and the scallops Norie ordered had an overpowering taste of lemon. I'd gladly suffer the small indignity of tuna cooked totally through, but other diners might not. So after our dishes were cleared, when Norie decided she wanted to visit the kitchen to say her good-byes, I decided to go along as well.

I made my way over to Jiro, who was bustling about. "Ah, Rei, Marshall told me you would be here. I have the check for you in the office. Let me finish the direction of this tuna dish, and I'll get it for you."

"Thank you." I was pleasantly surprised.

"*Do-itashimashite*," he replied. *You're welcome.*

Norie dug her elbow into me after he spoke. In Japanese, she murmured, "Rei-chan, come with me to say good-bye to the other staff."

It was unlike her to drag me off like that, so it had to be important. I followed, and sure enough she whispered in my ear. "*Do-itashimashite*. Did you hear him say it?"

"Yes. I guess he is trying to show that he's happy to give me the money. I feel a bit bad for having demanded it now that I've learned the restaurant's not doing well."

"*Do-itashimashite*! It means 'You are welcome.' Don't you see? A Japanese would never say that!"

With a sinking feeling, I realized that my aunt was correct. A Japanese would rather say *ie*, meaning "no," because he wanted to make it clear that he wasn't worthy of something as special as thanks. *Do-itashimashite* was an expression more commonly used by Japanese-speaking foreigners, who liked to use phrases that lined up with similar expressions in their own language.

"There could be a special reason he used the phrase," I said. "He might have been here so long he now thinks in English. Or maybe he said it because it actually *is* a sacrifice for the two of them to pay me."

"You believe in him." Norie sounded surprised. "You—the pearl diver!"

"What do you mean?"

"You go to great depths to look for beauty and truth. He's just a chef!" Norie exploded. "He could easily have escaped detection throughout his whole career. Chefs cook, they don't talk!"

"Hello to you both, Shimura-san and Rei-chan. What is the matter?" Jiro had come up behind us and spoke in Japanese.

Norie jumped about a thousand miles, and I hurried through my mind for a quick excuse. "Actually, I wanted to warn you that my tuna was overcooked. My aunt was saying you were so busy cooking, you probably didn't have time to talk to anyone in the dining room about how the tuna turned out."

"*Ah so desu ka.*" Jiro looked grieved. "I am sorry about that, Rei-chan, but the dish has changed. There was a health department inspector who visited, and we were told to cook the tuna until there is no more pink."

"But—but how could that be? You serve sashimi, right? That's raw. Lots of people serve sashimi in this town."

"I agree. This was a very strange situation. But one learns

quickly not to argue with the health inspector. Especially when he might be in a gangster's pocket."

"You mean Ken Chow, the man who owns Plum Ink?"

"Don't say the name." Jiro's eyes burned into mine.

What Detective Burns had talked about, this rivalry between the two restaurants, now came to mind. "Jiro, I'm so sorry. And by the way, I will wait to cash the check if that's helpful."

"Don't worry about that. Marshall has signed it. Come, I'll get it for you now."

"Rei-chan, I am going to the bar to say good-bye to that nice Vietnamese boy," Norie said.

I told my aunt that I'd meet her in a few minutes. The chance to follow Jiro into Marshall's office gave me a better opportunity to ask him some questions. "Where is Marshall tonight, anyway?"

"He is at Mandala." Jiro handed me the check. I almost dropped it when I read the amount on the dollar line, because it was for just the cost of the framing of the two pictures. Marshall still owed me almost ten thousand dollars for my work.

"How's business at Mandala?"

"Not so bad," Jiro said. "In fact, we've been using our gains at that place to prop up everything that's going on here."

"Do you think Bento will close?" I asked.

He looked at me dead-on. "We have that expression in Japanese, *gambaru*."

"Yes, to fight on. To try one's hardest." So that's what they were doing. They would put off paying every bill they possibly could, to keep the place afloat. Could I blame them?

"Right now, I still believe in this restaurant. If only more people would come and spread the word. Now that Andrea is back in front, I am very happy. She has a new attitude, and she knows just how to place people around a room."

"I noticed that the people who come here seem quite casual, and I've overheard some complaints about the prices," I said. "Have you thought about creating a few entrées under twenty dollars?"

"We can't lower our prices much." Jiro frowned.

"What about liquor?" I asked. "The bar is really popular."

"Yes, it is, but this is a restaurant. It is about food."

Jiro's reputation was based on the food becoming a hit. However, liquor was a big profit item. If they could drop prices anywhere, it was in the bar. But would that be worth it? I thought for a minute. "Jiro, I have an idea. You could sell every bottle of wine at half-price one or two nights a week. Slow nights, when you want more people to come in."

"They've done that at some other restaurants in the neighborhood, Andale and the Caucus Room," Jiro said slowly.

"And what about having a prix fixe menu for early birds—say the five-to-seven crowd?"

"Because they are afraid to come at night?"

"Yes, exactly." I was charging forward with my idea. "You could call it a pretheater supper, because the National Shakespeare Theatre is not very far away."

"I admire your ideas." Jiro sounded thoughtful. "Of course, I will have to talk to Marshall. But thank you for the ideas. We need some change to make this place work."

I almost said, "You're welcome," but that reminded me of Aunt Norie's obsession. "Oh, Jiro, just one more question."

"Of course." He seemed considerably more relaxed than when we'd started talking.

"Where were you born?" I smiled as I spoke. It was an innocuous question, after all.

"Why do you ask that?" His face seemed to freeze.

"Oh, you know, regional cooking styles and all that. I was just curious."

"I learned my cooking in the Kanto area. I thought I mentioned that to you earlier. Tokyo, *neh?*"

But he still hadn't told me where he'd been born. "Were you, ah, born in Tokyo?"

"Just outside. Sorry, I've got to check on the stock for the *yosen-abe*. It's that new menu item inspired by your aunt's." And he was gone.

29

Just outside could mean a nearby town, or another country. But I couldn't push him further without being obnoxious, I thought, as he veered away from me. But as I walked out of Jiro and Marshall's office along the route through the kitchen that led back into the dining room, I realized that strangers were on the premises: an older man with close-cropped, graying hair and a very young man in an oversized T-shirt and baggy jeans. As the younger one turned, I instantly recognized him as Davon, Andrea's half-brother, and then the identity of the older man, his father, slid into place.

The Nortons had come to Washington. It was a surprising move. And they were making it obvious, letting themselves be seen by so many witnesses.

I moved closer so I could hear the words spoken by Robert Norton to Alberto. It sounded as if he'd asked a question that ended with the word "tonight."

"Yes, yes. She is in front," Alberto replied. Robert and Davon seemed uncomprehending.

I chose that moment to enter the conversation. "Hello, may I help you?"

"You—you were at the house." Robert Norton looked at me as

if I were a nightmare that had returned.

"And the diner," Davon added. "You're everywhere!"

"I just finished dinner," I said, remembering all of a sudden that they thought I was a Japanese tourist. I couldn't let on that I was a quasi-restaurant worker. "Andrea-san gave my aunt and me a very nice table for supper. But we are finished. Are you here to see Andrea-san?"

"I want to ask her why she sent a carload of cops come by to see me," Robert Norton said. "They wanted to talk about a burglary at her place. But you know as well as she does that I gave you the papers you wanted. They were supposed to be in your care, in your hotel room."

"Let's just step outside, please," I said, mindless of the fact that this was where Kendall had been snatched. From the way the line of cooks had stopped chopping and sautéing, I knew we had become too much of a distraction.

Davon had a bit of a swagger as he walked out next to me, but Robert Norton showed his old injuries, moving slowly, and faltering as we passed the dishwashing station. Toro, the bull-like dishwasher, stepped back to avoid being tripped over and I caught Robert by the arm. I'd remembered his bad back and knees.

"Who's that guy?" Robert asked once we were outside, standing on the old cast-iron platform that had a few steps leading down to the Dumpster and the parking area. The parking space was filled, I noted, with a shiny black Mercedes that I knew belonged to Jiro and a silver Honda with Virginia plates. I could guess that the Honda was Lorraine's car. I looked at the trunk. Could I fit in it? Yes, without question.

"Alberto is the name of the Brazilian cook who was talking with you," I said.

"No, the dishwasher. Who's that?" Robert asked.

"I don't know," I said, wondering if Robert was trying to trap me into revealing that I worked at the restaurant and wasn't a Japanese tourist at all. "Are you all right, Norton-san? I was worried about your almost falling when we were leaving the kitchen. How is your health?"

"You didn't have to hold my hand like that when we were leaving. I'm not a cripple."

"Sorry," I said. "When somebody appears to be falling, I reach out to help."

"Even if you think that person is a burglar?"

I felt my face get warm. "I never said to anyone that I thought you were a burglar. It's just that since Andrea and I saw you, a couple of things have happened that probably wouldn't have happened if we hadn't gone to get those papers."

"So she got ripped off last night." Robert Norton sounded tired. "What's the other thing that happened?"

I looked at him coldly. "I was kidnapped on April twentieth by some men who threw me in the trunk of their car. I escaped near Quantico. They're still at large."

"Whoa, Dad, we heard about that on the news," Davon said excitedly. "I didn't catch that it was you."

"The cops asked us what we were doing on the night of the twentieth," Norton said. "I told them that I had choir rehearsal with Lorraine. Davon was playing basketball with the county rec league. Then we picked him up and went home and to bed."

I didn't answer him immediately, because I was laying out the situation in my mind. Robert and Lorraine and Davon all would have had witnesses for the early part of the evening. But as far as bedtime went, they could only speak for each other.

"Why are you here?" I asked, although I could guess. Robert wouldn't have driven the distance if he didn't want to convince Andrea he was innocent of the theft in her apartment.

"We came to tell you both to get out of our business," Davon said fiercely. "Our family was fine until Andrea and you-all showed up. Now the cops are all over us, and Momma's crying all the time."

"Settle down, Davon," Robert said. "And, Miss Shimura, I'm truly sorry about what happened to you."

"Thanks."

"You speak English pretty well for someone from Japan," Robert said after a beat.

I didn't answer. I'd forgotten about my fake accent for a moment.

"Davon, there's a map I need from the car." Robert handed him a key ring.

"What?" Davon said.

"Go find me the D.C. map. It's in the trunk or something."

Davon made an irritated face and trailed away to the car. I wished I was right behind him, so I could see if a rope lay inside. No, I told myself. That was dangerous. I shouldn't even be standing outside with them, I knew.

"Now listen here," Robert said in a low voice, when Davon was out of hearing range. "You and my daughter have got to stop looking into things. It's not safe. It didn't work out for my late wife, all right? You don't want to end up the same way."

Now I felt really sick. The man I'd decided was no risk was threatening me. Trying to maintain a relaxed demeanor, I said, "It sounds as if you don't think she committed suicide."

He nodded slightly.

"What do you think happened?" I asked.

"I don't know. I've said that a million times—"

"I know about the men. The ones who came around to the apartment and scared her nearly to death."

"How did you hear about that?" He looked at me intently.

"We read the letters. Sadako wrote to her sister about the men who wouldn't leave you alone. Who were they, old Marine Corps guys from your time at Sasebo?"

He shook his head.

"What were their names?"

"I can't tell you."

"You mean you won't," I said.

"If you knew, you wouldn't be safe." He spoke emphatically.

"If you think they killed your wife, for God's sake, why didn't you go to the police?" I spoke quickly, because Davon had shut the trunk and was ambling back. "Was it because you were secretly glad they erased a problem for you?"

"No." His body had started to tremble very slightly.

"I understand now." I remembered what the Naganos had told me. "After you settled in Virginia, the honeymoon was over. Sadako became a burden. Not to mention a new baby who'd cry at night and needed all kinds of attention."

"Don't talk to me about babies." There was a hint of wetness at the corners of Robert Norton's eyes. I'd gotten to him. He furiously brushed at his cheek as Davon came up.

"I got the map. Where we going to next?" Davon demanded.

"I just want to get out of here," Robert said in a low voice.

"Didn't you want to see Andrea?" I reminded him.

"I changed my mind," he said.

The conversation wasn't over yet. "Hang on. I'll go to the reception area and ask her if she can meet you after she's done. It'll be after midnight, but maybe there's a place where you could get a cup of coffee—"

"I don't think so."

"Just let me ask." If I lost him before Andrea even had a chance to see him, she would never forgive me.

I hurried back through the kitchen and out front, through the dining room. Norie waved at me from the bar. I'd forgotten about her again. What kind of niece was I? I gave her a just-a-minute signal with my hand, and hurried on to catch up with Andrea, who was returning to her stand after seating customers.

"I just had the nicest talk with your aunt. I can't believe she's going to Kyushu for me! What's up with you? You look like you ate something bad." Andrea didn't break stride as she continued toward the restaurant's foyer. Her words were as brisk as usual, but her expression was radiant. She was obviously happy to have her old position back.

"Your father and Davon are here," I said.

Now Andrea stopped and turned to stare at me. "I didn't see them come in."

I spoke quickly, because I could see new customers coming through the door, people Andrea would have to tend to in a few seconds. "They're out in the parking area behind the kitchen. I talked to them for a few minutes, and I think maybe you should talk to them, too."

"No kidding." Andrea sucked in her breath.

"Your father's upset about our—digging into things. But I think you should talk to him, maybe. That is, if you feel safe doing it."

"Of course I do," Andrea said. "But talk about bad timing. I'm in the middle of my shift. I don't think I'll be done until midnight."

She glanced at the foyer. A cute young couple wearing Lacoste polo shirts and, yes, shorts, had halted at the tall wooden pedestal table in the foyer and were looking around like hapless foreigners at the underground train station in Narita Airport.

"I've got to get back to my station. But tell him to be at Plum Ink around midnight." Andrea had already hurried off to meet the new patrons.

This time, instead of going through the whole dining room and kitchen, I went out the front door and around the back to see the Nortons. I didn't want my aunt to waylay me before I'd relayed Andrea's message.

But when I reached the parking pad, the Honda Accord was gone. I was alone with the Dumpster and a couple of rats scrabbling about in the twilight.

I dragged myself and all my regrets back into the kitchen. Alberto called out to me from his sauté pan.

"What is it?" I asked.

"You don't look so good, Rei. I'm worried. It can't be the tuna." Alberto slapped a breast of chicken on its other side, sending up a plume of fire.

"No, it's not," I said.

"What you doing going outside with those fellows?"

"Just talking," I said. He was too nosy.

"You shouldn't stand out there in the dark with them. You know that's where your cousin got took. After what happened to you, too, I can't believe you'd do something like that." Alberto raised his spatula toward me, shaking it for emphasis.

"I know, I know. I won't do it again." I flinched as a tiny hot-oil droplet hit my cheek.

"The older man, he was Andrea's father, huh?"

"Did he tell you that?" I countered.

"No, he didn't say that. But I thought that he looked like her. The boy, he looked a bit different, though."

"Different mother," I said. Lorraine. Nothing had been said about her. I still worried that she might have had something to do with the theft, even if Robert and Davon had done nothing.

"So where they go to?" Alberto persisted.

"I don't know where they went. Andrea was hoping to talk to them after she finished tonight, but they can't wait that long, they said. Will you tell her that for me?"

Alberto nodded. "It's a shame they couldn't see each other."

"Well, I can understand Andrea's choice," I said. "It's her first night back. She doesn't want to make a mistake."

Unlike me, I thought sourly. I was making faux pas right and left. As I drove my aunt back to Hugh's apartment for the last time, I tried to tell myself that tomorrow would be better. Andrea would telephone her father and sort things out with him, and my aunt would be en route to Japan and finding Sadako's Japanese relatives. And I'd have time to help my cousin before her own family came apart. I'd been hesitant to speak up before, but now I knew it was a necessity. I'd talk to Win.

30

After I dropped my aunt off at the airport the next morning, I headed straight for the Johnson house in Potomac. I'd already confirmed that Kendall was out of the house, and that Win was still at home. I'd gotten the news from Kendall when I'd reached her on her cell phone. If anything, her mood was worse than it had been the previous day.

Kendall's problems had started when she'd telephoned Senator Snowden's office that morning. Martina couldn't confirm that Kendall would be seated at Senator Snowden's table at the fund-raising dinner. Kendall had immediately rung Snowden's cell number to find out what was going on, but her call had gone into his voice mail. She suspected he was avoiding her because some of the couples she'd expected to commit to the fund-raising dinner had not come through after all.

I tried to reassure Kendall that the senator was probably in a hearing or doing something where he couldn't take her call. Then I asked her what she was going to do that day. She told me she was going to see an old employer about a paid part-time fund-raising position. Feeling relieved, I wished her luck at the interview and hung up. Rush hour was over, and the suburban freeways—267 and then 495, the Washington Beltway—were fairly empty, so I was able to roll along smoothly north to Potomac.

I was going to miss driving Hugh's car, which always had a delicious aroma of leather and good, strong tea. He'd left a travel mug of Darjeeling in the cup holder, and I was tempted to taste it. I'd left early so I could spend time with Norie in the airport, so early that I hadn't had any caffeine.

But Hugh put milk in his tea, which probably had soured and separated, so I left the tea alone. When I reached River Road, I began to mentally prepare myself for my visit. I would be dropping in with nothing in my hands, no excuse to give Win about why I'd come to see him. All I had with me were the rumors I'd heard, and I was sure he'd deny them.

I drove into Treetops via its main avenue lined with blooming dogwoods and azaleas. In daylight and the right season, the suburbs could be beautiful, but they still seemed too organized—just like the houses with their springtime wreaths on the door that would change to something different in the fall, and then again at Christmas.

The garage door was up, and I saw that Win's BMW was parked within, its vanity plate proclaiming LAXRULZ. Before, I'd thought that was just a reference to pride in lacrosse, since he had played for UVA. Now I thought about it in another context.

As I sat in the car thinking, the front door to the house swung open and Win emerged, dressed in a yellow polo shirt and khakis. He raked a hand through his clipped blond hair and squinted toward the street. I thought he was looking at me, but it turned out that he had spotted an errant daffodil, which had sprung up about a foot from the thick bank of them lining the walkway. He walked a few steps, tore off the top of the daffodil, and put it in the trash can at the front of the garage.

Not exactly the behavior of an addict, I thought. Or was it? The fact was, he hadn't gotten the bulb. The daffodil would be back the next spring. And there would be more of them out of line. Why didn't he transplant them, instead of cutting them off? What did it say about who he was, what he was capable of doing?

Win opened his car door, but before he could climb in, Win Junior had run out of the house and up to him.

"Daddy, Daddy's car, Win come," little Win cried out.

"No, you stay here with Lisa. Daddy's running late."

"Win no like Lisa. Win like Daddy's car."

"I don't have a child seat, so I can't take you. Besides, it's going to be bo-ring."

"Daddy going where?" Win demanded.

"I have to do some shopping. Like I said, bo-ring."

I relaxed inwardly. If Win were going to Whole Foods or Home Depot, it would be a snap to sidle up to him and get in the conversation that I wanted. I was afraid that he was going to work, and that would give me no opportunity whatsoever.

Win Senior and Junior argued a moment longer, and then the au pair ran out and grabbed the toddler up in her arms.

"Don't let him run out like that," Win said to her sternly. "Strangers drive through neighborhoods like this all the time, looking for opportunities."

Lisa bowed her head and mumbled an apology. I knew I could lay at least one worry to rest—the concern I'd had early on that there might be an affair going on between the two of them.

Win backed out without looking, so it was easy for me to pull out and follow him, once he was a block away.

As he'd said, strangers drove through the neighborhood all the time, looking for opportunities.

Instead of taking the beltway, Win headed into the city via Massachusetts Avenue. He passed through Dupont Circle, where following him became tricky. He made it out and continued to Scott Circle, where he headed north on Rhode Island Avenue. He hadn't stopped at any of the popular shopping areas. I began to realize that his shopping trip might not be for household necessities. And while I didn't really want to accompany him on a drug buy, if I saw him stop in his car and exchange money for a baggie or a vial of something, I'd know for sure the kind of man he was.

The BMW moved steadily on. When it entered Logan Circle, Win made a careful, slow, entire circle without exiting on any of the streets that spiked out of it. Did he suspect that he was being followed? I was trapped behind him, because I didn't want to lose him, but I didn't want him to know I was following. I took Vermont Avenue and quickly worked my way over to R Street, where I pulled in on a side street adjacent to the place where I'd seen the drug addicts. Sure enough, a few seconds later Win's car came by, though it surprised me by not stopping there. He continued on for three blocks, to stop at a handsome row house with a sign bearing the name of his real estate employer, but with a different real estate agent's name. It was a nineteenth-century three-story house similar to Andrea's, but grandly restored, with a garden full of tulips and jonquils, and shutters and doors painted a brilliant green. I stopped the Lexus a few houses back so I could watch. As Win pulled a key-ring out of his pocket, I remembered what I'd heard about his real estate practices. He must have gotten the house keys from another real estate agent, who probably believed Win was showing it to a client.

This was a safer situation than I'd anticipated, so just as Win disappeared through the doors, I got out of my car and marched up the steps and knocked.

Win opened it a long two minutes later. He was standing in a sparsely decorated living/dining room with recently stripped, gleaming pine floors. He looked at me blankly.

"Hi, Win."

"Hi, Rei," he said, quickly recovering. "I didn't expect to see you here. Are you interested in this house?"

"Not exactly," I said.

"What's taking so long, babe?" A slim blond woman walked into the room, a woman wearing just a tight tank top and shorts. She had a small object in her hand, something made of glass that she had folded her hand over when she saw me. I could guess that it was a crack pipe.

Now I was nervous. I'd thought he'd be alone, but the woman complicated things. And who knew, maybe she was a jealous mistress who had a gun.

"Who is she?" the woman said, coming up behind Win, wrapping an arm around his waist. He moved away at the touch, and she looked miffed.

"She's my wife's cousin," Win said. "Rei, ah, now isn't the best time to talk. I was going to go through some papers with my buddy who's listing the place."

"What buddy?" The woman sounded confused. Perhaps she'd already gotten to the place where everything was hazy.

"It's in your interests to talk to me right now or I'll make an immediate call to Kendall. I don't think she knew about this particular hideaway." I had already whipped out the cell phone, which was turning out to be quite a handy little accessory.

"Ah, Shelly, let me step out with Rei for a little talk." He looked at me directly and said, "I'll just go in the kitchen for a minute, and get the other set of keys—"

I listened carefully for the sound of a back door opening, because I wouldn't have put it past him to flee, but he returned a few seconds later. The front-left pocket of his khakis contained something small that made a slight outward indentation. It didn't look like a key to me, but a tube.

"I've gotta go, Shelly," Win said, walking swiftly to the door.

" 'Bye, Buddy," she replied.

As we headed down the walk, I said, "Why don't you get in my car and I'll drive."

"What are you talking about?" Win said. "I have my own car."

"Yes, but it's not worth the risk to let you drive. I know what you have in your pocket."

"What are you talking about?"

"I know about the crack cocaine." I used the remote-control feature on Hugh's car key to click open both doors of the Lexus.

"I'm not going with you for a harangue," Win said. "I get enough of that shit at home."

"Oh," I said. "So Kendall already knows what you're doing?"

Win glared at me. "Not exactly. And if you tell her anything about Shelly or her house, I'll make sure you never see Kendall again."

I glared back. "I'm giving you a chance, Win. Just get in the car and I'll take you somewhere that we can talk like two reasonable adults about your problem."

Win got in the car. I drove a few blocks and pulled into a space along the curb. It was quiet, the perfect place for a talk. I began, "So, how did it all start?"

"This is a bad block," Win objected. "The cops are always staking it out."

"Oh, so we might get picked up as suspected buyers from the suburbs?"

"Yeah," Win looked at me coldly. "And as you pointed out, I do have vials in my pocket."

I gave him a sidelong glare and started the car again. I drove the speed limit back to Adams-Morgan, curving around the alley behind Urban Grounds where I knew there was a Dumpster. I stopped by the Dumpster and said, "Throw it in."

"What?"

"Take the vial out of your pants pocket and put it in the Dumpster. I don't want it in the car."

Win's tone turned conniving. "I'll do it later. You don't want to be caught doing something stupid in public."

"I don't want you with that stuff!"

"I don't care what you want. I need it." Win's voice broke.

I turned the car off and looked at Win. To my surprise, there were tears in his hard blue eyes.

"How long have you been doing it?" I asked, consciously making my voice more sympathetic.

"I'd tried it once or twice, before the twins were born, but afterward, that's when I got into it. It helped me cope. Believe me, I've been cutting back. I smoke once or twice a week, now."

"That woman, Shelly. She gets it for you?" I asked.

"Yeah. And Shelly doesn't mean anything to me. Kendall's not at risk."

"But you're sleeping with Shelly," I said, and from the flush in his face, I knew I'd guessed right.

"I have to do whatever, you know, to keep things cool. I've been having some troubles with . . . credit. Shelly's helping me through."

"The guys you owe money to must be very dangerous."

Win nodded. "They don't play by the rules. It's not like the gentlemen's agreements my father made with the bank manager back in Lynchburg."

"They took Kendall from Bento that night, didn't they?"

Win's anguished look was my answer.

"My God! And what do you think they were going to do with her?"

"It was a warning," Win said in a low voice. "The day after it happened, I cleared the debt."

"With money from Kendall," I said, the pieces coming together. "She told me that you wanted to take money from her trust fund to support the candidacy of Harp Snowden. And then she said something about you giving loans to friends so they could buy their own tickets to the dinner. That money came from the trust as well, didn't it?"

"I didn't want to do it, but it was the only choice."

"And no checks have been delivered to Harp Snowden's office, have they?"

Win threw up his hands. "You're right. I didn't give the eight grand to Snowden. I used it to settle the debts. But don't you think the safety of my wife and kids is more important?"

"But they didn't stop kidnapping people. I was taken a few weeks later. How far will your dealer friends go to prove a point? Who will they grab next, Grandmother Howard in Baltimore? Or maybe your parents in Lynchburg?"

"They didn't take you!" Win protested. "What happened to you was completely unrelated."

"How could my kidnapping be unrelated? It was done in the exact same way, a woman thrown in a car trunk."

"Kendall's story was publicized on all the TV stations. The details were out there for anyone to take and use for their own purposes. I know it can't be the dealers because I asked. Believe me, if they'd wanted to keep me in line, they'd have let me know what they were up to."

I hesitated. I didn't trust Win, but he had made some plausible points.

"Rei, I'm sorry," Win said. "But you see, I paid my debts. I wish I could stop smoking, but I can't."

"What about trying drug treatment?"

"I heard it's, like, impossible to get into a center. And can you imagine me hanging out with all those lowlifes? What would people think?"

"They'd think that Winthrop Johnson's finally facing up to reality," I said. "Look, you've got to tell Kendall. She's the one who can help you through it all. I'm sure she'd go into her trust to get the money you need for private treatment. Then you wouldn't have to worry about having to socialize with poor people."

"Kendall would leave me," Win mumbled.

"She might not leave you, if you come forward and ask for help."

"People break up over much less than drugs," Win said glumly. "Look at you and Hugh."

"What about us?" I felt my guard go up.

"You miscarried! You had an accident, and now neither of you wants to stay together—"

"How did you know?" I was horrified.

"Kendall told me. She heard it from Hugh. I don't know why you treat it like some big shame. So you're not married. It's not like you're living in medieval Japan. Get over it."

"Leave my private life alone. Yours is enough of a mess, okay? You're going to have to tell Kendall what you did with the money, and why that terrible thing happened to her."

"Give me twenty-four hours, okay?"

"How can I know you'll do it?" I asked skeptically.

"Just watch this." Win stepped out of the car and hurled the vials filled with little chunks at the Dumpster. They hit the edge, and shattered into hundreds of tiny pieces. He'd created a hazard to the general public—but at least nobody could use the crack cocaine to get high.

I expected Win to come back to the car, but he bent over double, almost hugging himself. He was crying openly now.

"Win, I—" I didn't want to say that I was sorry, because I thought I'd done something necessary. "Come with me. I'll drive you back to your car."

He shook his head. "Just go. I'll find my own way back."

31

As I drove away, I began to worry that Win had tricked me with his big show of smashing the container of drugs. My words might have just flowed over him. From what I'd heard about addiction, supposedly someone like Win would have to hit rock bottom before he would want to change.

I was driving along Rock Creek, whose waters would flow into the Potomac, the river where Sadako had disappeared. Because I had nothing better to do, I followed the parkway out of the park itself, passing the Watergate complex and the Kennedy Center for the Performing Arts. I parked illegally just south of the bridge to Theodore Roosevelt Island. There, I stood, looking across the water to Virginia. Almost thirty years ago, Sadako Tsuchiya Norton had left her clothes on the sand and gotten in the water, to drown herself or swim to Washington. She'd have come out within a mile or so from where I was standing. She would have been dripping and bare in the midst of tourists and people who worked in the district.

I shook my head, remembering what she'd written in her diary about missing the water. Had her life really become so circum-scribed that she'd ended it by entering this puny stretch of the

Potomac—when, if she'd traveled an hour or two south, she'd have been able to enter the Chesapeake Bay, a substantial body of water?

Sadako didn't have a car, I reminded myself. She would have had to take a bus or a taxi to get to such an area, and at the time, a striking, young, Asian-looking woman traveling might have been remembered.

Still, the clothing detail bothered me. I had no sense anymore whether she'd put the clothes there, or the men had done it. Men—not necessarily. I shook myself. I'd been so focused on the men whom Sadako had mentioned in her note that I hadn't thought much about Lorraine. She'd known Robert Norton since high school, and she'd wanted him free to marry her. And Lorraine was a tall, muscular woman—I'd seen her pictures from the time of her wedding. With or without a helper, she could have hauled Sadako's lanky frame, which the police report said had weighed just 125 pounds. Maybe Lorraine had tricked Sadako into taking a drug that had made her sleep, made it possible to dump her somewhere, not the river, but perhaps an abandoned farm field or a wooded area where she'd decompose and never be found.

Lorraine might even have been driving the car that had picked me up. I had felt sure that it was a man's arms that had lifted me, but there had been another person, a driver.

I didn't think much of Win, but somehow, I'd believed him when he'd said so emphatically that the gang he'd owed money to had nothing to do with my kidnapping. There were two much stronger possibilities. Either my abduction was related to the restaurant feud, or to the Nortons. To throw off the police, the whole idea of my kidnapping could have been copied to make it look related to Kendall's kidnapping.

I stared into the rushing water, thinking about it. Only the siren of a police car whizzing by reminded me that I was parked illegally. I climbed into the Lexus and swung cautiously back into traffic, curving back on the roads that led to the Mall. I didn't know if the answer to my questions lay there, but it was worth a try.

• • •

Senator Harp Snowden's office was in the Hart Senate Office Building, I remembered Kendall mentioning to me once. Parking near it would be impossible, so I left the car in the Union Station garage. From there, I walked the couple of blocks to the imposing, modern building. I made it through the metal detector and over to a directory, where I learned that Snowden's office was on the third floor. A crowd of people were waiting at a bank of elevators, but there was still an elevator open that had only one man inside. I hurried forward and stepped in.

Just as I did, someone in the crowd said loudly, "That's for senators only."

I caught my breath, but the door had closed and I was riding upward with a dignified, gray-haired man in a pin-striped blue-and-black suit.

"Which floor do you need?" he asked.

"The same as you. Three," I said, trying to guess who he was. I should have known, but I was so awful at celebrity spotting. "I'm sorry. It's my first time in this place. I rushed in without really looking, something I do more than I should."

The mysterious senator nodded, but didn't reply. I was relieved to get out and dash off to Suite 321. The grand, airy feeling the building had downstairs was missing from the office's waiting room, which, while fitted with beautiful redwood furniture, was low ceilinged and lit too brightly. A television was going in the corner near the couches and chairs that were meant for the people waiting. There was a high desk behind which sat a young African-American woman with cornrowed hair and wearing a conservative blue suit. Kendall's words about dressing Republican came back to me.

"Yes?" she asked after I'd finished checking her out.

"Hello, Carla," I said, after spotting her name on a sign on her desk, "I'm Rei Shimura. I'm a—friend—of the senator."

From the way she looked at me, I guessed she'd heard that line a few times. "You're not on the agenda."

"Well, it's a matter that came up. Is he really busy?"

"He's always busy. At the moment, he's out. We have a policy asking lobbyists to make appointments several days in advance. Which group do you represent?"

"I'm not a lobbyist," I said. "I'm one of his California constituents and truly, I know him. It's hard to believe, but I do."

"You're welcome to wait for our chief of staff." Carla again bent her head to her work, which seemed to consist of opening letters, reading them, and placing them in different piles. I turned my attention to the television, which was playing some Snowden propaganda. It looked like a campaign advertisement, I thought, watching a celluloid Harp Snowden wave to a crowd from a stand in what seemed like a New England country village. Then he was striding slowly through an urban neighborhood, stopping to hug children and clap an adolescent boy on his back. In the background, I heard the swelling sounds of Coldplay.

"Is he already running for the Democratic nomination?" I asked after viewing the ad.

"Nope," the receptionist answered. "This is a sample ad, the one they might run on MTV if the focus group likes it. I like the music, do you? I hope the group will let us use it."

"Maybe they will," I said. "Do you mean to say that there are other ads, too?"

"You'll see them all. It's on a fifteen-minute loop."

The next ad was aimed at a more conservative market, and included an old photo of a twenty-something Harp in his military uniform, then in his thirties, with his wife and children, and now, in his fifties, helping a senior citizen across the street, and speaking on a bucolic New England town square. There was something about the picture of Harp in uniform that dogged me, but I was distracted by the appearance of Harp and Martina coming through the door.

I sprang to my feet. "Senator Snowden! I don't know if you remember me, I'm Kendall Johnson's cousin—"

"Of course I remember you, Rei Shimura." The senator beamed

at me. "Have you come to volunteer? That's done out of our campaign office, which is separate—"

"It relates to that," I said quickly. "It'll only take a few minutes."

"Rei, I'll be happy to give you the name of the proper person to whom you can report. The senator's too busy to talk." Martina was impatiently tapping the toe of her pump against the floor, as if she couldn't wait to whisk the senator back behind the heavy door leading to the office proper.

"Actually, it's a matter of some sensitivity—"

"Martina, why don't you make those calls we were discussing and I'll take Rei into my office for a few minutes."

"Not more than five," Martina said. "You're very busy this afternoon."

A moment later, I was in the inner sanctum: a large, rather preppily decorated room, all except for a poster commemorating a wine festival twenty years ago in Sonoma County, which hung on the wall amid an assortment of photos of the senator shaking hands with his friends: Nelson Mandela, Bill Clinton, and more faces I should have recognized but didn't have the time to ponder. The senator seated himself on one side of an antique mahogany partners desk and motioned for me to take the chair on the other side. It all felt very historic and civilized, but I knew Martina had probably set a timer on the visit and I'd have to rush forward in a twenty-first-century manner.

He beat me to the punch. "How has your recovery been? I couldn't ask you about that in public the other evening."

"I'm all right. I didn't know that you knew I was kidnapped."

"It was in the paper. Actually, it's a bit of a coincidence, isn't it, you seeing me that night, and then the abduction happening just as it happened with your cousin."

"The thought never occurred to me that you were a factor in either kidnapping." Though maybe it should have.

"I'm reassured that you feel that way." He paused. "Kendall told me she was worried it might look bad to the press, the coincidences, I mean—"

"I'm not interested in that. But I did want to talk to you about Kendall. She feels like—well, she's getting the cold shoulder all of a sudden."

"Really? I can't imagine why unless it's a misunderstanding. Maybe Martina's keeping her out because of this fear of too much association of me with young women, given some situations with politicians in recent years."

"She said you didn't answer her phone calls anymore. And I know that you can screen those calls yourself—"

Harp Snowden sighed. "Yes, I admit to doing that occasionally. I've been busy, and I admit I bypass calls from friends if I'm doing something important."

"You may have realized that there won't be as many contributors coming from Kendall's corner as she promised. In fact, there might be a legal problem if she persisted in bringing in those people and their funds. I just wanted to warn you—"

"You don't need to explain." Harp put a finger to his lips. "Thanks for the tip. We'll consider her work done."

"That's not what I mean." I was desperate. "*Please* make sure that Kendall isn't left on the outside. She's going through a lot of . . . trouble . . . right now. She needs to earn some money, and you know she has good ideas. After viewing the sample commercials in the reception room, I can tell that you followed her advice on music that would appeal to younger voters."

"The new music. I can't keep it straight. And of course, my staffers haven't a clue as to who recorded *L.A. Woman*."

"The Doors," I said. "In the late sixties, early seventies, right?"

"The year I got shipped home from Vietnam, 1971."

"Actually, I wanted to ask you something about Vietnam. Do I have a minute left?"

Harp Snowden glanced at his watch. "You have three. What else do you need to know?"

"I wanted to know more about what happened to you in Vietnam. You said that you'd been injured in a friendly-fire incident."

"It wasn't friendly fire, but fragging." He raised his eyebrows.

"I don't recognize the word. It sounds like some kind of hazing—"

"The lingo comes from the term for a specific kind of grenade that was the preferred weapon for angry soldiers to use against their own officers."

I sucked in my breath. "Who did it? And why? I can't imagine anyone doing that to someone like you."

"Oh, plenty of people would have loved to see me dead." He smiled ruefully. "I'd come down extra hard on some of the guys who'd been caught smoking heroin the month before, and of course they thought I'd been too easy in my punishment for another soldier who'd briefly gone AWOL. Not to mention, the platoon had caught on to the fact that I was reluctant to use my own weapon. But to answer your question, I didn't see who did it. It happened at night. I wouldn't even have known to react and take cover except for hearing the pop of the spoon on the grenade's safety lever. Then I knew I had four or five seconds until it exploded. I bolted instead of sticking around to figure out who'd thrown it."

"I can understand why, and thank God you only lost your foot." I realized how bad that sounded. "I don't mean to say only. It's just that, I mean, after what happened to me . . . I'm so glad to be alive. It could have been much worse."

Harp nodded. "I feel the same way. And because I lost my foot, I was sent home, which probably saved my life."

I knew I'd used up my five minutes, because I heard a sharp knock at the door. But I hadn't gotten what I really needed yet. "One last question. I'm trying to find out if something like that happened to another former Marine. How could I do the research, if he won't talk to me?"

Harp looked at me. "The Marine Corps Historical Center, in the Washington Navy Yard, has records from Vietnam. And the information is so old now that it's no longer classified."

"Thanks," I said, just as Martina appeared through the doorway. "You've been so helpful."

"As you've been to me. Thanks for the, ah, heads-up on your cousin."

"What about her cousin? Did I miss something?" Martina demanded.

"Let's see if we can't get Kendall on the payroll somehow. And back at my table at dinner. By the way," he said, turning to me, "will you and your fiancé be there?"

"Hugh's not my fiancé anymore. I'd come if I could afford it, but I don't have a trust fund like Kendall. I wish you luck with it." I realized how disjointed my words sounded. "The dinner, I mean."

He smiled again. "Thank you. And I'm sorry to hear things didn't work out with the Scotsman. I liked him."

I stood there for a moment, feeling strange. Harp Snowden did that to me—one time, he would turn me off with his smoothness, and then another time, he would say something that revealed character in a way that made me want to take a second look. He obviously had the power of a truly magnetic politician, someone who could make it to the White House no matter where his sound track came from.

32

My thoughts in a jumble, I drifted out of the building and back to Union Station. I placed a call to the Marine Corps Historical Center in the Navy Yard. I learned that they were going to close in an hour, but I was able to make an appointment for the following morning. As I drove home, I placed a second call to Andrea. I was beginning to forget that I'd survived for so long without a cell phone, and had once thought drivers who used them were supreme jerks. I was now one of them.

Andrea picked up on the third ring and said that she couldn't talk long, as she was going out the door to start her dinner shift at Bento.

"It'll just take a second," I promised. "Did you talk to your father on the phone yet?"

"No, I haven't. I got the message last night that he wouldn't stay to meet me, and I guess I was too mad to call him today."

"Well, I need some info from your father's service record to take with me to the Marine Corps Historical Center. Unless, of course, you want to go yourself—I don't mean to overstep."

"Oh, no. It would be great if you went. The problem is, I don't have the service record anymore, and the hell if that's what I'll bring up with him if we ever do talk on the phone. As you told me last night, he was upset about us digging into things—"

"What happened to your copy of the service record? I thought it had just come in, and you kept it in a different place from the box of papers that was stolen."

"I had them in my backpack, but remember how there was that break-in at my locker at work? The service record vanished along with my wallet. I didn't mention it yesterday because I was more concerned about not having money."

"I see," I said. "But what a shame. If you still had the record, you could have told me the name of his platoon."

"It was a long name, whatever he was with," Andrea said. "There was a division and a battalion and then a company name. The letter C sticks in my mind."

I was disappointed that she didn't remember more. "Do you remember his military service number?"

"Sorry. It was too long. But he was in Vietnam from sixty-eight to seventy, I can tell you that. That was before they started using social security numbers, because I would have recognized that."

So I'd go into the archives knowing a name, a set of dates, and the letter C. It wasn't much, but it was the best that I could do.

It was odd being alone at night. I ate exactly what I wanted for dinner, which tonight was a vegetarian empanada I'd carried out from Julia's, on Eighteenth Street. I drank a glass of wine, but that didn't improve my mood. It didn't feel like my apartment again, even though Norie was gone. The truth was that it had never really been my apartment. I decided I should do the right thing and take it back to its original masculine state. After I washed Norie's sheets and towels and returned the guest room, more or less, to the way it had been, I got started in the bathroom. Every single female toiletry I could think of went inside an old wine carton. Where I was going to take it all I didn't know, but it was mine.

The phone rang, and I jumped up to get it. It was Hugh on the other end, sounding surprised.

"You're home."

"You thought I should have moved out already?"

"No. It's just that you're usually out every night. I'm still in Boston, by the way. I was calling to check on your aunt, see what her plans are."

"She flew out this morning," I said.

"So soon! What brought about that rush?"

"She did. She wanted to go." I deliberated telling him that she was going to see Sadako's relatives, but decided against it.

"Back to normal, then," he said. "What are you doing tonight?"

"Returning your apartment to its formerly tidy and masculine state," I said. "Right now, I'm attacking the bathroom."

"I don't mind your bits and pieces," Hugh said. "I like waking up with your bra dangling off the edge of my shaving mirror."

"Hugh, I'm talking about . . . moving out. You do recall that you broke off our engagement, don't you?"

"I have the ring in my handkerchief box. Every time I reach for one, I remember."

"Don't be sarcastic," I said. "I've already gotten the picture that you'd be happier without me. Anyway, I've hardly seen you in the last week or so."

"Work's been hell," Hugh said. "And as far as the other things, well, I do recall taking a leave of absence to care for a woman who didn't say more than two dozen words to me for almost a full week. Now that your aunt's gone and we don't have to walk on eggshells, perhaps we can make a bona fide attempt at discussion."

"That sounds so businesslike, so legal," I said. "I wonder what kind of words you used when you told Kendall about the baby."

"I didn't know that would upset you," Hugh said. "If it did, I'm sorry. I told her because I think of her as family."

"But she's not part of your family," I said pointedly. "Since we're not getting married."

"You know," Hugh said, "I've heard that having children can

tear people apart. Whether you raise them or you lose them, they change who you are. I'm not the same, all right? And neither are you. Even though we never saw it or held it . . ." His voice trailed off, and I realized he was crying.

"Hugh." Suddenly I felt terrible.

"We aren't the same," he said. "Maybe it wasn't meant to be. Lord knows we've had our problems over the years. We've broken up how many times?"

"I can't count," I said. "Anyway, I didn't mean to start another fight. You still probably have work to do tonight, and there will be meetings tomorrow."

"I'm coming home tomorrow," he said. "After my morning meeting, I'm taking the shuttle straight back. I have to go to the office, but I will try to be home by six . . . that is, if you'll be there."

The archive closed at four. There would be no complication in getting home. I would even have time to make dinner. But what food do you cook for someone you're breaking up with? I would have consulted with Jiro if I hadn't been so unwelcome at the restaurant.

"I'll be waiting," I said to Hugh. "I promise."

I woke up the next morning with less than an hour to get to the Navy Yard. The Marine who'd made the appointment for me over the phone the previous day had warned me that there was no parking there, so I hustled off to the Metro without breakfast.

It took forever riding to the Navy Yard on the Green Line, a line that ran from Prince Georges County, Maryland, into southeast Washington. The stretch I rode was all tunnel—no scenery, nothing to take my mind off the challenge that lay ahead of me. I had dates and a hint at a company name, but nothing solid. If Andrea hadn't lost her father's service record, I'd be set. But she had lost it, or it had been stolen, by the same person, probably, who didn't want her to have her mother's papers. I imagined this phantom person showing up at the Marine Corps Historical Center and stealing the papers I needed just before I got to them—no. It would be impossible.

When I got out of the Metro station, I found a desolate neighborhood, not dangerous or dirty, just barely inhabited. And the Navy Yard was far from the Metro itself, at least half a mile. I followed a beautifully built old redbrick wall past several magnificent, closed entrances all the way to a gate for cars that was open at M Street and Sixth. I showed my California driver's license to a sentry who politely told me that because I didn't have any government identification, I would have to enter at Eleventh Street and O where there were police who would help me. Since when was a state driver's license not government identification? I thought furiously as I trudged on for a mile and a half longer. A homeless man wandered up to me with a plastic gas can and a sob story about needing money for fuel.

"I saw you last week!" I grumbled. I could swear he'd been in Adams-Morgan, blocking my way when I needed to park. Even if it hadn't been him, I'd heard the car-out-of-gas story almost a hundred times in urban America—whether San Francisco or Baltimore or Washington. Now I was wishing I'd come in Hugh's car instead of taking public transportation because the rejected beggar trailed me all the way to Eleventh Street, as if his presence might wear me down. Finally, when I was close to the Eleventh Street entrance, which turned out to be practically underneath Interstate 295, he wandered off. The military police were clearly present, and he must not have wanted a possible tangle with them.

Once approved, and given a visitor sticker to wear, I was allowed into the Yard. It was a vast campus with real streets and traffic lights and a variety of buildings, old and new. Building 58, the Marine Corps Historical Center, was an old Marine barracks that had been painted chalk-white and had on its first floor a nice museum devoted to Marine history. The lone attendant sent me up to the third floor. Once upstairs, in a suite of offices hung with historic portraits of various Marine officers, I wound my way to the reference historian's desk. The historian, a civilian in his thirties wearing a short-sleeved shirt, khakis, and wire-rimmed glasses, was on the phone. When he hung up, I told him I was the person who'd called for an appointment the day before. I gave him Robert Norton's name, the time I thought he'd been in Vietnam, and said that the letter C might have had to do with his company or battalion.

He nodded. "C was a very large company; beyond that, he had to have been in a platoon, and then a squad. The easiest thing might be to pull the casualty card for him. That will have the detail of the company name, and you can research the unit diaries from there."

"Casualty? Doesn't that mean—dead?" I asked.

"Wounded, missing, or dead." The man was looking at me strangely, as if he realized I was far removed from the typical researcher who came in.

"Well, he was wounded, he's not dead."

"If he's not dead, why don't you ask this former Marine the name of the company he was in?" the librarian asked in a reasonable tone.

I paused. "From what's happened so far, I don't think he'd tell me. And the situation is rather—urgent."

"Well, then, I'm sorry, but it'll be harder."

"Does that mean I can't get any information?" I shouldn't have confessed about not being on good terms with Robert Norton. I'd made it clear that I was a person up to no good.

"No, of course you can get information. But looking through hundreds of pages of unit diaries—well, that will be more tedious and time consuming."

"Hey, it's only ten in the morning." I smiled at him. "I need to consume time."

So I sat down at a microfilm reader in the Marine Corps library, under a portrait of a stern-looking former Marine commander. Now I really wished I'd eaten, because looking at tiny type whizzing past usually gave me motion sickness. If only I had a dollar for every time I'd gotten sick in the libraries at Hopkins and Berkeley, I wouldn't have to worry so much about Marshall not paying me.

The unit diaries were made up of pages divided into blocks of text that identified men, their ranks and company affiliations, and any movements they made—whether it was joining a unit, leaving it for a while because of hospitalization or rest and relaxation, or serving time as a punishment. I read through a number of pages before discovering that each monthly report had a personnel roster. From that point, I moved more quickly, and I was triumphant when I finally saw Robert Norton's name among a group of ten. Now, in addition to the division and battalion, I had his serial number and company. As I traced the unit diaries further into the year, I learned that he'd been wounded by sniper fire six months into his tour, after which time he'd been hospitalized for six weeks before being transferred to a different squad. This group he was with worked on land mines and building or bombing bridges. Half the team was gone after a year due to death or injury. But Norton was hanging on, and he was promoted to lance corporal. A lieutenant named Alan Martin was in charge. He certified each report and signed it, at the very end. About a year into his tenure, though, Martin's name was gone from the reports, replaced by a Lieutenant Russell.

I remembered what Harp Snowden had said about lieutenants losing their lives in fragging incidents. The unit diaries made it clear that Martin had enforced some punishments for Marines who had gone absent from their posts or had been caught with drugs. Could that have been enough to have caused his death? And, I thought with a mixture of excitement and dread, was that Robert Norton's big secret?

33

I needed more. I went back to the reference historian and asked him if a casualty card existed for Martin. It didn't.

"I'm frustrated because I can't find him," I said. "There's a new officer signing the reports starting in 1969."

"Maybe he was transferred out. Keep going." He looked at me carefully. "But you know, you look like you need something to eat. It's one already."

He gave me directions to a nearby canteen, where I went and drank a liter of orange juice and took the turkey off the submarine sandwich I'd bought. I sat there, in the midst of men in many different uniforms—Marines in their camouflage, naval officers in khaki polyester, and sailors in flared dungarees. I was wearing jeans, too—but the Yokohama Curry T-shirt I wore gave the truth away about me, that and my self-created vegetarian submarine sandwich.

Feeling stronger, I returned to the library and went back to my microfilm reader, where the light had been turned off but the tape had remained undisturbed. I went forward, and then I saw the notation: Martin had reported to battalion headquarters, along with five of the enlisted men serving under him. Another hour with the reader revealed that after this visit, the lieutenant had been sent to Okinawa, along with Norton and another of the Marines, while the three other Marines who'd gone to battalion headquarters were split up to go to new companies in different parts of Vietnam.

I went back to the reference historian, who suggested I go to a different historian—the chief archivist, another civilian who bore more than a passing resemblance to him—the glasses, preppy dress, and a calm, interested manner in all the proceedings.

"Something happened with this squad that was serious enough for them all to go to battalion headquarters. A few of them lost rank. They all moved to different places, and the Marine whose career I'm tracking was sent on to Japan. I'm trying to find a written account of what happened."

The archivist asked me a few more questions, then spoke. "We can look for a command chronology. This would be a written report that was filed by the officer daily, an accounting of everything that happened. You don't know a particular day an incident happened, it sounds like, but you could examine some chronologies for the larger time frame."

I settled down at a computer terminal this time, because the information was stored on a CD-ROM. The records that came up on the screen were scanned copies of original typed pages, and many of them were so faint as to be almost impossible to read.

But I was persistent, and the life of the squad was interesting enough to keep me spellbound. At the beginning, Martin wrote about the daily rituals of attempting to flush out Vietcong fighters in hiding. The Americans were fired upon, and predictably, fire was returned. Only rarely was the lieutenant able to report Vietcong who'd been killed. All too often, he was able to confirm his own men as dead. When the group's corpsman was killed, morale was seriously shaken. Now Captain Martin was writing about men in the group who were frequently disobeying orders and were angry.

And then there was the shooting incident. On a hot, rainy night in June, the lieutenant dispatched a squad consisting of Private Becher and Private Jones, Lance Corporal Norton, Corporal Davidson, and Sergeant Matthews to investigate the sound of voices. The men reported that they'd been fired upon, and had fired back in return. In the ensuing gun battle, an unknown number of Vietnamese nationals died. The next day, a reconnaissance of the dwelling revealed the presence of six dead adult and adolescent females, two teenage boys, and two babies, a boy and a girl.

Lieutenant Martin had written that he'd questioned the men separately about the incident and all had recounted the same story. In conclusion, he wrote, it was most likely that the Vietnamese civilians had been caught in the crossfire as the squad reacted with justified force to enemy attack. He and the men would travel to battalion headquarters the next week to discuss the situation with an investigating officer.

All shot and killed. If people were shooting in the dark, how could there be such a perfect kill rate? Wouldn't some of them have escaped the shooting or been wounded rather than dead?

There was no record of court-martial for any of the named men. I couldn't think of an obvious next step, so I returned to the reference section to check to see if there were casualty cards for any of them. Bingo. Private Jones had died in combat in 1971 and Corporal Davidson of natural causes in 1990. Thus, the surviving men who'd gone out were Robert Norton, Sergeant Cyrus Matthews, and Arnold Becher.

"I can't believe all these men were summoned to the battalion headquarters after so many civilians were killed, yet nothing happened," I said after the reference historian had given me the casualty report. "What's that famous army incident they made a movie about, My Lai? Justice was served in that case."

"Ma'am, even if there was no court-martial, there was probably an inquiry at battalion headquarters."

I thought about Hugh and the intense privacy with which he guarded his clients. "Who is allowed access to the inquiry records?"

"Well, most of those records were declassified years ago. We can't let people deal with the reel-to-reel tapes directly, because they're so fragile, so we've put everything on CD-ROM. The sound can be sketchy at times—just as the command chronology pages are sometimes illegible—but it's there. Just ask the chief archivist for the time period that you want."

Twenty minutes later I was walking out of the Navy Yard with a CD-ROM the staff told me was mine to keep. It would play on a personal computer, but not on a Walkman, they added, as if they'd deduced somehow or other—maybe from my jeans and Asics running shoes—that I was a Walkman kind of person.

The walk along M Street seemed faster, since I had so much to think about—and no conclusion about what it meant. I needed to talk to Robert Norton, but I doubted he'd tell me the truth. If he didn't tell it to an investigator over thirty years ago, why would he tell me now? I imagined he could still implicate himself and face a court-martial. That is, if he'd knowingly killed innocents. I'm not good with babies, he'd said to me once. And I now wondered whether the reason that Andrea's crying, as an infant, had disturbed him so much was because he was flashing back to the children killed in Vietnam. When I reached the Metro, its escalator was out of service. A repairman told me to take the elevator down. I did so, moving to the side to let in another person, for a minute, taking my mind off the words winding through my brain, just to make sure the person looked all right. I avoided elevators in secluded places, but today, I had no choice. As luck would have it, my fellow rider was a disheveled man with a heavy odor and tiny, reddened, angry-looking eyes.

Great, I thought, after I'd made the identification. It was gas-can bandit, the one who'd tried to get money from me in the morning. He had a cigarette clamped between his teeth. If he actually had gas in the can, he could blow us both up in the tiny elevator. Or he could get me, if he tossed the cigarette in the can and threw it grenade-style, the way I'd heard about from Harp Snowden.

The door opened before anything happened, and we were now downstairs in the Metro station. I shot another look at him but he had already moved on. He had thrown his cigarette on the ground in front of the fare-card machine, into which he was carefully dropping coins for a fare card. Fortunately, I had paid for a round-trip fare when I'd bought my fare card that morning, so I was able to scoot through the turnstile gate ahead of him. A train was coming in, not toward Greenbelt, the direction I needed, but farther into Anacostia. A sign on the platform told me that the next train to Greenbelt was six minutes away. I saw the gas-can bandit coming down the stairs to the platform, so I took a quick step onto the train. He started to hurry, but the train doors closed when he was twenty feet away. His small, mad eyes lingered on me as the train began moving. His mouth moved, too. I couldn't understand what he was saying, but from his expression, I didn't think it was a friendly good-bye.

I jumped off the train a few stops later to take the correct train back home. Of course, I had to worry about passing back through the Navy Yard station again, and running into my friend. So I stood in the compartment closest to the conductor, and kept a careful watch out the window as we drew into the Navy Yard platform. The crazy man was nowhere to be seen. Slowly my heartbeat returned to normal as I rode the rest of the way home.

My relaxed feelings ended an hour later, when I made it through the door of the apartment and realized I'd forgotten about making something for dinner. Hugh would be coming home and there would be nothing. He'd suggest going to a restaurant, and the last thing I could face was a candlelit table for two.

I wanted a simple, fast, no-frills meal to be at least under way before he got there. That way, the night wouldn't be too long. We could get to the discussion and the resolution.

I opened the fridge and started searching its shelves desperately. Norie had left her box of cherry blossom tea, but there were no delicious Japanese leftovers, as I'd hoped—she must have thrown them away before she left. There was the half-bottle of sauvignon blanc from the previous night, and lots of condiments—coconut milk, peanut butter, soy sauce—plus frozen vegetables, which could make a Southeast Asian soup.

I had started rifling through the pantry for a box of rice noodles I knew I had when I heard the door open.

"Hello?"

"You're back five minutes early," I said, not bothering to hide my distress.

"I'm sorry to do this to you without warning, but . . ." The rest of what Hugh said vanished in the crumpling sound of paper.

I walked into the small entry hall to face up to the situation. Hugh was almost disheveled, his tie half off and his shirtsleeves rolled up and spotted with wetness. He was trying to unpack a paper grocery-shopping bag that was dripping water out of its bottom.

"Ice melts," Hugh said. "You'd think someone who passed three A levels would remember that. But they're still cold."

"Never mind." I was glad he at least had a grocery bag. I could see from its labeling that it was a store in Boston, not Washington.

I left Hugh to mop up the foyer with a bathroom towel and took the decomposing bag to the kitchen counter. There, buried in bags of ice, was a very long white paper package. I opened it and caught my breath. Two crustaceans, but freakishly long. They didn't have claws like lobsters, and they had striping on their bodies that reminded me of tiger shrimp. Like shrimp, they had heads with beady eyes and long, trailing antennae.

"Is this a joke?" I said when Hugh came in.

"I don't make jokes at forty dollars a pound. What's wrong?" He looked stricken. "Are you off prawns now?"

"No, it's just . . . are they really prawns? They seem too big."

"These two are almost fifteen inches long. They come from the Atlantic Coast, off Nigeria. I know you believe in the sanctity of *terroir* and all that, but they seemed enticing. The fishmonger said they were best broiled or barbecued . . ." His voice trailed off.

"They won't fit in the broiler," I said, shaking my head. "And we can't barbecue in April. We don't even have a barbecue grill!"

"Why don't we make one?" Hugh asked.

So we did. We took one of my old blue-and-white hibachi, set it out on the fire escape, and filled it with coals that Hugh borrowed from the downstairs neighbors. While Hugh kept watch over the coals, I ran around the corner to the organic grocery to buy some field greens for a salad, and strawberries and cream for dessert.

When I returned, Hugh had already set the table in the dining room, poured wine, and melted butter with lemon. The prawns were grilling on the rack.

"I didn't know you liked to grill," I said.

"Oh, I think it's in the male genetic code to want to build fires. Is there any more of this wine?"

"Yes, but it's not chilled. Just take the glass you poured for me." I didn't want anything addling my brain. The discussion with Hugh still loomed ahead. After it was done, I planned to jump on the computer to read through the command chronologies I'd gotten on disc from the archives.

The prawns were luscious, rich beyond belief, and a perfect match with the butter. And one each really was enough, if you ate the salad.

I worked steadily at eating. It wasn't until we'd gotten to the strawberries that Hugh spoke. "Is there a reason you're avoiding it?"

"The wine? No, I had a little last night. But I can't drink tonight if I'm going to run tomorrow." I actually hadn't thought about running, but it made sense. It was about time I got moving again.

"Actually, what I meant to ask is why you're still avoiding me. Last night, after I talked to you on the phone, I thought everything might turn out all right, but since I've been home, it's just been . . . the same."

"Ah. So you thought this idea, making a special dinner, would change everything back to the way it was?" I paused. "It was a delicious meal, Hugh. Much better than even the Yin-Yang shrimp at Bento. Thank you."

"There's no point. Food—you can spend on it, slave over it, but in the end it all goes to waste." Hugh pushed away his plate.

"I try to think about what happened to us," I said. "Two months ago, we both had work. We were planning a wedding.

Then my aunt came and we weren't alone anymore. We started pretending we weren't cohabiting and, in a way, that led to it really being true that we weren't."

"The irony is that we weren't alone two months ago. There were three of us." He put his head in his hands.

"Oh, Hugh." I closed my eyes. "Don't. You know that if we had found out about it, we would have been in such a panic, the two of us pregnant and not married!"

"We would have married. We were on the verge, I thought."

"And I suppose you think I would have stayed in the apartment and carried out the pregnancy just right, no jogging or heavy lifting and certainly not jumping out of car trunks." My words came fast and hard.

"I wouldn't have made rules. How could I ever possibly impose anything on you?"

"Well, you've got me living in a city I've turned out not to like at all," I said. "And when we were at Andrea's that day, you said you wouldn't marry me if I didn't do what you wanted. You were different when you were wooing me, Hugh. You were so easy and agreeable. You let me breathe."

"Right," Hugh said thoughtfully. "I have changed. I fell in love with you and was delighted when you agreed to move in. Then, your aunt arrived for three weeks and I pretended this *wasn't* my flat, because that was what you wanted. Before I knew it, I was mediating your cousin's legal problems and hauling boxes of your friend's clothing. Yes, I've changed. And pardon me for trying to keep you alive. It's just that I love you."

"You can't mean that. You broke the engagement."

"I gave an ultimatum and you called my bluff. You threw the ring back at me." He paused. "But how proud are you, really? I'm finding that after this last week of hell, I'm not too proud to say that I'm sorry. That I want you back."

I couldn't answer. I stood up and began carrying plates into the kitchen. I couldn't be as bad as he'd said, one side of my brain told me. The other side said that he was all too right.

I was standing at the kitchen sink, quietly crying, when he came up behind me. I felt his hands on my shoulders, so tentative. His lips on my hair. Then I turned around and into his arms. This was it, the moment we'd needed weeks ago at the hospital. I'd been too broken up to take any more handling. But not now. I wanted it all.

Later that night, I wished for a cigarette. I'd never been a smoker, but now I longed for something to put a bridge between what had just happened and what I was thinking about now. Hugh had made love to me so slowly, so perfectly, but I'd felt as if he had only brushed the surface. As we had moved together I'd felt so serious, so sorrowful, that there was no room for anything else.

I loved him, but if my brain couldn't tell my body what pleasure meant anymore, what was the point? I had changed. I was not the same girl who'd once run across the streets of Tokyo ignoring the red lights. I was a woman like Sadako, someone who'd crossed an ocean she hadn't been meant to cross. I wasn't happy, but at least I was still alive. Sadako wasn't, but I was on the edge of a discovery of who had done that to her.

Hugh slept soundly on, a half-smile visible on his face in the sliver of light from the open door. But I couldn't lie still, not for another moment. I tied on a robe and got up and went into the guest room that was once again a study. I opened the envelope containing the photocopies, book, and disc that I'd been given at the Marine Corps library. I booted up the computer. It was time to listen.

34

"You poor thing." I felt the hand in my hair at the same time Hugh's voice spoke softly in my ear. I sprang up from where I'd fallen asleep at the keyboard. I'd spent the night at my desk. I'd started around midnight, and now it was light outside.

"Oh, hi." I shook off his hand, feeling embarrassed to be found this way. "I was listening to records of an inquiry."

"Can you give me a capsule report over breakfast?" As Hugh spoke, he was tying a Windsor knot in a new necktie, red and blue, with oversized dots. So it really was the morning. I squinted at the old Seiko clock hanging on the wall. It was already eight-thirty.

Hugh poured tea as I told him about Robert Norton's involvement in the civilian shooting. Then I described the taped recording of the inquiry into the events of the night of June 22, 1970. Sergeant Matthews, who was the highest-ranking of the men in the squad, had the platoon's sole pair of night-vision goggles to use. When he'd taken the patrol to the suspected enemy site, Sergeant Matthews told the investigator that they'd come under enemy sniper fire. He'd shouted for all to take cover, and then to return fire in the direction of a group of trees from which the shots had come. A high-pitched crying sound confirmed a strike.

They'd fired some more rounds just to make certain no accomplices had survived. Then all had retreated back to camp.

The next voice I recalled was that of Jones, the soldier who had died by the war's end. He gave, in almost the same words, a story identical to that of Sergeant Matthews. The investigator had asked him what he'd thought when he'd heard the high-pitched cry. "I guess I thought someone was wounded. And you know, I was glad we hit someone. We almost fell in a punji pit on the way over; if it hadn't been for the night-vision goggles, we would have. We came across three land mines the day before. It was a serious VC stronghold."

Becher barely got a word out. He stuck to yeses and nos and, upon being asked to describe the events of the night, offered, "It's like what Sergeant Matthews said."

When the investigator pointed out that no shells were found on the scene, along with no weapons, he had no answer. But Norton, when he was asked the same thing, suggested that other Vietcong might have picked up those weapons to use for themselves, along with the spent shells. And he hadn't seen any women or children on the patio outside the hut, either.

When I was done with the account, Hugh asked me for a definition of a punji pit. I told him he probably didn't want to know while eating breakfast, but he insisted, so I told him about how the guerillas smeared excrement on long, sharp spikes that they embedded in pits, hoping that their enemy would trip and fall into these pits at night.

Hugh made a face when I was through. "Let's talk about night-vision goggles, then."

"I fell asleep last night wondering about it. If Sergeant Matthews had night-vision goggles, he would have been able to see these people he gave the order to fire upon."

"I agree in principle," Hugh said slowly. "But you know, battle is supposed to be so chaotic—he really might not have seen them. And if they were wearing helmets, they might not have heard the difference between an adult cry and a child's."

"They should have been able to tell a baby's cry from an adult's. I would have."

We exchanged glances then, and I saw in his face what I'd felt in my gut for the last few weeks.

"I know," Hugh said. "And I'm sorry."

"It's not your fault," I said.

"And neither is it yours." He paused, then went on, "Are you going to the restaurant tonight?"

I shook my head. I couldn't begin to tell him about how badly things had gone with Marshall and my payment.

"Well, then, shall we try again?" He smiled at me.

"I don't really want to go to Bento," I began.

"No, I mean, trying—as in going back to bed. Tonight," he added, when I looked at him blankly. "Last night didn't work for you. I didn't push because I was—afraid of hurting you. But it must have been—a bore."

"It was fine." I felt myself start to blush.

"Well, it's not fine with me. I want another chance. Let's have a *mojito* at Café El Rincon first, just like old times."

"Actually, Hugh, I'll take a rain check on that." I knew there was nothing physically that should hold me back from intimacy. I loved him. I'd wanted to last night, with every ounce of my being—but it just hadn't been the same. I'd carried a child, and lost it. Sex would never be what it had once been, no matter how many *mojitos* I were to drink.

Hugh kissed the top of my head. "All right, then. But I'll see you tonight."

"You've been away from the home office for a while. I expect you'll need to stay late," I said.

"Why should I, when I want to see you?"

Ever since he'd returned from Boston, I'd felt so strange—filled with a mixture of excitement and despair. It wasn't the same. It never would be again. Since I didn't know how to answer him, I escaped to the shower.

And just as I'd expected, by the time I'd emerged and gotten dressed, he was gone.

• • •

I went to my warehouse that day to take inventory. Even if I wasn't leaving Washington and Hugh's apartment, it was high time that I revisited the goods Mr. Ishida had sent me in the hope that I'd sell them. Now it was time to see what I could afford to hang on to for a while, and what I really should press to sell—even if I had to do it online, or through classified ads. I was going to keep on earning a living—Marshall Zanger hadn't stopped me.

The thought of Bento, though, sent me off on a new tack. It seemed so clear that the things that had happened to me, and now Andrea, were linked. I wondered if there was a chance that someone connected to the long-ago scandal in Vietnam was actually working at Bento.

Ever since Andrea had mentioned that her father's service record had been stolen at work, I'd struggled with the idea that there might be a thief on the premises. For a long time, I'd felt there were a few suspicious characters there. Phong, I knew for sure, was Vietnamese, not only because of his name, but what he'd said about his parents running a Vietnamese restaurant in Arlington. Arlington, Virginia, was another connection to the Norton family, because they'd lived there when Andrea was young. It seemed crazy that Phong would be involved in suppressing any truth about brutality shown toward his own people, but of course, there were two kinds of Vietnamese fighting the battle—the Americans' South Vietnamese allies, and the Communists from North Vietnam. I remembered that there had been many Vietnamese names sprinkled through the command chronology that I'd read a day earlier. If I learned Phong's full family name, or his parents' names, I might find another link.

And what about Jiro? By now, I was almost certainly in agreement with my aunt that he was not Japanese. Could he be Vietnamese? It was a far-fetched idea, but worth looking up—as were the names of all the men working in the kitchen. Alberto, the observant one, the cook who'd seen Kendall walk through the kitchen right before her kidnapping—and who'd also been overly curious about my conversation with Andrea's father and brother. There was also the new dishwasher called Toro. His arm tattoo seemed more an old-fashioned military one than a fashion statement, and he also looked old enough to have served in Vietnam.

I knew that Marshall kept his employment records in his office, because I'd caught a glimpse of a folder labeled as such when Jiro had taken me in there to give me the check Marshall had finally made out to me. If I could get a glimpse of the employment records, I could learn more about Phong and Toro.

Andrea was right at her station as I made it into Bento around five-fifteen.

"Hi, sweetie," she purred, moving in to deliver a society-lady set of cheek-to-cheek air kisses, and indeed, she looked very Grace Kellyesque tonight, for a girl who was half-black and half-Japanese. Her curls had been lacquered behind her ears, and she wore a fluid silk charmeuse dress the color of a Cosmopolitan.

"You look stunning," I said, suddenly feeling self-conscious in my bootleg jeans and small T-shirt that barely grazed my navel. I was too casual, but I'd come straight from the warehouse and wasn't anticipating staying for dinner.

"Oh, thanks." She made a funny face. "I wouldn't be dressed like this if you hadn't helped save my wardrobe. So what's going on with the military records you've been looking at? I have to tell you that your timing is perfect, because we haven't opened for dinner yet."

True, but Phong was at the bar, a few steps away. He was polishing the zinc surface and looked up at me as if he, too, was interested in hearing what I had to say.

"I can't talk about that right now," I said in a low voice. "I've got to get into Jiro and Marshall's office to check up on something—without them knowing. Are the two of them in?"

"Well, Marshall's going off to Mandala for the night, but Jiro's in, and the kitchen guys are all eating dinner before the shift starts. Tonight it's a Japanese noodle soup, kind of like what your aunt made, but with shrimp. And speaking of your aunt, has she checked in yet?"

"No. I have her hotel number, though. I'll call her." I was distracted by Andrea's inquiry because I had wanted to make it into Marshall and Jiro's office. Too many people would see me. I should have arranged my trip to arrive later on, when it would be busy and nobody would have time to think about why I was there.

"Andrea, could you do me a favor?" I asked in a low voice.

"Sure. What do you need?"

"I want to look at the real names of the people who work here, where they were born and stuff like that—"

"Like the INS?" She frowned at me. "Oh, I know. You're still on that trip of your aunt's about Jiro not being Japanese."

"It's not that," I whispered, mindful of Phong hovering nearby. "Never mind."

"I'd like to help you," Andrea said, "but there's no way somebody like me could get away with being in that room. And I just got my job back. I don't want to risk losing it."

I nodded.

"Well, maybe later on, after the restaurant closes, we could get together at Plum Ink to talk about things," Andrea said.

I remembered that Hugh was making a special effort to be in that night. I couldn't just walk out afterward. "Andrea, I don't think I'll be able to drive over that late. I'm sorry."

"Oh, of course," Andrea said. "I'd almost forgotten about what happened to you. Can we just check in by phone or something?"

"That's a great idea. You have my home phone number," I said. "Call me tonight after eleven, okay?"

The kitchen door opened and Justin came out, once again dressed in waiter's garb: a lime-colored cotton shirt tucked into black wool-gabardine pants. He smirked at me. "Well, hello, sweetie. Come again to collect your hard-earned cash? Or are you going to add another dinner to your tab?"

I said in a carrying voice, "Actually, I needed to buff some furniture, but it turns out that the special wax I left here is gone. I'm going to have to get some more from my warehouse and come back either this evening or tomorrow."

"You have a warehouse?" Justin eyed me skeptically. "I thought you worked out of your home."

"I have a warehouse, Justin." I was losing my patience. "Believe it or not, I have a warehouse and a professional life outside this restaurant."

"Is that so?" Marshall's voice said. He'd come in right behind me, so I hadn't noticed. Now I was very glad I hadn't gone into his office.

"Yes, that's the way it is. I appreciate the payment you made for the picture framing, but I'm still waiting for the rest," I said.

"Speaking as one professional to another, it's a matter of courtesy to wait until things are solvent."

I thought of making a snippy remark about whether the Washington *City Paper*, or the *Post* would be interested in learning about fashionable Bento's insolvency. But I wanted to return to the restaurant that night, not subject to another permanent ban. With a tight smile, I said, "I'll return sometime soon to take care of the *tansu*, Marshall. I stand by my furniture, just as I stand by my word."

I left then, thinking for a split second of taking Hugh up on his offer to have a happy-hour drink. All of a sudden, I could use a *mojito*. But instead, I hopped a packed rush-hour subway train. Well, it wasn't really packed—it was crowded, I amended, as I stood with my hand on the overhead rail. Nothing was crowded the way Tokyo trains were. I closed my eyes, putting myself back on the Ginza Line for an instant. I opened them, looking for the brilliant banner of wedding and pharmaceutical advertisements that always lined the top of the Japanese subway cars. There was nothing except a blandly written transit authority reminder not to leave trash or personal possessions on the train.

I walked quickly from Dupont Circle, feeling goose bumps on

my skin as I approached the corner of Connecticut and Columbia Road. There were plenty of people walking—nothing would happen to me. And soon, I'd have all the information I needed to put those fears to rest forever. I'd already begun thinking about picking up the tin of wax I kept under the kitchen sink and heading straight back to Bento. If I got there around seven, the kitchen would be busy. Marshall would be at Mandala, so I'd be able to slip into his office via the kitchen entrance and look at the employment records.

Hugh wasn't home when I got in, but the light on the answering machine was blinking. When I pressed PLAY, I discovered that the call had come in from Japan. My aunt Norie had called hours earlier, in the morning, when I'd gone out. It was urgent that I call her back, she said, no matter the hour. She left a number with an unfamiliar city code. I cobbled the new number behind the country code for Japan, and, feeling guilty that I was calling her at six A.M. her time, made the call.

A sleepy-sounding person announced that I'd reached the Sakura Hotel. I apologized for disturbing him, and then asked to be connected to the room of Norie Shimura.

"I'm really sorry to disturb you and Ojisan," I said after my aunt answered in a sleepy voice.

"I wanted to speak to you! I found Atsuko-san!" My aunt sounded as triumphant as she'd been the first time I'd spoken a full Japanese sentence.

"Tell me," I said, getting out a pencil and paper.

Norie had taken the letters, and a gift of American candied nuts, to the address. Both had worked to sweeten the entry through the door of the house that had turned out to still be home to Atsuko, who had married, and had a grown son. In the house, Norie had instantly recognized Sadako's picture hanging in the alcove in their best reception room. Since contact between the two sisters had broken, Atsuko had assumed that her sister was dead.

"Now what is interesting," Norie said, "is that Atsuko-san had never seen those letters that her sister sent from America."

"Yes, of course. Those letters were returned unopened from Japan—"

"The handful of letters that *we* read were returned by the sisters' mother, who was the one who received the daily post. The mother and father were very much against the foreign marriage. Atsuko wasn't. But as you can imagine, after what happened with the one daughter, the parents married Atsuko-san quickly—an *omiai*," Norie added, using the word for an arranged marriage. "Atsuko-san lived with her husband's family a few miles away, early on in the marriage, but eventually, she wound up in her house for a few months taking care of her own mother after she'd had a stroke. And then, one day, a letter from Sadako-san came. And she knew what had happened to her sister, and wrote back with words of love and support, she told me. This letter writing went on for about a year. By this time, Sadako's letters did not come from Virginia, but from a place in Maryland called Kent Island."

"Kent Island! That's on the Eastern Shore. She could still be there!"

"Don't become too excited, my dear. As I just said, the letters stopped." Norie's voice was gentle. "Atsuko said that Sadako confessed that she had run away from the marriage and planned to go back for Akiko-chan—Andrea," Norie corrected herself. "But Atsuko never did receive a letter saying the two were reunited. The letters just stopped in late 1976."

"Does Atsuko-san believe her sister is dead?" I asked.

"She suspected that something terrible had happened. Through the copies of the letters that I took her, she learned about the men who had frightened Sadako-san. I felt quite bad for taking them to her, actually. She broke down. She insisted that Andrea come to her."

"She knows Andrea is still alive, then?"

"Of course! I showed her pictures on my digital camera. She wants her to come to Japan. They will pay for the trip, even."

So Andrea was wanted. I felt a bit of warmth in the midst of the gloom, but maybe it was unrealistic. "What about the family's reputation? Do they really think they can get along with an American niece?"

"Atsuko never bore the prejudice that her parents did. That's why Sadako kept writing to her, I'm sure."

I heard a car door slam and looked out of my window to see that Hugh had gotten a rare space on the street. If he walked into the apartment now, I'd find myself trapped in his idea of an intimate evening. On the other hand, if I slipped out, I could get what I needed at the restaurant and be back within an hour and a half. Hugh would never know the difference.

"I've got to hang up now, I'm sorry," I said to Norie.

"But wait! Atsuko-san must have Andrea's telephone number. Her son speaks English and wants to be the interpreter—"

"I'll call you back," I said, the receiver already on its way down.

35

I grabbed the tin of paste wax from under the kitchen sink. A buffing cloth, a buffing cloth. There wasn't a clean one around. I darted back to the bedroom and retrieved an undershirt from the laundry hamper. It would have to do. I had opened the kitchen door and had just stepped out on the fire escape when Hugh walked in the kitchen.

"What are you doing?" The puzzlement was clear in both his face and voice.

I tried to stuff his undershirt in my backpack so he wouldn't notice it. "Ah, I had to run out to do something quickly."

"Why didn't you use the front door instead? And did you forget that we had plans tonight?" With each step he took toward me, his concern seemed to grow.

"Well, Hugh, the world doesn't just revolve around you," I said, unable to hide my frustration that my quick exit was no longer possible.

"I see." He had dropped his briefcase on the floor, and was staring at me as if he'd seen a ghost. "Who is it, then?"

"What do you mean, who is it?" I tried to make a joke of things. "Don't tell me you've gone woo-woo on me."

"Who is it?" Hugh repeated in a steadier voice. "Obviously, you're going to spend the night, or a portion of the night, somewhere. But why on earth you want to sleep in one of my vests while you're in bed with another bloke mystifies me. Borrow his clothing, why don't you?"

"I'm sorry I took your precious undershirt or vest or whatever you want to call it. Here." Already I had balled it up and thrown it at him.

"Now I'm starting to understand. I've been gone too long." Hugh cocked his head and looked at me coldly. "All those restaurant people . . . which one is it? One of the waiters or that soulful Japanese chef? Or have you gone AC-DC? Is it Andrea who turns you on?"

"You can't be serious." I cocked my head at him, trying to figure out if his reaction was a joke. He was a pretty good practical joker, when he wanted to be.

"I wouldn't put anything past you, Rei. After all, you have no desire for me anymore."

"I do. I'm just in need of a little rest and relaxation, I told you that yesterday." I stepped back fully into the kitchen, closing the door behind me while I kept my attention on Hugh. I didn't know what he'd do next.

"Rest and relaxation, you say. Well, I've got the ticket for you." His Scottish accent burred the rs to a smooth, menacing edge. "Come here."

I didn't move.

"Well, if that's the way you want it." Hugh strode over to me, and picked me up in his arms as if I were as light as Jacquie or Win. Then he carried me to the bedroom, where he dumped me on the sleigh bed.

"Take off your clothes," he said.

"Okay, I know you've been weight lifting and all, but it seems out of character for you to use force on me—"

"Did it hurt when I carried you?"

"No, but it was rather—startling."

"Good. Now, take off your clothes, like I said."

"I'm not some army private, Hugh. I don't have to respond to orders." I was going to tell him that the kind of orders he was giving were what the military would deem illegal, but before I had a chance, the striped T-shirt I'd been wearing was halfway across the room, and he was yanking down my jeans. They went by the foot of the bed, followed by my bra, which he removed with a quick snap of one hand.

"Did you learn that move from watching *Happy Days?*" I said to defuse the tension.

"I don't watch American television," he said between gritted teeth.

I was scared, suddenly—but also, I admitted inwardly, a little excited. I watched Hugh loosen his tie, then pull it off. But instead of hanging it up, he tied it to another tie he pulled off his tie rack, and then another one. Within the space of two minutes, he'd created a long, thin length of multicolored silk.

"Um, isn't that the Aquascutum your mother sent you for your last birthday? You wouldn't want to ruin it by tying a knot you'll never get out."

"I know how to make good knots. I sailed when I was a boy."

He wasn't exaggerating about his ability with knots. Before I had time to grab my right wrist away, it was tied up. He slid the long rope he'd made under the mattress, then pulled it out on the other side, where I'd already stretched my other arm.

I couldn't quite believe what I'd done. To cover up my confusion, I told him he had me in an incorrect position.

"No," he said. "I have you right where I want you."

I couldn't see what he was doing anymore, but I felt my underwear slide off my legs. Then, the sound of more crisp knots and my ankles were bound. I could move up and down a bit, but I couldn't turn over.

"This is about my independence, isn't it?" I murmured. "The ultimate attempt to beat me down."

"Why would I do that?" said Hugh as he covered my back with his own body. I decided to experience it for a few seconds before coming out with any more protests.

As his tongue touched my skin, so lightly, experimentally that I had to struggle to hold still, I said, "You can't just make someone come."

"Can't I?" His hands were everywhere, detecting what I was afraid he would find out—that my reaction, tonight, was quite different from the night before.

"Oh!" I said, inadvertently. I was determined not to reward him with pleasure.

"That's right." He kissed me between the shoulder blades. "You have no choices tonight, no responsibility for the way that it feels. You can't help it if you like my hand inside like this—or my tongue over here."

No choices. There was absolutely nothing I could do but stay tethered in place, allowing his mouth and fingernails and palms to do what they wanted—no, I corrected myself, *what I wanted*. He was doing exactly what I wanted, but I would never have said that, not now.

The ordeal seemed to last for hours—my hovering on a precipice, his movement away from the one touch that would set me off, end it all. I forgot about being tired, I forgot about being angry and humiliated. I forgot everything except for what I was feeling at that moment, with Hugh.

I came the first time as the sun was setting outside the thin muslin curtains that were moving in the half-open window. All through the neighborhood, I imagined people were eating their dinners, reading newspapers, listening to the news on the radio. It was that kind of neighborhood. Somewhere, there was probably a couple arguing, another having sex. But not like this. I didn't know anyone who'd had sex like this.

I heard my voice raggedly asking him not to leave me, to give me more. Finally, he moved into me from behind. Like an animal, I thought, for a few great minutes before I coursed upward and felt myself break into a hundred sharp fragments. I was turning into a shooting star, a bomb, a grenade . . .

Hugh collapsed next to me ten minutes later. Or maybe it was an hour. I didn't know or care.

"Sorry," he said.

"What?" I murmured absently. It almost sounded as if he'd apologized.

"I really did think I could make you come."

"It happened. Twice, in case you wondered. For the record books."

"Yes, our private record book." His voice was tender. "But I think you're right, I probably did it—that way—because I was reacting to your independence. And I'm sorry about that. Shall I release you from captivity?"

There was a great deal of difference between being tied up and being delightfully serviced by—rather than servic*ing*—a man, but I wasn't in the mood to deliver a neo-feminist lecture. I was completely flustered as he moved around the bed, quickly releasing me from the silk bonds. When he was finished, I drew my legs together and curled up so I that was against his back. With my lips on his skin, I confessed how much I'd liked what had happened.

"If only it were all so easy." Hugh sighed heavily. "When I first met you, I knew you were the only one—but you turned out to think I was the stupidest Westerner on the island of Honshū. And then we got engaged last Christmas, and I thought things were finally going to be perfect, but they've turned out not to be. No matter how well we shag each other."

"Speaking of that, I was wondering—did you use protection?" I asked.

"Of course." Hugh reached back and patted my hip. "Although I hope you'll consider letting me ride bareback sometime after we get married."

I rubbed at my wrists. "But we *shouldn't* marry. This just proved it. People who are married never have sex like this."

"Oh, that worry again. Why can't it stay good? Don't you realize that this is what I want, too?" He rolled around so that he was facing me.

I was silent for a minute, then said, "When you're involved in raising a baby, you can't just drop everything and be hedonistic with each other."

"You can't," Hugh agreed. "Except when the baby's napping."

"Look, if monogamy is what you're after, you've got it. I just don't want to ruin it by becoming a Mrs."

"Did you know that the old English root of the word 'Mrs.' is 'mistress'? I'd think that might appeal to your provocative side."

"I can be your mistress *without* being married," I said. "Don't you think it might be . . . spicier . . . if we had separate residences?"

"No," Hugh said flatly.

"Come on, Hugh. It would mean the thrill of you laying your toothbrush and shaving things next to my toiletries on Friday nights. We'd go out for breakfast on Saturday mornings because I wouldn't have a huge tin of your favorite Darjeeling on the counter. And later on, there would be the thrill of my *not* having to wash your laundry, because you'd take it back to wash at your own place."

"Ah," said Hugh. "So I might enjoy the thrill of paying for your dinner, rather than budgeting for it out of my regular household account. Or the thrill of buying you lingerie on a business trip, hoping that you might wear it on a date sometime."

"Precisely!" I said, even though the things he'd chosen to be thrilled about seemed rather impersonal.

"The thrill of telling our parents that we've canceled our engagement for the sake of spicy shagging! The thrill of telling the same to our respected Japanese elders and friends. Yes, I can see the thrills arriving fast and furiously for the rest of our lives!"

"You're making fun of me." I kissed his neck.

"I'm not." Hugh pulled my face up to his, and kissed me on the mouth. "It's just that I really treasured the idea of living with you, forever. It made my heart race to see my old family ring on your left hand, and I dreamed about fixing up a flat in the city and perhaps even a small country house, after we had a—"

A child. A bairn or a wee one, a baby or an *aka-chan*. There were so many ways to say it, but he didn't. Nor did I. I just kissed his face, which was wetter than before, and fell asleep with him for a little while.

36

I awoke around eleven, when I heard a TV comedy show blaring in the apartment above. If I could hear them that clearly, how clearly could they hear our bedroom? But even worse than the embarrassment was my realization that Bento would be closing in roughly an hour without my getting in to research the employment records. Now was my chance.

I didn't shower because I didn't want to risk waking Hugh. Instead, I tiptoed to the dresser to get clean underwear and a little black dress. It made sense to go into Bento looking good, at the hour when I'd be entering it. Marshall wouldn't be there anymore, and if the last dinner orders had been placed, Jiro himself would have headed home. The bosses would be gone, and I'd do my thing without attracting staff attention.

As an added precaution, I picked a Hiroshige woodblock print right off Hugh's living room wall, and gathered up my tool kit. If anyone caught me in Marshall's office, I would say that I was hanging a picture. Then, taking one final sweep of the room, which included packing up the can of wax as well as a real buffing cloth, I decided to do one last thing. I wrote a note.

Dear Hugh,
Just in case you wake up before I return, I have borrowed your car for a
trip to Bento.

I imagined his face, so I added,

I knew you'd think this was safer than walking to the Metro. I have just a
little bit of paperwork to go through there. I'll be back as fast as I can, and
don't worry about me not finding a parking spot when I return, because I
know about the illegal spot at the end. Love from your rule-breaking mistress,
Rei.

That struck the right playful note. I headed outside, clicked the car open, and climbed in, locking up immediately. I was taking no chances. Once I got downtown, if I couldn't park in the pad right behind the kitchen, I would park in the bus-stop zone out front. I figured that I'd be in and out within the space of ten minutes.

The restaurant was blazing with light as I drove slowly past it. The sea-grass and aubergine-painted walls, hung with the old plates and pictures I'd found for them, looked beautiful—at least, to me. The front tables still had a few customers, but I couldn't tell what else was going on inside. I cut down the driveway that led to the back of the restaurant, where the parking pad was bare. The area was to be used for Marshall and Jiro's cars and any deliveries—so if it was empty, that meant I was in good shape. I took Jiro's spot and quickly hopped up the back staircase and into the kitchen.

One of the dishwashers, Toro, nodded at me, but the other guy practically had his head and shoulders buried in the stockpot he was washing. One of the vegetable prep guys was mopping the floor. I didn't see anyone else cooking. That meant, I guessed, that the kitchen and waitstaff had all either gone home or had moved on to Plum Ink. The couple in the front were the last stragglers. There was probably one waiter around to bring them cappuccino and hand them their bill, but the house was basically empty.

"How lucky I am," I murmured to myself as I swept with all

my things into Jiro and Marshall's office. I wasn't even going to bother with waxing the *tansu*. I'd just get to the papers I needed.

I moved to the file cabinet where Jiro had found my check the last time. I pulled on the door, but it didn't budge. Locked. I swept my hand along the top of the file cabinet, and came up with a small key. Very efficient security, I thought wryly. If it were my file cabinet, I'd put the key in a truly hard-to-think-of place. Hanging behind a picture, maybe.

I flipped through the files carefully. My fingers were almost perfectly healed, I realized. It made things easy. I examined bills to be paid, bills paid, vendor names and addresses, accounting, employees . . .

I picked up the folder marked "Employees" and opened it. I'd been hoping for a list of names and Social Security numbers, but it turned out to be a grab bag of applications, some of which carried the names of people I'd never heard of, names, perhaps, of people Marshall might hire someday. There were also odd slips of paper with people's names and phone numbers handwritten on them, and then, lots of photocopies of Social Security cards and green cards. Here were Alberto and Julio's cards, proving both of them foreign-born but legal. David Macauley, the Australian waiter with whom Andrea was staying, also had legal working papers. The U.S. citizens included people I'd expected, like Justin, and some I hadn't been sure of, like Phong. He'd been born in Arlington and his last name was Nguyen—just my luck, because it seemed there were even more Nguyens around than Shimuras. I wished I knew Toro's real name. There were many Social Security photocopies with names that I didn't recognize, names like Jiminez, Drake, Anders, Nebblet . . .

Nebblet. It was an odd, old-fashioned, English-sounding name that I'd heard somewhere. I hadn't seen it in the military records, I thought, but I had looked at hundreds of names in the last twenty-four hours. The *N* name I recalled was Norton, not Nebblet. But then, as I tried the names together in my mind, I remembered.

In Lorraine Norton's sorority photograph, her maiden name had been Nebblet. And hadn't Robert Norton said something about enlisting because a friend of his from boyhood had done so?

Maybe a relative of Lorraine's was working in the kitchen. But since when? I remembered when Robert Norton had hurriedly left the Bento kitchen with me. He'd asked about Toro, the dishwasher, how long he'd worked there. If Toro were a Neblett—a relative through marriage—he should have talked to him directly. What was going on?

Maybe they'd been in the military together. Maybe he'd been one of the two men stalking Robert and terrifying Sadako. I would look for the name. In my bag, I had not only the command chronology, but a unit diary from the first company that Robert Norton had served in. There was the name. "Michael Neblett." But who was he? I ran over the recognizably black employees in the kitchen. Dominic was Haitian, Luis was Brazilian, they both had green cards. Neither could be Neblett.

I sat down on the floor so I wouldn't be so visible through the glass window in the door, and went through the notes I'd made on another page. Here was Robert Norton's home phone number. I dialed it. On the fourth ring, just before I was ready to hear an answering machine and hang up, someone answered.

"Yeah?" The voice sounded like a young man's, slightly high-pitched.

"Davon, it's Rei Shimura, calling from Washington."

"Yeah. You aren't back in Japan yet?"

"No, there's some serious business going on. I want to ask you if you've ever heard of anyone called Michael Neblett."

"Sure. That's my crazy uncle Mike. He was in 'Nam with Dad."

"What do you mean, he's crazy?" I asked.

"I dunno. People just say that 'cause he can't hold a job. We haven't seen him in years. Why do you care? Do you want to play with his mind, too, tell him about that girl who's supposed to be my sister?"

"So whom did your father meet first, your uncle Mike or your mother?"

"Davon won't know the answer to that," a woman's voice said. "Hang up, honey."

I heard a clicking sound, and Lorraine and I were all alone on the long-distance line. I asked, "How long have you been listening in?"

"Long enough," said Lorraine. "Listen, Robert told you to leave well enough alone. I will, too, but yes, if you must know, my brother Mike and Robert both enlisted in the Marine Corps."

"What did your brother do in the military?" I asked.

"Oh, he went here and there. He's suffering from PTSD and basically is supported by Veterans Administration benefits. It's a very sad situation, actually, and I'd thank you not to pry any further or try to meet him."

"He was with Robert in Vietnam," I said, looking at the photocopied page of an old unit diary that I'd pulled. "He wasn't in the squad that killed the women and children that night, but he was in the company. He must have found out what really happened."

"You are out of line," Lorraine said. "And by the way, I know for a fact you're not really from Japan."

"How's that?" I asked.

"You've had a Social Security card since your birth in this country. Not that you've earned much toward your retirement allotment," she added unnecessarily. "Social Security numbers are important to keep confidential. It would be terrible if someone took over your name and Social Security number for themselves."

I laughed. "You're trying to scare me into thinking you'll screw with my Social Security number?"

"I said no such thing. But accidents do happen—"

"Lady," I said, "I had a miscarriage after escaping from some thug kidnappers, one of whom I'm almost certain is your precious brother. After that experience, I'm hardly afraid of—bureaucratic chicanery."

Lorraine started yelling then, but I was distracted by the appearance of a flash of color in the glass window of the office door. I looked up and saw Jiro Takeda standing outside, watching me. I hung up the phone immediately and got to my feet.

"What are you doing?" Jiro asked. He was dressed in civilian clothes, a black polo shirt and worn jeans. Obviously, he'd gone somewhere and come back, because he had his car keys in his hand.

I still had the picture right at my feet, the one I had planned to use as a ruse if anyone found me. But I wasn't touching the picture—I had my hand right in the employment papers. And the room was soundproof, I knew from my time in there before. Since Jiro hadn't heard the conversation, he probably believed I was there to steal the money that Marshall owed me.

I ran through possible explanations in my mind. I could pretend that I was looking in the employment records to find out someone's birthday. I could say that I'd forgotten to give Marshall my Social Security number, which he'd need if he were to issue me a check. I could also explain what I was really doing, but I knew it would sound unbelievable.

"What are you doing?" Jiro repeated.

"I—I wanted to know the names of some of the people working here," I said.

"If you wanted to learn names, why, then, didn't you ask Marshall or me?" Jiro was almost hyperventilating. "Anyway, that file is locked! How did you get inside?"

"I found the key. Jiro, I swear I didn't take any money. Check my bags. You'll see that I'm as broke as ever." I glanced out into the kitchen. The lights were still on, but in the time that I'd been searching the office, the remaining staff had left. At least I was all alone in this humiliation.

Jiro snorted. "I know you aren't after money. You have the rich lawyer boyfriend, *neh*? What you're after is something completely different. But it's not names."

"What do you think, then?"

He shook his head. "I am very disappointed in you. I thought you were a *yasashii-hito*, and I was wrong." He had used the phrase that meant "nice person," which had a connotation of comradeship. It was a lovely thing to call someone. And now I wasn't one anymore.

"Please don't tell Marshall," I begged. "I wish I'd never done this. But the reason, actually, is a matter of life and death."

"You talk like a chef or a waiter who doesn't want to work his shift. I have no time for such talk. Get out." Jiro was using rough Japanese with me, the kind only men used with each other, or inferiors. It was worse than any physical blow I could have received.

I bent my head to the task of gathering up my possessions. Jiro was the person at the restaurant I'd respected the most, and now he saw me as dirt. I could never come back, I knew now. After I'd picked up my backpack, I looked at the papers I'd had spread out on the floor.

"May I put the file back in place, at least?" I asked Jiro, only to find that he'd stormed off.

I ran a hand over my brow and put the papers back in the folder. Then the folder went into the file, the file into the drawer. I locked it with the key. Then I picked up my things and moved slowly out of the office.

Just as I did so, the lights went off. Jiro must have closed up and not cared that I was left behind. The framed woodblock slipped out of my grasp and the glass shattered. Damn it. I laid flat on the floor the remnants of the picture and made my way along the wall, trying to recall where the light switch was. I'd never had to turn the lights on or off anywhere in the restaurant because of the dilettante hours I worked. But I knew the kitchen met restaurant code, which meant there had to be plenty of light switches and outlets around. I could only hope Jiro hadn't set an alarm on the door. I would be able to go out an emergency exit, I was sure, they had to be kept open, by law. Where was it again? Down the hall, near the powder rooms.

Just as I reached the edge of where I thought the door into the dining area was, the light snapped on. I blinked in the harsh fluorescence and saw that Toro was standing in front of me.

My initial instinct to say thank goodness was thwarted when I saw his face. He was looking at me in a way that made Jiro's recent expression seem neutral. Now I filled my eyes with the sight of the man I'd barely glanced at before, except to catalog the ugly things about him: the tattoo, the graying ponytail, the love handles. He was wearing one of his usual, awful T-shirts, one that strained at his belly, but he didn't look too fat to move. Now I saw that his ponytail was black mixed with gray, and a kinky texture. And he had hard eyes, like Lorraine.

"Neblett," I said. "You're Mike Neblett. How did you choose the nickname Toro?"

"My old war buddy Garcia thought of it. Bull," he said, knocking on his chest with one fist. How had I missed seeing that he wore brass knuckles? Maybe because he'd had latex gloves on while he was washing dishes.

"Bull, as in tough? Or bull, as in that whole story about what happened when Norton and the others shot up the mothers and their children in Vietnam?"

He smiled at me, a thin smile that revealed spaces where some teeth were gone. "They shot 'em for fun—the sergeant's fun. I heard later about how they had to do it, from Robert, who had really wigged out. He thought he could trust me to help get the story to the judge advocate. But the sergeant stepped in first, 'cause he knew about our . . . conversation. And he made me an offer that was too good to resist."

"Which was?" I asked, playing for time.

"If I didn't say squat, I got released early, medical discharge, and VA benefits for the rest of my life. The others they split up to different places, better places than Vietnam. And afterward, when Robert was at the Pentagon, me and Garcia, we got the idea of how to make a little extra money off those guys. The guys who shot, and got away with it."

"You turned on your friend," I said.

"Hey, I helped him out. I even got him a good wife, one he could count on instead of that gook—yeah, I see your face. You don't like me talking like that, do you? Especially in a restaurant like this, full of gooks. Sneaky. That gook chef was trying to figure out if I was really legal to work—he almost messed up my VA benefit."

"That's a crime," I said dryly.

"And that VC kid who works the bar, he never brings drinks back for me or anyone else. And you—you're the worst one of all. Japanese, but not really Japanese, my sister said."

"She told you to put me away, didn't she?" I asked, sure of the answer.

"Lorraine's not stupid. She let me know about the problem, told me to get Garcia to help me put an end to it. She'd been holding Robert in check all those years—and now he's thinking of spilling. He says he don't care if he gets court-martialed. But we do."

So Robert Norton was a good man, fundamentally. Just as I'd thought. Andrea didn't have to be ashamed of her father. The only one who needed to be ashamed was Lorraine.

"Move." Mike Neblett hit me in the chest with the brass knuckles. I bent over with the pain, and choked out, "You hit me with those things when you got me in the car trunk. I felt them."

"And I'll hit you with them again. Then I'll drop them back off at your boyfriend's place. They won't have his prints, but that don't even matter. There's all that bondage crap lying around, and his DNA is gonna be all over you."

"You were there?" I felt like fainting.

"There's a fire escape that runs along his bedroom and kitchen wall." He laughed. "I made it to work late, but the show was worth it. I've been following you around for a while, as has my buddy. I lucked on that detail today. And I'm going to luck out tonight."

"Garcia was the man with the gas can, I bet." I wanted to keep him talking as long as possible.

"Yeah. You've stepped over him a few other times on the street, too. You tend to give money to women and children, you know that? It's discrimination!"

"So Garcia knew I'd gone to the Marine archives."

"Yeah. You were carrying stuff that said 'Marines' when you were walking down the street. He would've got the papers you were carrying and pushed you on the tracks, but there was people around and you were too damn quick. Took the wrong train, he said. But enough about all the misses. Tonight, we've scored a direct strike. And before we leave town, you need to chill."

"My mood's fine."

"That's not what I mean." He hit me in the back, between the shoulder blades. I stumbled forward across the shards of broken glass from the picture. It gave me an idea. I faked a fall so I could pick up a shard, but as I did that, he kicked me so I really fell across the glass. I lost the shard and was stabbed in half a dozen places, cuts that hurt, but that were nothing as searing as the pain of the miscarriage.

He'd dragged me up and was steering me toward a huge walk-in freezer. He opened the door.

Oh, no. "Why in the world would you leave me in there? It'll point straight to you, since you were here last. Jiro must have seen you when he was here a few minutes ago." I was angling to get outside, where I could run somewhere, anywhere. That was the key, putting distance between us. I hadn't run regularly in a while, but I knew the neighborhood, the Chinatown restaurants that drew big crowds, the place where the parking valets congregated.

"I don't plan on leaving you in the Sub-Zero for good. Just a little chill-out period while Garcia and I find a car we can hot-wire. There's a nice piece of land waiting for you in Virginia. You'll make good vegetarian fertilizer, huh? Will you be organic or whatever that crap is you always talk about?" He laughed shortly.

He wouldn't have to look for a car for long, because Hugh's was parked right out back. It was locked, with the alarm on. If he broke into it, the alarm would go off, but would that interest anybody in a city where screeching cars were considered an annoyance rather than a warning? I had to keep my mind on other things. "A human body is not organic fertilizer," I said. "And it's very hard to get away with dumping a body. Though I guess you did that with Sadako. But people know she was killed, it's become clear. It's probably just a matter of a few days before they catch you and dig up both our bodies. If I were you, I'd confess and save myself the death penalty for two murders."

"That's the one thing that you got wrong," Neblett said. "We didn't ice Norton's first wife."

"If I'm wrong about it, why were you so worried about what I was finding out? Why did you steal Andrea's papers?" I would have done almost anything to stall getting in the freezer, but he'd opened the door and was starting to shove me in.

"Yeah, I didn't know what was going to happen tonight, but it's all right," he said, as if to himself. "You got that guy's DNA all over you. It'll seem like you got hosed and then dumped. Even the knotted-up ties will help. Guess I'll hide those in the apartment, with the brass knuckles. Man, we've got a lot to do."

"But what about Andrea?" I called out just as the door slammed shut on me. Andrea was my last hope, because she was going to call me at the apartment to talk. She might have already, and if Hugh hadn't been too sleepy to pick up the phone, he might have actually gotten out of bed to look for me and found the note. If I disappeared, Hugh would be suspicious—but I'd taken the paperwork with the names Neblett and Garcia with me, so he wouldn't know whom to tell the police about. Even the good-bye note I'd left wouldn't necessarily help, because I hadn't dated it. The police might believe that it was from days or weeks earlier, or written under duress. If I were found dead, Hugh would be the leading suspect, especially since Kendall, Harp Snowden, and Win—all my Washington contacts, practically— knew we were having relationship problems. And if Andrea kept searching for the truth, she would be snatched up by Neblett and Garcia, too. Yes, I was sure they would like her to join me, along with her mother, in the plot of land Neblett had mentioned.

37

It was so silent in the freezer. Silent, and freezing. I hugged my hands into my armpits, the warmest part of my body. I had never minded the winter, but I'd had my winters in California and Japan, so mild as to be laughable. I laughed, just to hear that I could still breathe and speak. Oh, Hugh. I spoke to him as if he could hear me. You were so paranoid because you knew something would happen, you had a sixth sense! Standing in the kitchen, you saw the ghost that I would become.

Women were supposed to have a sixth sense, not men. I'd failed my gender. The surface of my watch glowed, and I watched the time tick past. How long would it take for Neblett to line up his friend and steal Hugh's car? Maybe twenty or thirty minutes, tops.

A grating sound caught my attention, and slowly the door of the freezer opened. I'd been crouched down in the farthest corner, as if that would keep me from being found. But as the door widened, a swath of light cut in. Behind it stood Jiro Takeda.

"So you are with Neblett," I said. "Well, I am surprised. But I guess it makes sense. You hired him."

"Get out!" Jiro sounded horrified. "You may be crazy. You may need the hospital. But you will not die in my clean Sub-Zero!"

I moved forward, awkwardly, into the light, and asked, "Jiro, why are you here?"

"I wanted to see what papers you had viewed. Have you seen mine yet? No? If you had found mine, you would see that I was born near Tokyo. I spent most of my life elsewhere, so I have no real Japanese accent and—my confidence."

"But I don't care where you were born!" I cried. "Jiro, we've got to leave. The man you know as Toro is coming back with his friend to take me away and kill me."

"*Heh*?" Jiro said. "I saw your bag and the broken picture on the floor. I knew something was wrong. Is it really the case that the dishwasher hurt you? I must tell you that I suspected him all along. He is a bad sort, working for pay when he is supposedly medically disabled—"

"Quick, Jiro!" I whispered. I'd just heard a big bang in the front of the restaurant. "We've got to get out, I don't know, some way."

"The kitchen door," Jiro said, grabbing his long knife from the roll next to his workstation. Then he used his empty hand to grab mine and lead me out the back door. But the door wouldn't budge.

"He must have blocked it," I said.

"We'll take the emergency exit, then. It's near the rest rooms. We must move through the kitchen door out to the dining room."

We changed direction. I felt reassured by Jiro's hand, toughened and callused from years of cooking, in mine. I was also glad for his knife. But Jiro was a chef, not a former Marine trained in guerilla combat. It would be two against two—Jiro and me against the two Vietnam vets, who probably understood hand-to-hand combat.

Jiro eased open the swinging door and I was at his side just as the glass in the front door shattered. How blatant did they dare to be? I guessed they didn't care about smashing up Marshall's restaurant. Too bad there were no businesses still open nearby, nobody right there to call the cops.

We had crept halfway down the hallway to the emergency exit

when the light came on in the front of the restaurant. I heard the sound of more than one person moving. I rushed toward the emergency exit, but when I pressed against it, it stayed resolutely shut.

"Oh, no!" Jiro said. "The door can't be locked. Ken Chow's boys must have done it to get us in trouble with the inspector—"

"Ssshh! We're just going to have to run for it—"

But before I could do that, the footsteps had crossed the dining room and I was staring at the intruders. Andrea and Hugh.

I shook my head, not understanding it for a moment. Then I realized that Andrea must have called the apartment as planned and spoken to Hugh. So the two of them had come to round me up. They would have saved me, if Jiro hadn't already.

But Hugh was looking at Jiro with a horrified expression, and then I remembered that the chef had a cleaver in one of his hands.

Hugh raised his cell phone in one hand. "Mr. Takeda, I'm prepared to call 911. And if you must take a hostage, I'll be the one."

"Do call 911, Hugh," I interrupted. "But it's not Jiro who's a danger, it's Neblett and Garcia."

"Who?" Andrea asked, looking at me as if I was speaking another language.

"Neblett's Toro, the dishwasher. Lorraine's brother. And Garcia's a fake-homeless man who carries around a gas can. I'll tell you more later, because we've got to leave this place very quickly. They're on their way back—" I cut myself off as I heard a door slam in the kitchen. They must have already opened the freezer and discovered I was gone.

"It might be Marshall," Andrea whispered. "There's no way to tell for sure."

Hugh had already dialed the police. "Emergency," he said in a low voice. "Send the police to a restaurant called Bento, on H Street."

"Finish on the way out!" I whispered loudly and motioned toward the front door, trying to coax all of them out. But nobody moved. It was so quiet that you could hear a pin drop, the sound of metal clinking against a floor.

I felt myself go cold as the pin dropping was followed by a

crisp pop. I whirled around to look at the door with the round window that separated the kitchen from the dining room. It was open, and something hard and metal hurled through it.

"Grenade!" I screamed, knowing there was no more time for us. It was too late to do anything but run. All four of us rushed for the front of the restaurant. Jiro, in the lead, was struggling to open the door—all the glass that Hugh and Andrea had broken, getting in, had complicated things. The grenade had rolled by the edge of one of the dining tables. I looked at it, keeping the mental count that I'd started since I'd heard the safety go off. One second had passed, now it was two—

"Come on!" Hugh bellowed as he struggled with the door. At this rate, we'd never all make it out in time.

"Get down!" I screamed at everyone, but they didn't understand. Nobody backed away from the shattered door, even as I held the grenade in my hand, intending to throw it through. I did the next best thing, which was to aim it as hard as I could through the plate-glass window in the front, which bore Bento's name.

I fell on top of Andrea, Hugh, and Jiro just as the grenade exploded. There was a thunderclap of noise, and along with it, lots of flying debris. Outside, I heard car alarms going off, and then, the sound of police sirens.

Now, as I lay entangled in bodies, I realized the impact of what I'd done. I'd launched the grenade into the street to keep it from killing us, but I had no idea if anyone was outside. I might have killed without intending to, the way I'd done before. I breathed in air slowly, trying to keep myself calm. War just didn't work, as Harp Snowden said. And like him, I was a lucky one: a survivor.

38

"Who taught you to throw like that?" Hugh asked me the next morning at breakfast. We'd gone out to Urban Grounds after spending much of the night in the hospital. He'd had a Christmas tree's worth of glass icicles pulled from the front of his body, as had Jiro, who'd been on the bottom, close to the broken glass from the door as well. Andrea had been in the middle, so all she'd gotten was a ripped-up dress and a ton of bruises. I'd suffered just a few lacerations on my back, and a nasty bump on the back of my head from a flying plate.

"Well, I did play some softball during my junior high years. I never formally joined a team, but in school, I did like to pitch."

"Well, pardon me for thinking that you needed protection," Hugh said. "One of the cops at the hospital said the grenade went off by the entrance to the vacant building next door. Nobody was hurt. It was the very best possible place, in such a difficult situation."

"It's hard to believe that, seeing how the restaurant fell apart," I said. The force of the grenade had blown the huge plate-glass window inward, knocking over tables, chairs, and everything else in its path. "Not only Marshall, but the cranky old owner of the place next door, could probably sue me if they wanted."

"Not if I have anything to do with it," Hugh said. "Besides, I'm sure they'll be delighted with the insurance payouts. Marshall will have enough money to redecorate, which you were saying was a plan of his anyway."

"It was, and I don't really care to be involved." I sighed heavily. "I'm just grateful to you and Andrea and Jiro for coming into the restaurant and saving me from another car ride to hell."

"I didn't do anything but bollocks up the getaway," Hugh said ruefully. "But we pulled together, like a regular bunch of troupers. Oh, look, the girl at the counter's waving at us. The toads must be ready. I don't suppose you could—"

"Of course." I got up to bring our two breakfast plates over to our table. Hugh's hands were so injured that he couldn't pick up most objects or use a keyboard. I'd be the one to button up his shirts in the morning, and knot his ties. I'd have to learn the Windsor knot, and some other knots, too. After that, I could have Hugh where I wanted him. I smiled to myself, thinking about the possibilities.

"You look as if you're daydreaming," Hugh said while I cut up his toast and egg.

"I am," I said. "I was just thinking that this whole business—people taking care of each other—is rather fun. Maybe it's the right thing to do."

"Yes," he said, and his eyes lingered on me. "I'm never going to propose again, though. The ball's in your court, darling."

"That's fine with me," I said.

"Well, then," Hugh said. "I'm looking forward to receiving your pitch—whenever it comes."

But there was a lot more to life than playing catch-up with Hugh. The police managed to locate Mike Neblett and Leon Garcia leaving Washington, D.C., on Interstate 295 in a stolen car that contained rope, like I remembered, and several firearms and extra grenades that, it turned out, they'd gotten from a friend assigned to guard weapons in Quantico. They also had a map of Virginia, with a small, remote state park circled. The place I was going to die, I knew. Perhaps the place where Sadako died.

But although the police had no trouble charging the two men on four counts of attempted murder, they were still reluctant to charge them in the disappearance of Sadako Norton. Mike Neblett, who'd admitted to kidnapping me and burglarizing Andrea's apartment, steadfastly denied he'd killed Sadako. His comrade Garcia didn't say anything, but he wasn't talking at all, not even to his public defender. Garcia was presenting the perfect picture of a catatonic, drug-addicted Vietnam veteran, although I remembered so well how he'd talked a mile a minute the day he'd followed me to the Navy Yard.

Other ends remained untied as well. Win was in a rehab center, Kendall said, and while it was supposed to be one of the nation's finest, there was no guarantee that it would change someone ambivalent about giving up drugs. And even though Kendall now understood the reason for her kidnapping, she wasn't going to tell the police about the drug lords in her husband's life. It would be too much scandal, she said, especially since she had been given a paying job as Harp Snowden's special-events planner. It was her dream job, she said, and every woman should have a chance in her life to get exactly what she wanted.

The only one who had not gotten what she wanted was Andrea. Even though the men who'd forced her mother to run were behind bars, she still didn't have a body to mourn. She had no closure. I brooded about this during the week I nursed Hugh, and then, when he was finally ready to go back to work, I told him about my idea. To my surprise, he had no arguments. He gave me the car keys and wished me Godspeed.

And so it came to pass that on a fine Wednesday morning, I was driving across the Chesapeake Bay Bridge headed for Kent Island, on Maryland's Eastern Shore. Andrea sat in the passenger seat with a tourist map on her lap. She'd figured out the route to Stevensville, the town where Sadako's last letters had been postmarked.

I squinted in the sun and started across the bridge, wincing a little at the feel of my back against the car seat. There were still a few sore patches on my back.

"Where do you think we should make the first stop?" I asked Andrea as we approached the turnoff sign for Stevensville. She had been fiddling with the radio for the last half hour, switching from station to station. She'd wanted a commercial pop music station, but I refused to budge from the local station I'd discovered, a public radio station operated by students at Kent County High School. KCHS played a fascinating mix of music ranging from Led Zeppelin to Lucinda Williams. Between these wide-ranging songs, the teen announcers tripped over the delivery of the nation's, and their high school's, news.

Andrea was looking out the window, as if she was lost in thought. She hadn't become closer to her father since the unraveling of the past; ironically, he wasn't upset about being court-martialed, but he was devastated that Lorraine was being considered as an accessory to the crimes against me. Already, she'd admitted to the police that she'd always thought her brother and Garcia had been behind Sadako's disappearance, and she'd warned them about me, in order to keep her life with Robert and Davon from changing forever.

I lowered the radio and repeated my question again about where Andrea thought I should stop.

"We could go to a seafood restaurant and find out about the oyster-diving scene. A really good seafood restaurant, serving the local catch."

"Great idea. I'll pull into the next gas station to ask for a recommendation."

The wiry young station attendant recommended Morrison's, which had the best crab cakes, with no filler. I wasn't sure we should take the recommendation of such a thin young person as gospel, so I made a second stop at the Main Tamer, a pet grooming and accessories shop on Main Street. The dog groomer who greeted us, a leathery-skinned blonde in her fifties, also recommended Morrison's, but for the fried oysters. So Morrison's it would be.

Morrison's was in the next hamlet over, a place called Leeville, which we reached by driving along a pretty, twisting road where farm fields were interspersed with marine service shops, a firehouse, and old, inexpensive-looking farmhouses that Hugh would have become very excited about. We'd come back some other time, I promised myself.

The restaurant was a neat, modern clapboard-sided structure built on ten-foot stilts, protection from the occasional surges of the bay, which kissed the edge of a dock behind the restaurant. On either side of the restaurant were seafood processing and packing buildings. The parking lot surrounding Morrison's empire was filled with trucks, mostly.

"Look at all those trucks. Florida, California," Andrea said, reading the plates. "The packing house must be a really good one, to ship to all these places."

"That, or they're selling seafood from those states to the restaurant," I said. "Remember the oyster shortage?"

It turned out that we were both right. The waitress who took our order vouched for the crabs and lobster being local, but the oysters came from the Pacific Northwest. Workers in the packing plant shucked, rinsed, and packed these Pacific oysters, just as they continued to steam, pick, and pack the local crab. Morrison's was the only seafood business left in Leeville. There had been many more places twenty years ago, Dottie said, when the bay was healthy and its marine population bountiful. Morrison's had survived because the family who owned it had been in the oyster-and-crabbing business for four generations and simply wouldn't give up. They had the infrastructure of the packing plant, and plenty of crab pickers and oyster shuckers, now that the watermen didn't have much to do on the bay.

"I find it amazing that this lobster really was caught in the bay," I said to our waitress when a two-pound lobster came out fifteen minutes later on a platter with a little butter and lemon on the side. I'd gone for broke when I'd heard they served lobster for less than $30. It was a bargain compared to Washington restaurants.

"Yep. The bay's kind of screwed up these days. The oysters are gone, and the crabs are fading, but the lobsters have swum in. When life gives you lemons, huh?"

"Actually, that sounds a lot like our lives," Andrea began, but the woman had already moved on to the next table. So we looked at each other and laughed.

"When life gives you lemons—" I began.

"Squeeze them over a lobster," Andrea said. "Speaking of which, did I tell you I'm applying to cooking school?"

"I had no idea! Is it because you want to do something at Marshall's new place?" Marshall had bought the building next to Bento, and was knocking down the wall between them to make one large restaurant. My heart had sunk when I'd learned he was scrapping the Japanese menu for Low Country cooking—a combination of North Carolina barbecue, grits, greens, mashed potatoes, corn pudding, and the like. But I couldn't be too angry. Marshall was grateful I'd thrown the grenade outside the restaurant instead of allowing his place to blow to pieces—so grateful that he'd finally paid me in full. I was flush again, so flush that I'd even bought myself a ticket to the Harp Snowden fund-raiser taking place in two weeks at Harp Snowden's own Kalorama residence. It would be a true *kaiseki ryoori* menu catered by Jiro with Andrea at his side, helping.

"I don't want to work for Marshall much longer," Andrea said, reminding me of what we'd been talking about. "Besides, I've got a really cool new option."

"Oh?"

"Did you hear where Jiro's going?"

"Sure. To Japan." Jiro had told Hugh and me over *mojitos* at El Rincon that he needed to face his demons back in the land of his birth. He was going to part ways with Marshall to create his own American seafood restaurant on a beach. I had already told Norie about it—and also about Jiro's true Japanese identity, and how he'd saved my life.

Andrea continued, "Because I want to see my Japanese relatives, I figured that maybe I could work while I was over there to pay for my trip. Jiro will need Japanese servers and hosts, but he could use a real American cook. And even if the thing with my Japanese aunt doesn't work out, I can just kick back with Jiro and drink saketinis."

"That sounds like fun," I said wistfully. "I wish I could go with you."

"I could use the help," Andrea said, taking a sip of iced tea. "This is really good tea. Presugared tea, the way restaurants are usually afraid to do it."

"Since when have you had a sweet tooth?" I demanded. "You used to look at me stirring sugar as if I was killing myself."

"I'm getting to like sugar more and more. I might even become a pastry chef. There are a lot of brilliant women in pastry."

After we'd paid our bill, we asked if there was an old-timer in the area who knew marine divers. We heard the whole spiel again about the scarcity of oysters, to which we nodded sympathetically. But in the end, we were sent over to the packing plant, where a red-faced man in overalls with a shock of white hair listened to our query.

Andrea had asked me to do the talking because she thought she'd get too nervous, blow the thing. So, trying to avoid having to tell the whole story, I asked if he remembered hearing anything about a Japanese woman who'd lived nearby in the 1970s. I thought she might have dived, but I wasn't sure. She probably had moved away and we were family, trying to get in touch.

He looked doubtfully from half-black Andrea to half-white me. I thought about telling him that race was about as impossible to define as the last remaining rock where the surviving oysters were hiding. I'd thought Mike Neblett was white, when he'd been black. Garcia had seemed African-American, but he'd turned out to be Puerto Rican. Norie had thought Jiro wasn't Japanese.

"There aren't many women oyster divers," he said. "There was one a long time ago, but she retired. And folks said that she was Korean."

That made sense, because Korean women were known for marine diving. There was a chance, maybe, that the two women, alone and Asian on a tiny American island, had bonded.

"What was her name?" I asked.

"I can't recall, but like I said, she retired. The oysters have got so scarce, there's not much business. The guys who'd been here before, well, they kept at it longer. She went in to work on land, I think. First grading oysters in the packing plant, and then she had enough money to take some college classes."

"Who knew her?" I was not going to give up on this woman.

He shrugged. "Polly Westerbrook—she's my cousin's wife—was friends with her. She said something about having dinner with her in Centerville a few months back. So this gal's still around, somewhere."

Centerville was one of the bigger towns on the Eastern Shore; it would take about a half hour to get there on Route 50. But I wanted to talk to Polly Westerbrook first, so we wound our way back to the place where she was said to work: the pet store we'd stopped at on our way into town. Polly was in fact the dog groomer we'd talked to earlier. At the moment, she was shearing a bored-looking poodle.

She looked up as we came through the door. "Well, hello again. How was lunch?"

"Excellent," I said. "I had the lobster. It's amazing that they swim this far south."

"A lot swim in places you think they don't belong."

I exchanged glances with Andrea, but the next thing that she said put me at ease.

"It's a good thing. Keeps us going, keeps us growing."

"I hear there's a chance of bringing in a new, nonnative oyster species so they could spread and repopulate," I said.

"That's right. The Asian oyster. A lot of people are afraid of it.

My husband's cousin Bobby, who works over at the crab-packing plant, says it's been bred over on the Virginia side of the bay for a while without causing problems. Too bad the brilliant minds running our state won't let us do it. What's the bay gotta turn into, a swamp or something, before they're willing to act?" She raised her eyebrows, making the creases in her forehead deeper.

"We talked to Bobby, actually." I was happy for the easy opening. "He mentioned a friend of yours, a Korean woman who used to dive around here. We'd like to meet her."

"Why's that?" She looked at us expectantly.

Andrea and I exchanged glances. She shook her head.

"I'd rather not say. I mean, I'll tell her, of course, because I'm hoping that she will be able to lead us to the person we are actually hoping to talk with. It might not pan out, but we've come so far, I thought it was worth a try."

"Well, it don't matter. I can't think of anyone who fits the description. Round these parts men do the diving, not women."

"But your cousin said—" Andrea protested.

"Bobby's never been able to remember anything right."

"But she was the only woman diver. He said that you used to have a beer with her, now and then, and you saw her recently in Centerville."

"He was confused." She'd stopped paying much attention to the dog, and the shearing continued over one of its ears, catching an ear corner on the edge. The dog yelped. She dropped the power razor.

She knew something. There was a buzzing in my ears that had nothing to do with the tool that was lying on the floor.

"It's my mother we're trying to find," Andrea said in a low voice. "This woman you know, we think, might have befriended my mom, back when she was here in the seventies, before she disappeared."

"It's so long ago. I'm sorry, I just don't know how to help you. Off the table, Daisy!" She grabbed the pooch around its middle and set it on the floor.

"You're still protecting her, aren't you?" I said. It had to be.

Polly's reaction to throw us off and protect her friend could only mean that the so-called Korean diver might not be the source we needed to lead us to Sadako. She might be Sadako herself.

"What do you mean? Daisy has her owner coming back in a half hour. The dog'll be fine." Polly sounded testy.

"No, I mean you're trying to protect your friend by not telling outsiders about her," I said. "You've been her ally all these years."

"Girls, I don't want to be rude or anything, but I've got to put this dog out in our short-term kennel. Good luck on the rest of your trip!"

"The men my mother was afraid of are finally in prison," Andrea said. "She—Rei, I mean—she was almost killed by them a few weeks ago. But they can't hurt anyone again."

Polly looked unconvinced.

I watched Andrea shut her eyes for a moment, then open them. She seemed to be gathering her courage for something. At last her voice came out, a little shaky. "Please help me. My mother's name was Sadako. She was married to a guy who'd been in Vietnam. I was born in Virginia in 1974. She liked to call me Akiko, but my American name is Andrea."

Polly swayed slightly, and put her hands on the dog-grooming table to steady herself.

"You know what she's talking about," I said softly.

Polly looked at me with a fierce expression. "You swear they're in prison?"

"My copy of the *Washington Post* containing the news story is back at my apartment," I said. "If you like, I can drive back to D.C. and fax it to you."

"No," Andrea said sharply. "I'm not leaving the shore until I've seen my mother. She walked away from me, but I still—" Andrea stopped speaking and buried her face in her hands.

Polly looked at me. Her careworn face suddenly looked even older. "There's not supposed to be a daughter anymore," she said. "Not one alive."

"Just as there's not supposed to be a mother alive, either," I said.

Polly sat down. "I—I better make a phone call."

I sensed that Polly wasn't going to send us unless it was clear that we were wanted. And there was a chance that this woman really was a stranger. All my instincts were screaming that Polly's friend was Andrea's mother, but it might not be the case. I'd been wrong about so much over the last few months.

Andrea was still weeping. I led her to a bench near the doorway and made her sit down. Daisy wandered over and nosed against her knees. This made Andrea cry even harder.

Polly disappeared with a cordless telephone into a back room. I wondered how she'd put the situation to her friend. Two strange city girls had wandered in, looking for her. They'd thrown around some Japanese names. Was that enough for her to agree to see us?

Polly came out again without the phone. Instead of saying anything, she went to Andrea and put her arms around her.

"She doesn't want to see me, does she? I knew it was a bad idea," Andrea said, her mouth wobbling.

"No, hon. She wants to see you right away. I'm going to give you directions to the marine center. She works in the lab on the first floor."

"There are Marines here on the Eastern Shore?" I asked.

"It's a marine biology research center," Polly clarified. "Pearl is working in the lab on an oyster cultivation project that's been going on for five years now. She got the job a while ago, when she stopped diving."

"Pearl," I said. "Her name is now Pearl?"

"Yes. It's not her given name, she said, but the one she chose to use ever since she moved out here. And it suits her more each year. You'll see."

"I feel sick," Andrea said as we started driving again, this time toward Centerville. "Sick as a dog. I wish—if I had known—I wouldn't be dressed like this, I'd be in something more conservative. And look at my hair." She touched her light gold curls. "She'll never believe I'm her daughter. I should have brought my birth certificate, some kind of proof."

I shook my head. "She's your mother. She'll recognize you."

39

The marine center was a modest two-story cinder-block building that I guessed must once have been a grade school, because of all the windows and the playground equipment in back. In front, there was a neatly clipped lawn decorated with a sculpture made from oyster cans. A boat, I realized belatedly. An oyster boat, made of the cans used to catch oysters.

We pulled into a large parking lot that was underoccupied by only a dozen cars, all of which bore "Treasure the Chesapeake" Maryland license plates. I was beginning to feel that some Americans were a lot like the Japanese, understanding that the value of nature was greater than all of us put together.

"I'm perfectly willing to wait in the car," I said to Andrea.

"No." She shook her head. "I'll lose my nerve if you aren't with me. Besides, you might need to translate something. Remember how she said in the letters that she couldn't speak English well?"

"She's been here for twenty-eight years, though," I said. "She's made friends and gotten a job. So don't worry about the English. I'll come along though, if you want the moral support."

The building had a wide central hallway with doors along both sides. I looked at the room directory, which was posted on a big board. There were offices for the study of sea grass, others for crabs, others examining salinity. The oyster recovery group worked at the rear of the first floor. I practically had to pull Andrea along with me. She was scared. Well, I'd be, too, if I were to meet my mother after twenty-eight years.

"I wish I wasn't meeting her in front of a crowd," Andrea said in a low voice.

"She might be alone. There were only about twelve cars in the lot. Divide that by the number of offices."

"You never know—" Andrea broke off. We were standing in front of the oyster-recovery-program door.

"Shall I knock?" I asked, because she hadn't moved.

"Yeah. You go first, because if she's there I—I don't know what I'll say." Andrea's face had tightened into the chilly expression I'd always seen on her in the old days, the days before I realized that was just the way she looked when she was nervous.

"Relax," I told her as I knocked. "Ten deep breaths. And you might want to smile."

"This is not a beauty pageant," she muttered.

The door opened, suddenly, and I found myself facing a tall, American boy—a man, I revised, a young man with glasses and blue jeans and an intense air. "Come on in. Are you the ones here to see Pearl?" he said. The room behind him was filled with marine equipment, books, and banks of computers and telephones.

"Yes," I said, squinting beyond him to see where she was.

"I work on the project with her. She wanted me to walk you out to where she's tending the oyster beds." He indicated the room's windows, which had a thrilling view of the blue bay.

"You mean—out to sea?" Andrea asked.

"Naw." He smiled. "We have the lab set up outdoors, along the pier. You'll see." We went back out in the hall, and then around to the back of the building. All along a wooden dock were round fiberglass containers that looked like small, aboveground swimming pools. A woman was standing with her back to us, leaning over one of the containers and examining something in a net. She was tall, and wore blue jeans and a purple-striped jersey. I'd been expecting black hair like my aunt's, but hers was silver.

"Is that Pearl?" Andrea asked him. I could hear the doubt in her voice.

"Yep," he said. "I'll leave you here, then. Take care."

When he was gone, Andrea gripped my hand. "I don't want to go up to her. I can't stand the disappointment."

"You mean, if it's not her?" I said, just as the woman turned. She looked at us without smiling. Her face was not the classic middle-aged Japanese woman's face at all. It was creased deeply with sun damage, and she wore a pair of tortoiseshell-rimmed glasses. But the eyes behind the glasses—they were Asian eyes. And they were looking at Andrea with intensity. Clearly she'd guessed which young woman was her daughter.

I kept hold of Andrea's hand and started walking forward. Now we were only three feet from the woman.

"Hello," Andrea said.

"Are you my Akiko?" She spoke softly, with a strong Japanese accent. There was no mistaking it, nor was there in the strong way she held her shoulders. This was Sadako.

Andrea nodded. "Andrea is the name on my birth certificate, but—yes. I learned a little while ago that Akiko was my baby name."

"How did you learn that?" Pearl asked. She was still on guard, it was clear.

"Letters. Your letters to Atsuko. Rei and her aunt translated them from Japanese for me."

Sadako looked at me as if she was startled to see anyone else standing next to Andrea. I bent my head, and in Japanese, introduced myself and said that we'd gotten the letters, which had been returned from her sister's home in Japan to Robert Norton.

"Yes, the early letters were returned. I learned that after some years," she said.

"And you stopped writing to your sister, Atsuko," I said. "My own aunt just met your sister a few weeks ago. Atsuko has thought, all these years, you were dead."

"Yes, I imagine she did." She let out her breath slowly. "Rei, I am very grateful for what you did. And yes, I am concerned about my sister. But how you found Akiko remains the most important thing."

"We found each other," I replied in English, smiling at Andrea.

"But I never found you. You were not there," Sadako said, turning to address Andrea directly. "I went back to get you, two months after I'd found my new life here. I went back in the night, slipping in with my old key. Robert was sleeping in the apartment, but you were not there, nor were any of your things. Because you were missing, I was sure that something terrible had happened to you. I went into such a—depression—after that. I stopped writing to my sister. I separated completely from my old life in Japan."

"I was in foster care," Andrea said. "You could have found that out if you'd asked my father."

"I should have." She bowed her head. "But I was frightened. I thought you were dead, that it was my punishment for what I had done."

"The river," I said. "Someone put your clothes by the river."

"I did that," she said in a low voice. "When I ran away, I wanted to make it look as if I'd died."

"But then, if you came back and got me, people would have thought I was kidnapped," Andrea said.

"But not by me, since I was supposed to be dead." Sadako sighed. "The plan sounds so crazy now. I was not the same person then. I thought I couldn't trust Robert to keep secret where I'd gone."

"What about Neblett and Garcia—the men who were in Vietnam?" I asked.

She nodded. "Those are the names of the Americans who had been with him there. And when he came back, they told him they'd reveal his secret about the killing, make it come out that he'd murdered the children. In exchange for their silence, he gave them so much! Money, weapons. He would even have given *me* to them, I think, if they hadn't thought I was so ugly."

"You're not ugly, Sadako-san," I said. "You are one of the loveliest, strongest women I've ever seen. In Japan or America."

"I prefer Pearl now, if you don't mind," she said softly. "I changed my name when I came here. I wanted a place where I could work without showing an identity card, and at that time, you could do that here. And in those days, the 1970s, there were many oyster boats working the bay. I decided to try. At first they didn't believe I could do it, because I was a woman—they use heavy machinery, not their hands. But after I showed a few of the boat owners what I could do with my hands, I had as much work as I wanted. The work, it was all I had. I never married again." She paused. "What about you, Andrea? You say that you were cared for by another family all these years. Were they kind?"

"There were several families," said Andrea carefully. "Some were kind, others—not. I survived, although I can't say that I've accomplished much. Not like you, becoming a scientist."

"Oh, I'm not a scientist. I never had the education for that. But because of what I'd done on the water, I was chosen for this laboratory-technician position. People call me the oyster mother, sometimes, because these are like my babies—" She broke off. "My words are stupid. I am no mother at all."

"It's okay," Andrea said dully.

"No, it isn't. I should have brought you here to the island with me on the day I ran away. I didn't because I wanted to make things—secure—first. I didn't want to be one of those women you see on the street, sitting with a child and begging for money."

As she spoke, I shivered, remembering the woman and baby I'd seen on my way to Mandala on that rainy day so long ago. Pearl and Andrea had both gone through tough lives, without a protector, but they'd emerged strong. And though their conversation was halting, it was clear how much Andrea's mother wanted to know her grown child. And I knew, from experience, that Andrea's reserve would thaw.

"I'm just going around front for a while," I said, knowing that I wasn't needed anymore. I turned and walked past the tubs of oysters, big clean shells to which tiny oysters were clinging. Asian oysters by way of California, and now, the bay. Too risky, some environmentalists said. Ha. I loved old things, but now I understood that you had to change to survive. I hoped the bay wouldn't turn into a lonely swamp before people realized that.

I passed the car and went straight across the street, where I'd noticed a small line of tourist shops when we'd driven in. There was a snack bar called Oyster Alley, and Body Art, a tattoo and piercing parlor. A neon sign in the window beckoned, saying that it was "Open 11–11."

It was three o'clock now, firmly in the window of operation. I stood close to the window for a few minutes, studying the pictures of tattoo designs, and pierced tongues and ears. My old roommate Richard had pierced his tongue when piercings really were radical. To get a piercing now, in the twenty-first century, was passé. Especially for a woman my age who didn't drink much, washed her darks and whites separately, and even gave money to a mainstream politician.

I pushed the door open and went in.

A woman in blue jeans and a tank top was moving through a yoga asana on a mat in the center of the room. She looked up at me from about knee level.

"I'm working. This is just what I do when it gets slow."

"It's better than watching TV," I said.

"So what can I do you for?" Slowly, she came up to a standing position, her arms outstretched. I saw now that she was over forty, but had the kind of long, straightened hair that was popular with high school and college girls. She had multiple hoops in both ears, a nostril pierced with a glittering red stone, and a tiny gold ring through her navel. A leafy vine tattoo wound its way around one ankle. There was a big-eyed moon on the other.

"I was wondering how much it is for a piercing," I said.

She cocked her head to the side. "Depends on where."

"Navel." It would serve as my mark, my memory of what had happened. My stomach pains had gone away, but I didn't ever want to forget that there had been a connection there—a cord that had briefly run from me to a baby, nourishing it for a few months of life.

"Oh, that's easy. Lots of gals your age are doing them, and the nice thing is, it can come out if you get pregnant. I charge forty bucks and that includes the ring itself."

I glanced around the parlor. It looked clean. "What kind of, ah, health precautions do you take?"

"We use a piercing gun, just like they do at the shopping mall when you get earrings. Everything's sterile. If you're nervous, our health department certificate is right by the door."

"I still don't know." I hesitated.

"You need your mom's permission, if you're younger than eighteen. In any event, I'll need to see a driver's license to verify your age."

Then I had to laugh. "What can I do to make it, well, not exactly the same as every other woman's belly piercing?"

"You could do gemstones. I'm wearing onyx." She raised her tank top so I could have a better look at two small black gems glittering in the middle. She was no flat-bellied nymph like Andrea, but the body jewelry was attractive on her, somehow serving to make her curves look more luxurious.

"Could I have a jewel on mine?" I was getting excited. What would Hugh think? If it was a genuine stone and completely tasteful, of course.

"Sure, but I don't have much of serious value. Right now, my stock is mostly onyx, amethyst, cubic zirconia, and freshwater pearl."

"Would it be a real freshwater pearl?" I asked.

"You can check it out if you're curious. Frankly, I don't know. I just buy the stuff from my supplier, who's always been reliable." She handed me a tiny box filled with the odd-shaped, small pearls. I scratched lightly at the surface of the one I liked best. It gave way slightly, so I knew that the pearl was real.

A few minutes later I was lying on a table that she'd flung a clean sheet over. I closed my eyes, knowing this couldn't be worse than a waxing. I didn't even have to get undressed. A swab of alcohol, and then a stabbing pain—but it was over quickly. I didn't look down until I sat up. Voilà, in my once plain belly button, a light smear of antibiotic ointment highlighted a curving wire of gold and two gleaming, Rice Krispy–shaped pearls. The body part that I'd hated so much a few months ago now looked almost magical. And like the woman said, when I had my next baby, it would come out.

There would be another baby, I said to myself as I walked out of the piercing parlor and back to the Marine center. And that child would learn about the one who hadn't made it.

It was time to catch up with Andrea and Pearl. I sensed that Andrea probably wouldn't need to ride back with me that evening. But I'd say good-bye, just to put a frame on her happily ever after, and my bittersweet one.

Relishing the secret under my shirt, I looked both ways before jogging across the street.

Here's a sneak preview of

The Typhoon Lover

by

Sujata Massey

Available in October 2005
in hardcover from
HarperCollins Publishers

1

I've never thought of myself as the blindfold type.

Not on planes, not in beds, and certainly not in restaurants. Especially not a place like DC Coast, where I was sitting on the evening of my thirtieth birthday, listening to my dinner companion trying his best to be persuasive.

"What happens next will be very special," Hugh said, picking up the small black mask that he'd placed next to our shared dessert. "You don't have to put the blindfold on inside here. Just a little later."

"You promised no party," I reminded him, but not sharply. My stomach was filled with a pleasant mélange of tuna tartare and crawfish risotto and crispy fried bass. It had been an orgy of seafood and good wine, just my kind of night.

"Hmm," Hugh said, studying the restaurant bill.

"If it's not a surprise party, where are you taking me?" I prodded.

"Let's just say I've got two tickets to paradise."

I rolled my eyes, thinking Hugh was showing his age, when I'd rather keep mine confidential. I didn't mind having a delicious, leisurely dinner, but he'd practically rushed me through cappuccino and crème brûlée. Hugh was frantic to leave, which made me think he definitely had something planned.

As we waited for the car to be brought to us on the busy corner of 14th and K Streets, Hugh folded the tiny black blindfold into my hand. "It's never been used, if that makes you more comfortable. I saved it from my last trip to Zurich."

"I thought you didn't believe in regifting?" I asked lightly.

"Well, you didn't want a ring. What else can I offer you?" The undercurrent of irritation in Hugh's voice was clear. I'd worn his beautiful, two-carat emerald for a short while, but ultimately returned it, because engagement rings scared me just as much as turning thirty did. Hugh was thirty-two; he'd been ready for the last three years. I wondered if I'd ever be.

The valet pulled up with the car and jumped out to open the passenger side for me. I got in, feeling a mixture of excitement and fear about what lay ahead. As we pulled off into traffic, I reclined my seat as far as it would go, hoping that this way, nobody would notice the girl with short black hair and a matching mask over her eyes. If anyone caught a glimpse, they might think I'd just come out of plastic surgery or something like that—though most Washington women who went in for that flew to Latin America, where the plastic surgeons were good and there were no neighbors to bump into.

"Are we headed for the airport?" I asked, with a sudden rush of hope.

"No chance." Hugh sounded regretful. "It would have been fun to get away, but I can't risk any absences when the partner track decisions are forthcoming."

Hugh was a lawyer at a high-pressure international firm a few blocks away. He'd been working for the last year on a class-action suit that still wasn't ready to roll. His work involved frequent travel back to Japan, the country of my heritage, where we'd met a few years earlier. I would have loved to travel with him, but couldn't because I was banned from Japan. It was a complicated story I didn't want to revisit on a night that I was supposed to be happy.

"Don't think about it," I muttered to myself. It was my habit to talk to myself sometimes, to try to shut out the bad thoughts that threatened what was a perfectly pleasant life.

"What don't you want to think about?"

"I'm getting nauseated from wearing a blindfold in a moving car," I said. "Not to mention, my nerves are shot because you won't tell me what's going to happen next."

"Oh, I'm sorry. Just hang on, I'll open the window." Hugh pressed the control that slid down the passenger-side window next to me. "We're just going around the corner to park. Will you survive another two minutes?"

I nodded, glad for a chance to listen to the sounds of the road. I could tell this wasn't our neighborhood of Adams-Morgan, with its mix of pulsating salsa music, honking horns, and shouting truck drivers. All I heard was a slow, steady purr of cars caught in traffic. After a while, the car moved again and turned a corner. Then it stopped. Hugh's window slid down.

"Paradise, sir?" a strange man's voice asked.

"That's right. We're staying till the wee morning hours," Hugh said. "Will this cover it?"

Before the parking valet could answer, I had a few words of my own. "Hugh, you *know* that I have a nine-thirty meeting at the Sackler Gallery tomorrow. You can very well stay until the wee hours, but I can't."

"Job interviews come and go. Thirtieth birthdays are only once!" He sounded positively gleeful.

My door was opened, and I unbuckled my seat belt. Then I felt a hand on my wrist, helping me out.

"You must be the girl getting the big birthday surprise." The valet's voice came from somewhere to the left.

I was busy working through the situation—was this a boutique hotel, maybe?—when Hugh tugged my hand. "There's going to be a downward flight of steps in a moment. Just take it slowly."

"What kind of a hotel has subterranean rooms?" I demanded.

"You'll know soon enough." Ten steps, and then a flat surface. "I'm going to hold the door open. Just step through."

I had no sight, but my other senses were bombarded. First, the sounds—a Dead Can Dance song pounding ominously on a stereo, and lots of voices—talking, laughing, shrieking. Then there were the smells—smoke from cigarettes and sandalwood incense.

Someone took my other hand and pressed briefly down on the area over my knuckles. I guessed that I was getting a hand-stamp, like what bouncers give at bars.

"Hugh, this is so silly," I complained. "I want to see where I am. If this is the S and M club we read about in *City Paper* I'm not going any farther."

Hugh sighed and said, "I'd hoped you'd stay blindfolded until the magic moment, but if you're that anxious, you may as well take it off. Go ahead."

Had I known about the series of events about to unfold—not that night, perhaps, but in the crazy, dangerous days that rolled out, right after my birthday—I might have just kept on the blindfold. I would have remained in Hugh's thrall, powerless to make my own choices, but secure—still twenty-nine and safe as houses.

But I'm not the kind of girl who stays in one place for long, whether it's a house or a nightclub vestibule.

I slid off the blindfold, and opened my eyes.

BOOKS BY SUJATA MASSEY

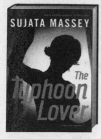

THE TYPHOON LOVER

ISBN 0-06-076512-7 (hardcover)

COMING SOON IN HARDCOVER

Through her chaotic twenties, antiques dealer Rei Shimura has gone anywhere that fortune and her unruly passions have led her. *The Typhoon Lover* takes her on her biggest adventure yet, a perilous journey that only Rei, with her experience in antiques and her foothold in two countries, can handle.

THE PEARL DIVER

ISBN 0-06-059790-9 (trade paperback)

A dazzling engagement ring is an added bonus for antiques dealer and sometime-sleuth Rei Shimura, who is commissioned to furnish a chic Japanese-fusion restaurant, where, in short order, things start to go haywire.

"A riveting story." —*Library Journal*

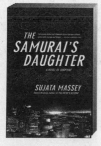

THE SAMURAI'S DAUGHTER

ISBN 0-06-059503-5 (trade paperback)

Antiques dealer Rei Shimura is in San Francisco tracing the story of 100 years of Japanese decorative arts through her family's history. Before long, Rei uncovers troubling facts about her own family's actions during the war.

"Absorbing cross-cultural puzzle." —*Publishers Weekly*

THE BRIDE'S KIMONO

ISBN 0-06-103115-1 (mass market paperback)

Rei Shimura has managed to snag one of the most lucrative jobs of her career: a renowned museum in Washington, D.C., has invited her to exhibit rare kimonos and give a lecture on them. Within hours one of the kimonos is stolen, and then a body is discovered in a shopping mall Dumpster.

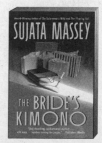

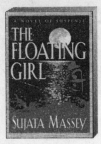

THE FLOATING GIRL

ISBN 0-06-109735-7 (mass market paperback)

During research for a comic-style magazine, Rei stumbles upon a disturbing social milieu of pre–World War II Japan. It evolves into something much darker when one of the comic's young creators is found dead—a murder that takes the tenacious Rei deep into the heart of Japan's youth underground.

THE FLOWER MASTER

ISBN 0-06-109734-9 (mass market paperback)

Life in Japan for a transplanted California girl with a fledgling antiques business and a nonexistent love life isn't always fun, but when the flower-arranging class Rei Shimura's aunt cajoles her into taking turns into a stage for murder, Rei finds plenty of excitement she's been missing.

ZEN ATTITUDE

ISBN 0-06-104444-X (mass market paperback)

When Rei overpays for a beautiful antique chest, she's in for the worst deal of her life. The con man who sold her the *tansu* is found dead, and like it or not Rei's opened a Pandora's box of mystery, theft, and murder.

THE SALARYMAN'S WIFE

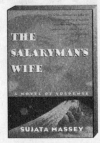

ISBN 0-06-104443-1 (mass market paperback)

Rei is the first to find the beautiful wife of a high-powered businessman dead in the snow. Taking charge as usual, Rei searches for clues by crashing a funeral, posing as a bar-girl, and somehow ending up pursued by police and paparazzi alike. In the meantime, she manages to piece together a strange, ever-changing puzzle.